the Secret Rise

Judith Briles
Brian Barnes

Book 3: The Secret Rise
The Harmonie Books Series
© 2025 Judith Briles and Brian Barnes

All rights reserved.

DO NOT TRAIN
Created by Human Intelligence

MileHigh Press

Published by Mile High Press

Editor: Barb Wilson, EditPartner.com
Proofreader: Peggie Ireland
Cover and Interior Design: Rebecca Finkel, F + P Graphic Design, FPGD.com
Book Publishing Expert: Judith Briles, TheBookShepherd.com

Books may be purchased in quantity by contacting the publisher through the author's website: www.HarmonieBooks.com

Library of Congress Control Number: 2025911092
ISBN trade paper: 978-1-959737-90-2
ISBN eBook: 978-1-885331-13-7
ISBN audiobook: 978-1-885331-14-4

Historical Fantasy Fiction | Women's Fiction | France

First Edition
Printed in the USA

To all the women who lead with

courage and crush through fear.

To our families and friends

who have given their encouragement and

support throughout the creation of The Secret Rise.

Contents

Celtic Sea
Engl
Cha
North
Atlantic
Ocean
Brittany
N
NW
NE
W
E
SW
SE
S
0 KM
50 KM
100 KM

WINCHESTER
and
SOUTHAMPTON
North
Sea
nnel
BOUNDARY
OF
NORMANDY
KINGDOM
OF
FRANCE
NEW HARMONIE
FECAMP
HARMONIE
LE HAVRE
Seine River
Normandy
ROUEN
PARIS

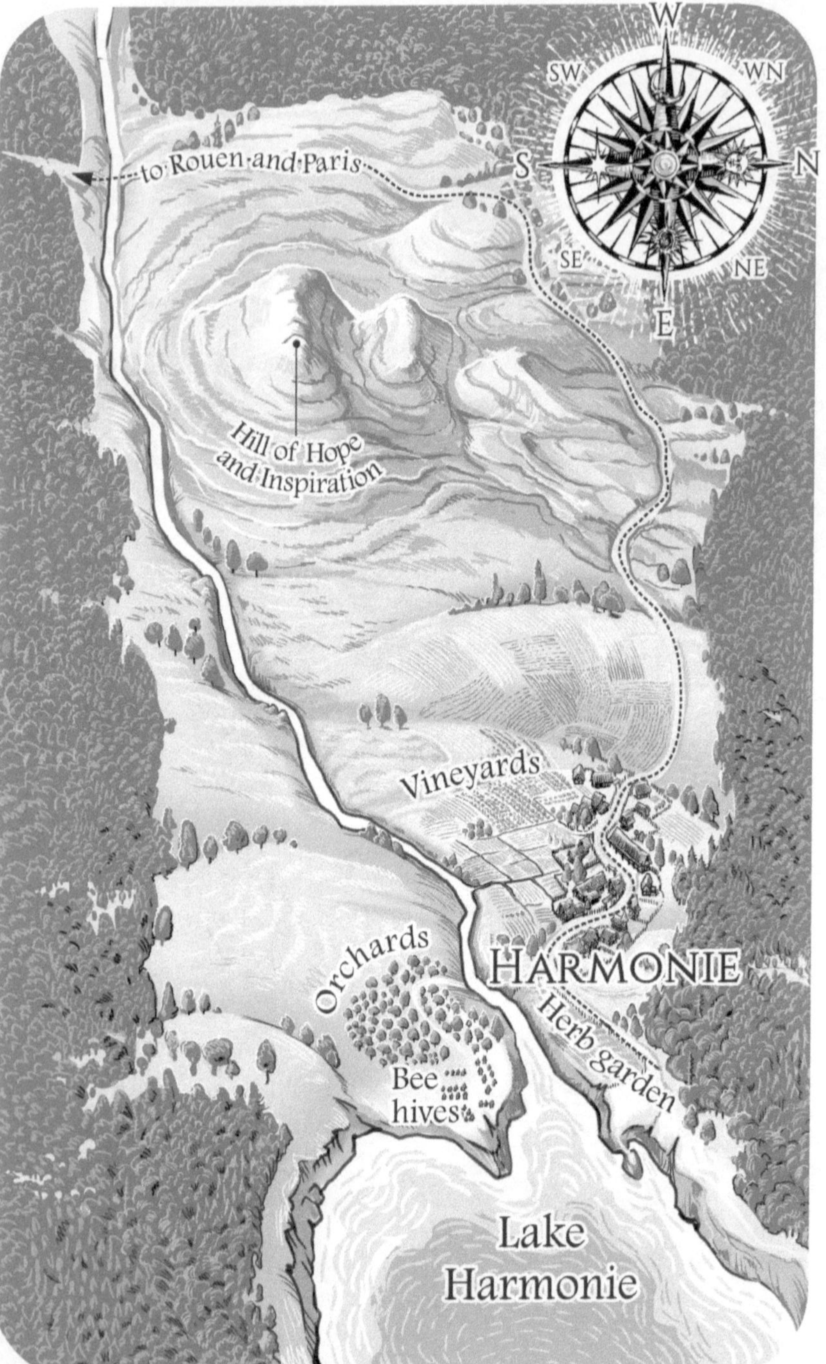

to Rouen and Paris
SW
W
WN
S
N
SE
NE
E
Hill of Hope
and Inspiration
Vineyards
Orchards
HARMONIE
Herb garden
Bee
hives
Lake
Harmonie

prologue

In the year 1002, Nichol and Robert and a small group of travelers founded Harmonie, a hamlet hidden deep in the kingdom of Normandy, less than three days ride northwest of Rouen.

Since childhood, Nichol has been gifted with her ability to see and hear people's true intentions. Alexander, her papa, valued her observations and advice and often sought them in his role as port commander and trade merchant in Marseilles, France.

In her early teens, she was trained to protect herself by Sir Roland, Alexander's most trusted soldier, after her brother Fredric and his friends assaulted her. Known then as Lisa, she became skilled with a bow and arrow, her use of a unique, jeweled dagger that only could be owned and used by the chosen one, and a powerful physical ability to outrun any man.

All her skills came into play when Nichol escaped to Paris after her papa was poisoned by her mother. Alexander had created a special map with instructions for her protection if she needed to escape. Upon his death, those he had advised to protect his daughter immediately gathered to move her away from her brother and her mother. The map she carried would lead her to Ezra, a moneylender and his partner in trade. When she departed Marseilles, a red-tailed hawk appeared overhead, seeming to oversee her actions.

Throughout her dangerous journey to Paris, she often heard a voice speak to her as she slept in the limbs of the tall trees she climbed each night, secured by her rope belt. Nichol referred to it as the *Lady* and often sought direction and assistance from what she came to believe was her protector. This voice was not new.

It has directed her actions and protected her from harm since she was a young girl.

Now, married to Robert and the mother of three, she is the chosen leader in the currently unknown valley hamlet of Harmonie, nearly three days journey north of Rouen, Normandy.

During her visits to Rouen, she met and befriended young Emma, destined to be future queen of England once she left Rouen. Emma's brother, Richard, the Duke of Normandy, owns the land where Harmonie resides, unbeknownst to him.

Nichol's vision and hard work in the hamlet has become a communal Harmonie House, a unique gathering place where Harmonie residents come to work, cook, and learn together, providing a haven for the adults and children.

Questions now surround Nichol:

• How can she protect her family?

• How can she protect her community?

• Does the *Lady* have other plans for her?

• Will Duke Richard provide his protection to Nichol and the hamlet of Harmonie?

• Will the alliance and sisterhood of now Queen Emma and Nichol continue?

• Will the merchants of Rouen, Paris, and the kingdom of England and Normandy accept a woman merchant when Ezra introduces her as his new partner?

• Will the red-tailed hawk continue to oversee Nichol and the children?

• Will the monk Timo become even more valuable as messenger Timo?

- Will Ezra's merchant and moneylending business thrive?

- Will the evil Priest Loupe's obsession to track Nichol and Lucette continue?

- Who will discover the secret hamlet of Harmonie?

Nichol knows that each of her three children has a special destiny.

Their destinies are revealed in *The Secret Rise*, Book 3, detailing their teenage years.

one

Harmonie

You will not fail; the Lady is with you.

In the morning darkness, the monk Timo awakened. There was no hint of the morning sun. Without hesitation, Timo sat up and then arose from his straw bedding.

Rubbing his eyes, he listened. Hearing no sound, he looked to the side, feeling his four-footed friend Moki's presence close by. A different feeling was running through his body and mind. He knew that today was different. It was a day that could soon bring an alliance between Nichol and Emma, the newly crowned Queen of England.

And much of it depended upon him.

"Moki, my friend, we have a long way to go today. This is a big day for us. Let us go pack for our journey and then find Nichol." When Moki heard Nichol's name, he lifted his head and let out a gentle bray and pushed Timo toward the entrance of the barn with his nose.

As they left the barn, Timo glanced at the horizon. His eyes scanned it, looking for weather warnings. His gaze came to rest on the shadow of Harmonie House, where a slight glow of light from the door emerged into the gloom.

Moki followed him to the entrance and when he entered, he was surprised to see Nichol and Helene surrounded by many glowing candles. They were busy preparing food for what was to be a large gathering. With both the sight and smell of food, Timo felt the growl of his belly.

Slowly, he approached the women. When the candlelight began to reveal his face, Nichol saw a worried look, one she had seen before, and stopped what she was doing. "What brings you and Moki here before the sunrise?"

"I had a strange dream that I cannot remember and that is what troubles me." And then words filled his mind.

What if I fail, Nichol? What if Emma will not see me?

Without hesitation, she got up from where she was seated and wrapped her arms around him. She whispered, "I can sense your concerns, Timo. You will not fail; the *Lady* is with you." And she felt him relax in her arms.

"Sit down. You must eat before you leave."

Helene brought him a bowl of broth with oats. As she placed it in front of him, she said, "We have packed bread, cheese, and salted meat for your trip." Timo put his hands around the bowl to lift and drink the broth as Helene gently placed a hand on his shoulder. In a voice that reminded him of his mother, she added, "You will charm Emma, just like you have Nichol and me. You will not fail, Timo."

The two women shared information about Emma that Timo hadn't heard before.

Showing him the red stone she wore around her neck that was given to her by Rose at the dock in Marseilles when she fled for Paris, Nichol said, "When Emma and I met in Rouen, we were able to communicate silently when I placed it in her hands. When we both touched the stone, Emma knew about Athena before her birth."

When Nichol revealed that, Timo raised his eyebrows.

She continued, "Emma and Duke Richard share a special sibling alliance that doesn't include their older brother, Archbishop William. Duke Richard protected her from his bullying."

Helene gave Timo a small package containing some of her husband Ezra's finer clothes to wear when he met Emma. As Timo refolded the articles into Moki's pack, Nichol shared her observations on the etiquette that would be appropriate when he first met Emma.

"Your training as a monk has taught you to listen carefully with your ears and to witness unspoken actions of those you meet. It will serve you well, showing you a person's true intentions. Do not speak to the king or Emma until you are spoken to. And always remember to bow when you greet them and when you leave.

"If you are alone with her, just be who you are. She knows of you through my tales about how I escaped from Marseilles and walked with you to Paris. She also knows of Shadow. She may not be fluent in English yet, but she will instantly recognize our language and using it will allow you privacy with your words. Those who serve her will most likely not understand it. She will understand you mean no harm and that you know me very well. Do not offer any information that is not part of the conversation or asked for.

"When she senses she can trust you, she will become more open. Most likely, she will want to know about me and Lucette. When I was last with her, she knew I was with child and she saw Aiden as if she was holding the stone as well. She felt I was her only friend."

As she said that, the door opened. Nichol's husband Robert entered, carrying Athena, and accompanied by Lucette and Aiden. "Athena is hungry," he murmured as he handed the infant to Nichol.

Shadow followed Robert in and plopped down on the cool floor. Lucette and Aiden ran to Timo and demanded his attention.

"Where you go?" Lucette asked.

Timo smiled and bent over so his eyes met theirs.

"I am going to see Granpapa Ezra and will be gone for many days. When I return, I will give you and Aiden a ride to the hill on Moki and we will pack food to take for all of us."

Picking them up, one in each arm, he took them outside and set them on Moki's back. Timo listened to the two of them chatter back and forth, amused at the clarity of the conversation, especially from Lucette.

She seems older than her years.

Joining them outside Harmonie House, Helene observed the patience Timo showed toward the children as she drew near.

"Come down, you two, Timo must pack and leave soon. He has a long trip ahead and will miss you both. Let us get some water for Moki."

As she spoke, Timo lifted them down and smiled as he quietly said to Helene, "I think Aiden and Lucette are creating their own language."

Laughing, Helene added, "Many mornings they wake when it is dark and no one else is awake. I listen to them converse with their own type of talk. You are right … it is almost like another language with Lucette telling Aiden new words and what they mean. If I do not know what Aiden wants, I turn to Lucette and she tells me. That little Lucette surprises me everyday."

Nichol had finished feeding Athena and passed her to Robert as she stood up from the chair. "Gunvor is excited about helping with Athena. As soon as you see her, watch how she reaches out to hold Athena."

Then she went to Timo, adding her final thoughts on ways he could communicate with Emma so she would understand that Nichol was sending her message through him.

"Timo, before you leave her, ask to pray with her. If you think it appropriate, remind her that you are also a monk. I will trust you to sense how much to reveal about how we met and continue to be connected. She and I are close in age."

Later that morning before he left, most residents of the valley knew where he was going and why.

Not only carrying nourishment for the journey and Timo's clothing, Moki's bags were loaded with cloth the women in the hamlet had made.

The cloth was intended for delivery to Joseph's and Rose's shop in Rouen. It has been the first shop Nichol had entered when she arrived from Paris, wearing the only breeches she had when they escaped in the middle of the night.

two

Rouen

You have the voice and similar features of your brother.

Late in the afternoon on his third day of travel, Timo arrived in Rouen and went directly to Ezra's home. He knocked on the door, announced himself, and watched as an eye appeared through a peephole. He remembered Ezra had a similar feature in his door in Paris, covered by a rabbit skin.

When the door opened, a man he didn't know stood in front of him.

Timo backed up a step and looked at the front of the building, ensuring he had the right place. As he gazed at the man for a moment, he appeared familiar. Then Timo realized who he was. A smile spread across his face.

Before he could speak, the man said, "I am Achim, Ezra's brother. Come in. Ezra is here as well."

For a moment, Timo observed Achim as he entered Ezra's home through the large front door.

When opened, the spacious interior welcomed gatherings where both Helene and Ezra loved to play host. Along the side wall were several pegs to hang cloaks.

To the left was the cooking area with a fire pit against the back wall, with stones built up the wall to protect it from the heat. Looking straight ahead from the large meeting room was a staircase that led to several sleep chambers.

Timo finally spoke. "You have the same voice and similar features of your brother."

Looking past the monk, Ezra saw the heavily-laden animal, waiting patiently. He turned to Gideon and Raisa, his brother's children.

"Take Timo's donkey to the warehouse. His name is Moki. Olaf and Marie will help you unload him. Then go to the stables where your horse and wagon are kept. The stable owners know Moki and will take him in."

Timo was then introduced to Dinah, Achim's wife.

Ezra and Roger, his protector, now housed a full family.

As they sat at the table in the main room, Dinah looked around, taking in the chaos and disarray she saw in the room. "Ezra, how long has Helene been in Harmonie? It doesn't look like anyone has cared for your home."

Sheepishly, Ezra lowered his voice. "Too long, Dinah. Roger and I have spent all our time between the warehouse and the docks. Some days, we don't even return here."

"Well, if we are to be here until we know where we will live, this place needs scrub brushes, soap, and water. Gideon and I will turn it back to a home. All the food here has gone bad. It will make anyone who eats it sick."

As she finished her words, she already had a wet cloth in hand wiping the table down and motioned all of them to sit at the now-cleaned table.

Relieved that he did not have to deal with cleaning the house while Achim's family was there, Ezra asked Timo, "Timo, what brings you to Rouen?"

"I am on my way to England to see Queen Emma and arrange a meeting for Nichol to follow. I will need your help to arrange passage on a ship to sail there. Once I arrive, I will beg for an audience with her.

"Before I left Harmonie, Nichol and I had an agreement. When I return from England, a message will be sent to Nichol to depart for Rouen. She will meet with the duke to secure his support and obtain passage to England. After that, she will leave to visit Emma in England to talk about trading with Harmonie and Rouen."

Ezra was quick to express his concern. "I need her here now. It is the right time to expand before winter sets in. She has the vision that is lacking here in Rouen."

Timo's response was equally fast. "She is the leader that Harmonie must have and she cannot be there and here at the same time. Nichol wants to inform the duke about Harmonie. All in Harmonie are worried that, with so much travel to and from the valley, one day someone will be followed. She will come here first and seek your advice before visiting the duke."

Timo paused, then added, "Together, I believe. You and Nichol both must go to see the duke at the same time."

Ezra smiled and nodded. "Yes, together we will go to see him. But first, we must go to the docks and find a ship leaving for England. Then we will book passage on that ship for you."

three

England

She sat on a silk cushion resting on a chair worthy of a queen.

Timo sailed for four days from Rouen to England. His destination was Winchester, where Queen Emma lived. Upon arrival in Southampton and after several careful inquiries, he learned that the new queen could indeed be found residing in Winchester, one day's ride north.

He waited for two days at the castle gates that were well appointed with guards surrounding the castle. Timo was patient. Finding a tree that was close to the entrance, he settled in after he delivered a wax-sealed parchment from the queen's brother, Duke Richard.

On the third morning, one of the guards approached him, saying, "My Queen will now see you."

Timo was granted entrance and led to a hall where Queen Emma was waiting. She was surrounded by rich tapestries of a variety of colors hanging from the walls. Large candles were lit, casting shadows throughout the room. With her was the castle steward on one side and her attendants on the other.

As Timo's eyes took it all in, he felt the coldness of the large room. He was also aware of the many guards that were stationed around the outer walls.

Richly garbed and wearing a glittering crown, Emma sat on a silk cushion, resting on a chair inlaid with gold. Across her shoulders was a cape with a fur collar to protect her from the cold drafts that were easily felt. Her feet rested on a red satin footstool on a dais two steps above the main floor.

Hands clasped in front of him, Timo approached and bowed from his waist.

"Your Majesty, I am here to bring you good wishes from Nichol of Rouen."

Hearing his words, Emma's heart leaped. With a wave of her hand, she dismissed the steward.

The man paused, obviously reluctant to depart.

Without hesitation, Emma spoke softly to Timo in French. She then turned and said in English to her attendants, "He is no danger and he is a friend of the queen."

As the steward left the hall, Emma slowly stepped down the two steps while her eyes never left Timo's. To his surprise, she took him by his arm and spoke again in her native French. "I have a limited understanding of their English language."

Then she turned to him. "I hear that you are a man who has great skill at making plants grow."

Timo smiled. "I am indeed that man, and I know someone who wishes to walk with you once again in a garden."

As they left the damp, cold castle hall, Emma escorted Timo to her garden and into the sunshine of a warm summer day. Her ladies followed, but kept their distance, as did the guards.

Whispering softly to him, she continued, "My attendants were picked because they spoke the language of Normandy. Do you speak old French?"

Timo nodded.

A sly smile appeared on her face. "Then we will speak openly."

She led him to a bench in the shade of a massive ancient oak tree.

As they approached the tree, Timo stopped, leaned back, and gazed at its breadth, its massive branches reaching and touching the sky. Then he asked, "If it could speak of men, what would this oak say?"

Without hesitation, Emma responded, "This oak is a *Lady* and speaks of women and men. She speaks to me."

"Of course, the tree does. She speaks to Nichol as well." As his last words were said, a light wove its way through the branches and onto Timo's face.

Queen Emma's entire body relaxed when she saw what the light revealed.

With a soft look and smile, Emma murmured gently, "I see you."

A phrase Timo had heard many times before from the lips of Nichol.

His time with the Queen passed too quickly. Emma told him of her isolation and her longing for the ways of Rouen and the friendship of Nichol.

Her attendants became agitated as the castle steward approached. Abruptly, he said, "The king wishes to see you."

Timo's last words to her were, "Nichol will come before the end of summer and before storms appear over the channel. Most likely, she will bring her new baby daughter with her."

Immediately, Emma stood and began to leave as two guards approached and began to escort Timo away.

Turning her head, Timo saw a smile grow quickly across her face as she heard his words. She leaned toward him, and murmured in French, "I would so love to hold baby Athena."

The guards stopped as their queen spoke and turned to hear if she had more to say.

Timo's eyebrows rose as he looked into her eyes. "How did you know the baby girl was called Athena?"

Stopping, she turned to him, the guards still at her side. Her smile remained.

"On our last visit, we both shared Nichol's stone. We always did that when we were together. I then knew she was with child and it was to be a sister to the young boy. I didn't know about Aiden until then. And that's when she told me of how he came to be her son."

Timo was taken back with what he had heard. *What else does Nichol see … and hear? Are these two women meant to have a destiny that will include us all? And perhaps England and Harmonie?*

"Queen Emma, is there a special message that you want me to take back to Nichol?"

"Just tell her I miss her and to come soon. And to bring Lucette and Aiden as well."

As Timo watched her departure, he saw the soft light forming above her head.

The Lady is with us … and me on this journey. And she is watching over Emma, too.

On his return to Southampton for his departure, Timo slowly rode and often stopped to make notes of all the crops, animals being raised, and the use of the land.

Nothing escaped his curious mind.

Finally, he remembered why he was there and rode without further delay to the waiting ship. He had much to tell Nichol … and Ezra.

One day, I will return.

four

Journey Home

*We have entered a place
we have never been before and can never leave.*

Timo was pleased to hear that the return trip would commence that afternoon when the tides were high. He boarded the ship that was laden with wool destined for the looms in Rouen. He was treated as though he was cargo, wedged between bundles of wool as the ship rose and dropped with each wave.

He found himself praying for many—himself and a safe passage.

For Queen Emma and what he began to foresee as a woman who would carry a heavy influence as their queen.

For Nichol, as a visionary who sought the greater good for those around her and was linked to the young queen.

And thankfulness for the presence of the *Lady* and the Light, that he was now known as a friend and not to be feared.

And for Nichol and her growing family that he had become part of.

Then he felt the words that he had been thinking. *Had the Lady seen me at the fair and brought us together on the road leading to Paris?*

His passage back allowed him the time to prepare for the bounty of questions he would receive from Nichol. Every word from Emma must be captured and repeated in the right order, every meaning must be precise.

When he arrived in Rouen four days later, Timo went directly to Ezra's. With a clenched fist, he pounded on the solid oak door.

"Ezra, it is Timo." Moments later, he heard the brace being removed and the door opened.

Ezra greeted him. "Come in and sit down. We have been anxiously waiting for your return. I knew that the ship would arrive back today."

Shortly after Ezra and Timo sat down, they heard another fist as it pounded on the door.

Young Raisa rushed to it, with Dinah behind her. As she opened it, Achim, Gideon, and Roger entered. They all gathered around Timo at the same time as Dinah put bread, cheese, and cups of ale on the table. The first mug was placed in Timo's hand.

While he had a long drink, Ezra became anxious. He couldn't wait any longer for Timo to offer information. "Did you see the queen?"

Timo nodded as he swallowed and put his cup down.

"Yes, and she is most eager to see Nichol. At first, she seemed distant and not too sure of her thoughts about what she should reveal to me. I saw that she could not speak freely with her attendants listening. We began to speak old French and our conversation became private. Calm came over her as words poured from her lips. She misses Rouen and her family."

Timo paused to choose his next words. With confidence he said, "She misses Nichol above all. And she knew about Athena … she even knew her name. The queen asked Nichol to bring Athena when she comes to see her. And I could see the Light around the queen as we approached a large oak tree to sit and talk.

"It was Nichol's Light … the one that I saw at the birth of Athena," Timo added. "I think the *Lady* and her light may be with the queen at times. She may not know it, but when I saw the Light, I did."

Low voices could be heard around the small table.

Ezra's normal stoic display changed while stroking his chin in thought. All were waiting for his reveal. A faint sign of elation appeared on his face.

"First the duke and now the queen." He then mumbled to himself, "I believe we have entered a place we have never been before and can never leave."

Dinah gasped, "The Queen of England …"

A loud knock on the door startled everyone and brought the men to their feet.

five

Discovered

We are all stronger now because you are here.

loud voice came through the door. "It is Robert …"
Another voice sounded: "… and Nichol."

Timo sprang from his chair before he heard Nichol's voice. Opening the door, he was alarmed at what he saw. Concern was etched on their weary faces. Helene had the same face. Then he saw that Gunvor, holding Lucette, and Tova, holding Aiden, had come as well.

He was worried. As he stepped back, he pulled the family within and shut the door quickly. "What brings the whole family to Rouen?"

Nichol saw Robert's family as she stepped through the door. Speaking so everyone could hear, she said, "I must see the duke, and then travel to England to see Emma. Robert felt that all of us must come at this time and stay for the winter."

Timo's eyes would not leave Nichol's. "What has happened?" He knew it was too soon for the family to arrive in Rouen.

Nichol shook her head. "The children need a bed to sleep in, and then we will talk."

Ezra went to Helene and as they embraced, she whispered in his ear, "Three riders were spotted at the south end of the stream, and one was a priest. I need to go rest now; take me upstairs. I'll tell you more there."

Gunvor and Tova held Lucette and Aiden in their arms, Robert pointed the way to a room upstairs where they went to lay down.

Dinah took Athena gently from Nichol and her smile broadened. "Finally, a grandchild in my arms."

Ale was brought to Robert and water to Nichol. Reaching for the cup, Nichol began to speak.

"Tova and I were taking food and water to workers in the field. Lucette and Aiden were with us and Shadow herded them to keep them from wandering off. As I approached Guvnor and her mother, Freyja, I looked past them. Then I heard shouts from other workers in the field. They were pointing south to where the stream flows from the lake.

"Three men just sat on their horses in the middle of the stream as their horses drank. I think they wanted to be seen as they observed the valley. At first, I thought they were spies, there to watch and report. Soon they turned and left.

"John and Cara left the field and headed to the barn. I followed him, knowing that he would rather fight than be discovered. He had saddled a horse and was ready to give chase with sword in hand. I grabbed the horse's reins and stopped him. Cara was there and pleaded with him to stop as well. As this was happening, Shadow had begun to move Lucette and Aiden, nosing them to follow me to the barn.

"Then I said, 'We cannot chase down and kill everyone that discovers Harmonie. It is time for me to go and talk to the duke.'

"By this time, we were surrounded by villagers. I could sense their fear along with their angry words—words that were directed at Garlyn and me. Garlyn then went to a wagon and climbed on the back. He shouted above all the angry noise, 'STOP!'

"The villagers quieted down. Then he said, 'We always knew that someday we would be discovered. Today, the day has finally come.'

"Garlyn was the one villager everyone always looked to for counsel—long before we came. They desperately wanted his advice. And he gave it.

"'Go back to the fields. There is work to be done. We will all meet in the Harmonie House in the morning.' And slowly, the villagers went back to the fields or to their homes. That left Robert, Garlyn, Helene, John, Cara, and me standing together. You could see that John still wanted to pursue and fight the intruders. I could see his anger seething with the intrusion of the outsiders. And now, Harald and Freyja joined in.

"Lucette and Aiden kept their eyes on us, waiting to see what would happen next … and then they acted. At the same time, each attacked one of John's legs, wrapping their arms around them. 'We got you, John,' Lucette said. 'Stay with Mama.'

"Shadow was jumping around wanting to be a part of the group. Then, I could see John's behavior change. He began to walk stiff-legged and slowly pulling Lucette around in a circle, crying out, 'You got me, Lucette.'

"That was the moment that made a difference for all of us, from our personal feelings of being found to what really matters. John's anger disappeared when he bent over and one at a time lifted Aiden and Lucette onto his shoulders and walked them to our home.

"When we gathered inside, I was now the one they looked to for leadership. It was a tense moment, with everyone standing inside, waiting for someone to speak. The air was filled with feelings of betrayal from being discovered.

"Words of encouragement were necessary, but I could find none. I simply revealed what was going through my head. And then I said: 'When I first saw the riders, I only thought of the danger for a moment.' I looked at the faces of those of us as they were watching the riders. When most in the field turned to me, I could tell that it was me they blamed for this happening. I could see them … fear, betrayal, and defeat on their faces.

"I then turned and looked closely at the riders. The rider in the middle was a priest. I carefully observed the other two men with him. The priest was clean-shaven; it was Loupe." As she said Loupe's name, there was a gasp in the room.

Nichol continued, "The others wore full beards. Suddenly, one stood in his saddle and leaned forward, then turned to the priest and pointed at me. It was Fredric.

"I think they saw Shadow and my children. Then they connected them to me. Before they turned to leave, the priest pointed and shook his finger at me. I also noticed that the red-tailed hawk was circling over Shadow and the children, as if ready to protect them.

"Rage and a sense of defeat filled my mind, but then a calm feeling came over me. With a slow and deliberate motion, I pulled my dagger—the one he and Fredric had seen me use before. I slowly lifted it for all to see, the sun reflecting from the blade, and jewels glittered like a torch. I then slowly lowered it at him and returned his finger point toward me with my blade. His anger was swift. He jerked his horse's head from drinking water, dug his heels into its flanks and left. The other two followed and they disappeared into the forest.

"My thoughts were vibrating in my head: *When I had the chance, I let you live. Next time I will not fail.*

"The villagers were right. I was the one that brought them to Harmonie. Wandering peasants did not discover Harmonie that day; it was evil men on horseback that discovered Harmonie. At that moment I knew I had to return to Rouen and seek an audience with the duke … for all of us."

Garlyn said, "Nichol, we would never have been able to remain hidden. We are all stronger now because you are here. Without your observations of your first trip to Rouen and how it was different this time, none of us would ever be experiencing what has happened to benefit us all."

As Nichol took in his words, she felt their impact. *It was Garlyn who had showed us that we were one. This is the one place that I've felt secure for the first time since Papa was murdered.*

That night in bed, a lone candle cast a dim circle of light while the children were asleep. Robert whispered, "Tell me what bothers you so … you need your sleep."

Turning her body toward him, Nichol spoke softly to him.

"Robert, do you remember when I said that, when you have an obstacle like a stream or a river, you build a bridge to cross over? I feel like I am that bridge from Harmonie to Rouen, but it is not ready for others to cross over. I must continue to build the bridge to benefit all, not just the powerful. The time to complete the bridge between our two worlds cannot wait—and I mean the peasant world of Harmonie and the world of the royals and church. Once I bring Harmonie into their world, there will be no return."

Robert took her into his arms. "You will not fail; it is not just your bridge to build. I know you worry about losing the trust that you have earned with the duke. I know what you have told me, just as I know he will wait for your return. He knows your value, just as I do, my dear wife."

With those words, he pulled her closer, leaving a kiss on her cheek. As he did, he could feel her relaxation. A smile crossed his lips.

She is a chosen one and I know that our children will carry her vision forward.

As his thoughts ended, he heard a gentle snore at his side.

Robert raised his head and gently let his lips brush her forehead before laying his head down and letting sleep overcome him.

six

The Nightmare

Where am I?

After the events of that day, it confirmed to Nichol that, for the first time, they were all vulnerable. No longer was Harmonie the safe place for her family that it had been when first discovered.

Lying in bed, exhausted from the travel and stress of the day, she fell fast asleep, even though her mind had not resolved what had just happened.

In the depth of her dream, Nichol felt as if she had awakened and found herself alone in a large windowless dark room with only one door. Slowly she walked to the door, not knowing how she got into the room. Suddenly, she felt terrified that she was a prisoner, with only one way out.

Taking a firm grip on the handle, she turned it while taking a deep breath. She pulled on the handle.

A slight opening emitted a bright light coming from behind the door before it was forcibly pulled shut.

Her heart now pounding in her chest, she didn't know what lay beyond the door. All that she knew was that it was her only way out. Rage replaced fear and her strength now doubled as she gripped the door handle again. With all her might, she wrestled the door open wider, but not enough to walk through.

Someone of great strength was pulling the door back … a man. She heard his voice. She pleaded with the voice behind the door to let her through, but to no avail.

Nothing but silence.

Despair set in. The empty room was all that she had … all that the man behind the door will allow her to have. Nichol sat down on the floor with her back leaning against the door. Looking up, she noticed a handle on the opposite wall … just a handle.

Rising to her feet, she walked briskly across the room, her sole focus on the handle. Closing her eyes, she visualized a door … her door … and when she opened her eyes, her hand had grasped the handle. Turning the handle gently, she was able to pull on it, without force.

The door opened wide and the valley—her valley—came into full view with women, men, and their children watching while she took her first step out of the windowless room.

Turning, she looked back to the door that had refused her entry and saw light as it began to open. She smiled and left her door open as she walked away.

Suddenly, Nichol woke up, filled with fear. Her bedroom was as dark as a moonless night.

Where am I?

She felt Robert by her side. Instinctively, she rose to her feet and rushed to the opened door.

Wiping cold sweat from her brow, she lit a candle and carried it to where each of her children slept. Holding it high over each one to see them in peace, she saw that they were cuddled together. The breath she had been holding escaped through her lips with a shallow hiss.

Shadow was lying at the foot of their bed, calmly watching her …

It was a nightmare that woke me.

Athena began to fuss. Picking up her infant, she returned to her bed to nurse her. As she cradled the babe to her breast, a warm hand reached out and rested at the top of her head, and she felt a gentle kiss brush her forehead.

Robert is with me. All the people I love are with me.

She closed her eyes. *We will be safe.*

seven

The Duchess

I see you are not wearing your fighting clothes today.

Morning arrived in Ezra's household that was now bulging with others, with not a room or floor unoccupied. Shadow's wet nose on Lucette's and Aiden's faces started them giggling and the noise woke up Athena. A stern look from Robert urged them out of the room and downstairs. Without hesitation, they pounced on Gunvor and Tova. The commotion woke everyone up. Athena, now squalling with hunger, welcomed Nichol's breast.

Dinah and Achim both sat up from their floor mat and watched the children's antics. Gideon jumped up and growled as he approached them. Their giggles turned to screams, to hide as Raisa joined in. The chase was on and Shadow joined the mayhem.

The noise brought Ezra and Helene to the top of the stairs. Watching the others, Ezra put his arm around Helene and kissed her cheek. "This house has been too quiet for too long, my love."

When Lucette and Aiden tired of the chase, Dinah stood, clapping her hands and demanded everyone's attention. She began giving orders.

"Gunvor and Tova, get the children dressed and take them and Shadow outside while we prepare the morning meal. Gideon, kindle a fire in the hearth. Helene and I will help prepare Nichol for her visit to the duke this morning."

After all were fed, Nichol was attended to by Helene and Dinah. She bathed and put on a purple dress, covering her hair with a mantle of white silk that draped around her neck and dropped to the middle of her back.

The dress was the same color that Emma so proudly wore when she lived in Rouen. She had told Nichol that her brother Richard would always comment on the color when she wore it. As her brother, and the one who had arranged her marriage, he reminded her that she would attract a man of royal blood with her beauty, equal to her birthright.

Before Nichol left, she encouraged Athena to nurse once more before she left. With full approval given by Robert and all in the house, and final words of support, knowing the importance for all their lives, she nodded her farewells.

Ezra took Nichol's hand as she approached the door and softly said, "Your duke does not stand a chance." Nichol laughed as she opened the door.

As usual, Shadow went first, sniffing the air for danger. "Shadow, let us go and visit Duke Richard. I wish you could talk and tell me of those your smell remembers; the ones that mean us harm."

Shadow walked just a few steps ahead of Nichol, flanking her on her left side. Nichol could smell the inviting aroma of fresh bread being baked and redirected their walk to the stall that offered it. She was amused by the attention she garnered. Most knew her as the young woman with the wolf dog that dressed in men's attire.

Their smiles and an occasional nod from some pleased her. The usual children followed her and Shadow, hoping for a treat, and they were not disappointed. Once they arrived, Nichol paid for four loaves of bread, breaking off large pieces until all the children had one. Having one loaf left, she continued walking.

As she passed the fish stalls, Shadow stopped. The fishmonger who knew them came from behind his display of fresh-caught fish.

"I saw you give bread to the children. For some, that is their only meal of the day." Picking up a fish, he offered it to Shadow. When Nichol tried to pay him, he refused.

Thanking him, she headed for the castle. As she approached the gate, Nichol was cautiously observed by the gate sentry. Shadow weaved in front and across her path with the fish still in her mouth, waiting for permission from Nichol to consume it.

Squinting at first, then as she moved closer, a broad smile appeared through the sentry's full beard.

"Nichol, I see you are not wearing your fighting clothes today."

Nichol took his hand and gave him the loaf of bread. "I am not expecting a fight today." Smiling as a devilish look appeared on her face, her eyes narrowed. "We did put fear in many that day, didn't we?"

Laughing out loud, the sentry replied, "I have missed your visits. Are you staying in Rouen for the winter?"

"Yes, but I must see the duke first and then I will travel to England and see Emma." Nichol paused, and then added, "You have saved my life and yet I do not know your name."

"My name is Victor."

"Victor, would you escort Shadow and me to the castle door after she consumes her fish?"

Nodding his head, Victor proffered his arm to Nichol while slowly walking to the castle, adding, "I believe the duke will be pleased to see you." Once at the door, he bowed his head slightly. He then returned to the gate. Shadow had finished her treat and followed Nichol into the castle.

Nichol lifted the door knocker and dropped it twice, announcing her arrival.

I like this knocker. Robert needs to make a knocker for Ezra's door.

The steward Thomas answered and just stood staring at Nichol, bewildered as he observed her new appearance. Nodding at her, a smile appeared, as if he approved of her new look.

"Nichol, I will announce your arrival to the duke." He bowed and turned on his heel to walk away.

Duchess Judith suddenly appeared and spoke loudly as she walked briskly toward her. "Nichol, what a surprise!" Judith's obvious joy in seeing Nichol was a welcome greeting. "Thomas, tell my husband we will be in the garden."

Taking Nichol by the hand, she led the way as they walked outside to the courtyard garden. In a lowered voice, she continued to speak. "We will have time together. The duke likes to make people wait."

They sat at the same bench where she and Emma had many closely guarded conversations while sharing the stone. Shadow lay at their feet.

Sitting close, a mere whisper away, the women clasped hands.

Nichol looked at Judith's belly. "I see you are with child." Nichol gently put her hands on both sides of the increased mound of the duchess. "The duke will be pleased to have his first son."

Her comforting words pleased the duchess. "Emma told me before she left that you would know and that I should listen to you. I know Richard values your thoughts, too."

Nichol's gaze was direct. "Soon I will sail to England to see Emma. I promised her that I would travel to England after the birth of Athena and before the end of summer. If she has not already heard of your coming birth, may I share your good news with her?"

"I know Emma will welcome you, and you may tell her of my news. If she has sent word here to the duke, I have not heard.

Men control her every word and action now. That is why she needs you more than ever. I even heard Richard say that she needs you." Hearing footsteps on the path, Judith looked up to see Thomas approach.

Nichol watched while Judith's whole body slumped, seemingly overcome with emotion. *She longs for close women companions who are not attendants, and who act as the ears and eyes of others.*

In response, Nichol grabbed her hand firmly and looked directly in her eyes.

"When I return, you will be the first one I visit. We must always remember your brave word spoken in defiance when I fought and defeated the pirate. I heard you shout out … NEVER."

That brought a smile to the wet eyes of the duchess. Both women stood and embraced.

Thomas cleared his throat. "The duke is waiting, my lady."

eight

The Duke

A son ... how do you know I will have a son?

Nichol climbed the stairs to Duke Richard's solar and stood in the doorway, waiting to be received. She moved through when she heard his voice calling her.

"Nichol, come in."

She entered and stood behind the chair that the duke once provided just for her. Slowly bowing, she greeted him. "Your Grace."

She returned to standing straight while watching for his reaction to her dress that was in his sister Emma's favorite color. To her dismay, what she saw in his gaze was a look that she did not want to see from him … not now, not ever.

A woman knew when a man felt desire for her. And this was a reaction that she did not expect or want.

She continued to speak. "The duchess was pleased with my dress. You will win favors if you surprise her with one in this royal color. Your Grace, I promised Emma that I would travel to England by the end of summer to visit and bring her news of Normandy. Would you like for me to deliver a private message to her?"

Richard shook his head to remove the thought that overtook him when Nichol entered. "How soon before you leave?"

"As soon as Ezra finds a ship that will take us to England; one that will take all my family. My husband Robert will be with me, along with my daughter and son, who are each under two years of age, and my baby Athena."

A stunned look crossed the duke's face and an uneasy silence filled with hesitation was in the air. "Your whole family? For what purpose does the whole family travel with you?"

I see him; he knows.

"Four days ago, three riders were seen at the edge of the valley where my family and I live. I recognized two of the riders: the Priest Loupe and my evil brother Fredric. For the last two years they have hunted me, endlessly pursuing me and my family as their prey." The more she talked, the angrier she became.

Her outburst of anger filled the room and was felt by Richard. Her fury had the effect she wanted. Her anger now became his concern.

Shadow rose from a prone position by Nichol's feet and assumed a wary, alert pose by her leg. It did not go unnoticed by the duke.

"Now they have threatened my family, and I can't leave them at risk now." Nichol looked down as rage filled her whole being. Slowly, she looked up and stared directly at Richard. "The priest and my brother have gone too far."

With effort, her rage subsided but her jaw remained tight.

Taking a deep breath, she added, "I want you to know where I … where I reside in your kingdom. My family has built a new hamlet; one that can bring wealth to you. We live in a valley north of Rouen, located within the kingdom of Normandy. The valley is subject to your authority; something I believe you knew before I came here today.

"I must know … under whose authority did the priest ride several days from here? Was it your authority, or did the priest take it on himself to travel north just to find me … *us?* Was it to bring us harm?"

Then she added one more thought in the form of a question. "Does not the priest have enough souls to save in Rouen and its surrounding villages without spreading his vile deeds in other places?"

Nichol paused, noticing Richard's outward agitation. He raised his hand to silence her.

"Shut the door, Nichol. I knew this day would come."

His eyes remained on her as she moved to the door and closed it. Returning, she sat down in the chair opposite him. A smile surfaced on his face.

"Emma told me how you taught her to sit in the right place and listen to conversations. Here, as in other places, the very walls have ears. I must thank you for helping to prepare her for her new role as queen. She is in a strange land and does not have kind ears around her."

Nodding to his words, Nichol waited for what he would add, knowing that he was using Emma as an example of what would come next. Richard needed someone he could trust—someone to be his ears.

Richard continued, "I have spies throughout the kingdom. Without them, I would be blind to what happens here in the kingdom and beyond. I knew you would arrange to travel to see Emma. She is waiting and you must leave soon. I also know of your friend Timo's visit to England.

"Take your family to England. When you return, tell Judith of Emma. She would be pleased because she admires who you are and how you have been a friend to my sister. I feel she is hoping that you will be a friend to her as well. We will have much to talk about when you get back.

"I ask you to remember that you are a woman, and, as such, you must temper your conversations with men. They will fear you. Use your wit; it is your most powerful weapon. I have had conversations with Ezra and he has told me about you. I have also observed your skills.

"Unknown to you, you are part of a dangerous struggle with the priest who is protected by my brother. I know you are aware that Archbishop William is my brother. I have cautioned him about the priest and your brother Fredric. I gave this warning with care and also as my last warning to him. You must be aware that I and my brother do not always agree."

He sat back in his chair, letting her take in his words.

"My authority is absolute over the land, but I must tread lightly with William. Do not corner me by demanding an answer and resolution that I'm presently at a loss to answer or provide. The actions I am planning will take time. When my plans come to fruition, they have personal consequences that could even affect Emma and the church. It requires much preparation."

Letting her absorb his last words, he added, "Is there something you wish to tell me before I see you again?"

"When I entered your solar this morning, you revealed to me that you knew my location away from Rouen. Do you think it is the priest's obsession of me—and now my family—that led him to the valley? I know much of his background through my father. The priest is not who you think he is and will only bring trouble for you and the archbishop. The only devotion he has is to himself, not to the church."

"How did I reveal that to you?"

"I saw you as I came into your solar. You know my ability to see people's intentions—yours included. I have displayed my ability to you and wish to be of counsel to you when you desire."

Counsel? What could she have in mind?

Richard sat up and then leaned forward. "Before you leave for England, I desire another discussion with you. You said that your hamlet could bring wealth to me. I need to know about your thoughts and how that can be executed.

"I will arrange your passage to England so that you will have my protection as you travel. How many will travel with you?"

Overwhelmed with his offer of protection, she responded, "Thank you," then added, "I will pay you in coin, whatever the cost is. Passage is needed for Robert and my children. Shadow. Then Timo and two older children; Gunvor and Tova, who care for my children.

"Once we return, we will go back to the hamlet that we call Harmonie to make sure the harvests are in and prepare it for the coming winter. Most will stay behind. I will then return to stay in Rouen with Robert and the children through the winter months."

Nichol stood and spoke with confidence. "I am pleased that you will have a son by then and Ezra and I will be able to expand on what we have learned and what we can do for you. There is a ship leaving for England within a few days. Ezra and I will see you before I depart."

A son … how would she know that I would have a son?

Richard turned his thoughts to words. "A son … how do you know I will have a son?"

Nichol paused and then smiled. "I knew him when I touched Judith in the garden. She knows as well."

Before leaving, Nichol's gaze fell upon a new tapestry hanging on what once was a barren stone wall, woven with richly colored thread.

The tapestry depicted Richard mounted on a majestic white horse with spear in hand. Hounds were at the horse's feet, sniffing the ground for the hunt's prey. A distance away, a boar was seen in the forest. Men on foot with spears stood by, ready for the chase.

Enchanted, Nichol stood and moved closer, taking in the tapestry's rich blend of colored thread, masterfully woven.

Richard watched Nichol's every move, attentively waiting for her thoughts.

Stepping back to study the tapestry's theme and aware that the duke was following her every move, she looked at Richard. He was obviously waiting for approval.

Lifting her eyebrows, Nichol bestowed upon him a smile and a nod.

"It is truly worthy of your solar. Whoever created this tapestry is a true master. I am drawn to your regal pose here. One day you will come to the valley and we will hunt together. You will not be disappointed."

Revealing and Opportunities

It's a beginning for all of us …
the secret rise of our knowledge and power.

After leaving the castle, Nichol slowly walked through cobblestone streets toward Ezra's home, lost in the moment with thoughts of the meeting with Richard.

In her father's solar, while hidden in her niche long ago, she listened only to spoken words at first and how they were uttered. She heard words spoken in anger, sorrow, regret, or words that told lies. When she emerged from the niche, she told her papa what she heard and what she believed their meaning to be.

Soon she realized that at times, she was wrong. Words alone did not always convey the whole story. She needed to see her papa's interaction with his visitors. After she cut a discreet hole in the tapestry covering the niche, she began to observe the faces and gestures. Thus, she learned to understand the spoken word also included seeing.

When Nichol said *I see you* to others, it bore a deeper meaning than what they understood.

Suddenly, Nichol found herself in front of Ezra's home.

Hearing a crying baby inside, she knocked on the door, announcing her arrival. At the same time, Shadow scratched her large paw on the door. Robert opened it with Athena in his arms, her cries turning to a whimper when she saw her mama.

Looking around the room, Nichol asked, "Where are Lucette and Aiden?"

"Helene, Dinah, Raisa, Gunvor, and Tova took them to the market. They needed to run outside. Ezra, Achim, and Gideon went to the docks and warehouse. Ezra wants them to become involved in the merchant business."

Reaching for Athena, she sat at the table and exposed her breast to the hungry infant. Robert sat next to her. Their eyes met as he said, "Tell me about your visit with the duke."

Nichol turned from Robert to observe Athena nursing, softly stroking her temple, then taking her small hand in hers. She began to share her morning.

"The duke is the older brother I wish I had. He was thrust into power at a young age and has been taught well. When I first met and spoke with him, he told me that a woman should know her place—to be seen, not heard. I was offended, then I thought I could use that to my advantage. As I continued to meet with him, he was asking my advice, using my listening and observation skills. And I freely gave it.

"When Emma's and my friendship increased, she would confide in him, telling him to trust me before she left for England. From my conversation with him this morning, he acknowledged that and encouraged me to meet with her in England. He offered to arrange our passage under his protection.

"When he said that, I told him that I would pay him in coins for our costs. He was surprised when I told him all who would accompany me, including Shadow and Ezra.

"Before I met with him, I sat with the duchess. She is with child and I know that she will bear him a son. He now knows this as well.

Robert was amazed at what he heard Nichol say.

Where did this wife of mine come from?

How does she know so much?

How can she communicate the way she does?

How does she get those in power to respect her as a woman and to be someone that can be trusted?

As his thoughts traveled forward, he was pulled back when she continued to speak.

"I would be part of his counsel and be unseen, with all the intimate knowledge of the kingdom. It's a beginning for all of us … the secret rise of our knowledge and power.

"When Loupe and Fredric came to Harmonie, I felt defeated but now I see we are in Rouen, and the bridge between Harmonie and Rouen is almost complete. The duke is part of it."

Lifting Athena to her shoulder and gently patting her on the back, she murmured, "I wonder what purpose the *Lady* will have for her?"

ten

The Beginning

We must maintain his confidence in us.
His path will be our path.

The next morning, Ezra's household was buzzing with activity. Plans for the day were being made.

Nichol and Ezra retreated to Ezra's room for a private conversation. In great detail, Nichol told him of the conversation and the thoughts she had with and about the duke. "On my way home, I thought that Harmonie needed a baron, one of our own choosing. Ezra, I think that should be you."

Ezra listened, then replied with words that could have come from her papa.

"I spent my life building my merchant and moneylending business, which is what I know and who I am. *You,* Nichol, must become someone who has a title; you are the one Harmonie needs and must have. When I propose this to the duke, I want you to remain silent while he thinks about it … or makes a ruling. His response will tell us a lot about his plans for us before we sail to England.

Nichol was aghast. "A title? No! No, Ezra! it must be you who has a title. He wants my advice but has also made it clear to me that a woman must know her place. My visits will be seen by most to be with Judith, but there is a place for me to hear conversations and not be seen. He desires this, and therefore it will happen. He is aware that actions against him from near or far are always in the making."

Nichol put her hand on Ezra's. He patiently watched and could tell she was searching for the right words to say.

"Ezra, do you remember when I was brought before Duke Richard to answer for the attack on Loupe? At first, he was upset and angry. I could see he did not want to be bothered. When he spoke, it was with anger. But then in the cold candlelit hall, with only narrow slits in the wall for outside light, the *Lady* appeared.

"As I watched her light flow forth, she settled over the duke's throne. I slowly turned my head and noticed that I was the only one to see that she was present. Suddenly, the duke changed his tone and ordered everyone out of the hall except me. Emma then entered the hall.

"I know that his abrupt change and acceptance of me was because of the *Lady*. The duke will see us today because the *Lady* has given us a voice. We must maintain his confidence in us. His path will be our path."

Ezra nodded in approval. "There have been few people in my life that I could confide in with delicate matters and rely on for advice. Until you came along, that was Helene and Alexander. Others I would not burden nor could I trust. But you are Alexander's daughter, a mirror of how he thought and treated others. I know of no one that can see a person's bearing at first meeting like you. Today our journey begins."

Their eyes held. Then Nichol added, "Duke Richard expects us when the noon bells are rung. At that time, we must be at the castle door. Today is a good day for walking; the weather is clear. There are no clouds or promises of bad weather. Let us leave early and walk through the village and say hello to the merchants along the way. It will be good to be seen by others. We can tell them of new items in the warehouse they may not know about."

Most days in Harmonie, Nichol dressed in breeches and tunic. Her dagger rested in its sheath, hidden from sight. When she was in a dress, it had no place to hide.

Her tresses peeked from her plain cloth head covering; they had darkened and were wavy much like Lucette's. Her sun-darkened skin separated her from women of privilege.

Where privileged women had access to items many in the villages did not … or did not think about … she did not understand why most chose to live with their body orders that could be cleansed with bathing. Their odor sometimes overwhelmed her.

Why did they not wash? often entered her mind. As a young girl, bathing was frequent in her father's villa. Margaux, the woman who was like a mother to her when she lived in Marseilles, had told her that keeping her body clean would keep illness away.

Nichol thought it was normal to bathe with buckets of warmed water and her young children looked forward to it. They loved the soap with olive oil that she routinely used.

As she thought of Margaux, she wondered if bathing frequently could be why her family did not get the sicknesses that other families get.

When she was in Rouen, Duke Richard advised her to wear dresses. When he first offered this suggestion, it was more of a demand.

At the same time, he warned her that she was coming under attack from powerful men but did not mention his brother, Archbishop William. Nichol knew who these attacks were coming from for Richard to have warned her.

Wearing men's clothes pleased her and gave her the strength while standing next to men, even knowing most would not accept her. Stories of her standing up to those who harmed others had been observed by many in Rouen and most in Harmonie. The confidence and defensive skills that her papa had encouraged after the assaults from her brother Fredric and his friends flowed through her.

She knew that she must heed his advice.

eleven

The Plan

Tell me of this valley where you live …
of the hamlet you are building.

nichol and Ezra arrived at the castle gate and were waved ahead by Victor, to the front of those gathered at the gate. The castle had thick walls with platforms and walkways that those within could use without going down the staircase to the lower section to move about.

The gate that Victor guarded was massive—oversized to allow carts and wagons in. There were two more guards in front of the gate. As he looked past them to the gathering crowd, he asked about Shadow.

"She is at home with the children. They are going to the markets today."

Victor looked at the overcast sky, with the sun streaming through holes in the thick, darkening clouds. "The air and skies promise rain this afternoon, midday. Bells will ring soon for you and your meeting with the duke, Nichol."

She gave him one silver coin, and leaned close, speaking in a hushed whisper, "What have you heard that I should know?"

"There are many men-at-arms training within these walls; more than most days." Opening the door to the inner castle, he added, "Let Thomas know that you are here to see the duke."

Now within the castle's outer walls, Nichol let her eyes take in the garden that was not fully awake from the winter months. When Emma lived here, she would meet with her and share the stone she wore around her neck.

As they approached the inner castle door that would lead to the duke's solar, the bell from the monastery could be heard. Guards were posted at the door of the solar and let them in.

Ezra lowered his voice and asked her, "Why do you think there are so many guards within the castle walls?" Steward Thomas was waiting and without delay, escorted them to the solar again, where private conversations were held.

Entering the solar, Nichol noticed light streaming in from a window, falling across two carefully positioned chairs. *Well-placed, like Papa's solar*, were her thoughts. Duke Richard was seated behind his heavy-planked oak table. Vellum documents were neatly stacked, wax and seal placed close by.

In unison, Ezra and Nichol both bowed. "Your Grace."

Duke Richard looked up, extending his right hand while indicating both should sit. Waiting for the duke to speak first, Nichol noticed that he appeared to be in good spirits.

"Tell me of this valley where you live … of the hamlet you are building. The one that you told me was called Harmonie."

Nichol smiled. *He is more than just interested.*

"The valley is three days ride north of here. There is no road into it, just a path that once was hidden. When you come to a stream, you must wade through its clear waters and continue to your right around a tall hill. A long gentle rise brings you to the crest of the trail where a grand valley comes to view."

Nichol closed her eyes while leaning back, breathing deeply through her nose. A calm came over her as she began to relate a story of affectionate longing.

"A sweet smell of wildflowers permeates the air and the clear view of tall meadow grasses touching the surrounding forest is unobstructed. You can see oak and birch as far as the eye can see, unspoiled by man. At the end of the valley is a hamlet we are building. This is Harmonie. In the distance there is a lake; the stream that runs through Harmonie is fed from that lake."

Nichol's soft tone drew Richard deeper to her, leaning in, reaching for each of her spoken words. His eyes glazed over, charmed by her spoken verse, painting a vivid canvas of Harmonie, one that her words easily evoked.

Opening her eyes, Nichol looked upon him, a willing captive to her words.

"When I saw Priest Loupe on the back of his horse, watering it in the stream of our valley, he shook his finger at me. It was not just a threat to me; it was meant for all in the valley as they were working in the fields. We are your subjects, not his.

"I have said before, Loupe does not do the Lord's work. We are good people who live in the valley, minding for ourselves and aware of the needs of others. With Timo's guidance, we have developed new farming methods that increase harvest production. I am here to offer you a way we both can benefit."

Nichol paused, waiting for Richard to speak.

Richard nodded. "The valley you speak of is in my domain. The land you describe may be under the control of Lord Charles and he is responsible for collecting taxes, giving justice, and raising an army if needed. He will say that you have no claim to this valley and this land is under his authority—granted to him by my father.

Nichol drew back. "No, this valley was unknown to you and Lord Charles until Loupe and Fredric rode in with another man.

"The reason we stayed hidden was because of him and the danger he posed to me and my family. We would have paid rents to you, but then we would give our location away.

"If the valley is not under the control of Lord Charles …" Nichol gestured toward Ezra, "… would you name him baron? There are many merchants who stand behind his honesty and loyalty. I believe you know and trust him."

"First, I must talk to Charles. Then I will decide."

"If you learn the name of the other rider, will you tell me?"

"I will. If one of them was Lord Charles, I will soon learn of it. Next spring when the meadows are in bloom, you will take me to this valley you speak of."

Richard paused. What came next was not a request, but a demand.

"You will attend the Archbishop's Sunday service and all in the family must be baptized."

Nichol listened to his demand and nodded in assent. "I was baptized as a baby in Marseilles. Ezra has been baptized. If this is something you desire for all the family, may we do it upon our return from England and at the archbishop's next service?"

Waving his hand, Richard said, "I agree."

Nichol's voice softened as she asked Richard, "Are you in any danger, Your Grace? Both Ezra and I noticed that there were more guards than usual as we approached the gate and then when we were within the walls."

"There will always be confrontations with others within and outside of the kingdom. You made me aware that we must be on alert to protect our residents from those who intend harm as the pirate did who you took down. The duchess has reminded me many times of your action.

"In your absence, I've met several times with Ezra about his warehouse and how he intends to work with the merchants in Rouen. We have come to an agreement on the taxes that will be paid forward. Ezra revealed that you would like to carry your goods beyond the kingdom, and possibly to England. He felt that it could also do some good for those who create goods here as well.

"Thomas and I have decided that those who have pledged fealty to me will have some training to protect me and others important to the kingdom."

Taking in his words, she sensed that there was more bothering him but held back in saying so. She then asked, "Is there a message you desire me to give to Emma?"

"I will have a sealed parchment ready for you to deliver to Emma, waiting for you at the ship in the morning. Then I will meet with you both upon your return to Rouen."

As they passed the castle gate, the streets were alive with people and chatter. The sun was at midday and aromas of fresh bread from the bakery wove through the air.

Ezra cautiously pulled Nichol to the side of a shop that had little foot traffic. Leaning in, he said, "You must be careful with him, Nichol. I could see that he has feelings for you."

Ezra pointed out to Nichol that Richard's demand to be baptized and attend church was a welcome into the flock.

"Nichol, with your agreement, there is no turning back. We must be on alert or find ourselves in the middle of a dangerous game of power in which we are the pawns."

Above them in the skies, the red-tailed hawk squawked, then took flight heading to Ezra's home.

twelve

The Curse of the Dagger

Shadow and I will know if you are telling the truth.

There was excitement and anticipation the morning of their journey to England. All clothing and food were packed and ready to go at first light.

The door opened and Shadow was first out the door. She turned to watch all in the house exit and begin their walk to the docks.

Lucette and Aiden babbled to each other in their secret words as they were carried on the hips of Tova and Gunvor toward the dock and the awaiting ship. Neither of their carriers had been on a ship before and were excited about the adventure that awaited them and the responsibility of caring for the little ones during the voyage.

Robert pulled a cart with their belongings that they would need for the next few weeks. Helene had packed food for several days for everyone in the party and had slipped it into the cart, along with a cask of water for the children.

As the family walked together, people followed them. Learning they were off to England to visit the Queen Emma, excitement grew. One woman asked Nichol, "Are you going to change what you wear when you meet the Queen?"

Nichol noticed Rose standing in front of her shop. Turning to the woman, she replied, "Rose has made me a fine dress to wear when we arrive in England."

Nichol's thoughts were on the trip until they turned a corner and docks came into view. Suddenly memories of Marseilles overcame her.

She could hear the gulls screeching while they hovered over the fishing boats. And her memories of the men rowing into the docks and those rowing out with sails opening, snapping as they caught the wind made her smile … always with hopes of a large caught on their minds.

There was joy and danger in their work, but once the river or sea entered a man's soul, there was no going back.

I watched with envy, wanting to be a man so I could go to sea, Papa. Nichol turned and scanned the rooftops. Sure enough, there was Papa watching her.

I wonder if the hawk can read my mind?

As they arrived at the ship that would take her family to England, the crew was putting the final packages on board.

Ezra turned to Nichol and took her hand. "You are in a world that is not ready for you. Know who you are with and measure your words, then the world will come to you."

Helene stood next to Ezra, tears streaming down her cheeks as she watched Nichol and the children board. All that was dear to her was about to sail away. Her thoughts were grim. *What if I never see them again?*

Nichol sat by the tiller, next to the man who piloted the ship in the middle of the river. The man looked to be about forty years old. His dark red, weather-beaten visage and hands scarred from years of work hid his true age.

Turning to Nichol with a welcoming grin, he greeted her.

"My name is Leiv. These four men and I have made the crossing many times. Coming from Normandy, the Norse raiders leave us alone. When we leave England for your return is another story."

Just as they were about to cast off their lines, three men hurried aboard. All three men were carrying swords and knives but not enough other personal baggage for a journey to England.

Their hardened appearance brought immediate alarm to Nichol's senses.

Nichol stood, her hand now on her jeweled dagger. In a loud threatening voice, she ordered, "This is a private passage. Leave now."

The three exchanged glances. A few inaudible words were spoken and then one man dropped a satchel. He scanned the faces in front of him and then stepped forward in front of Nichol.

"You must be Nichol. Duke Richard sent us to protect you."

Nichol felt the hair on the back of her neck rise. Richard had not said anything about sending guards on the journey. She was immediately on alert.

I know that these men are not from the duke.

As promised, a messenger brought a wax-sealed parchment letter from Richard for Emma. Nichol recognized him as one of the duke's messengers.

He stepped onto the ship and handed the letter to her. She watched him as he stepped from the ship to dock. Turning back toward the vessel, the messenger then paused, staring at the three men with a knowing look.

After watching them for a moment, he then turned to Nichol. Fearful anxiety spread across his face.

At that moment, the ship was pushed from the dock into the flow of the river. She heard Helene's words saying goodbye and raised her hand and waved in acknowledgment. Yet it was the messenger whose gaze she held longest. She and he held eye contact until distance separated them.

I saw him. He is warning me … us.

Nichol wanted to take in all the sights the river had to offer. Now she couldn't.

Every sense in her body was fully alert—ready for something she knew was going to happen. Instead of enjoying the river banks passing by, she watched over her family in front of her. She observed the look on each of their faces and saw not fear, but anxiety that matched her own. Without question, they had all stepped onto the ship that morning trusting her, placing their safety and future in her hands.

I will not fail. I will protect all of you, she murmured to herself as her hand touched the dagger at her side.

Slowly, they floated with the current of the Seine River as it meandered to the sea, where a new adventure awaited. Up until this voyage, Timo was the only one who had seen the sights the river had to offer.

From her vantage point at the ship's stern, Nichol watched Lucette and Aiden play and entertain the family. Careful oversight was needed to keep Aiden from falling in. He seemed determined to lean over the side and touch the water.

Nichol looked at both banks of the river and returned the occasional wave from those they passed.

Something she could not clearly define was troubling her. She began to focus on the three men and their unkempt appearance, now seated at the bow of the ship.

Richard told her there would be a letter, but he never mentioned sending guards. She could tell that their purses were bulging with a hefty number of coins—something guards usually did not have.

She knew—*she was certain*—that something was not right. Looking up, she saw the red-tailed hawk perched on top of the main masts looking down.

Richard had not sent these guards.

But who did …?

One of the guards kept his eyes on Gunvor, watching every move the young girl made. With a chill, Nichol remembered that look when Fredric's friends had attacked and attempted to rape her years ago.

Lust was being directed toward Gunvor.

Concerned, Nichol turned to Leiv. Their eyes met and in a low voice, she asked him, "Do you know these men?" He slowly shook his head, his face concerned.

Nichol remembered the fearful look from Richard's messenger as he glared at the three men. If her instincts were to be believed, the gaze of the messenger was a grim warning.

"They are dangerous and not with the duke. I feel they mean us harm, including you." As she spoke to Leiv, Gunvor brought Athena to Nichol. "I think she is hungry."

Thanking her, Nichol leaned in and whispered, "Stay close to your sister, Lucette, and Aiden. Keep Shadow by your side and move toward Timo. Those men are here to harm us."

Gunvor's eyes widened. "Are you sure?"

"Yes. Keep the children very close to you. They cannot wander on the ship with them here. If they move close to you, call out."

Settling against the inner side by the tiller, Nichol nursed Athena. Robert went to her side and quietly said, "I feel that there is trouble here."

Nodding, Nichol whispered, "These men are not from the duke. Their intent is as foul as their smell of drink. I believe they were sent to make sure we do not arrive in England. We cannot leave the river with these men aboard; and Leiv will help us. Take Athena and move over to where the children are."

Nichol took apples from a barrel and began to hand them out. When she got to Lucette and Aiden, she took out her dagger and sliced small pieces for them, making a showy display of her dagger for all to see. With the jeweled dagger in her right hand and cradling three apples in her left hand, she approached the three men.

The dazzling reflection off the jeweled dagger lit up their faces. The gems glistened, pulling the men into the dagger's spell and curse. Their eyes bulged—greed and envy had them in its grip.

Weak men cannot resist its appetite.

Nichol turned to leave when one grabbed her wrist of the arm holding the dagger.

"I will take that."

Nichol opened her hand and gave it to him. Loud enough for everyone to hear, she spoke. "It is yours. God can forgive your greed and envy, but I will not. The curse is now on you." She turned and walked back to Robert.

The ship was small, with no place to hide. All were now captive by the men's presence. Returning to Leiv, Nichol found herself surrounded: Lucette and Aiden by her side, Robert holding Athena.

Timo moved closer. "Nichol, we have no weapons and Leiv's men only have knives."

"We have different weapons, Timo. The dagger will soon be back in my hands. When night comes, we must attack them."

Nichol turned to Leiv. "When we arrive at Le Harve, will we go directly into the channel?"

"It depends upon the tide. We must wait for the right tide to begin the crossing."

Nichol leaned past Tova, who was standing in front of her, and observed the three men. Shadow had stationed herself at midship; as the huntress, she glared at the men, focused on her prey.

In a soft voice for only one to hear, Nichol spoke. "Leiv, we must not leave Le Havre to cross until late tomorrow."

Leiv spoke as he looked down the river, moving the helm and adjusting their bearing. "I have friends in Le Havre; we will dock there." Nichol put a hand on his arm in gratitude.

Sides were now drawn with only one resolution: retribution for their trespass.

Gunvor and Tova were aware of the attention emanating from the three men. They stayed with the children, close to Nichol. Robert brought Athena to Nichol to feed and went to prepare food for all. As he took out bowls to fill, he was approached by two of the men who pulled swords and seized control of all the food for the voyage.

Nichol observed how impulsive they were.

They were now showing their true intentions. These men have no plan to take over the ship; they are only here to kill us. They may act at any moment.

Nichol handed Athena to Tova. "Gunvor, you will guard the children. Leiv, have your men ready to charge them. Robert and Timo, be ready; I am going to distract them."

Turning to the three men, Nichol challenged them. "I see only one of you has the dagger that is worth a fortune. Is he going to share it with all of you?"

The other two were eating with their hands as food spattered their beards and dropped onto their tunics. Upon hearing her words, their gluttony stopped and their attention turned to the one with the dagger. Sweat began to form on his forehead and face.

Nichol focused on him. "You do not look well; it must be the curse. Are you going to share the dagger with your men?"

Not able to defend himself, he pulled the dagger from his belt. The weapon was quickly seized by another guard.

Nichol pulled the dagger's sheath from beneath her tunic and held it high. Her voice rang clearly across the deck.

"The gold and gems of this sheath are worth as much as the dagger. Which one of you wants it? There are three of you, so how are you going to share your fortune? You must leave when we dock at Le Havre."

The one clutching the dagger spoke. "We will travel to England where we can sell the dagger. We will not dock at Le Havre."

"My family is hungry and thirsty. Will you share the food and drink with them?"

"When we are done."

Nichol returned to the huddled group. She had seen a light reflected on the dagger; that same light was now weaving around them. With a thin smile she murmured, "The *Lady* is with us. Soon they will not be able to defend themselves," she said to Robert and Timo. "Two of the men have touched the dagger. The more vile they are, they curse of the dagger will create a weakness that they cannot overcome."

By her words, both men knew that Nichol was now in control.

When Le Havre was in sight, Nichol emerged from her huddled group. As she approached with Shadow at her side, all three men appeared weak and slow to move.

"My wolf is hungry and you did not feed her. Now you are food to her."

Halfhearted smiles strained to appear on their pale faces. "You poisoned us!"

She shook her head. "No, your greed, envy, and the lust for riches poisoned you."

Leiv's men on board rushed at the three men. All three were slow to draw their weapons to defend themselves. After a short struggle, weapons and purses were taken, their hands were bound, and they were lashed standing to the mast.

Nichol looked at the harbor and then to Leiv. "Is the tide right? Can we sail on to England?"

He gestured at the restrained men. "Yes, but the food is poison. We must stop to resupply."

"Only to them. It is safe for us to eat, and we all need to eat and drink." Nichol took a bowl and filled it with the same food the three men had been eating. Robert, Timo, Gunvor, and Tova did the same. She began feeding Lucette and Aiden. Cups were filled with water and all of them began to drink.

Water and food were given to Shadow, but she was not interested. Something else caught her attention. She went to the three men and began to smell their legs and boots. Shadow seemed especially focused on the first man to hold the dagger; standing on her back legs, paws on his chest, and her nose inches from his face.

He dropped his head to protect his throat and turned away, offering only a cheek. In response, Shadow began a deep-throated growl.

"She is hungry. You should have fed her. Have you seen how wolves tear their prey apart so it can slowly die?" Nichol moved closer. "I have questions for you. If your answers are truthful, she will not attack you. But if you lie, on my command, she will start by tearing the flesh from your face. First question: Who do you owe allegiance to?"

"A priest," was the man's weak response.

"What is the priest's name?"

"All I know is the name of the one who speaks for him, the one who paid us."

Before he answered, she knew. "What is his name?"

"Fredric. He told me that this priest was powerful and then he gave us more coin for this deed than we could earn in a year."

Robert stepped forward. "This is not the first time you have done the priest's bidding, is it? Shadow knows the lair from where you come by your scent. Others have had the same stench. Tell me where you gather."

Silence filled the air.

Robert turned to Nichol. "Let Shadow have him."

Nichol moved next to Shadow and put her hand on her pet's back. Now the three—woman, man, and animal—were face-to-face, inches apart.

"You know more about this priest and you will tell me. We have three days to travel before we reach Southampton. You will be given food and water only if you answer my questions. Shadow and I will know if you are telling the truth."

thirteen

The Answer ... The Danger

This one is just a sword for hire.
When the time comes, I will throw him overboard myself.

They passed Le Havre while Leiv's men set the sail. They were now on course for England as the sun slowly disappeared, its fire quenched by the ocean. Into the darkness, they sailed westward.

A small bed was prepared for the children, aft by the tiller. The swaying motion of the ship lulled them to sleep. Gunvor and Tova slept with the children between them. Shadow dozed at their feet.

Nichol, Robert, and Timo gathered next to Leiv. With no moon lighting the sky, their presence was felt more than seen. Leiv searched the sky for a break in the clouds, revealing the stars to guide them.

Moans and an occasional scream came from the three men standing, lashed to the mast.

Leiv cleared his throat. "We are a small ship and friends of the duke. To pirates and Norsemen, we are not worthy of their notice. We do not carry fighting swords to show that we have nothing of value to protect. We mostly transport wool to Normandy and bring back cloth."

He shifted his gaze. "Why were these men paid to kill you and your family, Nichol? This does not feel right. I think that they would have killed me and my men, leaving no survivors to tell of their treachery. What have you done to bring this about?"

"What have I done? Remember, it was the duke who hired you to take us to England. One of these men already confessed to me. They were not paid by the duke. I have done nothing wrong to bring these murderous men here to kill me and my family.

"Do not accuse me until you hear what I have to say. I will tell you my story. And when I am done, then you can judge me."

Nichol began her story of fleeing Marseilles after the murder of her papa. She told Leiv all the details of the dangerous journey to Paris: how Fredric and Priest Loupe chased her for the treasure they thought she possessed; how she met Robert, their marriage, and the creation of their home in the new hamlet of Harmonie.

Finally, she told Leiv about the letter she carried from Duke Richard to his sister Emma, now the Queen of England. She could feel his sudden interest in her words. Now he understood there was importance to the voyage.

"Why are these men trying to stop you from reaching England to deliver the duke's letter?"

"Tomorrow we will learn the answer to that. They will tell us all. But right now, we need some sleep."

Throughout the night Leiv's men took turns manning the tiller and adjusting the sails, keeping the ship on course. Nichol, Robert, Timo, and Shadow took turns as well, sleeping and guarding the three men.

Morning arrived. The mood on the ship matched the dark overcast sky. A southwesterly wind was behind them.

Quietly everyone went about their tasks. First the children were fed, then bowls of food and water passed around. The three men lashed to the mast were ignored as they begged for water.

Nichol went to Leiv. "Have one of your men take over for you. I want to question these men and I want you to hear their words as a witness." Turning to Gunvor and Tova, she place Athena in Gunvor's arms. "Move as far away as you can to shield the children from what is going to happen."

Nichol, Robert, Timo, and Leiv were face-to-face with the men. Nichol held a bowl of water. "If you tell the truth, you will be given water and food. I will release you when we reach Southampton. If you lie to me, none of what I just said will happen. Do you understand?"

Nichol held a bowl of water up so the three could see.

"This water is for the first to tell the truth."

The bound men were fixated on the water as she passed it close to their mouths. Nichol observed their faces for weakness, looking for the first to speak. She stopped at the one whose stare had frightened Gunvor and Tova. He glared back at her—a chilling cold cruel stare—with defiance.

She threw the water in his face.

This one is just a sword for hire. When the time comes, I will throw him overboard myself.

Robert refilled the bowl with water and handed it to Nichol. The second man answered her questions truthfully and was given water. He was just another sword for hire.

Nichol waited until last to question the apparent leader: the man who spoke when they first entered the ship and who later took the dagger from her. Holding the bowl of water, she stood in front of the one who took orders from Loupe; a soldier who Loupe trusted to carry out his orders.

She slowly observed every feature of his face. "I smell your fear. Choose your words wisely or they will be your last."

He sneered at her. "When Loupe hears of this, you will all die."

"Who will tell him?"

A condescending smile slid across his cracked lips.

Nichol turned to Leiv. "We must talk in private."

The two stepped out of hearing distance, and the three prisoners watched as Nichol spoke to Leiv and his men. Heads of the crew turned while fingers pointed at the bound men in anger and accusation.

The restrained men knew they were being judged and their fate was being decided. At first, the three tried to appear defiant, but as more of the crew turned and pointed at them, their fear became apparent.

Nichol returned with Robert and three of Leiv's crew. The crew began to untie the three captives. The men had been lashed so tightly they had no feeling in their legs and arms and collapsed to the deck.

Without a word said, two of Leiv's men picked up the first man Nichol questioned, dragged him to the ship's rail, and threw him overboard.

They watched him go under without speaking.

Nichol pointed to the second man. He was picked up and hauled to the rail, while trying to struggle and screaming for mercy.

He was also thrown overboard.

Nichol stood over the leader. "The vile Priest Loupe will not hear from them. Duke Richard will hear about you and your alliance with the priest."

Raising her voice, she demanded, "Tell me your name … now."

Silence was his response.

At her nod, Leiv's men began to drag him to the rail to throw him over. They hoisted him up, lifting his legs over the deck rail.

At the last possible moment, his plea tumbled out.

"Me name's Edgar an' the priest says he speaks for Lord Charles …"

fourteen

The Curse Is Lifted

Your evil is the reason you are tied to the mast.
The dagger is only safe in the hands of the rightful owner.

As the man was dangled over the side, Nichol heard him gasp out the name Lord Charles. Holding her hand up to Leiv's men, she directed, "Halt … bring him back to the deck."

Sprawled on the deck and gasping for air, Edgar glared at her.

"If you want water, you will tell me Charles' full name, how you know of him, and how he employed you. If not, you will get nothing. And I won't stop them from throwing you over the rail again."

All were frozen on the ship's deck, waiting for his response.

And then he spoke. "The priest and the man Fredric, they said you stole from 'em. They been chasin' your heels for near to three years. I was with 'em when they found ya finally. Afterward, we watched you for 'em … planned t' kill ya so we could get our gold. That Lord Charles—dunno his name, but he knows them other two, and they claimed they speak fer him. He wants the land you took. Says it's his, all rightful-like, and he's gonna kill all the folks tryin' to take it." He managed a grimace. "Twice th' coin fer one job."

Nichol was stunned.

So, Priest Loupe and Fredric somehow met and conspired with someone named Lord Charles to claim Harmonie, and to kill me and my family. Edgar must have been the third man on horseback that day I saw them at the stream.

A memory suddenly came to her. The duke had mentioned a lord named Charles in her last meeting with him.

Could this be the same Lord Charles?

Nichol turned to Robert and Timo. "I know nothing of this Lord Charles. His intent could be to undermine the duke. If he plots against the duke and wins, he could claim Harmonie for himself."

Both exchanged grim looks and nodded their heads as she spoke.

The three moved toward Edgar, the remaining hired killer. Robert pulled him to the mast and tied him against it. Nichol positioned her dagger above him and bound it to the mast to further lessen his physical and mental strength. She gave him a small bowl of water.

He begged ceaselessly to be released from the ropes that bound him. No one listened or looked his way, and he became more disturbed and delirious as the sun rose above.

Finally, he groaned out what were to be his final words, barely able to lift his head. "Yer a witch, you are … only witches can curse …"

Nichol looked at the faces of those on the ship and realized that the hired killer's presence and incoherent mumbling was affecting everyone. She moved to face Edgar and spoke loud enough for all to hear.

"Your evil is the reason you are tied to the mast. The dagger is safe in the hands of the rightful owner—be it a man or a woman—but only in his or her hands, no one else's.

"Wise men have known of the curse, created long ago by someone without a name. My papa made sure it was in my hands. He knew that it could be trusted and protected by me. Anyone else who takes it into his possession will become ill, go mad, and die, which is why I have kept it close to you while you are tied to the mast.

"I did not curse the dagger. You revived the curse when you touched it. You have failed in your quest. The dagger's justice saw your black soul and singled you out. Your lust and greed did not serve you well. You will soon die, Edgar."

Edgar's response was to lapse into unconsciousness.

Leiv approached her. "Tomorrow we will land in England. What do you want to do with him?"

"This is his last morning. He can join the others in the open sea."

Nichol cut the ties binding her dagger to the mast, returning it to its sheath, and walked away.

Timo sat at the ship's rail, staring out at the empty sea.

The fear and threats that rippled through the ship were not welcomed. He knew that the three men were bad and had been sent to do harm from worse, even evil men. He was aware of the power of the dagger and had seen it used in a variety of ways—but nothing like what had just unfolded. He was stunned with how swiftly the dagger had overtaken and incapacitated the men, particularly Edgar.

He wanted the memory of them to leave and this third man away from him … and the little ones. A soft light slowly wove around him, bringing the smell of the salt air. He could feel the movement of the ship reduced from the chop to quieter waters that gently slapped at its sides.

Nichol moved next to Timo, sensing he needed her. She knew he was hurting; the last two days had tested his faith. Nichol understood he was thinking about what had happened and trying to come to terms with it.

Looking out into the open sea, she waited for him to speak.

He glanced at her and then looked back to the sea.

"I remember the day we met at the fair, as though it was yesterday. When you left the fair, I watched you walk away, and a feeling came over me, as though I was parting with a longtime friend who felt like a sister to me.

"The next day, when you climbed down from the tree and caught up to Moki and me, a sudden change happened. I knew that we were meant to be in each other's lives: to learn from each other and to support each other. I had no idea where it would take the two of us, but I knew that we would be connected.

"I knew that you were disguised as a young man, though I did not know why. All I knew was that I was meant to travel forward with you as you moved toward your destination.

"When I saw certain … things … happen, I told no one, for fear of heresy charges if I spoke out. Now I know you have a higher calling, and it was destiny that brought us together. You, the dagger, and the *Lady* saved all of us on this voyage and have saved us many times."

Timo rose. "Robert and Leiv, please come to me. We have a task to perform."

The three men met at the mast and untied the body of the hired killer. Timo said a prayer of last rites over him.

Nodding at Robert and Leiv, he returned to Nichol's side. The two men looked at each other and without another word, lifted the body and threw it over the ship's rail.

Nichol went to her children in the vessel's stern. They had been protected and shielded by Tova and Gunvor from what had happened. Athena was wide awake and the other two were napping, sleepy from the warm sun and the lull of the ship's motion.

Picking up her infant daughter, Nichol settled in to feed her, leaning back against the side and closing her eyes to the warmth of the sun.

With the crisis averted, a sense of calm settled over all on the small ship. Leiv and his men were preparing for the final hours of their voyage.

A flickering light surrounded Nichol and her children and then danced over the side.

Thank you for being with us, were Nichol's thoughts as she took a deep breath and drifted off to sleep.

fifteen

Joshua and Roger

Joshua and now Roger are the keepers of a new secret.

Joshua had helped Nichol and family load food and clothing on the ship for their voyage to England. He had left before seeing the three other men approach the ship and board it.

Something that had been angering him of late; a recurring anger that clouded his mind and judgment. He knew there was the only one way to deal with his feelings. He must free the family of their ever-present danger, one that threatened even the children.

Now that the family was safely on the ship, he could turn his attention to the two men that he sensed were at the heart of the problem: Fredric and the priest.

Joshua had planned his first stop at Amos' Inn, where people gathered to eat, drink, and gossip. The tavern door was propped open, letting in the morning light.

Stepping inside the entrance, Joshua scanned the room. The innkeeper, Amos, turned to see who was blocking the light from the door.

"Joshua, what brings you here this morning?" As Joshua approached, Amos saw a troubled look on his friend's face, an expression not common to him. "What is troubling you, my friend? Did Nichol and her family set off on their voyage to England this morning?"

Joshua started in surprise. "How did you know they were leaving this morning for England?"

Amos leaned closer and lowered his voice. "Four men entered the tavern last night. They kept to themselves: secretive, careful, and leaning in to talk. The more drinks they consumed, the louder they became. I overheard their conversation of their voyage to England." Amos shrugged his shoulders. "I thought it was common knowledge at the docks that Nichol and her family would be on board."

"Do you know these men? Do you know their names?" Joshua's gaze was stern.

"No, they were not the usual men that come here." He paused for a moment, eyes narrowed while in thought, shaking his head. "I did not hear their names."

"If you see these men again, will you find out more about them?"

Amos nodded. "I will." He rubbed his chin. "There is one thing that I noticed; their coin purses were almost too small for the coin they carried. Men like these do not make that much coin for honest work. They are men for hire and here for but a short time. I do not think we will see them again."

Joshua thanked his friend and left. Remembering what Nichol had said about her half-brother Fredric and his weakness for drink, he set out to find which tavern he frequented.

He already knew that Loupe lived in a corner home at the intersections of two busy streets. If he lingered nearby, it would be easy to keep watch and see who came and went without being noticed.

At first glance, Loupe's home seemed not to be the desired location for someone who was carrying out treasonous activities. Then again, only a few had the power to question what he did or where he went. Such a place was perfect for a man of his character.

Joshua talked with peddlers while keeping an eye on the priest's door. He noticed a younger man stopping at the door of

Loupe. It opened before he could knock. He was let inside and the door was quickly shut behind him. Soon, the same man came out and turned away down the street and out of site.

Joshua promptly followed in his direction and lost sight of him. Stopping, he realized the man must have gone somewhere close by … but where? Many people were on the narrow street, so he stood and waited.

He is just a messenger and will soon reappear.

Moments later, a nearby door opened, and the messenger stepped out. Suddenly an arm reached out and yanked him back inside. Joshua moved slowly into hearing distance.

An angry shout sounded from inside. Just then, the messenger exited, and as he did, Joshua peered inside and saw two other men. The messenger was one step ahead when Joshua spoke, pretending to know the man.

"Was that Fredric that shouted?"

"No, it was the other one."

Tonight, I will drink with the devil's men.

Joshua waited until late evening. Strolling into the darkened streets, his destination was to a tavern frequented by dock men and other ruffians. He imagined Fredric would frequent such a place. Entering, he approached the tavern keeper, standing behind two barrels supporting a thick wood plank. He ordered a cup of ale and when the ale was being poured, asked the server if he had seen a man called Fredric.

The server slammed the pitcher down and glared at Joshua.

"He has been banned from this tavern. He starts fights and does not pay for what he drinks or the damage he causes. Fredric owes me coin, too … and I want it."

Joshua raised his chin in acknowledgment and clenched his hands around his cup.

After a moment, the server finished pouring and leaned in toward Joshua. "Get to the tavern closer to the docks. It is where men like him drink."

A patron standing next to him spoke a word of warning. "That is a bad place. Is what he owes you worth more than your life? The man you are talking about has friends that kill for pleasure and they are protected by powerful men. They are paid assassins. You best stay away from there."

Joshua shook his head. "It is not just my life … it is the lives of many. And there is much coin involved."

He knew of the tavern, located close to the docks and a place decent men avoided. After much thought, he decided that at least one person should know what his plan was. Someone who could share his motives, keep a secret and if there was failure, he would learn why.

His feet took him immediately to Ezra's door, where he knocked and announced himself. Opening the door, Ezra was surprised to see his cousin Joshua, who had been his private messenger, in front of him.

"What brings you? Has something happened?"

"No, but I need you to come with me. I have a task to do."

After a short explanation while Ezra donned his cloak, Joshua led his cousin in the direction of the tavern, speaking softly while telling him of his conversation with Amos. When the tavern came in view, Joshua stopped and took Ezra by the arm and pulled him aside, into a deserted alley.

Standing next to a building, Joshua quietly revealed his plan. "Loupe and Fredric must be stopped but before I stop them, I must learn who holds the power over them and what it is they want."

"How do you plan to stop them?"

"With my knife."

Ezra's eyes grew wide and his face flushed bright red. "No one will miss Fredric. There are many to take his place; but do not harm a priest, never a priest. We must convince the most powerful people of his danger to them and then let them decide his punishment.

"You must be careful, Joshua. Even the most powerful men in Rouen do not interfere with what happens in that tavern. Take Roger with you; he can wait here for you to come out. He is too well known to enter with you. Lure Fredric out on a pretext and take him to the warehouse to question him. No one will see or hear him there."

Joshua nodded. "Tell Roger what has occurred and that I will come to your home when darkness falls to walk with him toward the tavern." The two men parted, each heavy with thoughts of what could go wrong with their plan.

Later that night, Joshua left Roger standing at the same spot where he and Ezra spoke earlier in the day. Roger cautioned him, "If you feel danger, leave at once and come my way. I will have my sword out waiting."

The street was dimly lit. Joshua walked next to one side and felt his way touching the buildings as he went. The closer he came, he could hear loud voices and then saw an open door that was emitting candlelight. Just outside of the door, a man lay prone in the mud, stripped of his clothes and shoes.

Joshua stepped over the man's body and moved toward the barkeep, standing at the kegs of ale and wine. He asked for wine. When it was poured, he paid and asked, "Is there a man named *Fredric* here tonight?"

The server jerked his head at a table with three men. "He is the one with his back to the wall."

Joshua ordered one more cup of wine and approached the three men, two of them with their backs toward him. He made certain his full purse was visible to Fredric. He set a cup of wine in front of Fredric and pulled a stool next to him, close enough to observe his expressions in candlelight. "I have need for a man of your skills and I am willing to pay for your services."

Fredric glared at Joshua. He turned toward the two sitting with him. "Leave now. This man and me need to talk." He turned back to Joshua, and replied with slurred speech, "Do I know you? Where are you from?"

"I am from Paris and we both are friends with a certain priest. I told him of a woman who has a warehouse and in that warehouse, a large chest of gold and silver is stored. The priest told me that his share is one half and we can share the rest. It is hidden in the warehouse and I know how to find it. There is only one guard and he is probably drunk by now."

Fredric lifted his cup and gulped the wine without taking a breath. "A man can always use more gold. I will follow you."

They walked out of the tavern and down the street. Roger stood in the shadows and as they passed by him, Joshua spoke loudly so his words were heard. "This way to the warehouse."

Understanding Joshua's intent, Roger slipped away through the darkness, moving ahead to wake up Olaf and Marie. Olaf came to the door holding a candle and opened the door when Roger identified himself.

"Olaf, hurry and unlock the warehouse door and go back to bed. Whatever you hear, do not come in." Roger followed Olaf through their home and into the warehouse and watched while Olaf unlocked the outside door. "Now go back inside. Then you will have no knowledge of what is going to happen."

Joshua and Fredric arrived and slowly opened the door and stepped in. He took a candle from a pouch and struck flint to light it. Turning to Fredric, he raised the candle and saw the end of a knife blade pointing at his face.

"Show me the chest. The contents are rightfully mine." Fredric's voice was a harsh snarl. The candle cast a shadow across his face, exposing the darkness of his evil intent.

Joshua pretended astonishment. "You have no intention of sharing it with Loupe or me."

"I told you it is mine. Now show me where the chest is hidden or I will slit your throat."

"Nichol told me you were dim."

Fredric grabbed his tunic and raised his knife closer to his face.

Joshua leaned slightly to the side, looking past Fredric. "Who is that standing behind you?"

Fredric smiled. "You think I can be fooled."

In one swift motion, Roger's left arm wrapped around Fredric's head and pressed his knife to Fredric's throat hard enough to draw blood.

Joshua took the knife away from Fredric. "Get down on your knees and put your hands behind you." Joshua tied Fredric's hands securely with a long rope. He grabbed the other end of the rope and threw it over a beam. Working together, Roger and Joshua hoisted him up until his shoulders were wrenched upward and his feet could not touch the ground.

In obvious pain, Fredric glared at the two men. "When Priest Loupe hears about this, both you will lose your heads."

Roger grabbed him by the hair and pulled his head back. Looking into Fredric's eyes, he growled, "When the priest learns that you betrayed him, he will feed you to the pigs."

Roger held Fredric's head back as Joshua brought the candle closer to his face. "You are a fool. The priest knows there is no chest of gold and silver. What is it that this priest wants from Nichol?" He gave Fredric a grim smile. "We have all night. When you are ready to tell the truth, we will listen."

"I will tell you if you let me down."

Looking at Roger, Joshua announced, "I am thirsty. We should go to a tavern and return in the morning."

Whimpering and sniveling, his eyes wide, Fredric shrieked, "Do not leave me! I will tell you what you want to know."

Roger said, "We will not let your feet touch the ground until you talk."

Both put stools in front of Fredric, sat down, and started asking questions. Questions about his life in Marseilles and why he had threatened Nichol, chasing her all the way to Paris.

Nichol had told the two men that Fredric and his mother believed Nichol knew where her father's treasure was, and that she had taken it. Comparing Fredric's stories with what they had learned from Nichol, they agreed he was telling the truth.

Fredric cried out in pain and begged again to be let down.

"Not yet. Tell us more about Loupe," Roger insisted.

Joshua asked, "What is your connection to the Priest Loupe? How did you become involved with him?"

"Loupe was behind Alexander's murder. So was my mother."

That surprised both Joshua and Roger. Then Fredric kept speaking.

"The archbishop asked Loupe to create a private army, loyal only to him." Squirming, Fredric cried out again, "Let me down! I've told you everything, I swear."

Roger rose and loosened the rope so that Fredric's toes could now touch the ground … and stopped. He smiled. "Oh, I think you know much more." With a loud voice, he continued, "Tell us the rest."

Balancing awkwardly on his toes and gasping for breath, Fredric continued.

"He takes the coin given to the church by the peasants and uses it to pay people to do his bidding. Once they take his coin, there is no escape from his control and they must obey him. He rules with fear. There are many powerful men who support him. He has kept their identity secret even from me. Those who do not follow his every demand are never seen again. Most of his followers are rich men with titles. You have seen these men and know some of them. By the time you learn their intentions, it will be too late."

Joshua was alarmed when Fredric said *powerful people supported Loupe.* Some of the men had close ties to Archbishop William. He and Roger exchanged worried glances. The situation was worse than imagined.

Ezra and Nichol must hear this from me.

Struggling to talk, Fredric could not resist gloating.

"When that bitch and her family left for England, I saw three of Loupe's soldiers go on board as the boat pushed away from the dock. It was Loupe's chance to rid Rouen of her and he took it. Now, just Ezra remains to be dealt with and his time is limited." Fredric twisted against the ropes. "I have told you all I know. Now let me down."

Roger's face hardened, as if it had turned to stone with Frederic's words.

He stripped off his shirt and tossed it into a far corner. His hardened muscles twitched as if they were dancing. Rage seemed to vibrate through his body, emanating from his pores.

Joshua grabbed a handful of Fredric's greasy hair and lifted his head while moving the candle close to his face. Rivulets of sweat ran from his hair, dripping down his face in a steady flow. Creeping shadows moved on the walls, revealing a terrifying sight. Cold bulging eyes and a defiant sneer transformed into a sinister smile that highlighted Fredric's true self.

"Roger, look at this man-child who smirks at me with arrogant contempt. He is a fool who never understood." Joshua released Fredric's hair and his head dropped, chin resting on his chest.

For a moment, the warehouse was eerily quiet—the two men silent in their breathing, the man-child whimpering. The nearby river had made itself known with drunken voices skipping off the water.

Fredric mumbled loud enough for both to hear. "He will win and you will lose." As he spoke, the stench of loose feces filled the air.

Without emotion, Roger drew his sword and flexed his massive chest muscles. Taking several deep breaths, he glared at the dismal example of humanity in front of them.

He nodded at Joshua. Joshua loosened the rope, releasing Fredric's weight. Wobbling on his feet, Frederic's head fell forward exposing the back of his neck.

And then Roger struck quickly, with an executioner's precision, separating Fredric's head from his body. Blood spurted like vomit, its main target being Roger's chest.

Stunned, Joshua stepped back, knowing by the look on Roger's face that he was not done.

With two more slashing moves, accented by the grunts of effort Roger made as he dismembered the body, Fredric's legs were separated from his torso. Just as efficiently, he cut off his arms, leaving them still tied to the rope.

Rats began to gather, darting in and out of the candlelight to gnaw at the body parts. The stench from Fredric's bowels and piss permeated the air, combining with the existing musty smells within the warehouse. The heavy copper reek of blood overlaid it all.

Roger placed his sword point down on the ground with both hands on its hilt and calmly looked at what he had just done. Sweat trickled down his torso. He turned to Joshua. "Find a small basket. I have a gift for the priest."

Lighting another candle before searching hurriedly through the warehouse, Joshua finally found a basket and a dark cloth and brought it to Roger. He was followed by more rats, most likely attracted by the stench of fresh meat offered by Fredric's remains.

Roger placed Fredric's head in the basket, face up, and covered it with the cloth.

Both men were now covered in Fredric's blood. Roger looked at Joshua. "While it is still dark, I will deliver this basket to Loupe's. When I return, we will let the river have the rest of him."

Before stepping away from the warehouse door, Roger poured two full buckets of water over his head and body. He moved silently through the darkness of the night, ducking between buildings if he saw someone walking his way. The drunken night noises from the nearby tavern created a noisy distraction as he moved toward Loupe's front door, placing the basket in front of it.

Taking his sword, he struck the door with its hilt, loud enough to wake all inside. Turning, he melted quietly into the thick shadows, before making his way back to the warehouse and Joshua.

When Roger returned to the warehouse, he found Joshua had stacked the remainder of Fredric's body in a cart, along with empty buckets. Making sure they were not observed, the two men made their way to the river and discarded the torso and limbs into it.

Working in silence, they filled the buckets with water and washed down the cart and themselves. Filling the buckets again, they returned to the warehouse to clean up what they left behind.

Still without speaking, the two sat down to dry off as the sun rose to begin another sultry summer day.

Turning to Joshua, Roger broke the silence. "I put the basket in front of Loupe's door and beat on the door with my sword hilt. Then I walked away." His mouth tightened in resolve. "If harm has come to Nichol and her family, I will kill Loupe and deliver his head to the archbishop—his master—in the same way."

Joshua nodded his head in approval. "I am hungry and thirsty. Let us go to the inn and see what Amos has to offer." He held up Fredric's purse. "Fredric is paying for our food and drink."

"We will tell Ezra and Nichol later, after her safe return." Roger's tone was resolute.

Joshua and Roger were now the keepers of a new secret.

sixteen

The Secret of Silence

I do not know of a dagger with powers.

In the distance, a thin dark line appeared, extending across the horizon.

Leiv suddenly jumped up, sliding on the damp deck. While pointing to the horizon, he shouted, "England!" His words brought all on board to their feet.

This was a welcome sight, Robert thought, as he reached his hand to his wife, pulling her up to stand beside him. The sea was pitching and rolling the ship more frequently in the last two days, and he was glad to be closer to land.

Gunvor and Tova watched closely as Lucette and Aiden hopped and skipped around the deck. Their actions brought smiles and laughter from all on board, and that encouraged more silly behavior. Unfortunately, the children soon tired and displayed irritability brewing between them.

As they stood taking in the promise of land, Nichol looked at Robert and murmured, "Robert, Gunvor and Tova need our help."

Robert moved toward his children and picked up Lucette. Sinking into her father's chest, she then pushed back. "Down, Papa …"

"Not yet, little one. Let us see what Mama is doing." He brought her to Nichol.

Reaching for her daughter, she turned her toward the land that was now visible. "We will be on land soon and your legs will love how it feels to move about freely. Sit with me. I have a story to tell you before we get there."

As Nichol placed Lucette in her lap, Robert turned back to retrieve Aiden. Reaching for his son, he said, "Mama is telling Lucette a story. Let us go listen."

Returning to Nichol's side, he sat down close to Nichol with Aiden leaning his head against Robert's chest. Holding them tight, the children fussed a bit, and then let their eyelids drop as Nichol's voice soothed them.

Soon they fell asleep, including baby Athena, snugly settled in the sling that Nichol had placed around her neck when the last of the hired killers were gone.

Content with their family, Nichol and Robert watched over their sleeping children, quietly holding hands.

They arrived in the Port of Southampton on the morning of the fourth day. Before they stepped from the ship, Nichol brought everyone together.

"Do not talk of the three men and of this voyage. They were under the direction of powerful people in Rouen. If you do, you will put yourself and all the lives of those on this ship in danger. The men that sent them will make sure to silence all involved."

Nichol's gaze moved from Leiv and his crew … to all those whom she had brought with her. Their responses were unanimous: "Never will we tell, not anyone." Their oaths of silence became a blanket that engulfed them.

These men are honorable and yet one day the events of the voyage will be known. Perhaps when I tell the story.

When they stood on land, all were still swaying to the constant motion of the ship. For the first time, laughter was heard when

Lucette and Aiden tried to walk, staggering back and forth with smiles and giggles.

While waiting for Timo to bring a horse-drawn cart, Nichol took Leiv aside for a private conversation. Handing two of the three purses to him, she said, "This is for your men. I do not know when we will return." She smiled. "We will be your only passengers going back to Rouen."

From a hiding place in her tunic, she removed the third coin purse. "This is for you," she murmured as she placed it in his hand.

Leiv just stared at the coin purse. With respect, he murmured, "You have already paid for your return voyage."

She smiled again. "You and your men protected us, even though you could have easily sided with those men. I ask you to please not speak of the dagger and its powers."

Leiv shrugged. "I do not know of a dagger with powers. I am just a simple merchant."

seventeen

Finding Queen Emma

It is what women like us must do.

After Timo returned with a horse-drawn cart large enough for the children and clothes for the trip to Winchester, it was late in the day when they arrived at the King's Inn where Timo had stayed on his last trip.

The next morning, Nichol, Timo, and Shadow went to the castle. It was an imposing stone structure; a formidable stone wall protected those who dwelt behind it.

Timo noticed the guards at the gate were not the same two guards as before. Several merchants with their wares stood in front, awaiting admittance. The merchants were clearly expected by the guards and waved through the gate without delay.

Nichol and Timo stepped forward. Her breeches were no longer on her. She now wore a dress that had Emma's favorite color within the fabric—purple. At the front of her chest was a sling that carried a sleeping Athena.

Using the English language she learned from Cara, she addressed one of the guards.

"My name is Nichol and I would like you to give Queen Emma this letter. I am a friend of Queen Emma's and we have just arrived from Normandy. I wish to see the Queen, at her pleasure."

"Is that a wolf? Who are you again and why would the Queen want to see you?"

"My name is Nichol and I would like you to give a letter to Queen Emma that her brother, Richard, the Duke of Normandy, asked me to deliver to her. We are from Rouen in the kingdom of Normandy. We are staying at the King's Inn and wish to see her."

The guard's eyes narrowed, with an intimidating stare.

Ignoring the guard's silence, she said again, "I have word for her from her brother, Duke Richard of the kingdom of Normandy."

"Wait, what is your name again?"

"Nichol."

He has been standing in the sun far too long with that helmet on.

"I will tell the steward you are here. If you are lying, I will kill your wolf and kick both of you down the road."

The guard disappeared and when he returned, stood silently at the gate. No words came from him. The stare remained.

Moments later, Emma appeared rushing through the courtyard, her attendants trying to keep up. Arriving at the gate, she pushed all the guards aside but one.

As she faced the guard that had come to her, she gestured at Nichol, saying, "Whenever this woman, Nichol, comes to the gate, she is to be welcomed and announced to me without delay."

Queen Emma turned away from the guards. Her eyes were wet with tears of joy as she greeted the friend she had longed and hoped to see. Her smile was larger than any that the guards had ever seen.

Nichol and Timo bowed and before Nichol looked up, Emma had seized Nichol's hand. Turning her head toward Timo, the queen spoke through her tears. "Timo, you returned just as you promised."

"Yes, Your Grace, I came back as promised. And Nichol and her family have all come as well. We are staying at the King's Inn.

I will leave Nichol with you and return for her later." He bowed, turned, and walked away.

Emma reached her arms around Nichol whispering to her, "You came … you came." Stepping back, she now held her arms out for baby Athena. Once the babe was nestled in her arms, she placed a hand on the infant's tiny face and smiled.

Emma kissed the baby's cheek and gently brushed her cheek against the infant's. The two women connected their gazes, communicating in silence.

Nichol smiled. *We are now one …*

Quietly, Emma murmured to Nichol, "We must go inside; you must be tired and hungry."

Emma led them to her private chambers and ordered drink and food brought from the castle kitchens. Nichol nursed Athena as they ate and drank while exchanging the latest news from Normandy and of Emma's marriage to Ethelred. Athena fell asleep and Nichol carried her to Emma's bed with Shadow lying on the floor next to her.

Emma dismissed her attendants for a more private talk with Nichol. They placed chairs facing each other, and Nichol knew that further talk would have to wait until they embraced the stone. Leaning into each other, Emma slowly reached her hand forward with long-awaited anticipation.

Nichol lifted the red stone from her neck, now attached to a thin silver chain that Robert had created for her. It replaced the worn leather one that she had made when she ran from Marseilles to Paris years ago.

Pulling it from inside her dress, she placed the stone into the palm of Emma's hand and gave her a reassuring smile. Nichol then placed one hand over the stone and one hand under Emma's hand, with gentle pressure capturing their desired union.

Again, they rejoiced in a reunion of sisters, an exchange of who they were, and cherished a bond that would never be broken. Nichol's mystic life and her courage captivated Emma. She had tremendous respect for a woman on a perilous journey, at home and abroad. At once, they were of the same mind.

The stone led both women through Emma's beginning journey as Queen of England and gave them a glimpse into the alliance they would share.

Athena stirred and started to cry. The sound brought the women back from the stone's embrace.

Nichol's first words were, "It is what women like us must do."

Emma picked up Athena and handed her to Nichol. "I saw the valley where you live. One day I will come to you there for a visit."

As the two settled in to continue their chat, Emma revealed her gift of vast lands upon her marriage to the king. "I have been told I must visit one of the many villages, so that I may come to know more of the land that I own. Will you come with me while you are here?"

"I will. Tell me when and where to meet you."

eighteen

Emma and Nichol

I have waited long to hear your voice and words.

The next day, Emma went into the garden to await the arrival of her friend.

It was not often that the full sun was out and Emma raised her face to the sky, relishing the warm rays. Closing her eyes, she hoped for Nichol's arrival to come soon.

She instructed her servant to bring hot water laced with the herb spearmint for them to drink instead of the usual wine or ale. Discovering the herb in one of the shops in the village, Emma felt it was refreshing and looked forward to sharing the treat with Nichol.

Surrounded by the many varieties of flowers, a smile crossed her face as she breathed in their rich scents. Attracted by the fragrant blossoms, she heard the soft buzzing of the honeybees as they went about their business of gathering pollen.

They too are enjoying this warm day as I am … and then she heard the voice she had been waiting for.

"I am here to visit Queen Emma."

"Nichol, I am here."

She turned to see her friend approaching the garden. As Nichol entered the garden alone, the young queen gave instructions to her attendants to wait for her.

Approaching Emma, Nichol was bursting with thoughts and news to share.

She also knew that the royalty had its own protocol. Nichol was a commoner and Emma was royalty, thus the one who must initiate discussions and physical contact.

Reaching her hand out to Emma, Nichol found herself pulled into the embrace of the young queen as Emma hugged her only friend.

"Now … tell me everything, Nichol. Tell me about Richard. Of your new home. Of you … I have waited long to hear your voice and words."

"You are right. I have much to share with you about Rouen and what I am doing. And I bring a message for you from the duke."

As she said that, Nichol pulled a wax-sealed parchment out that she had placed in the hidden side cloth of her dress and placed it in Emma's hands.

Emma's eyes opened wider as she watched her friend, not knowing that Nichol had hidden side compartments in all her garments. Taking the parchment, her curiosity of what she had just seen grew.

"What is that you have in your garment? Where did this come from?"

Nichol smiled. "I have them in all my clothes—breeches and dresses. When I told Helene that I wanted a hidden place in all garments to carry things with me, she created a slit on the side and then added another layer of cloth to it, sewing each piece to a side of the cut so it formed a space—something like a purse—within my garments."

As Nichol spoke, she stood and placed her hand within the slit, showing Emma how it looked. "Put your hand in here and see how this concealed space feels."

As Emma did, her face lit with delight. "*Je veux aussi cela dans tous mes vêtements.* I want this in all my garments, too."

Gesturing to her attendant Mary, Emma showed her Nichol's slit in her dress. "Mary, I desire that all my garments now have a feature like Nichol's stitched in them. I wish you to add such a hidden pocket to every garment of mine."

Mary examined the side of Nichol's dress. "Yes, I will do this for you, Your Grace." With a slight bow, she moved back to the other attendants and communicated the wishes of the queen.

As Mary moved away, Emma asked about Rouen. "What are your plans there?"

"Ezra and I have decided to import spices and other goods to resell within the kingdom of Normandy and to other countries as well. We have made an agreement to do business with a man called Diego. He will bring in items from the Mediterranean. I think England would welcome much of what we are bringing in … and many beautiful goods are made in our hamlet, now called Harmonie."

"Tell me more about these items your villagers are making. This is something that you and I should discuss with the king."

Emma's attendants had gradually moved closer. Nichol was aware this did not please Emma. Switching smoothly to French, Emma reached for Nichol's hand.

"Can we share your stone again?"

Aware of her friend's need for privacy, Nichol responded in French as she slipped the stone off from around her neck. The two moved their heads close together.

Emma requested in English so that the attendants could overhear her words. "I have always loved the stone you wear. Can I touch it once more?"

With a smile, Nichol placed it in Emma's hand and moved her hand away from it as Emma said, "It is beautiful, Nichol. It reminds me of Rouen and my family."

The women listening seemed to relax when they heard the Queen's words. Emma reached out her hand to encase Nichol's, as friends would.

Emma let out a whispered gasp. "*Oh non …*" She lifted her eyes to Nichol's.

"*Qui …*" Nichol gave a slight nod.

When Emma asked her to tell her more, Nichol revealed all, including that no harm was done to her children and that the three men had been stopped and put overboard. As Nichol explained, Emma nodded her head. Nichol knew her friend could see the scene unfold through the stone.

When she looked up from the stone and their hands, Nichol continued in French. "*Connaissez-vous ce Lord Charles? Pourquoi voudrait-il me tuer, moi et ma famille?*"… Do you know of this Lord Charles? Why would he want to kill me and my family?

Emma's eyes widened. "*J'ai déjà entendu mes frères mentionner son nom. Il est l'un des seigneurs du royaume de Normandie.*" … I have heard my brothers mention his name before. He is one of the overseers in the kingdom of Normandy.

Nichol gently squeezed Emma's hand. "*Le roi vous traite-t-il équitablement? Timo a dit que vous avez maintenant des terres à votre nom.*" … Does the king treat you fairly? Timo said you now have lands in your name.

As Nichol asked her question, images filled both their minds of the king and lands. Emma switched to English. "Tomorrow, I will arrange for us to visit some of the land I now own and the crops we are growing."

"I would enjoy that. If you would permit, can I include Timo and Robert? Timo has great skills in crop development and use of water to support it. Robert is a skilled goldsmith. Do you remember the bracelet I gave you long ago? He made it for you. The chain I wear with the stone was made by his hands."

Without saying another word, Emma pulled the long sleeve of her luxuriant gown up, revealing Nichol's gift from long ago.

"I never take it off …"

nineteen

Taking to the Streets

This is what I have wanted ... to be connected with my subjects.

Still chatting in a mixture of French and English, Nichol took Emma for a leisurely walk on the streets of Winchester. They walked with soldiers from Emma's castle surrounding them.

The yeasty smell of bread baking garnered their attention. After following their noses for a short distance, they found the delicious aroma emanated from a small shop in the marketplace.

Nichol and Emma entered the shop, the shelves bursting with many loaves of bread. Several women were in the shop and they immediately recognized Queen Emma. At once, they bowed in unison.

Nichol nodded her head at the queen, as if to say, "Purchase bread from this woman ... greet the other women in her shop ..."

Emma picked up on Nichol's hand gestures and movement of her head.

In her primitive English and a smile on her face, Queen Emma said, "Good morrow, my lady ..." and then she turned to the other women and said, "Good morrow, ladies ..."

She turned back to the shop owner. "My lady, my soldiers have coin to buy half of all your bread. Will you fill my friend Nichol's baskets until they can hold no more?"

The woman in the shop was flustered, not knowing what to say.

The Queen? Here in my shop? She wants to buy my bread ... how could I possibly have her do that? I must give it to her ...

Nichol sensed the woman's dilemma. "Queen Emma desires to share your bread with many. She insists that you receive the proper coin for it."

A smile spread across the vendor's face. All she could say was, "Thank you, Your Majesty," as she let both her knees bend slightly and she bowed her head.

Then Nichol gave the grateful woman many coins. At the same time, the large baskets were placed on tables in front of the heavily-laden shelves, soon to be emptied by two of Queen Emma's soldiers.

As they departed the shop, they found a crowd had gathered outside, curious to see their new queen.

Puzzled at the actions of her friend, Emma said, "The ovens in the castle make bread every day."

"This bread is for your subjects. Not all of them have bread, or even food. Show them your generous heart and share your bounty with them."

Nichol and Emma led the slow procession, as her guards shouted, "Make way for the Queen!" Her attendants were by her side, followed by Nichol's children in the arms of Robert and Timo. Gunvor and Tova trailed behind, with Shadow nervously pacing back and forth.

The group began making their way down a narrow cobblestone street, Nichol and Emma each holding a loaf of bread. Nichol tore off a piece and handed it to a young girl who came to their side. Obviously hungry, the child crammed the bread into her mouth. Another child approached, holding her hands up for food.

Emma mirrored Nichol's actions, breaking off pieces of bread and dispensing one loaf after another to the children who gathered around her.

Two of the soldiers moved to the front and separated the crowd as they walked. Gunvor and Tova picked up and carried the children. Emma's loneliness, born behind the castle walls, grew less with every smile, each *bless you,* and all the gifts of sustenance.

The crowd grew larger and followed them all the way back to the castle gate. Emma sensed a new energy around her … and her subjects.

This is what I have wanted … to connect with my subjects. To know of them.

In the castle, King Ethelred had been alerted that Queen Emma had a large crowd following her back to the castle gates. Nodding to his steward, he moved to where she would enter. He was curious about the actions of his queen and her visitors.

He was curious for another reason. He had been told that a wolf accompanied the woman Nichol to the castle and he wanted to see this sight for himself.

His eyes widened as the queen was announced at the gate. Something was different about her. *She carries herself in a way that expresses a boldness about her.*

As Emma greeted the king, she noticed a change as he regarded her. *He looks at me with changed eyes.*

"Emma, I hear your visitor has a wolf with her. I would like to see both."

Emma curtsied. "Your Grace, I present Nichol, my friend from Normandy and her infant daughter. Shadow is her wolf dog and travels with her."

As Nichol stepped forward, her right hand was at her side. She turned it slightly so Shadow could see it. That was her signal for *stay back and sit.*

Keenly aware of Nichol, King Ethelred noticed the small movement of her hand and the wolf's obedient response. "I see that you give your wolf commands. Does it know many?"

There is more to him than I had been led to believe, was Nichol's immediate thought. "Yes, Your Grace. Shadow has been with me since she was a young pup. We have our own language."

Nichol hesitated, then added for his ears alone in a low voice, "I see you."

Turning to Shadow, Nichol made another movement, finishing with her hand directed toward King Ethelred. Tail wagging, Shadow rose and moved toward the king. The animal stopped in front of him with her head slightly bowed.

The crowd watching the scene unfold let out a low gasp. A smile spread across the king's face. "Can I touch her?" he asked Nichol.

"Yes, Your Majesty. You are now her friend. Shadow is my protector. She only bites bad people."

Never had King Ethelred seen such behavior between a wolf and human before.

As he leaned down to scratch behind her ears, he was intrigued about the wolf's obedient behavior and loyalty. He had no knowledge of a wolf being trained to respond to human commands.

"Shadow is as dark as night. A rightful name. I hope you stay with us here for a time. I believe we have much we can learn from you and of your ways."

"Your Majesty, we must return to Normandy before the week is over. We plan to see some of the lands of England with Queen Emma. One of the men with me—his name is Timo—has great knowledge and skills in plantings and managing farm crops. Some of what he knows may be of benefit to you, and what your men know could benefit our land as well. Timo will be with me when we look at them."

The monarch sat for a time, studying his visitors as he continued to stroke Shadow's head. At last, he repeated Nichol's words back to her.

"I think I may see you, too."

Turning to his queen, the king continued, "I wish to enjoy the company of Nichol and the rest of her party before they leave for their homeland. Tonight, we will sup in the Great Hall. There we will speak more about our countries."

twenty

The Great Hall

I do not know what a woman could advise a man more powerful.

Entering the Great Hall at the king's invitation, Nichol noticed there were two separated long tables facing each other with seating only on the outer side. One table was laden with breads, cheeses, rabbit, and chicken.

As Nichol was directed toward the main table with Robert and Timo, she was aware that everyone's gaze in the hall closely followed her and Shadow. As she reached her seat, the wolf followed her hand and immediately dropped to the floor by her side.

A hush fell over the hall. All eyes now turned toward the west wall where a huge door opened.

All in the hall stood, as the king and queen were announced. Nichol touched Robert's arm, signaling him that they should rise as well. King Ethelred and Queen Emma entered through the door and moved toward their guests.

One of the stewards pulled the king's chair out, next to where Nichol stood. At the same time, he nodded to her, then to the steward close to Emma to pull the queen's chair out. The monarch sat down and looked out to those standing, as if sending a signal to them to sit as well.

Noise and voices immediately filled the air. Nichol felt the heat on her face begin to rise. She knew some of it was directed toward her and her family—and Shadow.

With a wave of his hand, King Ethelred instructed the servants to bring food to the table. Turning to Nichol, he asked, "How did you train your wolf? I see she sits silently at your feet."

"Your Grace, she found me as a young pup when I was sleeping in the woods. I fed her scraps of dried meat and since then, we have rarely been separated. I taught her hand signals for many words and tasks. She accepted Robert and other family members and now protects my children as well. She only bites those who would harm me or my family. When I speak in her ear, she understands my directions."

"I would like to have a wolf dog someday like your Shadow, to protect my queen." Turning to Emma, he asked her, "Would you like a protector like Nichol has?"

Emma smiled at her husband. "I would, Your Grace. It would also make me think of Nichol and to remember her when she is far away."

Nichol was quick to respond. "Someday, Shadow may have pups. If she does, I promise one to you."

Emma's eyes glistened when she heard Nichol's words.

Picking up bread and cheese, the king said, "Before you depart for your homeland, you will meet with me after you view the land close by with my queen tomorrow. She has told me that you sometimes meet with her brother, the duke, and advise him. I do not understand how a woman could advise a man as powerful as a duke. You will enlighten me when we speak again."

twenty-one

Queen Emma's Land

Would this be something of trading interest to you? To the king?

Early the next morning, Nichol gathered everyone in the inn to eat with the children, and to give Gunvor and Tova suggestions for the morning while she met up with Emma to view her lands close to the castle. Robert and Timo planned to remain with Nichol.

Finishing feeding Athena, Nichol added the sling to her outerwear and nestled the small infant comfortably within it. Placing her hand on Shadow's head, she said, "Shadow, you stay with the children at all times." She instructed Gunvor and Tova, "Do not go anywhere without Shadow by your side."

At last, she turned to Robert and Timo. "We must go meet the queen. She will have horses ready for us."

Walking the short distance from the inn, Nichol was pleased to see Emma. She was even more pleased to see that Emma was sharing loaves of bread with the small crowd that had gathered.

Seeing Nichol arrive, Emma finished giving away the bread and moved toward her horse. One of the stewards offered his hand to help her mount. The queen's horse was a rich chestnut color with white stockings on its legs.

As Nichol drew closer, Emma said, "I am sharing my favorite horse with you, Nichol. I call him Duke."

A grin crossed Nichol's face when she heard Emma's words. "Duke is a perfect name. He is a beautiful horse with the white markings on his forehead and such a majestic tail."

Robert helped Nichol mount, and then he and Timo did the same for the two horses made available to them. Two of Emma's guards accompanied them as the small group headed north and away from Winchester into farmlands on a well-traveled paved road—something that Nichol longed to have in Harmonie.

Some of the fields were being harvested while others were laden with a variety of grains. They saw small thatched-roof houses with gardens that boasted of a variety of vegetables, fruit trees, and flowers.

As Nichol took in the scenery, her thoughts spoke to her. *Someday Harmonie will have all this … it will feel like this.*

"Your Grace, would it be possible for us to stop and see a few of the gardens more closely? And possibly speak to one of your tenants?" Timo asked.

Nichol was not surprised. She knew that the land spoke to Timo. To Emma, she said, "You know of Timo's interests of the land and crops when he first met you. Could we stop at one or two as he requested?"

"Of course." Emma directed her words to Timo. "Is there one you have a particular interest in?"

"I see clouds in the distance. Let us stop at the next one," he replied.

Nichol and Emma rode side by side, as Athena slept peacefully against her mother's chest. Robert and Timo were behind them with the two guards split—one in front, one in back.

"One day, I too will have a baby with me. When I do, I would like to have a baby holder like yours. Ever since I have known you, you have a baby with you."

"When I return to Harmonie, I will ask Helene to make a baby holder for you and bring it with me when next I visit. I promise.

"Emma, I see you are learning the language of your people; I understand it as well. When we were in the town yesterday, I was looking at the goods in many of the shops. I think that the goods we make in Harmonie would be something desirable to your people. And Ezra and I have access to spices, silks, and dyed cloth that we could bring to you as well, to use and to resell.

"Timo also excels at crafting leather goods and other items that he learned from his father. He is now teaching others in the trade. His work with the monasteries throughout the kingdom of Normandy enhanced the production of crops everywhere for many people. He made plant guides that were written on parchment, left behind for the monks to use in their fields. Robert creates jewelry others desire to possess when they see it. And the women in the hamlet are clever crafters and weavers.

"We could use your wool and spin it to make cloth. You have many other items that would prove to be useful in the lands that the duke oversees. Would any of this be of trading interest to you? To the king?"

Emma's nod was emphatic. "Yes. I believe it would. And I also believe the king would be interested as well. You and I could remain in contact, which is one thing I desire. You trust Timo and therefore I do as well. He could be a messenger between the two of us.

"I know you will be leaving to return in a few days. I would like to see Lucette and your son Aiden before you do. We can talk further about developing trade and spend more time together in my garden and with the stone.

"The king spoke to me this morning before I left, reminding me that he wanted to hear more about your meetings with my brother." Emma paused in thought. "He said to me, 'And why would your brother seek advice from a peasant woman?' I hope this does not offend you."

"No, I think of it as a challenge that all women face. A challenge we both can enjoy, especially against weak men. I see your brother, and he is not weak. He sees me as one who tells the truth and he knows I am not a threat to him."

Emma must have told him that I am a merchant. To him, a woman's purpose is only breeding male heirs, a place just above a slave. If he thinks that, he married the wrong woman.

"Your Grace … may we stop at this farm?" Timo asked.

Turning to where he was looking, as he and Robert slowed their horses, the queen nodded. Using English, she issued orders to the two guards.

"We will stop here. Go and see if the farmer is there."

Robert smiled. He could sense that Timo was excited to get off the horse and get his hands in the dirt. He was puzzled as he eyed the land nearest the road. There was much rock embedded in the soil; rock that didn't support plant growth.

As the six horses approached the cottage on the land, the door opened. The woman stayed at the door and the farmer moved in front.

It was clear to Nichol that neither of them recognized the queen; their gazes held fear and uncertainty as they looked at the two guards.

One guard spoke. "This is your Queen Emma, wife to King Ethelred. She desires to see your farm."

Hearing his words, the farmer's wife immediately came forth. Both bowed and the man spoke, "Your Majesty, you honor us with your presence."

With their words, everyone dismounted. The two guards moved closer to the queen as she said, "Timo is a man of the land and he knows much of plantings and growing crops."

Nichol's English was fluent. She added, "We are from far away. Timo has helped monasteries grow better crops and he may have suggestions for you. He also likes to take seeds he finds back to our hamlet."

Now, certain that there was no danger, the farmer and his wife gestured toward their garden. The wife spoke up, her voice timid. "I have many herbs on the side of our home. Would you like to see them?"

Nichol agreed and beckoned to Timo to follow her to the side of the cottage. The queen and Robert followed.

As they approached the area, Timo was talking and touching many plants. He was excited with what he saw and wanted to gather seeds of these plants. He was also curious about the soil. "Can I also take back a small sack of your soil so that I can compare it to ours?"

Pulling a small bag from his waist, he carefully placed the small seeds into the bag. Timo gently cut several sprigs and put them in another bag. Turning to the farmer's wife, he bowed and said, "Thank you."

He was pleased with his bounty. Heading back to the roadway, his thoughts returned to Harmonie.

Our soil is different. Now that I have the seeds, I can try to grow these seeds in our soil and then compare the findings. There is much to learn—which soil will yield more crops within the same size of land. With what I now know, we can show farmers in the entire kingdom of Normandy how to grow food we can send to other places. And we can sell it at the Fairs.

As the two women rode side by side, Nichol said to Emma in a low voice as they approached the castle walls, "I want to see you with the stone we share once more before we leave for Rouen. I will bring the children with me and their caregivers so the two of us may speak privately. I sense you have greater strength than your king, and it is you and I who should do any planning forward."

Emma turned her head and looked into her friend's eyes.

She has much to tell me—to advise me. Nodding her head, with a slight smile, she said, "Come after morning prayers. I will have bread and berries and drink for all."

Returning to the castle, each were caught up within their own thoughts.

For Timo, he imagined bringing new crops to Harmonie.

For Robert, he felt that his goldsmithing skills could once again be used.

And for Nichol, she saw opportunities for Emma … and for her. They were pleased with what they had seen.

twenty-two

The Next Day

I have created traders and merchants in my family.

As she readied a light meal for the children in the kitchen area of the King's Inn, Nichol turned her attention to Timo and Robert, revealing what she planned to talk with Emma about.

But before she said anything, Timo spoke.

"Their land will not produce the grapes needed for good wine. The weather here is questionable. Where we live, we could produce a variety of plants, even excellent grapes for wine. The vines I planted in Harmonie a year ago should start yielding next summer.

"Our homeland is far richer that what I saw here. If the cuttings I took yesterday do what I think they will when I replant them in Harmonie, they will produce far more than they can here. This will mean more for us to resell and different varieties to choose from in the marketplace."

As Nichol absorbed his words, Robert added to what Timo had said.

"Although the land does not appear rich, I believe there is wealth in England to support making jewelry for both women and men. When you see Emma, would you ask her if she thought jewelry and brooches would be desired by her class?"

Listening to both men, she couldn't help but smile. *I have created traders and merchants in my family.*

Calling out across the room to Shadow, she motioned to her to sit by the door leading outside and wait. Then she spoke to Gunvor and Tova who were at another table holding Lucette and Aiden and gestured for them to join her.

"You will come with me to see Queen Emma inside the castle walls. She wants to see the children; she knows Lucette but not Aiden. If it does not rain, we will meet in her garden. She may want to hold Lucette and Aiden and then talk with me alone. Follow what I say and tell you to do.

"The queen has said the king wants to speak with me. I do not know if it is with the queen present, or only me. We will see what occurs when we arrive."

With Athena fed and snug in her mother's sling, they set out toward the castle.

As they approached the castle, the townspeople were friendly as Nichol passed them and their shops. Some followed along behind her, murmuring as the group grew larger. She had brought extra loaves of bread from the inn's kitchen to share with any children she would meet as she walked.

Before departing, she asked the kitchen help to drip honey on the top of the loaves she would carry in a small satchel. Nichol knew it would be a treat for the young ones.

Pulling the bread out, she broke pieces off to give away. When Tova saw her giving the bread away, she joined in and became an extra pair of hands. The murmurs turned to laughter as the bread treat was eaten.

Reaching the castle gates, Nichol turned and said goodbye to her followers while distributing the last of the honey-dripped bread. She thanked them for escorting her safely to the queen.

The guards immediately recognized her and approached, welcoming her, the children, and Shadow through the gate, and closing it behind them. A steward immediately came to her and bowed his head slightly.

"The queen awaits you in her garden."

As they entered, Lucette and Aiden were held by Guvnor and Tova. Shadow was close to them.

Seeing Queen Emma, a broad smile spread across Nichol's face. She moved toward her, motioning Guvnor and Tova to sit at a close bench. At the same time, Emma rose, moving toward Nichol, with both women embracing each other and laughing.

Alarmed at what they were seeing, the queen's attendants began moving toward the queen to protect her. Emma held up her hand to stop them.

"This is my friend. I am safe."

Turning to Nichol, Emma sensed movement around her legs. *Lucette.*

Reaching her hand up to touch Emma's, Lucette asked, "Tu es l'amie de mamani. Es-tub aussi ma reine?" *You are Mama's friend. Are you my queen, too?*

Emma was charmed by what had just happened. *Comment ce petit enfant peut-il si bien parler?* How can this small child speak so well?

Emma laughed … and Lucette laughed with her.

Nichol smiled at her daughter, noticing a light enveloping her and Emma.

At the same time, Emma felt a warmth entering her body.

Nichol knew what happened. *The Lady is here … through Lucette to Emma. My children are protected and so is Emma.*

Nichol placed her hand on the top of Emma's and all were connected.

Suddenly, Aiden moved to Lucette's side and put his hand on top of Emma's. The halo of light wove around the women and the children.

Seeing the light, Gunvor stood to move toward the children. Tova stopped her by touching her sister's arm.

"It is all right, Gunvor. Remember the lake and Athena's birth? The light was there, too. They are all special, and because we are with them, we are as well."

Emma lifted Lucette and settled her into her lap. Nichol lifted Aiden as well to hers, repositioning Athena as she slept and placing him on her lap. His head found the crook of her arm with his eyes on Lucette.

Neither child squirmed nor displayed any restlessness.

The two women then spoke rapidly in French, as old friends would.

Nichol revealed that she would send Timo to Emma with messages from her when it was important and possibly messages from Duke Richard as well.

"If you would welcome it, Timo would like to help you make your lands more productive. He has done much for me … for everyone who lives in our hamlet … to increase the amount of food we grow. We are now taking our excess into Rouen and Paris and selling it at the marketplace. He plans to trade with other places that are far away, and to bring back more spices and herbs that we can learn how to grow.

"He has mastered a better way to bring water to the plants in our fields. And when I first met him, his role was to teach monks at monasteries how to better plant their fields and grow crops for the monastery and the people who lived around it."

Emma was silent. Then she said, "I saw Timo pray in a way that is different from others when he was here the first time. Is he a monk, too?"

"Yes. His real name at birth was Timothée. His younger sister called him Timo. He joined a monastery and was known as Brother Lemur when my brother Fredric and Priest Loupe were in pursuit of me and Papa's missing treasure after the poisoning of my papa. At first, I was leery of him. I felt he was another man who could harm me like others had tried to do. He didn't. His donkey Moki and I became friends.

"Through my eyes, he saw much of the injustice toward me and the cruelty of the church toward everyday people. He became my friend, and the brother I never had. I asked if I could call him Timo as his sister does, and not Brother Lemur.

"Timo told me his new calling was to develop justice and caring for everyday people outside the monastery after meeting me.

"When Lucette was not even a month old, he found Ezra's home in Paris in the middle of the night. Waking all of us, he came with a warning. At the monastery he was visiting, he had heard that Priest Loupe was in pursuit of a young woman who had given birth to a girl child and a mysterious light had appeared around her—a woman called Lisa and her new baby. Loupe's quest was to capture and destroy both.

"Because Timo and I walked together to Paris, he has seen a light weave around me. He never questioned me as to why I dressed as boy and called myself Nick. He knew that I was seeking my papa's business partner Ezra in Paris. Eventually, I told him more of what had happened. He knew that my name was Lisa before I changed it to Nick as part of my disguise when I escaped from Marseilles after Papa was murdered by my mother. When I admitted to not being a boy, I told him I would be called Nichol when I got to Paris. He did not know that Lucette had been born.

"Timo quickly figured out I—and anyone with me—was in danger. That night, we all escaped, including Robert, Ezra, and his wife. Since then, he has lived among us ever since we left Paris. The light led us to Rouen, and then to the hamlet we created beyond Rouen."

Taking in everything Nichol had said, Emma hugged Lucette tighter. "Nichol, I saw some of this when we shared your stone. Now I know much more. I promise you this: as long as I am the Queen of England, I will support you and your family. And I will send a message of my support of you to the duke as well."

The women continued to speak. Somehow, both Lucette and Aiden remained quiet. Nichol wondered, *Is the light of the Lady keeping them calm?*

Nichol shared more of her ideas about trading with England. "Timo brought back wool from his first visit here. He and I believe we can create beautiful cloth and resell it throughout the kingdom of Normandy, England, and other ports. Ezra has brought in beautiful dyes, silk, and spices from the East. Would you like us to trade them with you, too?"

Queen Emma's mind was filled with possibilities. Nichol had opened a new world to her … and for England.

Nichol lifted the stone and placed it in Emma's hand, covering it with hers.

Suddenly, Emma felt warmth flow through her once again.

"Emma … we will leave in two days. I must return home to Ezra and Helene and our hamlet's harvest. Can we have a final meal with your king and share what you and I have seen and talked about for future trade?"

Nodding her head, Emma declared, "I will arrange it."

Holding the queen's hand, Nichol added, "And there is one more thing I see for you. Your son will be born to you in the new year."

Hearing Nichol's final words, Emma's eyes glistened with unshed tears of joy.

twenty-three

King Ethelred

Is that an arrangement you would like?

Dressed in a long gown of light blue with a high collar and an embroidered head covering, Nichol handed Athena to Robert. "I should be back before her next feeding. Then we will go into the village before we leave tomorrow."

She crouched and put her arms out for Lucette and Aiden. They rushed to her and she pulled them close and held them tight. "Be good for Gunvor and Tova. I will be back soon."

Lucette touched Nichol's gold necklace. "Mama, can we go with you?"

"Not this time. I will be back soon."

When she stood, Robert embraced her as he whispered in her ear, "Watch those around the king. I fear they are more dangerous to you than he is. They will see you as an enemy from Normandy until you prove you are not a threat to their positions."

Releasing her husband from their embrace, Nichol said to him, "Friendship and trade are all I desire. I will know more after I meet with him."

Nichol patted her leg to get Shadow's attention who was next to the children. "Come, Shadow. We must go."

Nichol was lost in thought during her short walk to the castle. When she arrived, the guard escorted her to the inner door and announced her arrival.

I must have been expected.

When the steward opened the door, he looked at Shadow and frowned. Then he slowly moved his gaze to Nichol's feet, lifting his head from her feet to her face. His eyes never met Nichol's.

Nichol smiled. "Good day. I am Nichol."

"I know who you are," he responded gruffly. "The king is expecting you."

If Emma were by my side, he would not greet me that way.

The Great Hall had more than a hundred candles lit to augment the light coming from the small openings in the walls. Despite all the candlelight, the dampness of the castle could still be felt by anyone within its walls.

There were long rows of tables on either side of an aisle that led to where the king and queen were seated on a platform two steps above the main floor. And the smells emanating from the kitchen and bakery immediately overwhelmed her senses.

Two men were addressing the king as he sat, and Nichol could not hear what they were saying. Judging by the king's facial expression, she assumed they were in trouble.

Emma saw Nichol enter. Just for a moment, she began to stand and go to her. Instead, she sat back down and sat stiff in her chair.

The two men abruptly turned and rushed past Nichol. The king's expression did not change as the steward approached him, with Nichol trailing behind.

Standing next to the king was an advisor who bent over and whispered to the king just before the two men fled. Nichol stopped when the steward pulled on her arm signaling she was close enough. He turned to her with a threatening scowl. "Mind your wolf."

She curtsied low and bowed her head. "Your Majesty."

"Rise."

Nichol stood and exchanged a slight smile with Emma while waiting for the king to speak first.

King Ethelred turned to Emma and saw their exchange.

He looked back at Nichol—not as he saw her the first time but as a woman who stood before him with confidence, dressed as one of royal birth. An awkward silence ensued.

Nichol was used to being treated and seen as different. She took the silence as being either confused by her dress or a measure of respect. Which one was it?

I see you, King Ethelred.

The king stood. "I am hungry. We will talk over food and drink." He held out his hand to Emma as they descended the two stairs to the main floor and took a seat at the end of a long table with Nichol on one side and Emma on the other.

He dismissed his steward and advisor but before the advisor left, he whispered in the king's ear. His words were rebuked with a wave of his hand.

Does he not have the courage to speak so a woman can hear?

Nichol then let out a loud laugh that brought everyone's attention to her.

"Your Majesty … did he just imply I was a witch?"

Taken aback by her question, he responded quickly, "Are you?"

"No, I am a merchant trained by my father in Marseilles. Now I am a merchant with his longtime partner, Ezra of Rouen. I would like to trade with you and England's merchants. I have my father's merchants and trade routes to the east of Marseilles. I can bring you silk, wine from France, and furs that I have not seen here. Pepper and spices at a cost under those I have seen in your markets."

Eyeing a loaf of bread and cheese that was placed in front of him, the king reached for the food. "England would enjoy having better spices. Many would like better cloth to choose from."

"Yesterday, Emma showed me some of her land. We can produce fine cloth from the wool you produce. The cloth would be made rich in color with dyes from the far east.

"I do not wish to compete with your merchants in what you are exporting. My head hurts to think of it. What I would like is to bring goods that you don't have and buy goods we don't have from you. I also have access to fine jewelry that can be customized for the wearer.

"I meet with Emma's brother, Duke Richard, when I am in Rouen. I have the same agreement with him. Is that an arrangement you would like?"

The king paused in thought. "It may be. I would also like to know what advice you share with Richard. Emma told me that you have shown her how to meet and understand people better. Is that what you do with Richard?"

"What I showed Emma was how to see and understand people's intentions … ways to observe and to listen."

"You do that with the duke?"

"Yes."

As he continued to eat, Nichol realized the king was gazing at the gold necklace she was wearing. "My husband is a goldsmith and he made this necklace. He also makes brooches and other fine jewelry."

Ethelred then pulled a chunk of bread from the loaf. "When you return to England, bring the items that you have described. If they are what you say, I will bring in my merchant, Nigel, and he will work with you.

"Now, tell me about the place you were born in—Marseilles. I have heard of it."

Nichol told him of her love of the sea and the docks. She described the temperate climate and the arrival of the men from the east who spoke in different tongues. She told him of the villa she had grown up in and the orchard and lands that her father managed. "He kept order in the port and was a very kind and generous man. He made sure that the poor children were fed."

"Why are you in Rouen if Marseilles was as you described?"

Nichol's body tensed and her hands clenched. She looked directly at him, her gaze unwavering. "My evil mother poisoned my papa to steal his wealth. If any badness came to him, he created a plan to protect me and a map to use to escape with enough coin. He told me, 'If I die, those who killed me will come for you.' When he died, I followed his plan and used his map, and I fled to Paris and to Ezra, his trusted partner."

As Nichol revealed to the king of her father's death, Emma felt her friend's longing and sadness with every word she spoke. It was the same feelings she had as she watched Normandy disappear from her sight when she sailed to England to marry the king.

Ethelred listened to Nichol and watched Emma's reaction without visible emotion.

When she stopped and looked down at the food in front of her, she looked to Ethelred.

The king only heard my words.

Ethelred stared at Nichol to study her reaction when he asked, "What have you observed here today?"

"You should beware of the man who whispers."

Ethelred's eyes grew wide and his face flushed red. Moments later with short jerky movements, he pushed himself from the table, stood and left without a word to anyone.

Nichol watched his back stiffen as he left. *He is troubled by my words ... and he knows that the whisperer needs to be watched closely.*

Nichol and Emma reached toward each other across the table. Their hands met, bonding one last time before Nichol would leave at first light in the morning.

"We will stay connected, Emma. *Nous sommes sœurs... nous ne serons pas séparées pour toujours.* We are sisters ... we will not be apart forever."

Now understanding the deep feeling Nichol had for her father and childhood home, Emma felt every word she revealed to the king as if they were one.

Their friendship spanned two countries and a vast expanse of water. They both knew they would meet again but were uncertain when. No more words were spoken; distance would now become their enemy.

Emma was a captive of her heritage. Nichol was a free spirit in a dangerous time for women who defied expected behaviors of the day.

Gently squeezing Emma's hand, Nichol stood and silently walked away. Just before leaving the hall, she turned to see Emma sitting alone at the long table with her hands covering her face.

Nichol left the castle, walking briskly with her head down and tears flowing over her cheeks. She was overcome with feelings she now shared with Emma, combined with the lonely tears of her own journey.

twenty-four

Shopping

When it is rung, all in the valley would hear,
telling of gatherings or warning of danger.

When Nichol arrived at the King's Inn, Timo was the first to see her. Her flushed cheeks and forced smile worried him. "What happened?"

"The meeting with the king went well. I spoke to him about trade and now we must prove we can provide the goods I said we could. Diego's return trip is crucial to England opening their markets to us. If we succeed, then we will have the king's support. If we do, we will create expanded markets for Rouen, Paris, and Harmonie.

"Emma told him that I can observe and see people's intentions. He asked me what I saw and I told him something he did not want to hear. My words angered him and he left abruptly. He must now confront an advisor and question his loyalty." She looked down and murmured in a soft voice, "It was hard to leave Emma."

Timo immediately embraced her, feeling the sorrow of a close friend. He released her and with his hands gently on her upper arms, he smiled and spoke. "Robert has Athena who is hungry and will be happy to see you. The children are sleeping now but when they wake, I will take them and Shadow for a walk. Go be with Robert."

After feeding Athena, Robert slipped on the carrying sling and tucked the babe into it. Timo and Shadow sat next to the sleeping children. As Nichol and Robert walked out of the inn, Nichol stopped to give Gunvor and Tova coins to spend on their own.

Now, Robert asked Nichol where she wanted to go.

"Let us just walk and see what shops intrigue us. There was a shop I passed when walking with Emma that had bells in it. I would like to find that shop again."

Robert spied the shop first. Entering it, a large bell caught Robert's eye. "This is the one. It is large and will carry sound throughout the valley. When it is rung, all in the valley would hear, telling of gatherings or warning of danger."

The bell was mounted on a platform that had a wheel attached to one side of the yoke. When pulled, the cord attached to the wheel made the bell ring. Robert pulled on it gently. The sound vibrated within the store. The shutters across the windows shook.

A smile spread across Nichol's face as she heard and saw the result of Robert's cord pull. "This will become the Great Bell of Harmonie, Robert. You will need help in getting it to Harmonie once we return, but I think it will be of great help to us some day."

She paid what the shop owner requested and Robert quickly arranged with him to have it taken to the ship at the port before the light of the following morning.

At the end of the street was a bowyer's shop. Entering it, Nichol started a conversation with the owner. He was gruff and treated her with disdain until she began to speak of her bow and how it was made. Despite the bowyer's excellent craftsmanship, she saw nothing to compared to the ones she purchased in Rouen.

Turning to leave, she noticed what looked like a tall staff, propped up in a dark corner. Curiosity overcame her.

It could be a bow but it is much taller than me. What am I seeing?

As she moved closer, she noticed a string hanging from the top. It was indeed a bow, but a bow the likes of which she had not seen before. Taking it into her hands, she learned it was well made and sturdy, with metal nocks at the ends. Turning to the bowyer, she asked, "Where did this bow come from?"

The bowyer looked at Nichol and then at the bow. "There was a great battle with Norse raiders and when they retreated to their ships, it was left on the battlefield. A young man took it from the battlefield. He said it belonged to a Norse chieftain."

Nichol laughed. "You are a master bowyer but in need of practice when storytelling. It is in the corner because no one wants it." Nichol handed the bow to him. "Now tell me what you know about it and the wood it is made of."

For a moment, he slightly tilted his head, bearing a look given by a man not accustomed to dealing with a woman. Finally, he yielded to her question.

"The bow is a Norse bow made of one piece of yew. The ends are narrow and slightly curved with nocks made of metal. It has a long pull and I do not think you have the strength to pull it back."

Nichol was undeterred. "Will you sell it to me and for how much?"

"It is a very rare bow and worth double its weight in coin."

"I will pay you double the weight in coin or you will give it to me if I can string it and pull it back to where the string touches my cheek."

He handed the bow back to her and looked at Robert, slightly shaking his head.

With great effort and determination, Nichol strung the bow and began pulling the string. Every inch she pulled, the more she struggled. Her arm holding the bow began to shake and her face turned red as the string cut into her fingers.

The bowyer's mouth dropped open in shock and Robert inwardly struggled with her on every inch she pulled. Finally, the string touched her cheek. Slowly, she released it, still holding the bow as she turned toward the bowyer.

He was stunned. "I tried and could not pull it back. The bow is yours."

"How much did you pay for it?"

"The man who brought it to me was hungry. For it, I gave him the price of a meal."

Nichol paid the price of a meal with coin.

When the bowyer looked at the coin, he asked her, "Where are you from?"

"Rouen in the kingdom of Normandy across the channel." Then she added, "This bow needs arrows; I will pay for ten … and I will add the coin for ten meals for you to give to others."

When they left, Nichol looked down at her fingers and shook them. "I should have worn a glove. Did you doubt that I could string and pull the bow to my cheek?"

Robert laughed and gave her a slight bump as they walked. "Doubted you? No. But then you always amaze me. A back and shoulder rub tonight, I suppose, will be your reward."

Smiling, she leaned into him. "Of course. Long and slow. I would like that."

twenty-five

Creating Roots

What filled the air was a loud knock on the door.

Ezra woke with renewed energy for the day ahead. "Helene, wake up," he said while shaking his wife's arm.

"Goodness, what is wrong that you wake me from my sleep?"

"I have been thinking about our business in Rouen."

"And you woke me for your thoughts? Can it not wait for a decent hour to discuss? And perhaps wait for Nichol to return?"

"No, I have been thinking."

Helene now sensed that there was more to what was bothering Ezra. Sitting up now next to her husband, she reached her hand to grasp his. "Tell me what troubles you."

"Nothing … nothing troubles me. I have been visiting many of the merchants, shop owners, and guilds here in Rouen. Not all of them. I am the newcomer here; the others are established.

"But I see things changing with Diego and now with what Timo is learning about England and what Nichol will know after she speaks with Queen Emma … I think we need to prepare now on working with those who have shops in Rouen. We must let them know that there will be more items to sell and a greater variety.

"I won't know what Diego will be bringing to the docks of Rouen. The best way to sell what we receive from him and trade with England will only work if we organize with the merchants and guilds here. We still can have overland routes from Marseilles north to Paris. At the same time, bring goods in from lands to the south in the kingdom of France to the kingdom of Normandy. At times, the goods can be shipped directly to Harmonie."

Helene was surprised, and yet not because of what she heard Ezra say. He had always reached out for offering his moneylending services beyond Paris where they lived before leaving for Rouen.

He is right … he needs to bring as many here together so that they can work cooperatively with selling their goods.

"It is time for us to rise. And with what you say, much to do. I will prepare a meal before we leave. Dinah told me yesterday that they have found a vacant house that needs work but might be suitable for them. I know she wants a place of their own and wanted to ask what I thought. We had planned on going to see Joseph and Rose with Achim."

Suddenly, the quiet house had noise in all corners. Helene and Dinah prepared a meal while they all gathered in the kitchen. Raisa was the center of attention. At five years of age, she was inquisitive and asked questions that meant she had overheard adult conversations.

Gideon helped her onto a tall stool at the kitchen table. "When I get older, can I go to England and see Queen Emma, too?"

Everyone stopped what they were thinking or saying and turned their attention to Raisa. Helene smiled and winked at her. Dinah quickly changed the subject of Gideon's question.

"Raisa, after we eat, we are going to the cloth shop. Rose wants to show us a home we can have for our own."

"I do not want to go! I want to live with Auntie Helene." Helene covered her mouth and turned away as her shoulders began to shake.

Dinah turned to Raisa. "We will live close by and see Auntie Helene every day. Now, eat your meal." She turned to the men with a stern look, not amused with their enjoyment of the conversation.

While they ate, Ezra tried to be vague when he spoke. "When they return, some must go back and help with the harvest. We can plan the journey."

Not looking up from her food, Raisa spoke again. "I want to go to Harmonie, too."

Not another word was spoken about the harvest or Harmonie. What filled the air was a loud knock on the door.

Roger and Joshua had arrived, agreeing not to tell anyone of their night's activities. Helene noticed that their clothes were wet and their bodies reeked of sweat. Seeing the questioning look she bestowed on Joshua and Roger in their wet clothes, Roger was quick to explain.

"We disposed of much of the waste from the warehouse last night to make room for the new merchandise Ezra said Diego would bring in. Then we got water from the river to dampen the wooden floors. Joshua dumped one of the buckets on me … and well, one bucket led to another."

Ezra chuckled when he heard Joshua tell of the water dumping between the two men. But now he was eager to tell them of his expansion ideas for E & N and suggested that they talk after they return from Joseph's and the warehouse. "Roger, will you stay here until we return?"

Nodding yes, Roger understood what he was being asked to do. It was his custom to guard a large oak and metal-strapped chest with a lock, secured to the floor in the bedroom. Within the chest was the treasury of E & N Merchants. And Ezra and Nichol were the only ones who knew where the key was hidden.

Joshua joined their walk to the cloth shop. Rain had stopped and that brought out peddlers, merchants, and people standing in groups to converse. Still, the streets were still wet and scattered with puddles to be avoided.

Finally, they entered the cloth shop and greeted Joseph and Rose.

Helene looked at Ezra and was beginning to feel that he had taken on too much. With a sigh, she said, "You men go do what you have to do. Rose and I will look at the house. We will make the decision without you. And we will look at cloth, too."

Smiling, Ezra gave her a kiss on the cheek. Before he left, he said, "We will meet you back home."

Rose, Helene, and Dinah watched as they left. Helene said, "They did just what I wanted them to do. The guilt he felt by leaving us, I will remind him of someday."

Ezra had thought about the route he wanted to take, and there were shops he wanted to visit. Some shops were small so Joshua and Gideon stayed outside, while Ezra and Achim struck up a conversation with the owner. Joshua had met a merchant at Amos' Inn that he wanted to meet again and left.

Gideon could hear the ringing sound of a hammer striking metal and decided to investigate. He knew it was a blacksmith shop the moment he entered. Walking to where a man was hammering a piece of glowing red iron, he stood and watched the iron change color with the heat. The whooshing sound from the bellows entered his ears and a smile spread across Gideon's face. The blacksmith put the iron back into the coals.

Gideon approached him. "You could use another hammer on that iron."

The blacksmith grunted. "My apprentice left two days ago, and I have more work than I can finish. Everyone that walks in here wants their work done yesterday."

"I know how to work with iron … I can help."

Looking Gideon over from head to toe, the blacksmith said, "Show me your hands."

Gideon held out his hands. The man grabbed his right hand at the wrist and pushed up the sleeve of his tunic, feeling his forearm. He examined the calluses on Gideon's hands and nodded.

"Put on that leather apron and join me."

Ezra and Achim came out and saw Joshua and Gideon had left. They continued moving through the marketplace, going shop to shop.

Achim heard the familiar sound of a hammer against red-hot iron and knew where Gideon had gone. They entered the black-smith's shop and went directly to where the forge was. When the iron went back into the coals, Gideon looked up with a smile on his face. Achim's fatherly pride was evident.

The blacksmith said to Gideon, "Your father?"

"Yes, he is a blacksmith. We lived in a small town south of Paris and I worked with him as long as I can remember. My Uncle Ezra is next to him; he is a merchant in Rouen."

"Yes, your uncle—I know of him. Put the iron into the coals and use the bellows to get it hotter."

He approached Ezra and Achim. "My name is Vilfred." He turned to Achim. "You are his father; he looks like you. You trained him well and I could use him."

Achim looked past Vilfred and saw Gideon's immediate positive response. "He will tell you what he is willing to work for."

Vilfred turned and said, "We must continue and not waste the coals."

Leaving Gideon at the blacksmith's, the three men moved forward. As they walked, Ezra then told Joshua of his plans for him to run the merchant business in Paris and become his eyes and ears there. Joshua was pleased to return to the place he knew best, the city where he was born. Above all, he was pleased with the thought of reestablishing Ezra's business again.

Listening to the plans for Joshua, Ezra's brother Achim added, "And I can be part of your eyes and ears here in Rouen. Dinah told me last night she would like to go to Harmonie with Nichol, Robert, and the children when they return from England to get ready for the harvest with Timo. She will take Raisa with her and return to Rouen when Timo sets up the fair."

As he heard his brother's words, Ezra thought of Helene. *She is not going to want to be away from all the children.*

Soon, they were at the warehouse. Ezra was surprised to see much of it in order, as Roger and Joshua said they had done. As he looked around, he saw Olaf open the large bay door to the warehouse. Marie was by his side.

When Ezra, Achim, and Joseph arrived at the warehouse, Marie and Olaf had just returned from their quest to find land outside the Rouen walls for Timo's fair idea. Before leaving for England with Nichol, Timo had told them he wanted to plan it for All Saint's Day, the first day in November.

"Ezra, we found land outside the Rouen walls for Timo's fair. We have been talking to many of the merchants and asked them to participate for the first winter fair in November if they wish. The merchants, shop owners, and guilds are interested."

"This is good news, Marie." Pleased to see her, his eyes fell to her rising belly. "I see that you are with child."

Olaf reached for his wife's hand. "We are."

Walking back toward his home, Ezra said, "Achim, tomorrow we can revisit all merchants, shop owners, and guilds and seek if any are interested in participating in this fair, and any others that are planned."

When they walked by Joseph and Rose's, Ezra was surprised to see Helene, Dinah, and Raisa still inside. Large pieces of cloth were spread around and the three women were talking with more energy and words than he had seen or heard in some time. Raisa had wrapped herself in one that she hugged closely. Rose was holding the wool that Timo had brought back from his first trip to England. It had been dyed and woven into fabric with colors that were unusual.

Helene turned and saw Ezra. A broad smile spread across her face. Walking across the store, she said, "We will see you at supper. Dinah likes the house and we can easily fix what needs to be done. Go."

That evening at Ezra's and Helene's home two more were added —Olaf and Marie. As Helene walked toward the house, she could hear laughter.

It's been a long time.

twenty-six

Rouen

Tell me what you and Joshua are keeping secret.

Fourteen days had passed since Nichol and family had sailed from Rouen to England.

Ezra woke from a restless night's sleep. He was dressing in the bedroom's darkness, not wanting to wake Helene, as her voice broke the silence.

"What is troubling you, my dear?"

Ezra sat back down. "Give me your hand," and Helene firmly grasped his hand. "I know what troubles you; you talked in your sleep, I too worry."

Ezra's quiet sob brought her to him. Face-to-face in the darkness they both shared their grief and wept with their concern.

Ezra's voice was broken. "What have I done? It has been many days since they left. They should be home by now."

"The decision to go to England was not yours alone. Let us go down to the docks this morning to greet them as they arrive. We will do this every day until they do."

Midmorning when Ezra and Helene arrived at the docks, there were no ships coming or sailing away. While they were scanning the horizon, they heard a friendly voice call out to them. It was Roger and standing next to him was Joshua.

Helene turned to Ezra. "They are here for the same reason we are."

Roger has a frown and that is not like him when he greets us.

As they approached, Joshua whispered to Roger, "We must not tell them of what we know. We must have faith that with the grace of the *Lady*, they will return unharmed."

"If they do not, I will personally give Loupe's head to the archbishop on a platter," said Roger.

Once together, they all silently looked toward the east. Helene broke the silence. "The *Lady* will protect them."

Her words brought a moment of cheer to Ezra. Joshua and Roger exchanged long glances. Both were thinking … *if only they knew what Fredric had revealed …*

It did not go unnoticed by Helene. "It has only been fourteen days since they left—four days there and four days back with good weather. That leaves six days to visit Emma and see the land."

Helene paused in thought. "It may be a good sign that they have not returned. Emma will want her to stay. When she returns, Nichol will have made an alliance with the Queen of England. That is what you should prepare for. Any day now they will arrive and sail up the river, and we must be ready to greet them. I know they will have many stories to tell. Ezra, you and Joshua stay here and keep watch. Roger will see me home."

When they turned a corner out of eyesight, Helene stopped and turned to Roger, her anger apparent. "Joshua can easily hide his knowledge; it is what he is trained to do. Your eyes betrayed you and now I believe you are not telling me what you know about their voyage."

"I will tell you but we must be in the privacy of your home."

When they entered Helene's home and as Roger closed the door, Helene looked him in the eyes, pointing to a stool at the kitchen table and in a demanding voice, ordered, "Sit."

Knowing her from years of service to Ezra, Roger had never seen her as angry as she now displayed before him. He obeyed her command and sat down. A soldier and a man of action, he could not look across the table at Helene.

The silence that he felt, her glare, a wound greater than a loss in battle, a feeling of betrayal.

In a harsh voice, Helene snapped, "Tell me what you and Joshua are keeping secret from Ezra and me."

Roger could barely find his words and stuttered as he began to tell what he knew of the voyage. He would only tell of Fredric's demise and then stopped. "I do not know if they made it to England safely. I will know more soon. I can tell you that Fredric will no longer trouble Nichol. Those words will be welcome ones for her to hear."

"I feel there is much more." Her eyes narrowed. "What else did Fredric tell you?"

Roger summoned his strength. Keeping his voice even and his face expressionless, he said, "For now, let us find comfort knowing he is no longer a threat to Nichol and her family. When they arrive, Nichol will have a story for everyone to hear."

Roger's words were not convincing.

There is more to tell but he is right. When they return their story will be told.

Helene was not fully convinced. "I want you to return to the docks and one of you must keep vigil, day and night until they sail in. I want to greet them when they arrive."

twenty-seven

The Return Voyage

You protected us. We will protect you and your story.

On the return trip while the children slept, there was time for Nichol to reflect and plan. For her, it was not only necessary but a must. When they landed, it would be a new day for E & N Merchants.

The beautiful sights of never-ending water by day and glittering stars in the dark heavens by night reminded all how small they actually were.

When Leiv and his men were in England, they purchased a cloak for Nichol and wool covers for the children. Gunvor and Tova were wearing their new shoes and the simple dresses that they bought in Winchester. No longer did they look like children helping with the babe and toddlers in the family. Without the everyday breeches and tunics, they now had their first longer dresses from materials the colors of summer flowers. They were excited with their new look.

Amused, Nichol watched Gunvor and one of the young sailors as their eyes flirted with each other. The ship's cargo was Nichol, Robert and their family, the Harmonie bell that Nichol and Robert had purchased in England, the new bow, and countless bales of wool.

Nichol filled the hours on board with lengthy discussions of trade, especially with Leiv, between England and Harmonie.

On the third morning at sea, boredom set in. They were confined to a small area surrounded by the bales of wool cargo. Aiden had become a climber and was up and down the bales, scratching his legs until they bled. Nichol sensed the children were becoming restless and all of them were anxious for the sight of Normandy.

Nichol struggled to her feet and stumbled with the roll of the ship, dropping her hand for balance onto Robert's shoulder. She was grateful they were only a few steps away from Leiv, stationed at the tiller.

With the help of Robert, she moved next to Leiv and sat down. She noticed Robert and Timo turned to hear the conversation between her and Leiv.

With an inviting grin, Leiv said, "My hearing is not what it used to be. I see you have something to say, and you have my interest and that of Robert and Timo as well."

Nichol motioned with her arm and hand to include all her family with her.

"What you have seen of me and my family on this trip is who we are. We live in a valley north and east of Fécamp, a day's walk, maybe two, into a once-hidden valley. In that valley is a hamlet we call Harmonie."

Leiv nodded. "Before this trip, I heard of you and Ezra through gossip on the docks. I was told that he was a merchant and moneylender in Paris. It seems you are new to Rouen and there are some respected merchants in Rouen that do not wish you well because of your private meetings with the duke. Now you have Queen Emma as a friend and a future trading partner." He rubbed his nose. "Very few merchants and moneylenders I know have private meetings with nobles. Or royals."

Nichol paused in thought, surprised at his words. *The knowledge of my private meetings with the duke can only come from someone inside the duke's castle and I know who it is. I will use this person to my advantage.*

"Duke Richard chose you to take us across the channel to England. His trust in you is all I need and it is enough for me. The help you gave us on the voyage seals a trusted bond between us. If you agree with my words, I propose to have you ship goods for us from England directly to Fécamp. There are docks there, and we can load finished cloth and other goods onto your ship for a return trip to England."

Leiv seemed pleased with Nichol's words. "Many merchants I sail for always find a reason not to pay me the agreed-upon cost at the journey's end. You have been more than fair with me, and I will gladly carry cargo for you."

After a long silence Nichol brought all in the ship together. All eyes were on the young man that Gunvor had been flirting with and who had moved close to her.

Nichol cleared her throat. "You who sail for Leiv know the danger that lurks in the waters between Normandy and England. Norsemen and pirates may appear at any time. None of us thought that the danger to all was on this ship when we left Rouen. The three men did not just appear without cause. They were sent by a powerful man to stop me and my family from arriving in England.

"Leiv and this crew, you men who stand before me, are brave sailors and my family gives praise to you for keeping us safe. One day you will be able to tell of this voyage and the coin you have earned but not now. Not yet. Do you agree?"

Leiv spoke first. "Aye, Nichol, I agree."

His crew of four each spoke up. "Aye," was echoed by each.

"Thank you. I will now tell you about our voyage to England, the only story you can tell. We left Rouen and sailed toward England and just before we left, three armed men stepped onto the ship. They stayed to themselves and we all thought they were running from trouble because of their coin-filled purses. When asked who they were or about the purses, they refused to say. When we landed in England, they quickly disappeared and did not come back for the return voyage.

"Any other story than what I just said would put our lives in danger and yours as well. Only show your normal wages for the trip, do not show the extra coin you received from me. If anyone —especially a stranger—approaches you and asks for details about the voyage, let me know who it is."

Each of the men again said, "Aye."

Leiv added, "You protected us. We will protect you and your story."

Lucette and Aiden became the ship's entertainment on the trip home. The children decided to follow one of Leiv's men. They became his shadow, attempting to do everything he did.

Timo was sitting next to Nichol, peacefully staring into the distance. Then his eyes closed as though he was in prayer. He seemed unaware of those around him and was gently swaying to and fro with the ship's motion.

Nichol turned to fully face him. She noticed his eye movement under his eyelids, along with his hand and body changing positions. These motions were the same motions he normally displayed while telling a story.

In Papa's solar, I observed a person's body and hand movement together while they were speaking. What story is Timo telling? Is he awake or asleep? Will he remember?

Time passed and everyone settled in for another long afternoon at sea. Even the children seemed weary; gone was the excitement and danger of the first voyage. Thoughts of home were on all their minds.

Timo woke and nudged Nichol and smiled.

She was curious about the actions of her friend. "You appeared to be in a trance. Do you wish to share your thoughts with me?"

Timo's eyes narrowed in thought. "It was a dream … and not a dream. I was writing your story and now I will include this voyage."

Nichol was surprised. "I have not seen you write. Where do you keep this story? I trust it is well hidden?"

Timo pointed to his head. "From the day we met at the fair and every day after, all that I have observed and even your stories, told by you and others. One day I will write your story on vellum, but it is far from complete. Everything will be told."

Nichol's eyes got big. "Everything?"

"Everything and in great detail, even the *Lady*."

"You know we could be hanged or burned at a stake for heresy if this story is revealed."

"Your story must be told and your children's story as well because of who you are and what they will become—the voice of the people. Your story is not just about who you are but what you have done and will do. You are too humble to take praise, and you are steadfast when you and your family are threatened."

Nichol was still wary. "May I read it before you decide to share it?"

"Yes." Timo smiled. "But only to read. The words are mine." He paused, then cast his gaze to the horizon where the sky and the sea met. "When we are gone, your story must be revealed. It will give courage and inspiration to others and women. Only the truth will be told, and it will be a story like no other."

Nichol looked at her friend, her gaze calm and steady. "When we return, I will go to the archbishop's service and sit on the first bench in front of him. When our eyes meet, I will know if he sent these men. If he avoids me, then he becomes a dangerous coward and an adversary to me and to us all."

twenty-eight

The Reunion

I believe you both have much to talk about.

The afternoon of the fifteenth day, a lone ship was seen approaching the docks. Nothing unusual was noted, only that the ship's deep draft showed that it was laden heavily with cargo.

Ezra, Helene, Joshua, and Roger were standing silently, waiting at the docks.

It had started three days ago when the sun was high. Marie and Olaf arrived to join the waiting vigil. A child's voice could be heard over the din of the dock, shouting "Granmama!" Everyone turned to see Raisa running toward them, followed by Dinah, Achim, and Gideon.

Marie stood next to Helene and grasped her hand. Both women were relieved to see the ship returning. Only Helene and Ezra were aware of the events in the warehouse that caused the cleanup by Roger and Joshua, and that Fredric had revealed that killers had been sent to the ship to kill Nichol and her family.

What the four of them didn't know was whether the hired killers had succeeded.

Raisa hugged Helene and asked, "Granmama, what are you looking at? Why are you crying?"

Just then, Marie peered at a distant ship approaching under full sail and recognized it as the ship they unloaded when Timo first returned. Kneeling next to Raisa, she pointed to the ship and said, "There, that is them! They are back!"

All remained silent until Nichol could be seen waving from the deck. Then, one by one, they emulated her actions until all were waving back. Robert stood by Nichol's side, holding both Lucette and Aiden.

The closer the ship sailed to the docks, everyone's spirits rose higher and higher. A celebration would take place that evening, and all were looking forward to feasting and telling stories of the journey.

Nichol was not expecting anyone to greet them when they docked. *How did they know that this was to be the day we returned?* The weary travelers were surrounded by those eager to welcome them as they stepped off the ship.

Nichol could not hold back her tears, seeing tangible proof of how much she and her family were missed while they were gone. Stepping from the ship, the tired passengers were embraced one by one.

Finally, Leiv commanded in a loud voice, "Move aside, everyone. We must unload as much as we can before dark." His announcement came just as Olaf returned from the warehouse with wagons waiting to unload the ship and take the cargo to be stored.

Nichol gestured to Leiv to join them. In a voice all could hear, she introduced him to her people. "This is Leiv, a merchant who will carry our goods from Rouen to England and return with wool whenever we ship. I have asked him to do this for us on a regular basis."

Ezra was now standing next to them. Nichol introduced Leiv to Ezra. "I believe you both have much to talk about."

All the men helped unload the ship while Nichol and the women went with Helene to her home. Helene and Dinah started preparing food for when the men returned, knowing it would be the first good meal for those who were on the voyage.

To the delight of Helene and Dinah, Lucette and Aiden ran around both, staying close to them. Darkness slowly fell as everyone worked hard to accomplish his or her tasks.

Outside, voices filled the air as the men approached Ezra's door. Knowing that the door would be barred on the inside, he banged loudly. "I have hungry men with me."

Helene peered out through the hole in the door. "Who goes there claiming they want food?"

Ezra stepped forward, with his eye to hers and the moon behind him. "Very important friends who will start eating this door if you don't open it, woman!"

Laughing, Helene unbarred and pulled the door open and now Lucette and Aiden each grabbed Ezra's legs. "Granpapa!" they said together, giggling.

Picking them both up, Ezra moved into the warm house and took a deep breath, letting the aroma of a rich stew fill his nostrils. "Tomorrow, Granpapa will spend the morning with you two after you have a long sleep. First, I need to talk with your mama and papa, and everyone must eat."

Lucette hugged him, saying, "I know, Granpapa. Good night." She wiggled down and reached for Aiden's hand. "Come. We will play with him tomorrow."

My granddaughter is wise.

Nichol had finished feeding Athena and then motioned to Gideon, Gunvor and Tova. "You are all tired. Take the children to bed and you sleep, too. We have much to do tomorrow."

Signaling to Shadow to follow the six, she turned to Helene. "I am famished; let us all eat."

Ezra, Robert, Achim, Olaf, and Timo sat on stools at the table, eating bowlfuls of the stew and hunks of fresh bread. Roger,

John, and Joshua stood with plates in hand as did Helene, Nichol, Dinah, and Marie, who served the men and themselves. They all knew that there was much to tell.

The stew tasted good after the work the men had done unloading the ship. Along with bread and cooked apples with cinnamon, Ezra declared it a repast fit for a king.

When they were done, the table was cleared and cups were filled with wine. More candles were lit as they all gathered in a tight circle.

Nichol looked at each one and began with her story of the warm welcome from Emma and the king.

"I told King Ethelred we could bring silk, dyes, and spices to him from lands in the east. There is much more to tell; that is for another day." She stopped. "The attack and what happened after we left … "

Then she stopped again. "Why was everyone on the dock waiting for us today?"

Helene hugged her so tight, it was hard for her breathe.

She then looked across the table to Joshua and Roger standing together.

I see you.

"Both of you … tell me what you know, then I will tell you of our voyage to England."

Joshua hesitated and Roger's anger erupted into harsh words. "We uncovered a plan to kill you and everyone on board."

Nichol struggled to control her surprise. "Who did you hear this from?"

"Your brother, Fredric. His head was left on Loupe's doorstep and the rest of him made a generous meal for the fish in the river." Looking down to the floor, then up and into Nichol's eyes, his expression burned with residual emotion. "Fredric angered me."

"Nichol, I saw a light around us when we were dealing with Fredric's demise. We knew your *Lady* was with us. And we decided not to tell Ezra and Helene until after your return. We knew you would tell them," Joshua quietly added.

Nichol immediately went and embraced them and whispered to them, "You did what I could not do." She stood between them and began to speak.

"Three men had been watching and waiting and came onto the ship just before we left, staying to themselves. The purses attached to their belts were heavy with coins. These men were sent to make sure we did not arrive in England. Before the dagger took the third one, he revealed that someone named Lord Charles was conspiring with the Priest Loupe. I knew then that they were planning to kill everyone. Thanks to the power of the dagger, all three of them ended as meals for the creatures of the ocean.

"Tomorrow morning, I am going to attend Mass. I want to look Archbishop William in the eye and see his reaction when he sees me. If he shows no surprise that I am there, then I believe that Loupe and this Lord Charles who sent men to kill us may have acted alone. They cannot hide because they are arrogant and will soon reveal themselves. That is just how they behave.

"What is important is that we are all here and safe. We must stay vigilant because whoever is responsible is not going to stop."

twenty-nine

Archbishop William

I know it is a dangerous game I am playing.

The next morning Nichol woke to Athena's hungry cry.

"Shush, shush, Athena, you will wake the whole house," she murmured as she got up and went to the crib. Changing the baby's cloth, Nichol sang softly to her daughter. Picking her up, she settled on the stool by the crib and pressed her engorged breast to the baby's waiting lips. Rocking back and forth, Athena settled down as she nursed.

Nichol returned to bed, nestling Athena between Robert and her. He sat up next and gently took Athena's hand in his. Athena turned her head toward him, her smile spreading across her face. "This one will be will be daddy's girl," he cooed to her as he leaned down and kissed her cheek. Now her little legs started to kick and Nichol laughed out loud.

Just then, Lucette and Aiden burst through the door and jumped into bed with them. Robert began to wrestle and tickle them until their laughter and screams woke everyone up.

Nichol was not enjoying the wrestling so close to Athena. "Robert, would you take them to the kitchen and feed them?"

Robert jumped up and put on his tunic and then dressed the children. By then, Helene and Dinah were up and greeting them as they ran into the kitchen. A small piece of bread was given to Lucette and Aiden to satisfy them until the porridge with apples could be cooked.

Nichol soon entered, ready to leave for church service. Placing Athena into Dinah's outstretched arms, she reached for a piece of bread and cheese. All eyes were on her now standing next to Robert. "I do not want to be late," Nichol said as she turned to leave.

"Are you sure you do not want me to go with you?" Robert asked her.

"Not this time. Come with me when I go next."

He went to the door and lifted the brace from its bracket and opened the door. Nichol stopped and gave him a kiss. He handed her an apple and held her hand in his.

"Remember, the *Lady* is with you."

Her worried look disappeared, as Robert's words had provided her with a burst of confidence. Still, she was consumed in thought as she slowly walked to the church.

I am not alone. I have never been alone and now I have a family who surrounds me with love. Who are these wretched men who threaten my family? They will rue the day, I swear it.

Nichol put aside her worrisome thoughts while moving with a crowd entering the church.

I must sit where I can see the archbishop and he can see me.

Nichol entered and paused. To her surprise, there was no room to sit, both sides of the aisle were fully occupied.

I will stand at the back next to the entrance. I will make sure he sees me before he leaves the service.

She did not have to wait long. From her place at the rear, she moved forward as Archbishop William entered. Everyone stood and turned to face him as he passed. Priest Loupe and another priest were side by side, walking right behind William.

Loupe walked with a pious, arrogant face and was closest to where she was, as they moved forward down the center aisle.

A sudden pounding vibrated within her chest. *A fraud. A man who prays in church and then preys on the weakest of the flock.* Nichol loudly cleared her throat and before they passed, both turned to her.

She leaned toward Loupe and mouthed the words: *I see you. You are a fraud.*

Loupe knew what she had mouthed.

Did others see her lips move?

Could they tell what her lips said?

Loupe felt exposed and trapped in his once-protected church sanctuary. His only choice was to continue forward to the altar, under the protection of the archbishop.

I have to be rid of this woman before she brings me harm.

Nichol could sense his unease.

I will take communion and look the archbishop in the eyes and only speak if I am spoken to.

Once at the altar, Archbishop William turned to the gathered congregation. The archbishop's priest delivered his sermon in Latin. It took her back to her days as a young girl in Marseilles. Margaux had taught her Latin, so she could follow any sermon and was able to read scriptures that her father had collected.

She looked over the congregation and knew they did not understand any words that were being said, yet they held onto every word uttered by the priest, mesmerized by the whole ceremony.

When the sermon was over, a line formed to receive holy communion. Pew by pew, the attendees approached and knelt to receive communion before the altar. The line was very long, extending out the door of the church. The crowd moved forward at a slow pace to receive the archbishop's blessing.

Nichol stepped outside the church.

I will wait and then join them so I will be the last to receive communion.

When the line was down to the last two people, Nichol slowly walked down the aisle. The three men at the altar watched her approach.

The young priest smiled at her and she returned his smile with one of her own. She knew him by the name of Samuel. She turned her direction now to Priest Loupe and Archbishop William. Both glared at her as she approached. Nichol saw a look of dread spreading across their faces.

A smile was still on the young priest's face, oblivious to the shared past history.

Archbishop William dismissed the last person as Nichol stepped in front of him to kneel. His voice and hands began shaking with anger as their eyes met.

I challenged him and he did not know what to do.

Before she knelt, he said, "I cannot give you communion. You are with sin."

"I have committed no grave sin and now I stand before you. Tell me, what sin do you speak of?" Nichol paused and glared at William.

Not accustomed to being disobeyed, and never by a woman, he responded, "There is no communion for you today. Now leave."

"I am a Christian, just as you are, Archbishop. I was baptized as an infant in Marseilles …" She paused, then added, "Priest Loupe is aware of this."

Silence filled the air, a seething silence laced with heavy breathing.

Nichol then added, "I thought that you would ask me about your sister, the Queen of England."

William stood motionless, unable to order her removal and paralyzed by her words.

She then turned her attention to Loupe, mouthing *I see you, fraud,* yet not saying a word aloud that the young priest or archbishop could hear.

Turning back to Archbishop William, she spoke boldly. Her voice rising, she pointed her finger at Loupe. "Yet you let this wicked and evil man stand next to you—giving and most likely taking communion from you.

"My family and I were on a ship ready to leave on our journey to see Queen Emma. Three heavily armed men came on board just as we pushed away from the dock. These men were sent by this Priest Loupe to kill my family, the captain, and his crew. Each had a large purse loaded with coin that we later learned were filled by my brother Fredric, Priest Loupe, and a certain Lord Charles. The three men confessed to this before we killed them and dropped their bodies into the sea, and I have no doubt their words are true."

Her voice was loud enough to carry throughout the church. All shuffling and chatter stopped as the people knew something other than communion was taking place.

The outwardly visual anger displayed by Archbishop William was not toward the woman standing in front of him. He could no longer ignore the years of rumors that were woven with greed and abuse.

William glared at Loupe, his face flushed and teeth clenched. In a low growl, he muttered, "Priest … you dare embarrass me in front of my congregation? I will not forget."

Nichol smiled. Her work was done.

Turning on her heel, she walked out of the church without taking communion. A crowd was still outside the main doors to exchange greetings with the archbishop, patiently waiting for the archbishop and priest to arrive at the church entrance.

Nichol was almost out of sight of the church before she turned to look back. Only the young priest and the archbishop were greeting those coming from the church. Loupe was not visible.

A sense of satisfaction filled her.

This will be the talk of Rouen for days.

I stood before him and told the truth. I could see him change, beginning to see that my words spoke the truth. Now he must confront his evil Priest Loupe.

I know it is a dangerous game I am playing. I must take my family back to the safety of Harmonie soon.

If it was not the archbishop, could there be other merchants who worked with Loupe and Lord Charles who so desperately wanted us dead? Did I remove the protection the church gives Loupe? Or is the archbishop the leader?

Only time will tell.

thirty

Nichol's Truth

And I did not have a disagreement … I gave him a revelation.

Achim, Dinah, and Gideon had moved to their new home the previous afternoon. Gunvor was with her brother Olaf and Marie. Nichol looked forward to not being surrounded by so many people in Ezra's home.

Fed and wide awake, Athena let her mother know that sleep was not happening any time soon. Moving her arms and kicking her feet, her gummy little smile was broad. Athena was rapidly learning to observe her surroundings and the people within them. As Nichol descended the stairs, Athena's eyes widened as she recognized her siblings' voices and laughter.

The sense of calmness she felt holding her infant daughter was what she needed after yesterday's encounter with Loupe and the Archbishop William—one that she only shared with Robert. The two of them decided that she would tell the others after she met with the duke later today.

Entering the kitchen area, Helene was on a stool and holding Lucette. Raisa and Tova were seated on the floor with Tova, play-ing a counting game and asking, "How many fingers am I holding up, Raisa?"

Smiling at the scene in front of her, Nichol leaned and kissed the top of her daughter's head. As if it was a sign, Lucette wiggled out of Helene's arms and moved to Ezra's side. Pulling on his tunic to be noticed, she looked up and coaxed, "Granpapa, up."

He happily stretched his arms out, lifting her into his embrace. The two quickly were in their own world with silly sounds and words, moving to a stool. As he held her, he noted her darkening, curly hair and her strong resemblance to Nichol.

Happiness filled Nichol as she looked at them. *They are meant for each other. I have never seen Ezra so happy.*

Eyes connecting, Nichol and Helene communicated silently.

Nichol spoke first. "I need to see Duke Richard this morning and give him news of Emma … I must also ask if I can be of assistance to him. I want to see his reaction to yesterday's church service."

"Church service? Did something unusual happen at the church service yesterday?" Helene asked.

"After the children are settled to sleep, I will tell everyone at the same time." She lowered her voice. "Loupe was there."

Nodding and knowing that there was much to tell, Helene responded, "Eat a little something before you set out. The girls are fine with us. Robert is out with Aiden and Shadow."

Chatter filled the kitchen area as Nichol ate the cheese, bread, and fish from the previous night's meal that Helene set in front of her. With Athena now sound asleep, she passed her baby to Helene, whispering, "I'll be back soon."

Smelling and feeling the dampness of rain as she opened the door, Nichol gathered her sheepskin cloak, closing the door behind her. Lucette was so absorbed in all things Ezra, she did not notice that her mother had left.

Once outside the door, Nichol looked upward at the low-hanging dark clouds. She took a deep breath of the damp air, allowing her senses to take over as she observed the changing leaves of the trees.

I will miss the long days of summer. I am glad we went to England when we did.

Rousing from her thoughts, she heard a child call out, "Mama! Mama!" Aiden ran toward her with Shadow by his side. She smiled, seeing that he did not miss a single puddle on the way. Robert was close behind.

Nichol bent over and hugged him. "You both need to go inside and dry off and get warm." She kissed Robert and whispered in his ear, "We will have much to discuss when I get home. I have more thoughts about the archbishop from yesterday. He is not to be ever trusted."

Raising his eyebrows, he looked at her. "And you walked away. I need to hear the rest. So will everyone else. Where are you headed now?"

"To the castle to meet with the duke. I will return soon."

Nodding to his wife, Robert picked up Aiden and called Shadow to come with him. As he did, Nichol began walking toward the castle.

By the time she reached the end of the street, Timo was at her side.

"I know where you are heading, and I did not want you to go alone. There may be memories of what you did to the priest when you were here and I feel it is best that you have a man on your side in case there is trouble. And I have heard the news of what happened yesterday."

Stopping, she said, "What have you heard?"

"The gossip is that you had a disagreement with the archbishop and he turned you away."

As they walked along the cobblestones, Nichol realized he was right.

"Thank you, Timo. I will need your support when I tell the duke about our voyage. And I did not have a disagreement … I gave him a revelation."

thirty-one

The Duke and Duchess

With only the truth can I protect you.

pproaching the gate, the guard recognized her. A smile crossed his face. "Welcome back, Nichol. Go to the door and announce your arrival."

"Good morning, Victor. My brother Timo is with me today." Thanking him, she turned and nodded toward Timo and headed toward the castle door.

Looking toward the garden, she again recognized the signs that the fall was close. The beautiful summer garden that she and Emma shared was in the past. Melancholy came over her.

Now in front of the door, Nichol did not immediately knock. Instead, she turned to Timo. "I will not leave before the duke hears the truth. There is danger for us if it is not well received. Do you agree?"

To Nichol's surprise, Timo laughed. "Our whole journey has been filled with danger and we have survived." He lifted the large door knocker and dropped it twice.

Steward Thomas answered and stood back to let them in. "You have come before the duke sent a guard to bring you here. The duke is in the Great Hall." Looking at Timo, he ordered, "You will wait here."

"No, Thomas, he needs to come with me." Nichol was resolute.

The steward shrugged his shoulders. "It is you he wishes to see. If he is displeased, you will be receiving his anger promptly."

The steward led them to the Great Hall where the duke was seated in his chair. A clerk stood to his side and a man stood before him, speaking.

The duke turned to the side to see who was following Thomas and saw Nichol. With a wave of his hand, he dismissed the man in front of him and motioned Nichol to come forward.

Thomas joined Richard on the opposite side of the clerk. Once in front of the duke, Nichol and Timo bent at the waist, looking down. They both said, "Your Grace," then looked up at the seated man.

Duke Richard knew of Timo's agriculture skills through Nichol and that he was a monk. He knew he had accompanied Nichol to England … but he did not know that he had already made a visit to Queen Emma prior to the recent voyage. He was surprised that Timo was with Nichol at her first visit with him since her return.

Is there something more I do not know or are they here to share news of England?

As both stood in front of him, he said, "Tell me of Emma."

"She is in good health and well; but you must know she struggles with the language. Also, she misses you. She is strong and I believe she will become a great queen." Nichol paused. "Your Grace, she offered me and my family land and protection if we would stay with her."

Richard's concern was immediate. "What did you tell her?"

"I told her that we are both victims of our own destinies. Her destiny is being Queen of England and mine … well, she has seen mine. That does not mean we cannot be lifelong sisters and our love for one another is greater than the distance that separates us."

"What has she seen of yours?"

Nichol stood silently in front of him, her face blank. Her thoughts were distant thoughts.

I cannot reveal our sharing of my stone …

I must protect Harmonie and those that live there …

I cannot let him know of the light …

Then she spoke. "She has seen of my love of the land and of fairness for women when I share with her how I have had to defend my family from thieves with my bow. And she has seen that I will advise you if you desire it. She has seen my skill of observation, and I have worked with her so she can communicate and interpret what the intent may be of others by their actions, nonactions, words, and behaviors."

Richard sat back in his chair. "I knew you were back, as soon as you stepped off the ship and then William told me about Sunday's Mass. You publicly embarrassed William—a high-ranking and powerful member of the clergy—in front of a church full of worshipers.

"These actions—and you—are now the gossip around Rouen. What has been told to me from your words is that you said you killed three men and got Loupe sent into seclusion for his actions —and all of this in just one day! Now that you are in front of me, you can explain your actions. With only the truth can I protect you."

Nichol squared her shoulders and looked Richard directly in the eyes before replying.

"It is why I brought Timo with me as he was on the ship when the hired killers came on board."

She raised her chin. "I am sure William told you that he refused communion to me because 'of my great sin.' I told him that I was not guilty of any great sin and that three men boarded the ship to kill me, my family, the captain, and the crew. I also told him that they were sent by his evil Priest Loupe and Lord Charles. This was revealed to me by the third man before he was killed by my dagger and thrown to the fishes.

"William embarrassed himself, Your Grace, when I confronted Priest Loupe in front of the congregation at the altar. He knew I was telling the truth—*I saw him*. He had knowledge of Loupe's behavior in the past and he chose to ignore it. If your words are true and he is in seclusion, Rouen is now safer with him gone."

No one in the Great Hall moved, spellbound by Nichol's words that resounded from the hard stone walls to those listening in every corner. The very world seemed to pause, waiting for the duke's next words.

From the corner of her eyes, Nichol saw Judith edge closer to them with every word spoken.

Richard seemed to relax in his chair, his posture easing.

"I had Leiv and his crew brought before me. He started to tell me the story that you told him to say, and I tell you now that he is a poor liar. I told him that I must have the truth. He then related to me the same story that William heard from you yesterday. And he added that it was you who had created the strategy that saved everyone but the killers on the ship."

His fingers tapped a quick rhythm on the arm of his great chair. "You and your family are now under my protection. You will come back tomorrow for a private conversation at midday."

He once again stiffened, leaning forward. "No one will escape punishment for his actions."

"Yes, Your Grace. I will be here. Thank you." Nichol and Timo bowed, turned, and began to leave when Nichol saw Judith waiting at the entrance to the hall.

Judith whispered, "Follow me." She led them to a more secluded spot for conversation, away from prying ears to spread castle gossip and lies.

When she stopped and turned around, Nichol and Timo bowed and said in unison, "Your Grace."

Judith leaned to the side to see a clerk stationed to listen to their conversation. She sighed.

Taking Nichol's hands in hers, she leaned close and spoke softly.

"Archbishop William gave Richard and I our private Mass after your confrontation with him at the altar." Her smile broadened.

She continued, "I wish I had been there. William knew of Priest Loupe's bad deeds and he chose not to discipline him. He uses him to keep others in line. For now, no one dares to harm you, but your name is on everyone's lips. Soon you must go back to Harmonie until the gossip stops. I support you and I believe that Richard will trust you to tell the truth. Go now."

Nichol gently squeezed Judith's hands. "I see you are well, with your belly beginning to swell." Without saying another word, Nichol and Timo left the castle and began walking toward Ezra's.

Timo stopped and began to shake his head. Realizing he was no longer beside her, Nichol turned to face him. "Timo, what are you thinking that must be said?"

"This morning when I joined you, I was not sure that we would be coming home at all and now we have the duke's protection. This is … extraordinary.

"I now believe you possess more insight than any of us realize. You are someone that most people of power do not see as a threat. Only evil is threatened by your presence."

Nichol took his arm as they continued walking home. "Tonight when the children are asleep, we must all gather and fully discuss what has happened since yesterday. And what plans we should consider for Harmonie … and for all of us. Soon, we must return to Harmonie for the harvest and you must start planning for your fair. There is so much to talk about. Everyone will have a voice."

Now at Ezra's door, Nichol stopped and turned to Timo.

"We have many challenges ahead. With our growing Harmonie family and E & N, the core of a new generation is now here. It was there on the docks that day we returned from England. For now, let us celebrate our new beginning.

"It is our time."

thirty-two

The Tell at Ezra's

"Never back down!"
In unison all raised their cups, "Never back down!"

Athena was fed and sleeping in her cradle. Lucette and Aiden were settled in another small room with Guvnor and Tova singing softly to them and coaxing them to sleep. Gideon and Raisa had walked back to their home.

Stools were set around the kitchen table, while others stood behind those seated. Wine was poured, and the group awaited what Nichol had to share about her encounter with the archbishop and Loupe on Sunday. Now that they were all together, it was time to disclose what had really happened on the ship.

Nichol raised her hand and the small talk stopped. She stood next to Robert and behind Marie who was sitting at the table. Nichol gently placed a hand on her shoulders.

"I am gossip of all in Rouen because of the Mass at the church Sunday. You must understand that I did not go there to confront the archbishop. I just wanted to see him and determine if I could if he was involved in any way with the three men who attacked us on the ship. When he refused to give me communion, my words flowed.

"As I entered through the large open doors of the church, I could see that it was crowded. Many were standing and the archbishop had not entered. There was no one at the front. I found a standing place along the wall so I could see him when he entered. Soon the archbishop moved through the door, dressed in flowing purple robes that reached his ankles. He was followed by the Priest Loupe and another young priest I had not seen before. Neither were dressed as richly as the archbishop; instead, they were dressed in white priestly garments.

"As Loupe passed by me, I loudly cleared my throat and Loupe turned toward me. His eyes focused on me and his false saintly look turned to fear. He looked like a cornered animal, trapped with nowhere to run. I mouthed, '*I see you.*'

"The archbishop spoke to the people in the church in Latin, a language I understood. He then told those who were there for communion to come forward. Many of the parishioners lined up. Loupe and the other priest assisted him. Loupe looked toward the back and side often, searching the church walls. I knew he was looking for me.

"As people started moving toward the front of the church, I had slowly moved to the back. I wanted to be the last to take communion. The archbishop's eyes were filled with anger when I stepped in front of him. I saw his hands shaking.

"What he said to me, he should not have said. He told me I was with sin and could not receive communion. I asked him what grave sin I had committed to exclude me from receiving it. All he said was, 'There is no communion for you today, now leave.'

"The villagers were still in the church. Now they were listening and watching. I reminded him I was a Christian and baptized as an infant, and Priest Loupe knew this. Silence filled the air. I heard his heavy breathing, and Loupe's as well.

"I then said, 'Priest Loupe sent three men to kill me and my family after we boarded the ship to take us to visit Queen Emma.'

"The young priest's eyes looked like they would pop out. I then added, 'I thought that you would ask me about your sister, the Queen of England.'

"There was no response. Only silence. I turned and walked out of the church."

Roger raised his cup, "Never back down!"

In unison, all raised their cups, "Never back down!"

Then Nichol added, "In front of the worshipers, I accused Loupe of sending those men to kill us and all on board the ship. The archbishop did not question my words, and he did not seem surprised when I told him of Loupe's actions.

"I learned from Duke Richard today that Loupe has been sent away. But like a nightmare, I know he will reappear. The archbishop is like most men of power. What they do best is blame others or maybe claim that God is testing their faith.

"I do know what is to come. Loupe may be away for now, but he will come for me … for us … again. It is time for all of us to think of protection for here … and for Harmonie."

thirty-three

The Women

Sitting down at the table,
it felt right to be there with each other.

The next morning, Nichol awoke before any of her family. Leaning over the cradle that held Athena, her daughter's eyes opened and her innocent face immediately curved in a smile.

A mother's smile was Nichol's answer as she lifted her baby and nuzzled her. Quietly she moved to the door and descended the stairs. To her surprise, candles were lit in the kitchen area and Helene was heating water.

"I have been waiting for you," was Helene's greeting.

Shadow was immediately by Nichol's side. Moving to the front door, she opened it so Shadow could slip out and relieve herself.

Helene chuckled and reached for Athena. "Let me change her cloth from the night. I have made us both a bowl of herbed hot water."

Sitting down at the table, it felt right to be there with each other. Helene looked down at Athena, now nursing, and spoke first. "I do not like it that I will no longer live with you. And that I am not with the children as much as before."

Reaching out, Nichol placed her hand on top of Helene's. "I know and I do not like it that you do not live with us as well. Summer is coming to an end and we must return to Harmonie to finish the harvest and meet with everyone in the hamlet.

"We have much to transport to Harmonie so that the women can start spinning and weaving the wool we brought back from

England. When I know that all is taken care of, I promise you Robert and I and the children will return here for the winter months. We will live with you and Ezra. Timo will also return to set up his fairs outside the wall with some of the finished goods. Other merchants in Rouen will display goods as well. I know that one fair will be held around All Saints' Day long before the Solstice.

"Ezra and I will meet today or tomorrow to talk about E & N. Hopefully, he has some word when Diego will return. If Diego has been successful, E & N will have much to do with new goods and reselling them.

"Lastly, I will meet with the duke tomorrow and learn much more about how he can help and protect us—something he does not know I will be asking and—making suggestions as well."

Helene let out a sigh of relief. Knowing that Nichol would be back in Rouen within two months of her return to Harmonie had done much to lessen her sense of loneliness. She placed her other hand on top of Nichol's. "I will be happy when you are here for much longer. I worry about you and the children."

"Helene … I feel safer in Harmonie and know that I must return. And I think my children will be safer in Harmonie than here. I know that both Lucette and Athena are special children. I see the light around them. And I know that Aiden has some of it, too. In Harmonie, I will be able to see whatever it is developing in them without concern for bad men intending to do us harm. In my heart, I feel you know that as well.

"During our time in England, Robert and I purchased a loud bell that he will position in a central place in the valley. The bell can be rung to send out warnings if any one of us is threatened. And we can also use it to call everyone together.

"You will have Dinah and Marie here to be with. The men will be working with the port, warehouse, and merchants as soon as Diego arrives. By then, I will be headed back to Harmonie with the children.

"And someday, I would like all of us to live together at the same time in the same place."

When Helene heard Nichol's words, tears freely flowed and she murmured, "You are my daughter. I will do anything to support you."

Planning Forward

*E & N will prosper not because of me but your connection
with the duke and Queen Emma.*

The morning began with Helene heating herbed water. Nichol had joined her on a stool, nursing a wide-awake Athena. Noise from upstairs meant Lucette and Aiden were up and would be down soon. The morning quiet was broken.

Helene cut apples and brought bread to the table; the porridge was already warming. Aiden and Shadow appeared first.

"Me hungry," were the first words out of Aiden's mouth. Lucette followed Tova and moved toward Nichol. Her first words were, "We want to go to the river."

Helene and Nichol exchanged glances and Nichol nodded her head lightly up and down. "Eat first, then we will go," Helene said, giving Lucette a hug. She then looked at Nichol. "You and Ezra have much to talk about before you go back to Harmonie. I will take the children with me today to the river. Gunvor and Tova will help me. I need to buy more food and visit the cloth shop for cloth to stitch warm clothes together for the children before winter sets in."

"They will like that. And I know Lucette loves bright colors for her tunics. When I am out with Ezra, I will stop at the tannery to get more skins to make larger foot coverings for Aiden's and Lucette's growing feet. Helene, what if I got lighter skins to create breeches for each of them? Could you stitch them as well?"

As Helene filled the table with food, Robert and Ezra joined them. Pulling up a stool, Ezra addressed the table.

"Nichol, I would like you and Robert to join me this morning at the dock. There is much to discuss before you leave for Harmonie. We must not dwell on recent events, but we must learn from them. We cannot be caught off guard by the priest and others he recruits to help do his deeds. We must stay alert so that we won't be fooled. Others will come for us and we will be ready for them.

"Olaf and Marie have been very busy at the warehouse. If the stars have been good to Diego, he should be coming into port soon with his ship laden with goods for E & N to resell to merchants. It would be good if you are still here when he arrives.

"Finish your hot herbed water and feed Athena if she wants more of you. Then we will set out."

Securing Athena in her sling, Robert carried her first, freeing Nichol to talk with Ezra. Stopping outside of one shop, a merchant stood by a table that displayed jewelry.

Nichol was intrigued and drew Ezra closer to the table. "Did you make these?" she asked the merchant. Robert stood silently by her side, waiting for the man's response.

"Some, I make. Most I get from others."

Nichol pushed up her sleeve. "Would pieces like this be of interest to you and your customers?"

Eyeing the bracelet that Robert made for her, the merchant's eyes widened. "I could sell many like this. Where did you get it?"

Gesturing at Robert, she said, "My husband is a goldsmith and he made it for me. He also made one identical to this for Queen Emma of England. He could make more jewelry and brooches for you to sell."

Looking at Robert, the merchant said, "When can you bring me more of what your wife has on her arm?"

Robert nodded. "I will be working on more pieces and returning here before winter. I will bring them for you at that time and you can decide what you would like to offer to your customers. Would that be agreeable?"

"My name is Sam. I look forward to your return." The two men shook hands.

Ezra was pleased with what he was hearing. *Robert has his first merchant to carry his work.*

Silently, they continued through the busy streets toward the river, closer to the warehouse.

All of them stopped at a quiet place at the riverbank and sat down.

Ezra's voice was serious as he spoke up. "The bottom of the box that contains our treasury is visible. Soon I will see nothing but wood. It is important that Diego arrive soon with his ship heavy with merchandise to fatten our treasury.

"We still have your father's gems, gold, and silver. With the precious stones and metals, Robert can make brooches, necklaces, bracelets, and rings with what you have of your father's."

Nichol was distracted by a screech from the sky. Looking up and pointing at the hawk, she said softly, "Papa ..."

Silence followed. Seeing her serene gaze at the hawk, Robert knew she was reliving moments with her father from long ago. The men waited for her to return from her memory.

Moments later, she smiled. "Ezra, you were saying ...?"

"Your father was a caring and generous man. I miss him, too." He patted Nichol's hand. "Now we must create a plan for Robert to become a successful goldsmith. He could make plain items for Sam's shop, and at the same time create more elaborate ones for his own." He patted her hand again. "I will find a shop for him by the time you come back.

"And you must have time to become the merchant you are destined to become. E & N will prosper but not because of me. It is your connection with the duke and Queen Emma. Even though you are a woman, daring to speak the truth to the Archbishop William and Richard, the duke, trusts you."

Ezra laughed. "The archbishop does not respect you but I think he will listen to you. Possibly it is through his brother, the duke that he hears. If Robert has the goods to make something that you can present to him without spending any coin, it would be wise. The archbishop is a vain man and can be easily flattered."

Ezra stopped talking to let her absorb what he had said. Then, switching what he was suggesting, he added, "I know a man who has pack animals and he can transport the sheep's wool stored in the warehouse to Harmonie if you will lead the way."

Ezra looked at Nichol. "What are your thoughts?"

She laughed loudly.

"We have been gone too long. I have forgotten how you change what you are talking about with how you speak," Nichol said, shaking her head. "A messenger is needed if we are going to have Harmonie be a part of E & N Merchants and for me to be able to communicate with the duke, to Leiv at the docks, or even Helene. And I know that people will arrive if land and work is there for them. If we have the need in Harmonie, you need to know. That need might have already started after we returned here to go to England.

"In Harmonie, I remember overcast days when the wind was blowing from the west, and I could smell the channel. I remember as a child when I was at the docks and smell of the water; the air smelled just like the Mediterranean Sea. If it was just a day's journey from Harmonie to the channel, Leiv could sail to a spot on the coast and unload wool, moving it to Harmonie and then returning to England with cloth. No longer will Harmonie be in a hidden valley. I see growth coming, Ezra, and I am sure you do as well.

"And one day soon, the children must stay in Harmonie for their protection until they are grown. Timo is concerned for them and has encouraged me to leave them there under his protection as they get older, along with John and Cara. I know that they will be different than the other children in how they talk, think, and act. We have always had plans to gather the children and teach them to write and how to defend themselves as I was taught.

"I now have three young children. Athena is still a baby—but look at Lucette and Aiden. Lucette talks as an older child would, like one more than twice her age. Aiden mimics her. We need to think beyond the ages they are now."

She paused, then asked, "Tell me, Ezra … how is it with Helene when she doesn't have the children around her?"

"She is lonely and unhappy. She doesn't have the women friends she had in Paris here in Rouen. And she misses you."

Nichol was silent for a moment. "Do you think Helene would prefer to stay with the children in Harmonie?"

"If that is what she wants, she will have my support."

"Helene is like a mother to me. I think it would be best just to ask her."

"As we traveled back from England, I thought about how best we could work with the duke. If the duke meets with me today, I will ask him if he has decided on giving you a title."

Ezra paused. "I think you should have a title to set you apart."

With his words, Nichol laughed. "I am a woman. It will not be me; I cannot have a title. Now that Harmonie has been discovered, it will not be long before the duke appoints someone to rule over us and to protect what he sees as his, and we will be under the thumb of that person. If you are the one he appoints, you will be responsible for collecting rent and taxes. John could assist you. You will be someone we trust to be fair in applying laws. You are also one that would not spy on us or interfere with our progress."

"You make a good argument. If he accepts what you say, I will accept. I will ask him to go to Harmonie. The valley would welcome him."

Midday, Robert joined Nichol and Ezra at the warehouse where they settled after leaving the house. The skies were still clear and talk was of when Diego would arrive with his next shipment.

Nichol spotted the red-tailed hawk on a roof top close by. *Hello, Papa …*

Athena woke with her plaintive *feed-me* cry and Robert gently hugged her.

"Let us sit on the stools so I can talk with your Mama and Granpapa, and she can feed you, little one."

As he passed the baby to Nichol, she was already unbuttoning the flap on her upper tunic. Nichol lifted her baby to her breast.

Once Athena settled in, their discussion turned to what she would say to the duke when she saw him later in the afternoon and guessing when Diego would come into port.

The three of them knew it had to be soon.

They planned how the next few hours needed to be spent. With Athena fed, Nichol slipped her into the sling Robert was wearing.

"I will go to the castle and see if the duke will see me now. I will return before Athena needs to be fed again, then I will meet you back at Ezra's."

As the two men watched her move quickly toward the castle, Ezra said, "I have never seen a woman like your wife, Robert. Her strength has carried us all. She has truly become the son her father wanted."

He slapped Robert on the back. "Come, we need to find the man who could transport wool to Harmonie to be made into cloth. If he comes by the warehouse, we can ask Olaf if he has had news of Diego and his ship."

Suddenly, both men heard a friendly voice. They stopped and turned to see Joshua approaching, his broad smile beaming. He spoke words that didn't make sense to them.

"Joshua, what are you saying?" asked Ezra.

Grinning larger, he repeated, "A headless torso, with arms and legs missing, was found by a fisherman tangled in bushes at the river's edge."

Both Ezra and Robert were confused. "And why does this make you amused, Joshua?" Ezra asked, noting that Robert seemed to be cradling Athena closer to his chest as Joshua repeated his words.

Lowering his voice, Joshua continued, "I went to where the torso was and a crowd had gathered around it. When I looked at it, I knew who it was. The cuts were clean, like what Roger does. And a small piece of tunic cloth was attached to it, cloth I recognized. It was Fredric.

"Then I then spoke in a loud voice for all to hear … 'At Sunday's Mass, I heard that Priest Loupe had something to do with this body.' As I spoke, I watched the faces of those gathered."

Pausing in thought, his smile turned devilish.

"And now the gossip begins that I took care to plant. Fredric's stench was horrible, too much to endure, so I left. Tonight, I will visit a few taverns that he frequented and say that I heard it was Fredric's torso. I will also include Loupe and Archbishop William's name in my remarks.

"I will make sure that the gossip reaches the duke and archbishop by repeating what I say in every tavern I'm in."

Then he added, "I wonder how long the stench stays with the archbishop. Will it stick?"

thirty-five

Duke Richard

You will have two shadows and that dagger of yours.
Only a fool would attack you now.

ichol approached Victor at the gate through the castle's outer wall. An afternoon chill had settled in. Victor's smile was always a welcome sight to her and added warmth to the air as she tightened her wrap around her.

"Nichol, you are alone today. Where is your faithful companion, Shadow?"

"She is with the children. I am here to see the duke."

Victor leaned in close to Nichol. "Beware. He has had many visitors today and none have left as cheerful as they arrived."

"Then I will cheer him and tell him only good things." Nichol placed a silver coin in his hand, a gift to him for his observations. She lifted and dropped the knocker on the door twice and stepped back.

Suddenly the door jerked open and a man came striding out and bumped into her, nearly knocking her over.

Startled, Nichol almost fell to her knees. "Bastard ..."

The man spun around, spitting his words. "What did you say?"

Steward Thomas was at the door, watching her.

Nichol glanced at Thomas as the man grabbed her arm. She turned and in one smooth motion, hit him in the throat and then stepped back. He let go of her and bent over, gasping for air.

"It is a good thing her dog is not here. If she was, your throat would be ripped open," Thomas said as he glanced at the man.

The man glared at Nichol, his eyes narrowed, while struggling to talk. He pointed at her. "I know who you are. This is not the last you will see of me, BITCH."

Nichol stepped inside the castle. Closing the door behind her, the steward said, "The duke is in the hall; I will let him know you are here. I think today he will want to see you."

She leaned against a stone wall and thought of what had just occurred outside.

Who was that man? Should I be worried? He did not know me until 'her dog' was mentioned by Thomas.

Moments later, Thomas reappeared. "The duke will see you in his solar."

Nichol slowly walked up the wide stairs to the solar, entered, and curtsied.

"Your Grace."

"Sit." The duke uttered the single word, not forcibly but with concern in his voice.

Nichol walked to the chair and sat down. *The placement of the chair is the same distance to the table as Richard's. Why? He looks troubled.*

Calmly, Nichol spoke. "Your Grace, you looked troubled today. Can I help you?"

Richard sat back in his chair. He looked at Nichol in silence.

"Your Grace … you should know. That man who just left nearly knocked me down as he exited. I called him a bastard and he grabbed my arm. I turned around and struck him in the throat."

Richard started laughing. When he managed to control his mirth, he looked at Nichol. "Thomas told me what happened. That was a lord you struck. You could be seriously punished for that. I do not think he will charge you, as he would be embarrassed to tell a story of a woman who defeated him.

"I can tell you why he left mad," the duke continued. "He claimed Harmonie was on his land, and he wanted to appoint his own person to your hamlet of Harmonie."

Nichol began to speak, and he put his hand up to stop her. "He is an arrogant fool and I do not trust him. I do trust you … Baroness Nichol of Harmonie."

He chuckled. "And you just hit Lord Charles."

Amazed at his words, Nichol stopped, her mouth gaping open. *Baroness of Harmonie …*

A smile appeared on her face as she curtsied again. dropped back to one knee, bowing before him. "Your Grace, my loyalty and service I pledge to you." She inhaled. "And I saw Lord Charles— who he was and is."

Without hesitation, Richard put his hand up to stop Nichol from further talk. "What did you see of him?"

"He is arrogant but not a fool. He is a dangerous adversary to you and to Harmonie. Now I know who he is protecting: the Priest Loupe."

Both paused in thought. At last, Richard leaned forward.

"I promised you safe passage to England and he sent three men to see that you and all on board disappeared at sea. He denied knowing anything about the three men, but I knew he was lying. I told him if anything happened to you, I would hold him responsible. He did not take my threat seriously.

"He has many soldiers and threatens others around him to get his way. Now he has threatened you. Most lords can repel his attack but I fear for your Harmonie. He will attack soon after the harvest when your barns are full, and then he will blame you for not protecting Harmonie. Then he will lead soldiers into Harmonie and proclaim to be the new lord and protector. You will have no choice but to give in to his demands."

Nichol was alarmed. "How do you know this? The attack on Harmonie … did he tell you?"

Duke Richard's smile was grim. "No, it is what I would do if I were him: attack soon, before you can prepare to defend yourself and take your harvest. He just wants the land."

"Would you keep him a lord if he takes Harmonie by force?"

"I would. He is a lord and I am a duke. I rule by fear, just as he does to those under him. Fortunately, he fears me more than I fear him. He has made many enemies. I will bring them together to rid him of his power, and possibly his title."

Nichol stood. "If you cannot stop him, I will. I know how. We will … I will … be ready. I promise … we will protect your land from the known enemy."

He nodded his assent.

She added, "I will see you once again before I travel to Harmonie for the harvest."

Moving toward the door, she turned. "You have a son coming soon. Is Judith well? May I see her before I return to my family?"

"Yes, she is well and she will want to see you. You have charmed her and Emma. They both seek the comfort you bring to them. It seems you are wanted by so many for different reasons."

The duke snorted and then said seriously, "And it seems you are the only one that comes before me without demands. I have someone that will protect you; his name is Otto. He would have enjoyed seeing you hit Lord Charles in the throat."

Richard abruptly stood, signaling it was time for Nichol to leave. "He will be at Ezra's home tomorrow morning. Now you will have two shadows and that dagger of yours. Only a fool would attack you now."

I will welcome Otto … but at no time can I let my guard down.

thirty-six

The Coming Threat

*He will have people watching us. They want me
in Harmonie when they attack.*

Many thoughts raced through Nichol's mind as she bid goodbye to Victor, left the duke's residence and headed toward Ezra's.

I have now become Baroness Nichol and brought the wrath of Lord Charles down on my head … and on Harmonie.

The burden this title carries is heavy.

When do I tell my family?

I know that our coin is almost gone. Will Diego arrive soon with goods that will restore it?

Timo's fair must be a success.

We must be ready to harvest what the earth has brought forth.

There are too many decisions to be made right now.

Harmonie does not have an army; they are just farmers.

How can Harmonie defend itself against a violent army?

I know that I can kill this count and save many.

I must …

Almost before she knew it, Nichol stood at Ezra's door, knocked, and announced herself. Thinking about her worries had made her apprehensive.

Suddenly, she sensed that the *Lady* was with her.

A calming feeling flowed through her body. Leaning her head on the side of doorframe, she saw a shimmer of light move from the ground to the top of her head. As she stepped inside, she heard the words: *Never forget, I am with you.*

When she fully entered, she was surprised to see Roger, Timo, and Joshua sitting close together on stools, the tops of their heads almost touching as they spoke.

Suddenly, Lucette and Aiden moved together from Ezra and Helene's laps, squealing with delight, "Mama is home … Mama is home." Both wrapped their arms around each of her legs, each of them hugging her.

Aiden had gained so much strength in his little arms, he almost toppled her over. She kneeled and hugged them both, picking each up as she laughed with them. Even Shadow leaned against her, nuzzling her head against a now-available leg.

I've not been gone long … What is going on here?

Puzzled, her eyes moved from the kitchen area where Joshua, Roger, and Timo were to her right. Ezra, Robert and Helene were watching, seated in the great room on the benches that Robert had made. She had stitched wool-filled cushions for them as she had done for their Harmonie home.

At last, her gaze settled on Helene. She gave Nichol a slight nod and a comforting smile.

They are all staring at me. Were they waiting for me? Is there news I do not know about?

"Helene, would you take Tova, the children, and Shadow to the market? I think we should have fish tonight and buy one for Shadow as well. Please leave the door open when you leave. The castle was quite dark where I sat with the duke today for the conversation we shared, and I want the light of day around me as I tell of my conversation with him."

"Save some of your conversation for me when I return," Helene said as she gathered Tova and the children. As if she knew she was included, Shadow walked to the door to wait for Helene. "I will also bring more candles for light so we can all sit in this room together," she added.

As Nichol settled on one of the benches in the great room, Timo brought over two of the kitchen stools. Opening the door for more daylight to flow in, they gathered with anticipation of what was to come.

Nichol looked into their eyes as she began her story. Quietly she spoke so her words would not venture outside the walls. All in the house leaned in to hear every word.

"When the *Lady* guided us across a stream and around the hill to a high point looking down into a valley, I had a feeling I had never had before: a husband, children and now you all as my family. I no longer had to hide who I was. I could stop running from those who were after me. A valley filled with good people. I did not know then that we would name it Harmonie."

Her head dropped.

"How fast times have changed. Today, as the duke's castle door opened, an angry man charged out. He ran into me, almost knocked me down, and so I called him a 'bastard' for his carelessness. When he demanded me to repeat what I said, I chose not to. He then grabbed my arm and I instantly reacted and hit him in the throat with a closed fist.

"He was struggling to breathe and then Thomas, the duke's steward, told him that he was lucky my dog was not with me to rip his throat open. His eyes changed. He squinted at me and I felt his rotten breath on my face. Then he hissed at me and said, 'I know who you are. This is not the last you see of me.' Then he ended by calling me a bitch.

"I told Duke Richard what happened with the man who had just left. That was when he said that the man was Lord Charles—the same Lord Charles who was responsible for the attack on us as we left for England. The duke then motioned for me to sit down.

"He confided that Lord Charles knew about Harmonie and the growth of it. And the duke told him that he was not to have any control over Harmonie. The duke wanted to be able to award the valley and its lands to someone of his choice to govern it. That's when the man left, very angry at the duke's refusal to name him as the authority: the one who collects rents and taxes and then transfers the monies to the duke."

Nichol paused. She knew that what she would say next would take them all by surprise.

"The duke then said to me, 'I want you to be Baroness Nichol of Harmonie. You will report directly to me and collect what is due.'"

Nichol stopped and looked around the room at the mouths that had dropped open. All remained silent, knowing there was more to come.

Ezra spoke up, breaking the silence. "Nichol, I think the duke is wise. You are the right choice. Those in Harmonie trust you. Those who know you here in Rouen do as well. And so does the duke."

Nichol continued to speak. "Then Duke Richard continued, 'After your harvest, you must be prepared. Lord Charles will attempt to take what he feels is rightfully his with or without a baron I selected in place. I have no doubt that Lord Charles will come for Harmonie; we have not seen the last of him. A man like him does not honor his commitments or responsibilities. Charles was to collect taxes on his land and merchants in the village. I have seen none.'

"I then told the duke that I saw Lord Charles in the brief encounter with him before he felt my fist. The duke asked what

I saw. I told him, 'He is arrogant but no fool. He will not stop at Harmonie. He wants what you—the duke—have.' What surprised me was that the duke nodded his head when I said this to him. I sense that the duke does not trust the man or like him at all."

Taking a deep breath, Nichol let her feelings out. "Priest Loupe, together with the powerful and now-vengeful Lord Charles, is not something I saw coming nor did any of you. I cannot ask you to put your lives in danger because of the threat to Harmonie. We can walk away. We can build another hamlet …"

Robert took Nichol's hand. "I will not walk away. It is our home."

Everyone agreed in unison.

Timo spoke above all the others. "Nichol, I think you have another plan for us to consider. What has the *Lady* told you? Tell us."

"The *Lady* came to me as I walked back from the duke's to be with you now. I'm sure of it. When Charles hears that I, a mere woman, is now a baroness, he will send a small group of men to threaten all in the valley. He will act as a hero and stage a march in, chasing the original threatening men away. All in the valley will cheer; he wants to be seen as Harmonie's protector. I believe he will have people watching us. They want me present in Harmonie when they attack.

"He then will accuse me of not protecting Duke Richard's land and ask the duke to name someone that shows fealty to him and the duke, meaning him."

Her head dropped. "Once they capture me, I will never be seen again. That would be their plan." Lifting her head, she added, "We will stop them."

Everyone started talking at once. Robert looked at his wife and knew that she was already planning her next move. Nichol directed her words to Joshua.

"Joshua, we must learn who his spies are and how Charles does business with others. Watch and listen, but do not interfere with them as you probe. Then, we will send wool to Harmonie and bring back grain from the harvest and take it to Richard's water mill. Eventually, I will go to Harmonie alone. With Joshua's insight, we will know when the time is right. There is only one way in and out, so we will know when Charles' men arrive."

Nichol added, "Richard is sending one of his men to protect me. His name is Otto."

Her words got Roger's attention. "Otto? He is one of Richard's best."

Joshua leaned back, tilting his head toward the door. "I hear children approaching."

Ezra put up his hand to speak. "I think I can speak for all here, I am angry and very tired of the nobles and the clergy taking while leaving little for everyone else. The *Lady*—Nichol's *Lady*—does not do that."

"The clergy tells us over and over what God wants, and dukes and kings then tell us they are anointed by God. That God gives them the right to steal." He turned to Nichol. "Nichol, has the *Lady* told you what she wants?"

"She brought all of us together and led us to Harmonie. Harmonie is ours. We have created it, and our efforts will protect it. She does not want or make demands, only gives hope, not hate or fear. She gives me knowledge to make decisions for the good of all of us … and for others.

"We have much to talk about and to do. We will talk more in the morning," Nichol said as her eyes moved from one person to the next. "For now, let us be with our children."

As she spoke, Robert moved to her, putting his arms around her as he pulled her closer. "There is no one I would rather be with, to love, than you."

All eyes turned to the door. Lucette burst in, demanding attention for her stories, followed by Aiden, who was picked up by Roger. Behind them was Achim and his family.

Helene chased the men outside. "We will prepare the evening meal and we do not need you underfoot. Take the children with you and do not let Aiden annoy Shadow while she eats her fish."

Before Timo left, Nichol took him aside. "I look forward to all of us going to Harmonie for the harvest." She paused and gave a heavy sigh. "Can you find workers who will go with you to help with the harvest?"

"Yes, I will find workers. And I long for the day we all can stay in Harmonie. It is where we belong."

Ezra and Robert's eyes met.

Both knew that Nichol was the core to their survival and they would do everything in their power to support and protect her.

thirty-seven

Diego Returns

Good fortune smiles on them.

Five days after Nichol's confrontation with Archbishop William and Loupe, there was rapid knocking on Ezra's door. As moments passed, the knocking grew louder.

Inside the house, Helene was immediately fearful of who was on the other side of the door.

Roger went to the door and lifted the flap covering the hole in the door to peek out. He turned toward Helene, relief on his face. "It's all right, Helene. It is Olaf."

Roger yanked the door open. Olaf stood bent over with his hands on his hips and gasping for breath. "Come … Hurry. Get Ezra! He is here. Diego is sailing into the harbor, and I think he has two ships, not only one! Marie is waiting for them at the dock."

Ezra rose from his seat at the table, moving at a speed seldom seen before. In a voice that could be heard outside, he began issuing instructions.

"Helene, I must go to the dock right away. Olaf—find Nichol and Robert; they are at Joseph's and Rose's cloth shop. Have them bring the children here for Helene to watch. Timo is at the stables. Find Joshua … who knows where he is … and tell them to meet us there. Our cargo must be protected and moved to the warehouse as soon as it is unloaded."

When Ezra and Roger arrived at the dock, a crowd was beginning to form, craning their necks to see as the ships drew closer. Merchants and dock workers recognized Diego's smaller ship, but the bigger ship was a mystery; much larger than the ships which normally sailed into Rouen. Both ships were heavily laden and sat low in the water.

Excitement grew, along with speculation of the cargo that Diego was transporting.

"Wine, leather … mayhap rare wools for cloth …"

Other voices could be heard from those gathered.

"No, it is silk, pearls, spices, and gems …"

"Fabrics from the east … mayhap some kegs of ale and exotic cheeses …"

Of course, no one knew, but the air was filled with excitement … and hope.

The speculation heightened and the noise level increased as all on shore waited for the ships to toss their lines and tie off at the dock.

Ezra followed Roger as he pushed his way through the crowd to the front of those gathered. He saw Diego standing on the bow of the ship and waved to draw his attention.

Diego scanned the crowd and when he saw Ezra standing at the end of the dock, waved and smiled. In a loud voice that everyone could hear, he exclaimed, "Ezra, my friend!" He gestured in a sweeping motion from the front to back of the ship.

"We have returned from Greece, and Italy, with all the treasures you requested. We have silk, cotton, and linen cloth from the royals of Persia that we found in Italy. Spices and sweet salt, swords from the finest forges in Italy. Leather, furs, and casks of wine only the Greek gods drink."

Pulling a large pouch from his belt and holding it high, he continued to speak.

"Gems that few have ever seen, their color only found in heaven." As the ships finished being secured to the docks, Diego's men brandished knifes and swords as a warning to the crowd that was closing in.

Diego stepped off the ship in front of Ezra. Together they began to walk away, followed by a crowd of merchants and peddlers. Olaf had found Nichol and Robert, and as they approached the docks they were greeted by Ezra and Diego.

Ezra turned to face those following him. "I know each and every one of you will share in the ship's bounty." This pronounce-ment pushed the excitement to new levels of speculation.

Finally, the curious crowd was persuaded to disperse.

Ezra turned to Nichol.

"We need carts and bearers to unload the ships and take as much as we can to the warehouse before nightfall. The rest of the goods we will protect on the ships. I already have guards for the ship and warehouse."

Listening to Ezra, Nichol agreed with him. "Robert and I will stay at the warehouse with Marie and Olaf. Otto will be there, too. I believe that we will be able to handle any looters that dare to come during the night. Diego can decide where he wants to be."

Bales of silk and cloth were delivered to Joseph's and Rose's shop. As Nichol examined the goods, she saw colors richer and more vibrant than even what her father had imported.

She said to Ezra, "This is finer than anything I saw in Paris and Marseilles. I want Judith, Duke Richard's wife, to be given first choice of our goods."

Robert delivered a cask of wine to Amos the innkeeper, where Diego's men would stay when not in the taverns or on the ships. Ezra always gifted those who showed their kindness to his family.

Diego motioned to Nichol as she watched the men unload. He gestured to her, drawing her attention and said, "In my travels, I found a special sword and a dagger in Italy, made of a metal unknown to where we live. Choose one of these for yourself. I thought you may want to gift the other to Duke Richard."

Opening a small wooden box, he revealed two beautifully crafted weapons, both with leather-wrapped hilts and sheaths.

Taking first the dagger in her hand, she turned it and made a motion as if she were fighting. "This was wise of you, Diego. Of course, the dagger is my choice for me.

"For the duke, I think he would think it befitting of his title to have this majestic sword. Much has happened since we returned from England. The duke has assigned Otto, one of his guards, to me. This gift for him will bring us and Harmonie great goodwill. Ezra and I will share ale with you after the ships are unloaded tomorrow when the unloading of the ships is complete."

Nichol spied Otto nearby, leaning against a dock post and casting a wary eye over the few lingering people near the ship. Nichol motioned him over.

"Otto, I need to get a message to the duke. Who should I trust to carry it?"

"I will carry it. I have a meeting early with him tomorrow before I come to you."

Thanking him, Nichol walked the short distance to their warehouse. She called out to Marie, who was watching goods beginning to be transported through the warehouse doors for inventory and storage.

"Marie, would you store and protect these for me until I meet with Duke Richard tomorrow?"

As Nichol handed the two items to Marie, Marie gasped in surprise. "These are so heavy, Nichol, and so ornate. I have never seen anything like them, not even when I lived in Paris. They are safe with me."

"Robert and I will sleep here in the warehouse tonight and until all the merchandise has been dealt with. With you and Olaf, we will act as the guards inside the warehouse. On the outside, Ezra has several heavily armed guards stationed around the warehouse protecting the goods inside and Diego's ships."

That evening inside the warehouse, the four of them talked about the needs of Harmonie and what the people of Harmonie could make and return for resale in Rouen, Paris, and even Timo's fairs. Dinah had brought Athena to be with Nichol so she could be fed throughout the night.

With lanterns lit, they were able to see many of the items while they unpacked and examined Diego's cargo. As more and more items were revealed, they grew as excited as the crowd when the ships first arrived.

Diego had brought back a wide variety of goods that were unusual and unexpected. Nichol and Marie found themselves making piles of goods to be packed on the horses to take to Harmonie.

thirty-eight

The Caravan Leaves for Harmonie

Gunvor, Tova, and Gideon will travel with you.

The next morning as the sun rose on the ships in the harbor, Nichol, Robert, Achim, Ezra, and Timo met with Diego. He reported that all had been quiet during the night. Together, they watched as the final cargo from the second ship was unloaded.

Following the last wagon to the warehouse, Robert was surprised to see that twelve pack animals were already loaded with bales of wool destined for Harmonie. A large cart was also stacked with extra weaving supplies, but with room for the remaining cargo being unloaded. Nichol made sure that the huge bell she purchased in England was secured in the cart bound for Harmonie, along with her new bow.

With the ship's manifest in hand, Ezra and Achim found room for the entire ship's cargo, sectioning off where items were placed, and identifying the type and count of each. By the afternoon, many of Rouen's merchants and vendors had arrived at the warehouse, waiting to speak with Ezra.

As he read from the manifest, enthusiastic words filled the air. Many repeated what Ezra said, as if to make sure they were hearing right.

Silk … pepper … gems …

Standing nearby, Diego listened as orders were placed. The whole cargo would be sold within days; more successful than he imagined.

The market for these goods is bigger than I thought it could be. Paris is ideal and Ezra was right. We need more ships!

Nichol separated herself from the group and looked around. Joshua was approaching with a big smile.

"I see that grin. What young woman gave you that smile, Joshua?"

His smile deepened. "A gentleman never betrays a lady's identity. I see that a caravan is being packed with goods. The timing is fortuitous; I will lead it to Harmonie."

Nichol arched an eyebrow. "How close is the woman's husband?"

"Close." His smile grew even broader. "You know me well."

"The caravan belongs to Hugh. Find him and help him leave soon. Gunvor, Tova, and Gideon will travel with you and they will stay in Harmonie to help with the harvest. I need for you to return here with fresh news from Harmonie; we have been gone too long and I worry."

Nichol slipped away to feed Athena. When she finished, she walked to Ezra's with her daughter strapped to her chest in the sling, humming as she walked.

Helene opened the door as soon as she heard Nichol's voice. Lucette and Aiden were chasing Shadow around with little success of catching her. Nichol sat down and described the morning's events, seeing Helene's and Dinah's interest. Then she added, "Most likely, horses and carts will be packed up by this afternoon to travel to Harmonie."

Later, all of them returned to the warehouse with the children. Nichol was surprised to see the caravan was already set to leave. Gunvor, Gideon, and Tova were leading horses packed with wine, leather, spices, and cloth from Rose's shop. The procession and the heavy cart gradually moved out of sight.

Timo had helped them pack the horses and he stood, watching them leave. Nichol stepped next to him, and he turned to her. "That should be us. Harmonie is where we belong. That is where the children belong."

With tears in her eyes, she knew he was right. "Life does not give us easy choices. You know that from the first time we met we were selected to serve a purpose other than our own choosing. Our destiny will become clearer to us as time passes, Timo."

Timo chuckled. "I must continue with you on your journey. Your children will continue this story, and it is one that I will not miss."

At that moment, Diego stood at the entrance to the warehouse and waved to Nichol and Timo to join him. He pointed to a chest sitting on the ground, partially covered with a cloth.

"Something for both of you."

Robert came over along with the children and Shadow smelled the chest.

Timo lifted the cloth and a small book rested on top of the wooden chest.

Nichol's excitement was apparent.

Diego just said, "For you."

Nichol picked it up and without opening it, pulled the treasure to her breast.

Diego continued, "Someday you will go to Cordoba in the kingdom of the Iberian Peninsula. There is a man that has more books than your eyes can see. When I told him about you, he said a woman's voice came to him and spoke your name. He said the voice said to him that you speak her words as though they were yours and understood their true meaning."

As he spoke, Nichol felt giddy. It had been many years since she had felt a book in her hands as a child. Now she knew that Cordoba would become part of her travels and of her children's someday.

Again, Diego pointed to the chest. "Timo, my friend, the chest is for you."

Timo's mouth dropped open. Clearly, he was overwhelmed. "A gift for me?"

He opened the chest and what he saw seemed to bewilder him. He picked up what looked like a sheet of parchment, held it up to the light, and felt the texture.

"Is this what I think it is? A new type of parchment?"

Diego nodded. "It is not made from animals …. it is made from plants."

"Plants? I must learn this new method. How wonderful!"

Both were stunned with the thoughtful gifts from Diego.

Thanking him profusely, they dropped into their own thoughts.

What other wonders will he bring back each time he returns?

thirty-nine

Protected by Richard

Nichol, you have a sword. Did you leave your dagger at home?

In the middle of the night, Nichol immediately sat straight up, wiping a cold sweat from her brow. Her heart was pounding in her chest.

Was it a dream? What was real?

Next to her, Athena began to stir in her cradle. A lone candle burned the last inch of its wax, and the sound of horse hooves pulling a wagon on the cobblestone street outside could be heard.

Close by in their sleep room attached at the rear of the warehouse, Marie and Olaf were sleeping on their pallet.

Her heart stopped racing when a hand gently touched her arm. "What troubles you, my love? Robert whispered. "You have been talking in your sleep. Is it to the *Lady?*"

Nichol lay back down and pulled up her sleeping tunic. She rolled on top of him, burying her face into his chest and breathing heavily. Slowly, she moved her hips back and forth in a rhythmic motion. Robert put both arms around her and began to move with her.

Nichol opened her eyes and quietly kissed Robert. A smile crossed both their lips.

Athena began to cry, awakening Marie in her nearby quarters. Getting up, she quickly moved to tend the baby, whispering, "Shhh, little one. Let your mama and papa sleep."

Picking Athena up, she whispered, "You need a dry cloth." Removing the wet night cloth, Marie quickly slipped a clean dry one under Athena, humming softly as she did.

Nichol sat up and softly said to Marie, "Thank you. I know Athena thanks you as well." The women smiled at each other.

Cooing sounds came from Athena and Marie lifted her and kissed her on her cheek. "It's time for you to be with your mama." Handing her to Nichol, she added, "We have a long day ahead."

Marie moved toward a bowl holding water and splashed her face. Reaching for a head covering, she picked up a basket and turned to Nichol. Taking in the scene in front of her—of Robert now sitting up with his arm around Nichol and the baby nursing, she thought, *Someday I will have this for me.*

"I am going to the market. Olaf, will you brace the door after I leave?"

Marie opened the door to the outside. Glancing upward, she turned her head back toward Nichol and said, "It will rain soon." Stepping through the door, she closed it and left for the bakery as the morning light broke. She could hear the brace dropping into the brackets, securing the family and goods within.

Athena was in no rush as she nursed. Mornings had become a time when Nichol and her daughter snuggled. Athena loved to grasp her mother's nipple, smiling and laughing as milk spilled out of her mouth. Nichol laughed with her.

Robert had left the bed and finished dressing. Olaf was up and did the same.

The two men looked around the many goods that had been carried into the warehouse. Olaf said, "We have much to do here. I know that Timo and Ezra will be here soon to start filling the orders from yesterday. Marie will be back soon with something for us to eat before we start what will be a long day ahead."

Within a short time, Marie returned and announced herself. The brace was lifted, welcoming her to the warmth within and replaced as soon as she entered. She placed her basket on the table.

The aroma of fresh bread produced belly grumbles from all of them. They were hungry.

Nichol, now holding her daughter and patting her on her back, moved toward Marie, thanking her for the food and laughing. "We are all hungry, as you can hear …"

Then she noticed tears in Marie's eyes. "Olaf and I would like a child of our own. We try, but … he knows of Aiden and my past."

Embracing her, Nichol said, "You will have children, Marie. I know you will. Remember, you birthed Aiden and now I raise him as mine. He is still your son and you have feelings for him; I see it when you are with him. He will have two mothers and two fathers. I don't think we should keep secrets from him or from the girls. You and I will both know when it is time to tell them … but that will be many years from now."

Marie absorbed Nichol's words.

Relacing her tunic to cover her breast, Nichol held Athena out to her. "Hold Athena while I prepare our morning meal. I know that both Athena and Lucette will love you as they do Helene. We are all family here."

Tears flowed from Marie's eyes. She embraced Athena as if she was her own.

A knock sounded from the door. Otto announced himself and was let in.

"Have you eaten anything, Otto?" Nichol asked. After he shook his head, she encouraged him to eat the bread, cheese, and apples that were laid out and offered him his choice of ale or water to drink.

She sensed his bewilderment with being openly included within the small room.

Otto sat down and hungrily ate what was on the table. When he finished, Nichol handed the new sword to Otto that Diego had given her. "This is for the duke. Will you carry it for me? Shall we go see him now?"

Otto nodded. "He will be in the Great Hall this morning."

When they arrived at the castle gate, there was a variety of people in front of Victor—some dressed shabbily and others appeared to be of title.

He was pleased to see Nichol and Otto approaching, and he gestured to them to come through the gate without waiting.

As they entered the hall, Richard looked past those in front of him and acknowledged them. He nodded at the seats near the rear of the hall. Nichol and Otto sat on a bench and waited their turn to speak.

She turned to Otto. *Who is this quiet man, with a beard that hides scars, a prominent nose and piercing dark eyes and why do I not see him?*

"Otto, this morning, I am going to ask the duke to allow you to travel with me to Harmonie."

Otto just looked down at the sword on his lap, then spoke. "I will go with you if you wish and the duke approves."

Then he looked up. "Baroness, I have a wife and two children here in Rouen. I would like for them to see this land of yours. Can they come as well?"

"They are welcome to join us, but we will need the duke's permission for them to travel with us. I will add them to my request."

After a time, Duke Richard waved for them to approach.

Otto handed the sword to Nichol, and they approached and bowed.

"Nichol, you have a sword. Did you leave your dagger at home?" the duke quipped. That remark brought smiles and laughter from those in the hall.

Nichol laughed as well. Holding the sword flat, lying on her palms, she slowly walked in front of Richard and curtsied while lifting it above her head.

"Your Grace, no finer sword exists. It comes from the forges in Italy and is made from metal of an unknown origin. I have chosen it for you."

Richard took the sword and carefully inspected it and then raised it for all in the hall to see. "It truly is a masterpiece."

He stood, carrying the sword toward a large stool in the room. Lifting it above his head, he swiftly brought the weapon down on the stool, separating it into two parts with no splintering. Inspecting the blade closely, he saw no nicks or warping from his blow to the wood.

Running his fingers across the blade, he pulled them back quickly as blood appeared. A grin spread across his face as he turned to Nichol.

"Thank you … this is the finest sword in my possession."

Excusing everyone in the hall, he said, "Nichol, I need a private word with you."

Richard and Nichol sat across from each other at the end of the table.

The duke looked up at Otto to dismiss him and immediately Nichol said, "If he is to guard me, I need for him to hear what you have to say. I now trust him."

After a moment of consideration, Richard agreed to her request. His next words, however, did not please Nichol.

"You must stay in Rouen this winter. In the spring I plan to travel to Harmonie and then on to Fécamp."

Dismayed, Nichol stiffened and sat up straight. "I plan to return to Rouen after the harvest is completed in Harmonie and before the winter solstice. Am I to be your prisoner?"

Otto nervously shuffled his feet.

Laughing, Richard shook his head. "Yes … and no. How can I protect you, your family, and Harmonie if you expose yourself with no protection? Even with Otto by your side to protect you, they will come at you. There are powerful people that would like to see you go away forever.

"I have many people that I must see every day. They come to me with requests and complaints. Rarely do they tell the truth behind them. I would like you to see them as only you can and guide me with what I grant and don't grant."

"I will but there can be no secrets between us. If you are right, Lord Charles will arrive soon, and that is why I must go back to Harmonie and prepare the hamlet for him. Which means I should be leaving soon. If this man could attack at any time, I would want Otto there. If his family would like to join us, do they have your permission?"

Richard looked at his guard. "You will go with her and take your family. If Lord Charles sees you with Nichol, he will know to take the warning I gave him seriously."

With his response, Nichol continued, "The pack horses have already left for Harmonie. Before I depart, I would like my husband and children baptized by the archbishop.

The duke nodded his head in approval of the baptism. "I will tell the archbishop that you desire baptisms for your husband and children and to have this completed before you leave."

"Thank you. I will leave go and await the time for the baptism. I would like to see Duchess Judith before I leave. We have special silks and spices for her selection. Is she well enough to see me?"

As she left with the steward, the duke thought, *Nichol knows us. A gift for the duchess will please her.*

forty

Duchess Judith

I don't trust Richard's brother.

Leaving the hall after concluding her audience with Duke Richard, Nichol headed to the garden, where she thought she would find Duchess Judith. She did.

Otto stepped away and noted that there was a solid friendship between the two women. *How did that happen*, he wondered.

As the women sat down on the bench together, the summer flowers were still in bloom. The sun's warmth felt good on their backs. Both women turned and held their faces to the sun's rays, as if they might leave suddenly after only a few moments of the morning.

The duchess spoke first. "I am happy that you have returned from England safely. The duke was worried that there would be trouble."

"There was. Three men came on board and threatened to kill all of us, including my children. They attacked us shortly after we left the port. We were able to overcome them with the help of the captain. I was thankful that my children knew to stay in the stern of the small ship when the attack happened as they were told to do so."

"Did you have your dagger?"

"Yes. We would not have lived without it."

Judith understood Nichol's words. She had overheard Richard and William arguing before Nichol and her family departed.

As Nichol talked, Judith's hands drifted to her bulging belly, gently caressing it. "I don't trust Richard's brother."

Nichol reached out to touch her. "Nor do I. I fear that the archbishop surrounds himself with people who will do ill will to others." She did not want to linger on the archbishop or the attack that he had supported. "Your Grace, are you well and past the time of feeling ill in the mornings?"

"I am. Richard is looking forward to the birth of his first son."

When she said that, Nichol added, "Next time I come, I will bring more of the herb to add to hot water in your cup for comfort."

When Judith heard her friend's words, she smiled.

"Your Grace, I have promised to be at the shop of Joseph and Rose this afternoon. Could you join me? I have silks and cotton that I think you would like, and spices as well from Italy. And from England, wool that we will weave in Harmonie and bring to you later as warm, sturdy cloth. I will also bring you news from Queen Emma before I leave."

Getting up, she said, "I must go. There is much to do before we depart for Harmonie in a few days. I will see you at Joseph's and Rose's shop later, Your Grace."

forty-one

Otto and Gabrielle

This Nichol ... will she welcome us and our boys, Otto?

Seeing Nichol stand with the duchess, Otto moved toward the gate and waited for her. Victor had the gate open, awaiting their arrival. As they exited, Nichol said goodbye to him as they walked through.

Outside the door, she heard the latch drop and spoke in a quiet voice. "Otto, your wife and children should wait to come to Harmonie when we return there after winter and the land is ready for the spring planting. I fear it may not be safe right now."

"My wife is very strong. There are times when she scares me. My boys are ten and eleven, and they can take care of themselves." Otto's voice was laced with certainty.

Nichol patted him on the back and said, "Then your family will go when I go. If you like what you see, a home could be built."

On their way to the warehouse, Nichol stopped by the church. There, she found a priest to speak with her and she paid for the baptism of Robert and the children in two days.

When she walked out of the church, Otto was there. His posture was tense and expectant, as if he were doing more than waiting for her, and Nichol could tell he had something to say that could not wait.

It was clear to Nichol that Otto was searching for exactly the right words to say so she patiently waited for him to speak. "Most men could not make demands of the duke the way you do. He does not see you as a threat, only an ally. Counts and lords come to him with masked motives and selfish requests. I have heard him say you see people. One day I hope you tell me what that means."

Nichol put her hand on Otto's arm. "Right now, we must go to the warehouse; I have a hungry daughter to feed. And I promise you, you will indeed learn what the duke's words mean.

"Leave me at the warehouse and go to your home. Bring your wife and boys to eat with us there at the end of the day."

Leaving Nichol at the warehouse, Otto walked quickly to his small home. He was excited to share his news with Gabrielle and the boys. Calling out to her as he opened the front door, both his boys stopped drinking from their cups at the table and turned their heads toward their papa.

"I had news for my family."

"What news, Papa?" both the boys said together.

"News … what news could you have, Otto?" Gabrielle said as she joined Otto and the boys at the table.

"Nichol will be returning to Harmonie in a few days. The duke has told me to go with her and her family and has given me permission to take my family there as well. I have heard much of what is being built there. I believe it would be a better place for all of us to live."

Gabrielle took in his words. The boys watched their mother's face, as Otto did.

"This Nichol … will she welcome us and our boys, Otto?" Gabrielle's words were hopeful.

"Yes … I told her how strong you were and the ages of our boys. She and the others are building a hamlet. Knowing what I do about her now, I think it will be a village others will want to come to.

"She wants all of us to come and sup with them tonight. Her husband Robert and their three children will be there."

After a moment, Gabrielle nodded slowly. "I think I want to be part of this new adventure. We will eat with them later today. If all goes well, the boys and I will be ready to travel to our new home when you say it is time to go."

That afternoon, Helene and Dinah brought Lucette and Aiden to the warehouse to spend the night. They stayed to help prepare the evening meal.

When the door opened, Shadow was first inside, almost rolling Nichol over when she rushed to greet her. The men were already in the warehouse, sorting the orders to be picked up or delivered to merchants and vendors.

The sun was setting in the west when the sky cleared and the rain clouds moved away. Otto had returned with his wife Gabrielle and his sons Henrik and Siebert. Nichol welcomed Gabrielle, taking her arm and introducing her to all of the others.

After the food was served, Nichol acted as the host and moved from one group to another. Throughout the gathering, the conversations were of better days to come for all of them. Diego, Leiv, E & N Merchants and Harmonie the chief topics being discussed.

Helene had created quite a feast. Wine was out for all to enjoy. With candles lit, the conversation went long into the night.

Otto and Gabrielle quickly blended in, becoming part of the larger group. Otto already had a sense of who everyone was and what was important to them. Gabrielle had grown up on a farm and Nichol learned that she longed to be in the country again.

She confided to Nicol that when Otto told her that she and the boys would come with him when they left for Harmonie, she felt full of optimism and joy.

Lucette and Aiden made immediate friends with the new boys. They followed them around the warehouse after the meal was concluded. Shadow stayed close by.

That evening after the last worker left the warehouse, Lucette and Aiden were sound asleep on Nichol's bed.

Nichol gently picked up Aiden and placed him next to Marie as she lay on her palette. Marie pulled the child closer to her, cuddling him.

In the darkness of the room, Nichol could hear Marie's soft sobbing.

Two days later Robert and the children were baptized.

forty-two

To Harmonie

I will ring our new bell to call all together.

The morning after the baptism, there was a gathering at the warehouse.

Helene and Dinah arrived, laden with food for their journey. A small horse-drawn cart was already loaded and waiting.

Timo brought Moki with the basket for the children strapped to the animal's back. When Lucette saw Moki, she let out a joyful shout. She and Aiden ran to Timo and held their hands for him to lift them into the empty basket awaiting them.

Leiv and two of his men also joined the caravan heading to Harmonie. When he and Nichol last spoke, they discussed bringing cargo into a bay that was north of Fécamp.

"I have been in that area before, Nichol. Once we get to Harmonie, I plan to head toward the channel to explore the possibilities of digging a channel in a small port to unload future cargo that Diego brings in," he reassured her.

Excitement filled the air. The little ones were jumping up and down in the basket and Timo had to calm them down, reminding them to not be so active with the rest of the load Moki would be carrying. The older children wanted to just run. They wanted to see what changes had happened in Harmonie since they were last there. And the adults … they felt like they were going to a promised land.

Those who had never traveled this far were in awe of the difference of the forest in front of them and what they left in

Rouen. The canopy of emerging colors from the cascading trees was breathtaking to them. The clutter, stench, and grime of so many people living close together was not here.

Leaving Rouen for the beauty and serenity of the valley was the reward for those who already knew it. For those who had never seen the valley, Nichol said, "Your eyes will welcome the openness and the people who await you. It is a new community where all think of themselves as part of a large family. They watch out for each other."

Even the children had smiles on their faces as they viewed the passing landscape. Lucette and Aiden clapped their hands at the same time. "Home is near," could be heard coming from Lucette's mouth as she hugged her brother.

At the end of the second day, they left the road and entered the forest as the light began to dim. Shadow led the way with Otto's sons right behind her.

Suddenly, Shadow stopped and smelled the air.

Everyone halted and remained silent. The animal glanced back at Nichol.

"Friend or foe, Shadow?" were Nichol's cautious words.

Otto moved next to Shadow and drew his sword. All in the caravan stayed still.

A lone rider came into view. Shadow's tail began to wag.

Nichol recognized Joshua. She exhaled with relief at seeing her friend, hopeful that he had news from Harmonie.

Joshua dismounted and moved toward Nichol, with a wary expression on his face and his hand on his weapon. Nichol hastened to reassure him.

"Joshua, this is my friend, Otto. The duke ordered him to protect me. And now he brings his family to Harmonie. There is no need for your sword."

Nichol's eyes met Joshua's. "I think you like the Harmonie valley. You do not seem in a hurry to return to Rouen."

"Again, you know me well, Nichol. This will be a good place for everyone to settle for the night. I scouted it and there is a clearing behind me where a fire can be built for warmth and any cooking you want to do.

"I will return to Harmonie with you and tell you what I learned since you were there last. Much has happened and we have completed the harvest. It is beyond anything we expected."

Looking at the men and women in front of him, he didn't recognize all of the faces. "I see Moki … but where is Timo?"

"He is setting up for what we are calling Timo's Fair., talking to the merchants in Rouen to participate," Nichol said. "We will know soon if we have permission to create it."

Robert picked up both Aiden and Lucette, giving Moki a rest from the active children, and moved toward Nichol and Joshua.

"Joshua, tell us of Harmonie," Robert said. Aiden and Lucette both settled into Robert's arms as if they wanted to hear what was said. Shadow leaned against Nichol, then dropped to the ground, her watchful gaze on her mistress.

"The crops that were planted were more bountiful than we ever imagined. The waterways Timo created in the fields fed the seedlings well and everything grew sooner and faster that what anyone had seen before. The young apple trees will produce next year and the vines of grapes and berries will come in as well. And wait until you see where the large bell is now placed."

As Robert and Nichol heard his words, their gazes joined together. "It is just as you saw, Nichol." Turning, he said to Joshua, "The wool you brought up earlier will keep the weavers busy during the winter months. Tell me how Gideon has done while we were away."

With Joshua and Robert deep into conversation and the little ones still engrossed with what was said, Nichol turned toward the others as they settled into the clearing.

"I would like to hear that news as well. And Tova and Guvnor can help get food set up for everyone."

Everyone seemed to know their tasks. They were tired, but laughter filled the air.

Joshua was the center of attention, telling everyone of the changes in Harmonie that were happening, as the light from the fire illuminated the eager faces.

Traveling through the forest and finally leaving it toward the end of the third day, everyone stopped once again. What laid in front of them was something that only those who had been to Harmonie had seen.

At they crossed the stream, they came to the hill of Hope and Inspiration. The splendor of the valley now came into full view.

The group moved forward slowly and then stopped, transfixed by the view. The sparse clouds hanging above the valley moved, blocking the full sun and casting shadows that wove slowly amongst the dark forests and valley. The vista they viewed had become a moving picture to their eyes.

Otto turned to Gabrielle and smiled, and they embraced as she whispered to him.

Nichol turned to Robert. Joy and calm came over her and the pent-up anxiety of events of the past months seemed to disappear.

Suddenly Timo's words returned to her. *This is where we belong; this is where the children belong.*

Descending further into the valley, it appeared all the residents of Harmonie were working in the fields or around their homes. As the caravan walked down the road and entered the valley, Shadow howled, announcing their arrival. People stopped what they were doing and waved. Some of the residents followed them as they traveled the road to their home.

Garlyn cupped his hands to his mouth and yelled, "Nichol! Robert!"

Hearing his voice, Nichol saw him waving from a distance and waved back. "Robert, take Moki and the children to our home. Garlyn and I will follow."

Garlyn hurried to Nichol's side, beaming with an ear-to-ear grin. "Welcome back! We all have missed you! So much has happened since you were last here. The harvest was plentiful enough that everyone survived through the winter, with extra to spare. Eight new families have arrived and settled into the village. New homes are being built for them before winter comes again. Right now, I have a family living with me until their home is done. Many of us began spinning the wool and started using the looms that arrived to make cloth." He stopped to catch a breath. "Oh, and when we are not in the fields, we gather in the longhouse."

"I must tell you news from Rouen before we reach our home." Nichol stopped and turned to Garlyn, facing him. "Duke Richard has named me Baroness of Harmonie."

Garlyn looked perplexed. "Your voice tells me you are not pleased? You must explain."

"A man named Lord Charles has claimed that Harmonie is in his county and wants to name another person, someone under his control. Duke Richard does not trust Charles. That is why he titled me Baroness of Harmonie—to protect the land from Charles' greed and to help protect us.

"Charles intentionally bumped into me as he left a meeting with the duke at his castle. He threatened me, which means all of us. I believe he will send men after me … after us … and the duke believes this as well. How many men I do not know. But if there are too many, I will go with them to save this valley."

As the two people continued on their slow walk to her home, Garlyn took Nichol by the arm. Moments passed without words.

He looked down at the road in thought. "When you and your family arrived in the valley, we knew that the day of discovery would come. As I remember that day, we all felt saddened that our peaceful valley would be no more. I soon realized that you and I were of the same mind. And I am thankful it was you who arrived.

"This valley is worth fighting for. With you as the Baroness of Harmonie, we will prosper. I know the good people of this valley will fight for you and for what we have."

The two of them faced each other and nodded their heads. They were like-minded.

"Now let us help you unpack and gather to celebrate your arrival in the longhouse. I will ring our new bell to call everyone together. Welcome home."

forty-three

The Legend of the Rise Begins

The constant clanging was the sign, warning of danger.

Gunvor's father Harald sat on his horse, surveying the valley. Nichol had asked several of the men to keep watch over the valley throughout the day and night since she had returned from Rouen. Harald had volunteered to keep watch daily during the morning hours. His reins in hand, he positioned himself at the stream where the road into Harmonie left the forest.

Wearing a cloak with a hood to protect him from the cold drizzle that had descended onto the valley that morning, he stared into the forest. Clouds clung to the very top of the forest canopy and he was thankful for the gloves he wore. There was no break in the solid gray sky.

The forest was alive with sound. The range of bird calls told their stories or warned of enemies that were on the hunt. Sometimes it was the screech of a hawk that frightened the forest creatures.

A sudden silence in the forest chatter alarmed Harald.

Pushing his hood back, he leaned forward in the saddle, his ears and eyes alert. The hair on the back of his neck stiffened.

What is that … ?

Within moments he recognized the sound.

An unwelcome one.

The rumble of horse hooves pounding the road echoed out from the dense forest. The sound increased in volume, and Harald knew that meant the sound of many riders approaching.

Turning his horse, Harald galloped toward Harmonie. He paused, just at the turn of the hill, taking the last chance to view those who were approaching.

There are ten …

His horse swiftly moved through the valley. His destination: the huge bell that Robert and Nichol had brought from England, positioned outside the Harmonie longhouse.

Leaping off his horse, he yanked at the rope repeatedly, bringing all in the valley from their homes. The constant ringing of the deep-toned bell sent an ominous message throughout the valley. Everyone knew the constant clanging warned them of danger.

Almost at the same time, the clouds overhead darkened.

Nichol was nursing Athena when the clanging started. Her body tensed immediately. She knew the bell's message. Quickly moving toward Robert, she placed Athena in his arms.

Deep in her heart, she had known this day would come.

Nichol put on her breeches, strapped her dagger in its sheath to her side, and slipped into her tunic. Then she reached for her bow and grabbed a quiver of arrows.

"Robert, take the children to the forest. You know the place. You must protect them. Go now."

As he began to protest, she put her hand up. "There is no time to talk … they are coming." She moved quickly to the road. In the distance, she could see riders approaching.

Nichol positioned herself in the middle of the road in plain sight. She knew she was the reason they were there.

A sudden bump on the leg made Nichol glance down to see Shadow looking up at her. Reaching down, she scratched her faithful companion behind the ear.

"You are not one to miss a good fight."

Around her, people with children were headed for the safety of the forest.

Nichol looked down the road to see the riders now at Garlyn's, and coming fast. Harald stopped ringing the bell and joined Nichol.

They are not slowing down. How did they know exactly where I would be?

Nichol closed her eyes.

A feeling of calm came over her, and she relaxed.

I am not alone. The Lady is here, too.

John stepped next to her with sword in hand and was joined by Cara. Then Otto stepped in to position himself on Nichol's other side, along with Harald.

All eyes were focused on the soldiers approaching. John put a hand on Nichol's shoulder. "There are only ten of them."

Her eyebrows raised quizzically, Nichol turned to John.

He gave her a wink. "They should have sent more."

The soldiers remained on their horses, fanning out into a straight line fifteen feet away and stopped.

A soldier in the center of the men urged his mount forward and pointed at Nichol. "You there—with the wolf dog—you are Nichol, are you not?"

She raised her chin. "I am. Who sent you?"

He glared at her and ignored her question. "You are to come with me."

"I will not … nor will anyone else here. What is the reason you are here? And who sent you?"

"Lord Charles wants you off his land. He gave us orders to bring you in front of him," the soldier spoke again.

Nichol took a step forward. "This is not Lord Charles' land."

As her words flowed, she concentrated on her thoughts, focusing on him.

I will not go. I will not go. I will not go …

Clearly stunned, unable to speak, the soldier was silenced with her words. His mouth opened, then shut, then opened again, but no words emerged.

Amused, Nichol thought, *He looks like a fish out of the water.*

With a slightly mocking tone, she continued to speak.

"I am honored that Lord Charles sent ten soldiers to kill me, but that is not the real reason you are here. Say your true purpose."

The soldier was confused. He turned to Otto. "What are you doing here?"

"Edric … Nichol is now Baroness of Harmonie, appointed by Duke Richard himself, and now under Duke Richard's protection. She does not answer to you or your count. Go back to him and tell him so. This is not his land. Now leave. You are not welcome here."

Nichol listened to the exchange between the two men. There was a past between them. And this exchange? To Otto, it seemed personal.

I must talk with him later. He may be able to give me insight into Charles and how to destroy his power.

Edric hesitated; now Otto was in control. Edric's men turned to their leader, as if urging him to take back control from this mere woman.

He seems confused as I want him to be.

Nichol seized on Edric's hesitation. "Your lord is a coward. Why is he not here with you? Is he hiding where the forest meets the stream?" Nichol heard the men laugh at her words.

She scanned the faces of the leader and his followers. "I see by those faces in front of me that there is truth in what I say. Your lord sent you ten men to arrest or kill me—like the three that tried to kill me months ago. Those men are the ones that met their fate in the depths of the ocean."

With her words, the men in front of her exchanged worried glances. A murmur rose. A few pulled the reins on their horses, preparing to back them away from the leader.

Nichol spoke again.

"Tell your lord that if he wants Harmonie, he must come himself to take it from me. Duke Richard decreed that I am Baroness of the Harmonie valley. Lord Charles knows this and you should as well. If any harm comes to me, or to others in the Harmonie valley, the duke will know. He has the final authority over this land."

She took a step back. "I suggest you honor the duke, not your lord ..."

When Nichol spoke, John and Otto glared at the men in front of them. Their glare intimated all but the two in front.

Otto pointed his finger at the man next to Edric—a challenge to be taken seriously.

The longer she spoke, more people in the valley joined her by her side. Leiv and his men and other villagers began to surround the soldiers, encircling them while carrying a variety of weapons.

Nichol tilted her head back and smelled the air. John knew what she was doing.

"Nichol, what do you smell?"

Her eyes narrowed as she looked directly at Edric. "I smell a stench."

She lifted her nose in the air again and took an exaggerated inhale. "Yes, it is the stench of fear."

Shifting her glance, she lowered her tone and quietly spoke for only John and Otto to hear. "He has no way out. Be ready; he will attack at any moment."

Turning her head slightly to the side, she saw more villagers joining them. Now Gideon, Joshua, Leiv and his men stood by her.

Edric and his men quickly lost their initial advantage of greater numbers and horses.

Nichol stood, watching him try to decide what to do. "Go back and tell Lord Charles that I will meet him and Duke Richard in Rouen at the duke's pleasure."

She watched his reaction to her demand, knowing Edric would be a dead man if he came back without her. Dropping her voice, she said, "I know that you will not go back without me."

Edric shook his head at her, attempting to clear his mind. His men watched him while Nichol could see the indecision and lack of confidence.

John raised the sword in his hand, extending it in front of Nichol. Otto brought his sword into contact with John's. They both knew what was next.

When they pulled their swords away, Nichol immediately raised her bow and let the first arrow penetrate Edric's chest. The second arrow pierced the soldier to his left.

Shadow attacked two horses, causing the riders to struggle for control. The animals began to buck, attempting to dislodge their riders.

John and Otto worked together, taking one soldier down, and then another. Villagers with pitchforks, axes, and knives battled Charles' men with a frenzy. No mercy was given in their united protection of their hamlet.

Nichol released two more arrows, wounding two more before they were pulled from their horses.

Only one rider was still mounted, backing his horse with sword slashing on either side.

Everyone backed away. The soldiers had hesitated and waited too long to collectively attack. They never had a chance from the Harmonites. Those on the ground wouldn't live long.

A sudden silence came over the battle as all looked up and turned to Nichol.

Standing alone, she calmly nocked an arrow and pulled the string to her cheek, with steadfast focus on the last mounted soldier.

Frozen with fear, his stunned look met Nichol's gaze. With his death imminent, he threw down his sword and nodded to the victor to accept his fate.

Nichol released the tension on the bow and pointed the arrow toward the ground. "Tell your lord I will be in Rouen for the winter. He can find me there. I do not think Duke Richard will be pleased when he hears of what has occurred here. Dismount now and walk away. Your horses now belong to us—the victors."

Nichol looked around. Most of the Harmonites stood in shock, blood on their hands, weapons, and clothes.

Otto and John found two soldiers still breathing and hastily slit their throats.

The soldier Nichol had spared took to his heels, running toward the woods and away from death.

Nichol took control and calmly began giving orders. "Cara, go tell those that fled into the forest that it is safe to return. Gideon, tend to the horses, and find places for them in the stable.

"Otto and John, collect the weapons and take them to the longhouse. And Garlyn, these men must be buried soon. Strip them of coins and clothes that can be used. Dig one grave for all of them. All who can dig and help, do so. Ring the bell when it is done. After they are buried, we will all meet in the Harmonie House."

forty-four

Harmonie Longhouse

We want you Baroness; it has always been you.

Later that day, all the valley's residents gathered in the Harmonie longhouse. The fallen men were buried and the villagers had walked to the river close by to wash up and clean their bloodied clothes.

There were no serious injuries from the battle and much talk of heroism and courage. For most Harmonites, it was the first time they had fought together for a cause. Collective pride in the defense of their valley featured in most conversations.

The room was aglow with a profusion of candlelight. Food was prepared and a cask of wine was tapped. Ale was plentiful. Gunvor and Tova brought the children to Nichol. With her arms around all three of them, she pulled them to her chest, kissing the top of each of their heads.

Athena clung to her, pushing her head at Nichol's breast. She was hungry.

The wine and ale began to loosen tongues. Not all were pleased with the attack and a few began to voice their thoughts. Some shouts blamed Nichol for the attack.

In turn, Garlyn shouted back for them to be silent.

Nichol stood on a stool and held her hand up. With her other, she placed two of her fingers in her mouth and let out a loud whistle that penetrated every corner of the room to quiet everyone.

Then she spoke, addressing all in the room.

"You should all know that those men who attacked us were from Lord Charles. He wants to steal your home and gardens.

Understand that. No one inside this room is the enemy. The true enemy is the others who seek what we are building … what *you* are building and working for. Charles and men like him are guided by greed.

"Everyone should be thankful for Harald's ringing of the Great Bell. You all heard it immediately, and you knew that it carried an urgent warning because of the constant ringing. If Harald had not succeeded in sounding the bell to warn us, Charles may have been successful in taking over Harmonie and killing many."

"I have only one question for you. It is a simple one. Do you want me as your leader, answering only to Duke Richard, or do you want Lord Charles and his men to rule over Harmonie and over you?"

Those in the hall absorbed her words. Silence filled the air.

Why are they not responding? Has fear and doubt overtaken them?

Nichol began to step down when a woman's loud voice from the crowd broke the silence. Her voice was laced with determination and urgency.

"We want you, Baroness; it has always been you!"

Cheers broke out as Nichol rose and held up her hand.

"Soon, I will go to Rouen to meet with Duke Richard and tell him of what has happened today. And I will plead for his continued protection and support of Harmonie.

"You should all know that Timo has obtained permission to hold a fair just outside of Rouen. We will represent Harmonie with tents filled with our cloth and crafts. It will bring coin to you. Others will buy what you make and we sell on your behalf."

Nichol looked over at those attending, and stopped at a table where John, Cara, Otto, Gabrielle, Joshua, Leiv and his men sat.

Their eyes met when they raised their cups and repeatedly yelled her name out loud.

Unseen to most, a soft light bounced around the room.

All the conversations stopped when everyone in the longhouse started yelling her name in unison, holding their ale cups up to her and slamming their hands on the table.

 Nichol put her hand on her heart, bowed, and mouthed the words *thank you.*

She looked across the table at Joshua and raised her hand to signal that there was more she must say.

"Joshua, Duke Richard must hear of today. The valley needs you to leave in the morning and deliver a message to him, a message for his ears only. All that you have witnessed today must be told to him, in detail as only you can do. Tell of the brave women and men of this valley who risked their lives for his just decision to make me Baroness of Harmonie. Tell him of the betrayal and treachery of Lord Charles.

"Tell him that I will be in Rouen within the week. I plan to stay for the winter with my family at Ezra's. And—as before—I will pledge my fealty to him."

Joshua bowed his head. "I will leave at daybreak, Baroness. The duke will hear of all that happened here and that you will arrive within the week with the harvest to grind our grain at his watermill. I will tell Ezra and Helene that you, Robert, and the children will arrive soon with the harvest and goods that will be available for sale in their stalls and at Timo's fair."

"Good," Nichol said, nodding her head as he described his plans. "I will see you before you leave in the morning."

Turning to those in the room, she added, "Charles' men are buried. All their belongings of clothes and boots, along with knives and whatever else they had was removed. Garlyn and I will meet tomorrow to decide what we do with it."

Hearing his name, Garlyn stood and directed his words to the people in the room. "You all should be thankful to Nichol and Robert for finding and bringing the bell to Harmonie. Without it and without Harald pulling the cord, Harmonie could have been destroyed. I think we should call it the Great Bell from now on."

Nichol and Robert laughed and then both clapped their hands at the same time. Soon, the entire room was filled with praise.

Nichol held up her hands. "It has been a long day. I need to tend to my children and sleep. Thank you all for your support."

Robert was holding Athena. Moving toward him, Nichol lifted Lucette to her right hip, took Aiden's hand, and went out the door.

They were homeward bound, needing time to be just them.

forty-five

The Harmonie House

I think most of the swords and knives
should be kept here in Harmonie.

The next morning, the brisk valley air remained but the cloud covering of the past days were gone.

When people entered the longhouse, the warmth from the ovens and smell of bread baking immediately lifted their spirits. Most came to spin wool and weave cloth, but that was not the only reason. It had become a gathering place to contribute ideas in support of Harmonie.

Joshua had already headed back to Rouen. Nichol had given him cheese, bread, dried rabbit, a few apples, and a wineskin so he had food for the journey. His last words to her were, "I will be in Rouen before dark tomorrow. I will contact Ezra immediately so he knows of the attack and then go to the castle at first light the next morning to see the duke. He needs to know the truth of what happened here before Lord Charles gets to him."

"Take this coin, Joshua, and give it to Victor at the castle gate and tell him it is from me. He will make sure that the duke knows your message comes from me."

After placing the children in the care of Gunvor and Tova, Nichol, Robert, Otto, and Garlyn sat down after Joshua left. It was time to decide what to do with the weapons, clothes, and horses collected from the soldiers.

Garlyn placed the purse filled with coin that was collected from the soldiers and placed it on the table. "We need to agree on what to do with the horses we kept," was the first thing he said. "They are valuable and would be used by most in Harmonie. And for those who travel to Rouen when needed."

Both Nichol's and Robert's heads nodded as he spoke. He then added, "They will be ideal to load with grain and then taken to the mill at Duke Richard's water mill in Rouen. I think most of the swords and knives should be kept here in Harmonie."

"John and Gideon like to build things. We need several carts to take goods back and forth. Garlyn, is there anyone you know of within your group of houses that have skills to build carts?" Robert asked.

"The coin collected could go to building carts for Harmonie for taking goods back and forth to Rouen as Garlyn suggested."

Nichol liked what she was hearing. Others were taking responsibility and ownership that would benefit Harmonie.

"I will coordinate washing of the dead soldiers' clothing and boots with the other women. Nothing will be wasted. When we are done, we will call the community together with the Great Bell to the Longhouse and tell them that anyone can take what they need.

"The weapons should be distributed to those who can handle them," she added. "I think that we should consider teaching others some of the defense skills I was taught to protect themselves and others. I can teach archery to women and men; the valley could have a tournament to test those skills. It would be advantageous if others should shoot a bow like I can," she stated, with a decisive nod.

"When the bell rang to warn us of the danger, Harald rang it for what seemed a long time. It would be ideal to set up a system so that the bell would be a way to communicate. Continuous ringing means danger and to gather any weapons each person has and be prepared to use them.

"If there are two rings, a pause, and then two more, it would mean to come to the longhouse for a meeting. If there are four rings, a pause and then four more, it would mean that help was needed. Someone is injured or one of the buildings is on fire.

"We could create a big flag or banner that wherever they were to go, it would be quickly displayed so those would know what is happening."

Nichol, Robert, and Garlyn all agreed. Having an organized system would continue to build trust with the others who now lived there.

"Nichol, more are coming here. We should be thinking of where they will live until they have their own home," Garlyn said.

"Some who are already here may welcome a few people into their home for a short time. When I left Marseilles, I slept in trees, barns, and the longhouses at monasteries. We could allow the use of our longhouse here for sleeping for a limited number until they had a home of their own. Is that something you could oversee, Garlyn?"

"I would need help. If there are many needing a place to sleep and eat, I'm sure others will come forth to help. I think it would be good to have someone here, like Cara and John, and then I could get another closer to where my home is. That way the valley is covered," Garlyn added.

"I like the way you are thinking and planning, Garlyn. Just like a mayor would."

Otto had listened closely to the three of them. Finally, he spoke up. "My family has come to live here as well. Gabrielle and my young sons are already here and don't want to leave. They will remain here when I go back to Rouen with Nichol.

"I could work with Garlyn and John to train those who live here of all ages for how to protect themselves and others in the hamlet."

As Garlyn looked around the table, it was the first time he felt that the community could be strong and protected.

Did Nichol refer to me as mayor?

Relishing his newly appointed role, he continued to speak.

"Otto … your family can stay in the longhouse. The other men and I will work together to build a home for your family that they can move into soon. When you return, we can add to it. As the mayor …" he lifted his chin, "… I welcome you to Harmonie."

With his words, they all slapped the table in approval.

Just then, Gideon came to the longhouse, looking for Robert.

Seeing him, Robert said, "We have much to do. I want you to help me repair and sharpen the knives and swords of the fallen men of Lord Charles."

Together, Robert and Gideon left for the forge.

Cara entered the longhouse with Gabriel, Otto's wife. Gunvor and Tova were busily tending to the children. Nichol greeted them and invited them to the table where John, Otto, and Garlyn were seated.

It was time to talk about Timo's fair.

"Garlyn, we will be leaving in a few days to return to Rouen. The duke knows of the fair and told me that he thinks it will be good for those living there and surrounding areas. We need to plan what we are bringing and who is going to go with Robert and I when we leave," Nichol said.

John was the first to speak. "We want to go down to the fair." As she said it, Cara nodded her head in agreement.

"You will be surprised when I say this, Nichol. I would like to go, too," were Garlyn's words.

"I like that, Garlyn. I know that Duke Richard will be there. I want him to know of you," was her response.

Quickly the group came up with items to carry to Rouen to sell from those living in Harmonie. There was excitement and energy in the room.

After the horrendous encounter with Lord Charles' men, the idea of relief and adventure was welcome.

What started as a bad thing had united all in Harmonie.

Nichol locked eyes with Garlyn. A smile crossed both their faces at the same time.

They were all in agreement.

forty-six

Otto

He will protect me and our boys with his life and you as well.

nichol looked at Otto. "Tell us how you know this man you called Edric. I could tell when you spoke to him when Charles' men were here that you share a past with him."

"My father and mother were peasants and could not feed all of us. I was the oldest and because of my size and constant fighting, one of the duke's soldiers saw me and took me to Duke Richard's father for training. I was first trained as a page, then a squire, and eventually became a knight.

"Edric came from a noble family and entered service at the same time as me. He always thought he was better than me because his father was a noble. During my training, I became the best of those around me and was noticed by the duke. Of all the knights, Richard chose me to be part of his personal guard.

"Nichol, I saw you when you came to the castle but our paths never crossed until Richard made me your personal guard. The only reason Edric was knighted was because of his father. The best way to describe him is to say he was weak-minded and not trustworthy. He was always jealous of the skills I honed, and he became his own worst enemy. No one will miss him—not Lord Charles, who I know of from conversations I heard in the duke's Great Hall. He uses people for his own personal gain, then throws them away when not needed.

"You saw the eyes of Edric's men. They did not have their heart in what they were sent to do. Did you see their faces when

I said that Duke Richard made you Baroness of Harmonie? They knew then to turn around and leave, but it was too late. Your arrow was already in flight."

John's softly-spoken words brought silence and reflection from all at the table. "They died for the vanity of one man. There would be no victory celebration for Harmonie. There was no winner, only the determined reaction to protect a way of life."

All at the table went silent, contemplating John's words.

Nichol's head tilted. Her eyebrows and face were lowered in concentrated thought. John, Cara and Garlyn watched her; they had seen her like this before. They knew the next words to come from Nichol must be heard.

"Lessons that I received at an early age taught me to listen carefully to people, observe them while they talked. No detail was too small. There is little written about the past, only stories that are passed from one generation to another till there is little truth to them. What we are told of the past bears little truth to what actually happened.

"True knowledge of the past is important but people do not change. Lord Charles will not stop; in his mind, he has been wronged. There is no length that he will not go to rule us—to destroy us if necessary. Harmonie is not the prize. He seeks the power to control people. We are the prize and it is the conquest that he seeks.

"Lord Charles will not give up. He is a little man with too much power. Too much blood will be spilled before his end comes."

"You are right, Baroness. And I will be at your side," Otto said.

Two days later, in the early hours of the morning, they were packed and ready to leave Harmonie. Twenty-five people and twelve pack horses began the trip that would take three days of travel.

Shadow, as was her habit, led the way with Otto's boys, Henrik and Siebert, close behind her. Robert led Moki, burdened with children in the basket. Gabrielle walked with Nichol and helped carry Athena.

Throughout the three days, the two walked together most of the time. Sometimes, they separated themselves from the rest.

During one of those times, Nichol said, "Tell me about you and Otto."

"He is kind to me and a good father and loyal to the duke. His size and looks tell most to stay away. When you shot the first arrow into that man, I knew that was not the first time that you killed someone. Then later, you nursed your baby with your children close to you. I am amazed that you can take down a bad person and moments later, become the loving, caring mother to your baby. I have known of no other woman like you. Neither has Otto.

"The night of the attack when we were in bed, we talked of you and Harmonie. I told him I wished to live and raise our boys in the Harmonie he described—the one you are creating. He agreed with me. Otto will protect me and our boys with his life, and you as well. Know this, if you are ever threatened, stand back; he will not yield in his protection of you and now your children."

Nichol listened to Gabrielle and let her words resonate within her.

"The duke wishes that wherever I go, Otto will be with me. That means we will also be close and I like that, Gabrielle. I like that I've gotten to know you better as we have walked." She then laughed. "You will hear many stories about me. It's wise to not believe everything you hear."

The first night, they stopped in a small meadow before the sun set over the forest trees. With few words spoken, those who packed the horses unpacked and tended to them. Those who had packed food began to prepare the evening meal. Gabrielle's boys Henrik and Seibert collected firewood. When they brought it back to their mother, she gave them the flint Nichol had given her to start the fire.

"When it is started, gather more dry wood to last the night."

Bread, apples, cheese, and salted meat was the evening meal, with a one cup of ale for each. Most were tired from the day's travel and sat on the ground eating and staring at the fire that cast flickering silhouettes on the meadow and surrounding forest trees. The children were in awe of the lightning bugs that filled the early night light.

Shadow lay next to the Nichol, Robert, and the children. Abruptly, she stood looking first at Nichol, then back into the forest from where they came.

Nichol and Robert came to their feet at once. "Someone is coming."

Out of the forest darkness came a familiar voice.

"Nichol, put your dagger away. It is me, Leiv, and we are hungry."

Shadow was the first to greet them, her tail wagging in recognition.

A spot was made by Nichol for Leiv and two crewmen from his ship, then food was placed in front of them.

Leiv then stood as he talked for everyone to hear.

"I have good word from our travels. Nichol, you asked me to find a port on the channel close to Harmonie for trade to England. I am here to tell you that a place exists. The channel is only one day of travel west from your valley. When we arrived, we traveled up and down the coast and found the best place to drop anchor to load and unload cargo. The bay we chose will protect the ship from the channels' weather and eventually build a port.

"We returned to Harmonie, only to find you had left. With the full moon, there was just enough light for us to follow the road you had taken. When we heard voices in the distance, we knew you were close by. I am glad we found you. I would rather be at sea with only the stars to guide me than in a forest surrounded by trees."

That night, as the fire dimmed and the cool air surrounded them, the children were sound asleep between Robert and Nichol. Shadow crept in at the children's feet and received Nichol's attention. She rubbed Shadow's head and neck, then lay back down gazing at the night sky. Tired from the day's journey, but for the first time in days feeling alone with her thoughts.

Most people in the valley just want to live in peace and that is my goal, too.

Turning her head to the children, she let her eyes move slowly over their sleeping bodies.

The Lady is with each of you now and I possess knowledge and skill from her. The Lady will bestow upon you more gifts than she gave me. Use them wisely, little ones. Robert and I will guide you as you grow.

Turning her eyes to the sky, she enjoyed the sparkle of the stars in their dance across the heavens.

When we arrive, I must first meet with Richard. It will be expected of me.

Her last thoughts before giving into her body's fatigue were Ezra's words: *You are in a world that is not ready for you.*

They would travel three days more to Rouen.

While they walked, Nichol talked to everyone about their wants and needs.

Most simply wanted a home and a small parcel of land of their own. All agreed that the Harmonie longhouse was an important part of their lives: a place to work, meet, and stay warm in the winter. It was a place for a growing community that would welcome them. It was a place for support.

Arriving in Rouen on the fourth day, Nichol and Robert went directly to Ezra's and received a warm welcome from Helene and Ezra.

The next morning, Otto arrived at Ezra's, both Otto and Nichol aware that they must see Duke Richard. Athena had nursed and Helene did not notice them leave, as she was enjoying every minute with the children.

Before she left with Otto, Ezra reminded Nichol that they must meet with Timo that morning. The fair was only days away.

When they approached the outer gate, Victor had many supplicants in front of him and he waved them through. Nichol made a point to give him a silver coin, and Otto asked her what favor Victor did in return to earn it.

"Victor was one of the few that was kind to me and my family when we first arrived in Rouen. And he defended me against a pirate. I will never forget him or his kindness to me."

Once through the castle door and in front of Duke Richard, both of them bowed and said, "Your Grace."

Richard dismissed those in front of him and called all in the castle to the Great Hall.

In a loud voice, he said, "To all present this morning …"

With his hand, he gestured toward Nichol. "This woman standing in front of me, Nichol of Harmonie, I name as Lady

Nichol Baron of a valley and surrounding forest and a hamlet within called Harmonie. She is to receive all the respect of any baron or noble in Normandy. She and Otto defended Harmonie from ten armed soldiers sent to kill her."

With a wave of his hand, he dismissed the hall and invited Nichol and Otto to his solar. Nichol passed Judith, bowed and said, "Your Grace, we must meet soon."

Judith smiled and nodded. "Go with the duke. We will meet soon; I promise."

forty-seven

Timo's Fair

Someday, these men will learn
that you are more than their equal.

Timo had been given permission by Duke Richard to hold a fair just outside the walls of Rouen. Ezra, Achim, Helene, and Dinah were going door to door in Rouen telling of the coming fair.

For a small fee to the duke, a merchant or vendor could set up a table or tent and sell their wares, sharpen knives, give haircuts, or shave a face. Displays of dyed cloth, clothes, leather shoes and boots, and many other things would be featured.

The food would be plentiful; livestock would be bought and sold. The wonders of Persian spices, silks, cotton, and wool cloth would be displayed by the many merchants that purchased from E & N Merchants.

Robert would display the gems imported from Persia. The gems were the attraction Robert desired, along with his brooches and bracelets displayed beside the goods of another goldsmith.

Timo's tent would display Harmonie's crafts and cloth. He planned to tell tales of orchards, grapevines, and beehives in a valley that would bring delicious cider and wine and honey to other fairs in the future. Wine and ale would be plentiful.

The morning of the fair started with overcast skies but soon gave way to scattered billowing clouds and a promise of warmth. Everyone dressed in their best clothes. Many from Harmonie came. John, Cara, and Garlyn stayed at Ezra's, others at Amos' Inn.

At first light, Otto was at Ezra's door to escort Nichol and the children to the fair. Robert was already there with Timo under a large cloth tent that Timo had erected the day before.

When they arrived, Nichol took Lucette, Aiden and Athena to Timo's tent and left them there with Helene and Dinah. Ezra joined her and they went to meet with all the many merchants and vendors who had set up stalls with tables and goods spread out.

The air was exciting with happy voices and people calling out to each other. They were flanked by John, Cara, Otto, and Gabrielle. Merchants would bark their goods to passersby and invite them to their stand.

Garlyn saw them and approached with a concerned look. "I just came from the pasture next to the stable where our horses are kept. A man approached me and asked who those horses belonged to. The man who stopped knew the horses and questioned me, and I told him I just brought them here for the owner. He then asked me who the owner was and I told him I did not know. He then gave me a threatening look. As he left, he said he would be back."

Otto did not hesitate. "Go back and tell the stable owner that I own the horses and if someone wants them, tell them to come find me and bring a sword."

Nichol heard a commotion and turned to see Duke Richard and Duchess Judith, surrounded by an entourage. Richard's silk tunic vibrated with colors of red, blue, and yellow. She recognized the fabric used to craft Judith's tunic—greens, blues, and violet danced as she moved. It was what she gave her from Diego's first shipment.

Each wore finely woven wool cloaks with hoods, held together with jeweled clasps of Robert's making. Both had leather belts and purses.

When the duke approached, they bowed and said in unison, "Your Grace."

Nichol's and Judith's eyes met. Judith lightly touched her belly and Nichol smiled as she did. She turned and her eyes met the duke's.

"Your Grace, I hope you are enjoying the fair. Your presence bring joy and honor to the fair and those who are already present."

Richard extended his hand to Nichol. "Walk with us. Nichol, I have been thinking about our meeting in my solar yesterday."

As he moved away from the group that closely followed him, he added, "I want Joshua to deliver a message to Lord Charles. Once it is delivered, he will not harm you or attack Harmonie again. Two knights will go with him with my written demands.

"Charles must respond. If Joshua and the knights do not return unharmed and with his response within four days, I will send an army to bring him in front of me here in Rouen."

Nichol looked at Richard. "Joshua told you …"

Richard nodded. "Joshua told me how the ringing of the large bell warned of the attack; to you on the road with bow in hand and arrow ready; to you taking down a few of the knights; to the others fighting with their axes, rakes, and pitchforks. He told me about Otto and John by your side.

"I know why you sent him ahead of your arrival to tell me. Joshua spoke with clarity and great detail about what occurred. When he was done, I felt I was a part of the battle. His emphasis on words and actions was so real that I could see the arrows fly and blood flowing with the men dying in front of me."

"Your Grace, they came just like you said they would … except they were going to capture me. I believe their orders were to kill me after we left Harmonie."

The duke nodded. "Joshua and Otto told the same story of the attack on you and those who live in Harmonie. Someday, these men will learn that you are more than their equal."

He clasped his hands behind his back as they strolled. Then he stopped and turned to speak directly to her.

"I need your gift to see people. Timo's fair has been welcomed by all and is a good thing for Rouen. Judith was excited to come … and to see you again. When the fair is over and you are settled in Rouen again, I want you to attend meetings in the Great Hall and be hidden in the solar for more private meetings—much like you once did in your father's solar.

"I have told Simon, my chancellor, of my desire to have you in attendance. He did not approve. Simon will soon see that you do not pose danger to his position in the castle. My steward told him that you could be trusted. In fact, I believe that he will find you an ally."

Turning to Judith, he reached out his hand to bring her closer to Nichol as he spoke to her. "Now let us enjoy this fair …"

Judith came from Richard's other side, and Nichol offered her arm as they continued walking, as two women friends would do.

As Nichol walked with Judith at her side, she saw people looking not just at the duke or duchess … but at her. Her eyes met the gazes of many as they walked.

I walk with the royals but I am not of them. I must never lose the trust of those people whose eyes met mine.

A strange feeling of calm came over her. There was an increase in her smell, sight, and the clear sense of the intentions of those around her. It was the same feeling she had felt just before the attack. Now the feeling appealed to her.

I remember the Lady telling me that I would experience this. She has brought those in my life for a reason; they are of her choosing.

Intentions of harm, intrigues—even sensations of love and jealousy can be felt or seen in my observations. These feelings are far greater than I ever felt when in Papa's solar. My role for the duke will be a spy tasked to unmask treachery, to discover conspiracy, and to discern truth from falsehoods.

Nichol smiled slightly with the thought, *a new game to play.*

Richard felt her silence and noted the two women weren't talking, yet they seemed to be communicating, as Nichol had linked her arm with Judith's. Nichol seemed to be lost in distant thought.

Breaking the silence, he said, "Remember, Nichol, Lord Charles is an ambitious and dangerous adversary. He has many spies. When in Harmonie, you must be watchful and when you leave it as those who are left behind must be. His next attack could be on the road.

"I know that Joshua is your messenger. There are times I need someone as discreet as he is; someone who can move quickly; and someone who I can trust. I would like to be able to use his services as well."

Nichol nodded her head with his words.

She then looked at Judith and then at Richard. "I know. There is danger with him. Let us enjoy this day together and tell of the intrigues of Normandy when the fair is over. Possibly Fécamp would be a place that would celebrate having a fair next year. There is so much to see.

"And by this time next year, your son will be here."

forty-eight

Eight Years Later ... the Evening Meal

We have coins but when there is no food to buy,
everyone but the nobles go hungry.

For the next eight years, Nichol and her family lived in Rouen with Ezra in the winter months.

The Harmonie House continued to be an active community gathering place and Helene was at the heart of it. Her sewing skills were welcomed by the women in Harmonie. Her enthusiasm for children created an environment where the women met and brought their families as they cooked and sewed together.

As one of the few educated women who could read and write, she made sure that the children had ongoing lessons each week. Nichol encouraged the mothers to join in the lessons. Several of them are now reading. And Helene wasentrenched with her year-round role as Granmama, filling in for Nichol, and helping Cara with her little ones as well.

Lucette and Aiden were ten and Athena was nine. All were fiercely independent. Cara stayed busy within the longhouse and was also pregnant with her and John's third child.

Nichol and Robert would have lived in Harmonie year-round if it were not for Duke Richard's insistence that she acted as his seer.

Their time was divided. From spring to fall harvest, they resided in Harmonie. As soon as the harvest was completed in October, they relocated to Rouen and prepared for Timo's fair on All Saints' Day. Nichol returned to Rouen when Diego arrived with more shipments of silks, spices, and cloth along with other supplies that could be used in Harmonie.

Sharing what she uncovered and any conversations Diego and she had would remain private. Knowledge about her insightful gifts to others could put her life and family in danger.

E & N Merchants prospered. Ezra traveled occasionally, accompanied by his brother Achim, now a business partner in some of Ezra's ventures.

As their company traded with England and the Mediterranean countries, their share in Rouen's economy expanded. Yearly, Nichol would travel to England to spend a few days with Emma and support the trade that had been established. Often, Lucette would accompany her. Through Ezra's past business connections in Paris, he introduced Diego's luxury items brought from the Far East. As the years passed by, Nichol became more of a silent partner to Ezra, using her connection with the duke to build its influence.

Along with Achim, Marie and Olaf became Ezra's associates and were now responsible for ordering and providing goods to the markets.

That fall, when Nichol and family arrived back in Rouen, her children began to draw interest from other residents. They were different. Villagers were talking about Lucette, Athena and Aiden —sometimes not in a complimentary way. They were just too different than children their age, even the older ones. For one thing, they could read and write, far better than most of the adults.

Some of the mothers had picked up what their children were learning during the time that they spent at the Harmonie House.

At the evening meal when they were seated, only Aiden began to eat.

Lucette and Athena just stared at their bowls, then watched Aiden until he looked up.

"What? I didn't do anything wrong. Why are you looking at me?"

Lucette put her spoon in the bowl and turned it as she lifted it out. "Mama, there is nothing but broth. There is no meat and nothing from the garden in this broth. Is our food gone?"

Helene and Ezra stayed quiet, knowing that it was a teaching moment for Nichol.

Aiden and Athena repeated what their sister said.

Seated with her family, Nichol looked around the table, making eye contact with each. She then said, "You noticed." Rising, she brought dried fish and cheese to the table.

"Outside, the street stalls are mostly empty. Did you notice that when you were out today? We do have food, but many don't. Throughout this winter, I bought bread and dried or salted fish for you to hand out to those in need.

"There are many hungry people who live close to us. Granmama Helene and I make sure that food finds its way to them with our own breads and any extra we have. We have coins but when there is no food to buy, everyone but the nobles go hungry. The duke does not let people hunt or forage for food in his forest.

"When Timo, Moki, and I were traveling to Paris, late in the day we would seek a place in the forest to stay for the night. Timo gathered plants, berries, and mushrooms to add to our meals. If you had his knowledge, you could survive on what the forest provides. I want you to seek him out and ask if he will teach you about these things. You can learn which plants are safe to eat and those to avoid. It is important that you take him to the forest; it would please him to share his knowledge with you.

"We will return to Harmonie soon, where you will help me plant our garden. Granmama will help and we will plant many foods and herbs that can be stored for the winter months when little can be grown."

Athena and Ezra looked at each other and a smile appeared on her face. "Granpapa, I see you have a story you want to tell us, too."

Ezra cleared his throat, and his quiet voice brought the children closer.

"When your mama was your age, she would walk to the docks in Marseilles by herself, the same age all of you are. It was a dangerous place for a young girl to be alone. Her papa knew she was there and encouraged her to go."

His voice now is just above a whisper. "Pirates—very bad men they were—roamed the docks and frightened everyone but your mama."

Ezra glanced at Nichol. Her eyebrows narrowed and glared while slowly shaking her head. Helene put her hand under the table and dug her nails into his leg.

Ezra ignored both women.

"Your mama was not afraid. Your Granpapa Alexander was the port commander. And he had eyes on your mama at all times so he could protect her ... She just didn't know it." Ezra paused and took a deep breath.

Aiden's eyes widened and he fidgeted on his stool. "Tell us more. Did any of those pirates hurt Mama?"

"Ahh ... there was an old woman at the docks. Her name was Rose. When your mama was there, Rose looked out for her. Granpapa Alexander gave Rose coin to feed and clothe poor children. Rose was a healer and, in her shop, she taught your mama about herbs and how to treat sickness.

"One time, a bad man dragged your mama by her hair to one of the taverns. Rose saw it happen and got one of the orphan children to run to your granpapa for help. He rushed to the tavern and saved your mama that day. All because of Rose's eyes.

"Rose was a special person to Alexander. Her eyes would let him know what families needed food, clothing, and the coin to get them. She told him if there was anything he should know about happenings at the port. Because of that, he made sure that she had what she needed to help others.

"Just before your mama left Marseilles for Paris, Rose gave her a very special stone." Ezra glanced again at Nichol. Her eyes welled with tears and a faraway gaze revealed to him she was back in long-ago Marseilles with her beloved Rose.

"Rose taught your mama much. Her compassion and caring for those without all began from her time when she was a young girl, growing up on the docks of Port Marseilles.

"Tomorrow I will tell another story. I will tell you how she helped your mama escape from the evil men who were coming after her. But now … it is time for bed."

Outside, even though they were warm in their beds, everyone could hear the wind blowing.

Inside, sleep would eventually come. But first, the children would dream of pirates; a faraway place called Marseilles; the old women named Rose; and the stone their mama wore.

Lucette, the Apprentice

You are like your papa.

Timo's fair in Rouen on All Saints' Day was now a tradition. There were entertainers, tournaments and contests, a week-long festival with days of activities that brought people from as far away as Paris to buy and sell or just enjoy the food, ale, and wine.

Duke Richard and Duchess Judith had just left to return to the castle. Nichol and Robert were slowly walking from booth to booth when Nichol looked around and saw their children with Raisa. She pointed toward them.

"Robert, do you see what I see?"

"Yes, Lucette, Aiden, and Athena with Cousin Raisa."

"Here is what I see … I see four children that need to be kept busy this winter."

Amused, Robert stopped walking and turned to her. "What do you suggest we do?"

"We will find work for them to keep them separated and out of mischief. I have a plan, and it starts with that table over there."

Moving toward the table that had a rack of bows next to it, Nichol focused on the old man sitting behind the table. She had known this man since she had first arrived in Rouen, and she relied on him. His age was evident as she observed his shaking hands. He sat alone, without an apprentice near him, even though his skill at his craft made him a master. He was Hubert the Bowyer.

Nichol smiled as she approached Hubert's table. When he looked up, it was apparent he did not recognize the figure in front of him.

Nichol saw his blank glaze and she felt sadness. Moving closer, she reached for his hand and gently touched it.

"Hubert, it is Nichol and Robert."

A smile appeared on his heavily lined face. "Apologies, my friends. My eyesight is failing me."

With sadness in his voice, he added, "I do not have a new bow for you this year. I had wanted to make a special one that you would like for the fair, knowing that you would be here. My apprentice left me this past week, and I fear my shop will soon close."

"I believe I have an answer to help you, Hubert. You have met all our children and made bows for them. Our daughter Lucette has my desire to use a bow as I do. Would you welcome her as your new apprentice?"

Hubert slowly rocked back and forth on his stool. His hand reached out and picked up one of the arrows on display. A smile spread across his face. "I remember her, a very curious child. Before my eyesight began to fail, she looked like you when you were young. How old is she today?"

"Ten years and she is wiser than other children her age. I know that you will have no regrets taking her as your apprentice and training her in your workshop."

"Does she know of your plans?"

"No, but I know she will agree."

"There is another bowyer in Rouen that has taken my apprentice and much of my trade from me."

"I know of the other bowyer and his bows and arrows are inferior to yours. If you agree, she will be at your shop when the fair is over."

In thought, Hubert began to stroke his beard. Nichol anxiously awaited his response.

"I will return to my shop at the end of the day. Have her come there in the morning. If she truly wants to be a bowyer, I will teach her all I know."

Nichol reached over his table and clasped his hand in both of hers. For a few moments, she gently held it. "She will be there."

She and Robert then walked away.

Robert had questions. As they distanced from Hubert's table, they spilled out.

"What can she learn over the winter and before we return to Harmonie? What will Hubert do when she returns with us? What if she no longer has interest? What …"

Now Nichol stopped and turned to face Robert.

"When we approached his table, I could see he was not well and his hands were shaking. When I held his hand, I knew he will not live past this winter." Robert felt her sadness and pulled her into his arms.

Her voice trembling, "I saw him. I know his needs. In the morning, Lucette will take food and drink to him. She will learn. She will become his apprentice and care for him."

Robert surprised her when he said, "You are like your papa. You see people's needs. You make sure that there is food for others and children are watched over. Your papa encouraged you as a child on the docks and now you are doing it with our children, teaching them compassion and caring."

As he said his words, a hawk's screech could be heard. Looking up, the red-tailed hawk circled high above.

They both looked up at the sky and smiled.

That night over the evening meal, Nichol told Lucette of her conversation with Hubert. She and Robert wanted her to be part of the decision for her to work with him.

"Would you like to learn from Hubert, Lucette?" was all she asked.

"Mama, his bows are always the best. I would like to learn from him to make bows and arrows for our own use. And I like the old man's stories. I can bring him food and wood for his fire each day."

Nichol was pleased with her daughter's thoughtful and caring response.

fifty

Athena, the Apprentice

What have you learned today?

"What about me, Mama?" Athena could hardly contain herself when she heard what her big sister was going to be doing. "I could help Lucette with the caring of Hubert."

"No, Athena. You have special skills, just as your sister and brother do. I was aware of what Lucette could do with a bow. There is a woman I want to meet with tomorrow and then I will tell you about her."

Athena danced up and down with impatience. "Tell me now … I cannot wait …"

Everyone laughed. "Be patient … It will come soon," was all Nichol would say.

The next morning, Athena was anxious to leave. She had a plan and was stopped with her mama's words, "Where are you going this morning?"

Athena proudly said, "I am going to find my own work."

Robert sighed and then turned to her. "Take Shadow with you."

Shadow heard her name and was up by Athena's side in an instant. It was obvious she was ready for an adventure.

Athena was giddy with her thoughts. As she left and closed the door behind her, she signaled to Shadow to stay close.

Inside the house, Helene, Ezra, Robert, and Nichol experienced a brief moment of sadness together, quietly looking at each other for comfort.

"Our babies are growing up," came out of Helene's mouth. Her words carried a sense of pride and sadness at the same time.

Athena knew exactly where she was headed. She rehearsed what she would say all the way to her destination before she entered the small shop, a shop that she visited many times before with her mother. It was a place that always felt like another safe home to her.

The front door had paintings of flowers around the frame, using colors that made young Athena smile. When she opened the door, a scent came to her, one that she was familiar with.

Zita, the owner, looked up and smiled when Athena entered. "Where is your mother? I see you have brought the beast Shadow with you." Shadow went to her and put her head on Zita's lap and received a head rub.

"Mama is home. Lucette and Aiden are working, and I would like to work for you."

Zita smiled. "What is it that you would do for me?"

"I will do whatever you need. I would like to learn how to become a healer, which herbs should be used for healing, and to do what you do."

Amused, Zita pointed to a shelf. She said to Athena, "Do you know the names of plants, spices, and herbs that I have here on the shelf? Do you know what ailment they are for?"

Athena went to the shelf and began to name each item. She described the spices, the plants, the lotions, the balms, each of the herb concoctions, and then named what aliment the item was intended to treat.

When she finished, she turned to Zita. "That is all I know."

Zita was astounded. *This one knows as much as her mother does, and more.*

The woman and the child both stood silently, gazing at each other.

Observing Zita, Athena began to see her. No longer did she observe a hunched-over old woman. *I see kindness and wisdom in her face, a gentle woman weathered by her years. Her graying hair is peeking out from under her light blue veil. Now her soft brown eyes are watching me. I see passion in them.*

Athena waited for Zita to speak.

"I know that you will go back to Harmonie in the spring—why would I want you to work here through the winter when I know you will leave?" Zita's words were firm.

"I want to be a healer like you. I know Mama has brought you herbs and spices from the east that cannot be found here in Rouen. One day, I want to sail to the Far East with the merchant Diego. I think there are many different spices and herbs that I want to bring here, and to gain knowledge that explain their uses."

Zita did not seem to hear Athena's words, a slight smile and twinkle in her eyes. "Athena, come with me to the back of the store."

Athena followed her and stopped where Zita began to light candles revealing a bed, shelves, and a small table with a cloth covering something hidden beneath. Zita stepped to the table and slowly lifted and folded the cloth, uncovering ancient parchments.

Athena's eyes widened. *What are these?*

Carefully showing the parchments to Athena, Zita said, "These are treasures worth more than gold, Athena. They will reveal much about your namesake … about you. This winter, you will read all this to me as you work within the shop each day you are here."

Athena was beaming with pride as she bid goodbye to Zita, promising she would return in the morning.

Opening the door to Ezra's house, she burst in, full of excitement and news.

"Mama, Zita is a kind old woman and she wants me to come back every day. I think she is just like the woman—Rose—in Marseilles you told me about."

Nichol smiled and reached out to hug her daughter.

Yes, Zita is like Rose; they are special women. Her presence in our lives—and now guiding Athena—is meant to be.

Athena could hardly contain her thoughts and feelings. "She showed me old parchments … I do not believe many people have seen them before. I could read the words, Mama, all of them, but some had meanings that I did not know. Zita carefully moved the top ones and then stopped at one that had my name at the top of it. *Athena.* The parchment was about me!"

"I know of the parchment. The *Lady* told me that they would be revealed to you someday to begin your learning of healing." Nichol's smile was full of pride.

At their evening meals the children talked about their daily activities: who they met; what they learned; and the work they had accomplished. Everything brought smiles to Nichol and Robert.

Nichol remembered her papa asking her at the end of a meeting or at the close of the day: "What have you learned today?" She decided that from that day forward, she would ask each of her children that question … and when she saw children in Harmonie, she would ask them as well: *What have you learned today?*

Bedtime would not be complete without a story, preferably from Ezra. His stories captivated all the children, even Aiden, who could already read and write.

"Granpapa Ezra, tell me about Granpapa Alexander fighting the pirates and the ships they sailed."

Ezra stood and blew out all but two candles and sat back down, his face in shadows. In a low voice, he began to speak.

"Your Granpapa Alexander was trusted by all the merchants. He was an honest man and made sure that those in need did not go hungry, especially the children. He taught your mama to care for many who were in need. His job as Port Commander was to keep order and to protect all the merchants from pirates and thieves.

"Many of the merchants had come to him for help. They told your Granpapa that a mean pirate was causing them great damage and harm. One had his ship stolen; many others had their ships raided. All the goods were taken and sold to other people. These wicked pirates harmed women and children. When the pirates came to Marseilles, no one was safe.

"Your Granpapa called several of the merchants to his villa. It was decided that they would go into the port area and asked at the inns and taverns where they were. Your granpapa told them there was one tavern where the worst men went and to start looking there.

"That night, your Granpapa Alexander and his men entered the tavern he named earlier. When they went in, the tavern smelled sour, like spilled beer and bitter pipe smoke. The only light came from guttering candles secured to the tables with melted wax. There was no fire burning in the hearth.

"The dim light created shadows, concealing the faces of the evil men. There, he found the worst pirate of all. His name was Trebilock and he was the pirate leader. That night, with great courage, Alexander and his men fought with the evil Trebilock and his pirates. Alexander and his men won, ending the thieving ways of the pirates forever.

"Another day, I will tell you more of the story. I can see your mama is signaling to stop … that it is time for bed."

All three children began to complain. "No … tell us more …"

Aiden turned to Nichol. "Mama, what happened to your papa? Why is he not here with us?"

Nichol spoke in a firm voice. "It is time for bed."

Once in bed, the children fell fast asleep, tired from their new apprenticeships and another story from Granpapa Ezra.

It was the best day ever.

fifty-one

Aiden, the Apprentice

Mama knows that the Lady is speaking to me at night.

It was early morning in Ezra and Helene's home.

Hearing a knock on the door, Robert peered out the hole in the door. It was Otto. Opening the door, Otto entered as he did every morning to escort Nichol throughout the day.

Aiden was sitting at the kitchen table that Robert had recently expanded by adding two planks of wood for more room. Lucette and Athena ate in a hurry, anxious to begin their apprenticeships. Between mouthfuls, they two girls jabbered excitedly about what they would be doing.

Aiden just stared at his bowl. Observing her children, Nichol noticed Aiden was quiet and in his own thoughts. She cleared her throat to get his attention.

Looking up, he noticed his mama smiling at him. "Aiden, do you have something you want to share with us?"

Aiden began to fidget on his stool. In an unsure voice, he began to speak.

"When I wake from dreams that I have, I remember being in the dream. They are as real as all of us sitting here together now. I do not know if they are of the past or things to come, Mama. I just see through my eyes different things that I remember when I wake. Last night, all of us were on a ship sailing to a distant land."

Nichol interrupted, "When did these dreams begin?"

"I have had them for a long time, but now they are becoming more real. At night as I fall asleep, they come to me, but not every night. As I close my eyes, I say to myself, *I am ready for my next adventure.*

"Two nights ago, I was in a battle. Now, I want to return to that dream."

Looking at Otto, he gave a hopeful grin. "I must talk to John or Otto on what to do to survive the battle."

Becoming more animated, Aiden kept speaking. "I like to tell stories. Some stories come from my dreams and sometimes new worlds just come to me. The dreams do not always feel like stories; I think they are real."

No one at the table moved. Even Lucette and Athena stopped talking to look at their brother.

Nichol sensed that something was stirring in her son—something that was different from the behaviors that Lucette and Athena displayed.

I know that the Lady is now guiding him.

"Lucette … Athena … Aiden … you are old enough now to learn that it is wise to measure your words when you speak out loud. Do not let your words make you stand out from others. Understand that you children act and think differently from many of the children here in Rouen. What you say and how you express yourself may be challenging to other children and adults as well."

Taking extra time to bid farewell to her daughters, Nichol turned to Aiden.

"I know that Papa has plans for you today. You have been working with him and Gideon for many months. You were his first apprentice. Now that you are here, he will expand what you have been doing. You will gain the skills to make swords and daggers that many people will want to buy. Go to his forge and he will bring food to have midday. Take Shadow with you."

Looking at both his parents, Aiden nodded his head and reached for his cloak as he opened the door to head out. *I want a dagger like Mama's and I will make one for my sister. I need to know how to master making daggers and swords. Mama knows that the Lady is speaking to me at night.*

Nichol turned to Otto. "Otto, you know that our children are different from many children, as I am different from most women. It is important to both Robert and I that you will have the same loyalty to them as you do to me. For the growth and survival of Harmonie, but also for their own."

Otto nodded. "The duke told me that you were different and important to him. I see that. And I also see how you protect others and the hamlet. My family now lives in Harmonie and I look forward to our return when winter passes. You and your family are important to me. I will protect you all."

"Thank you. I felt that you would."

Turning to Robert, she continued, "Take this food and go be with our son. I know that there is much truth to his dreams. I also feel Aiden's dreams are not just dreams. They are like the visions that the *Lady* gave to me as a young girl. The dreams continued when I escaped after my papa was murdered.

"We need to have an ongoing conversation with him every day. It was something I didn't have and having someone to talk to would have clarified much to me. We both need to know what he is hearing, feeling, and thinking."

Thoughtfully, Robert murmured, for Nichol's ears only. "Who would have thought that Aiden would be like Lucette and Athena, created from the two of us the way our daughters were? I believe that the *Lady* made sure that Marie was desperate and distraught on the road so that we would find her and the newborn baby boy. Aiden was meant for us. I am sure of it—our son."

As she heard his words, Nichol knew that what he said was true.

Reaching for his hand, she smiled. "We have a special family, Robert. It is a gift."

fifty-two

The Family

Children … my papa always asked me when we sat down for supper,
'What did you learn today?'

There was a different feeling in the house as they sat down for their supper that evening. Helene had created a pottage with fresh fish and vegetables. She had taken bread crusts she got from the bakery, warmed them, and broken them on top of each bowl.

The seven of them—Nichol, Robert, their children, Helene, and Ezra—were hungry. Of course, Shadow was hungry, too.

Glancing around the table, Ezra looked at each of their faces and a smile spread across his face. "My family … this is what Helene and I always wanted," he said as he lifted the bowl to his lips to drink the delicious broth.

"Helene and I are excited that you each have apprenticeships. We would like to hear what you are learning. What do you like? Is there anything that surprised you as Zita, Hubert, and Robert worked with you?"

Aiden could hardly contain himself as Ezra posed his questions. With a twinkle in his eye, Ezra turned to him. "Aiden … how about you? What did you do today?"

"Papa taught me about the bellows and how to use them. I learned how to keep the coals hot so that whatever Papa or Vilfred were working on would be at the right heat. Today, we made nails." As he said that, he proudly placed three nails on the table. "Papa said that we will need many more to build the houses in Harmonie this summer."

"My turn … my turn!" Athena burst out. "I made something special with Zita today. We took dried berries and dropped them into hot water. I added a little honey and waited for a little time to blend the flavors. Zita called it Athena's Brew. It warmed me inside and tasted good. I wanted more. I think that we could offer it at Timo's next fair and I think people will buy it."

"Oh my, Athena. You are like your mama," Ezra said with a chuckle. "A merchant we did not know about!" Everyone laughed, including Athena.

Nichol turned to Lucette. "And what did you learn from your day?" she asked.

A serious look settled on her face. "Hubert is not well. I must keep it warm for him in his shop so he is more comfortable and not cold. I gathered firewood to keep the fire going and will do that each day. He was grateful for the food I brought and I will do it every day. I will bring extra so he has something to eat before I come the next day. He taught me about different woods today and which wood would be best for Mama's arrows. I plan on making many for her. He seemed happier when I left."

Looking at her daughter, Nichol reached out and touched her hand.

"You have learned how important it is to take care of others when they can no longer do it for themselves. Thank you for doing that for Hubert."

She then turned to her other children.

"Athena, Zita is old as well. Listen closely to her words. She has much wisdom to pass on to you with her knowledge of herbs. Creating a warm brew like you did will be welcomed in our home and I think in many others as you share. She may have some herbs that would help Hubert now. Ask her when you are there in the morning."

Aiden knew that his mama was coming to him next.

I will tell her this has been my best day. I like working closely with Papa and just being all together as we are now.

"Aiden, Papa has much to teach you. You will be an expert in so many things."

Her eyes meeting Robert's, she added, "He's not just good at nails and horseshoes, he is a craftsman and a goldsmith. One thing I cherish is the special seating with armrests he made for me when you children were babies, and the seats in front of our house in Harmonie. What is created in his mind and comes from his hands is beautiful and will be desired by many.

"Children … my papa always asked me when we sat down for supper, 'What did you learn today?' I learned much from each of you. which pleases your papa and I, as well as Granpapa and Granmama.

"I think that, at the end of each day, we will promise each other that we will always share what was learned during the day. And that includes everyone, not just the children."

Around the table, seven heads nodded. Shadow barked, as if to agree.

fifty-three

Ezra and Helene

As Helene spoke,
Ezra felt the strength in her words and decision.

In the morning before Otto arrived and without being told to get up, the children were up, washed and dressed for the day. They were seated at the kitchen table and chattering, excited about what the day would offer. Robert and Nichol watched them as their bowls were emptied quickly.

Lucette packed boiled eggs in the shell, bread, salted fish, and cheese with Helene's guidance. When Athena and Aiden saw the food being packed, they wanted the same. Aiden asked, "Would you make packs for Athena and me, too?"

Before another word was said, Helene gave them a cloth like Lucette's filled with their food. "When your mama first traveled to Paris by herself, she had made a pack with Timo's help. She wore this pack on her back to carry things so her arms were free. I will make each of you children one so that you will be able to carry food and other items every day, just like your mama did."

Lucette was the first to respond to Helene's words. "Granmama … we would all like that." As she spoke, the other two nodded *yes* at the same time.

Helene and Ezra joined Nichol at the table, while Robert took Shadow for a walk.

Without a word from Robert, Shadow headed to the butcher down the street. Along the way, merchants would come to their door or rise from their tables and greet the two before they reached the butcher shop. Shadow was well known.

"Hello Shadow …. I saved a huge bone for you this morning," the butcher said as they entered his door. When Robert returned, Shadow had a large bone in her mouth, her tail happily wagging as she settled at the open door with her prize. The meat had already been gnawed off.

Hugs were given to all as the children left, with Robert and Aiden out first to join Vilfred at his forge shop. Nichol planned to escort Lucette and Athena to Hubert's and Zita's. Otto arrived just as they were leaving.

Nichol turned to Ezra and Helene. "Otto and I are going to meet with the duke this morning. Then from the castle, we will go to the warehouse."

"I will meet you there," Ezra replied to her. "We have much to discuss before you go back to Harmonie."

Ezra shut the door behind Nichol as their family left for the day. Ezra turned to Helene and he watched her facial expression change from joy to despair, then her eyes welled in tears.

"What am I to do when they leave?"

He heard the pain in her words as he went to her and they embraced. "They are my life. You have your merchant business, and I have Nichol, Robert and the children."

Ezra moved back and placed his hands on her arms. "Is it time for you to go with them to Harmonie and make that your home? That is where you are needed. Watching you with the children this morning, it is not just the children. Nichol and Robert need you as well. I will miss them and especially you, my wife."

Helene's words were slow but filled with certainty.

"Dinah has told me that she wants to go to Harmonie to be with Gideon. Raisa has said she wants to work with Achim at the E & N warehouse. Gunvor and Tova will be in Harmonie as well.

"I think Harmonie is now where I belong. There is much to do with the children and Nichol has told me about the expansion planned for Harmonie House. I am part of that as well. I will miss you, but I will come back to Rouen with them when they return after the harvest."

As Helene spoke, Ezra felt the strength in her words and decision.

"Yes, this will be our new plan. It will be good for all. I will talk to Achim this morning and you can talk to Dinah and tell her that I thought that you should go to Harmonie when she goes."

Reaching for her hands, he said, "Now, let the two of us sit at the table. There is much more to talk about this morning. Would you make Athena's Brew for us?"

Helene hugged Ezra and softly said, "You have charmed me from the first day."

Getting up from her stool, she kissed him and moved to heat the water for the special mixture of dried berries and honey that Athena had collected and kept in a bowl just for her concoction.

She brought two cups of brew to the table and sat across from him.

Ezra took a sip and smiled with approval. "Never could I imagine when Robert and Nichol came to our door in Paris that it would lead to us sitting at this table in Rouen. I think they saved us. Then, all I could think of being was a merchant and moneylender. Now I think about you, our family, and being together. Never had I dreamed when the two arrived that they would create a new community and be protected by the duke.

"Marie, Olaf, and Achim are not only managing the warehouse, but they also go from shop to shop and take care of what the owners' needs are. The last time Diego sailed in, they gave him a list of things needed in Rouen and now even as far away as

Paris. Other merchants have placed orders from them and now Raisa wants to become a merchant. When Joshua is not used as a messenger, he wants to help; he understands the moneylending business. It is a family business and soon—maybe this summer or fall—I will step away and join you in Harmonie."

Helene reached across the table and placed her hands on his. "Ezra, you remember when we were fleeing Paris from the bad Priest Loupe and the church?"

She paused to express the emotion she felt. "I have tried to express what I saw, my true feelings I had at that moment, but words failed me. All I could think was how could all of this happened? We had a good life in Paris. I had women friends. We had plenty of coin that you shared with others."

She stopped to find her words to continue, and then revealed, " I wondered if Nichol had tricked us with this runaway scheme. I felt frightened and afraid."

Tears were forming in Helene's eyes. She squeezed Ezra's hand and continued to speak. "After my experience with her at the cottage, when she was suddenly attacked, she showed the kind of power in a woman … or a man … that I have never seen before. She stopped the two men who had come to kill her. She and Shadow saved my life and hers. And now I know, she has guided and saved us all. The *Lady* is at her side, and now ours.

"When my eyes saw the valley for the first time that would become Harmonie, it was as though a spirit entered me. I have never before felt so at peace and filled with joy as I did at that moment. My fear disappeared as my eyes and heart spoke to me.

"Nichol's courage with her baby and now another she has embraced as her own led us to that valley. She protected us from the bad Priest Loupe and now Lord Charles. Eventually, she befriended Emma and her brother Duke Richard and his wife,

Duchess Judith. Nichol has done what few men have done—never a woman. She is who she is. She does not lie or deceive others.

"I want to be with her, Ezra, all the time. And with Robert and the children. I want to be part of their lives, no matter what danger may come."

"Helene, your words make me want to leave for Harmonie with you." Pausing, he pondered her words, then added, "I know that Lucette, Aiden, and Athena are different from other children … and I think they are special, in the same way their mother is special. It would be wise for you to be there to help the children temper their impulses.

"We must be alert whenever the church is involved or tries to reach out. It demands the complete control of what people think or do. It controls and rules through fear and hate. Anyone who thinks or says something different than their doctrine will be swiftly dealt with. It is clear to me—and I believe Duke Richard— the church fears Nichol. Eventually, it will see that the children are like her and should be feared as well.

"The only reason Harmonie safely exists today is because of Nichol's relationship with the duke and the personal protection he provides with the bodyguard he assigned her. Nichol has told me that Otto desires to join his wife and children and live in Harmonie so he can be with family and protect her as well. With her vision of Harmonie and the duke's coffers expanding with the money produced from the goods Harmonie sells, the duke will continue to support her."

The two went silent, both deep in their thoughts.

Then Ezra said, "How long the calm we have now will last, no one knows. But, with Nichol and the *Lady*, we will always side with them."

fifty-four

The Duke

Only let in people you know.

Nichol and Otto began their walk to the duke's castle with Lucette, Athena, and Shadow scampering ahead of them.

The first stop was at Hubert's shop. Nichol hugged and kissed Lucette before she entered. Then on to Zita's shop, where Nichol gave Athena coins to spend on herbs and berries to buy for her new brew.

When Athena opened the door, Nichol signaled for Shadow to follow her daughter. Athena gave her mama a hug goodbye; then she entered and shut the door behind her.

Continuing to the castle, Nichol noticed Otto's cheerful mood. Nichol took his arm and looked at him as they walked. "Your usual morning scowl has disappeared. What pleases you this morning?"

A smile appeared through his unkempt beard. "Soon we will leave for Harmonie, where Gabrielle and my sons wait for me."

Before they turned the last corner with the castle in view, Nichol murmured to Otto, "We are all alone on the street; everyone has disappeared."

Otto turned around and glared at a man behind them, His eyes narrowed with a chilling stare and he spoke loudly, "Why are you following us?"

The man stopped and stared back at them.

"How long has he been following us?" Nichol asked.

"Since I arrived at Ezra's this morning, I wanted him closer so I could question him, but he has stayed far away. Now he is just behind us."

Nichol looked over her shoulder and then faced ahead.

In an urgent voice, she whispered to Otto, "There are two more in front looking directly at us as they approach. I will take my dagger to the one behind us … you take the two in front."

Now standing back-to-back with Nichol, Otto pulled his sword and knife at the same time. With a sinister smile, he shouted, "I am going to enjoy killing both of you, but first I am going to skin you alive!"

Fear gripped one man. Eyes wide and mouth agape, he turned and ran. The other hesitated for a moment and then followed.

Otto turned back to the man behind them, now lying on his back with Nichol's dagger half-buried in his shoulder. Her foot was braced on the wrist of the man's arm, with his hand still holding a knife. She glared at him.

Otto approached and placed the tip of his sword on his chest. The man winced in pain. "What shall we do with him?"

Nichol looked around. "Otto, there are people in the street watching us. They went inside when they saw the men because they knew there would be trouble. The duke will hear about this, so we must be the first to tell what happened before rumors and gossip start."

Otto thought for a moment. "The dagger will make him tell us the truth. Shall we drag him to the castle and he can tell the duke who sent him?" Nichol nodded.

As the two of them neared the castle's outer gate, bearing their burden, they could see Victor was surrounded by vendors and suppliers, and a lord who wanted to be heard by the duke. When they drew closer, heads turned toward them.

Otto yelled, "Move aside! We must see the duke!"

Once the waiting people saw Otto and Nichol dragging a man moaning in pain, begging someone to remove the dagger from his shoulder, they gave way and let them pass. Victor immediately opened the gate for them to enter.

Once inside, their commotion brought everyone in the castle to them. Upon their entry into the hall, Richard stood as they approached.

Nichol and Otto dropped the man at his feet.

"This man tried to kill me. There were two men with him that Otto chased away. If Otto had not been with me, I would be dead."

Richard's anger was apparent. "I know that dagger. It belongs to you, Nichol."

"Yes, he came at us from behind and two others appeared in front. When I turned to confront him, he rushed me with his knife. I had to stop him and I threw my dagger at his shoulder, not his heart. I wanted to know who sent those men. The two in front did not want to fight Otto and they fled."

She nudged the man with her toe. "He will talk before he loses all his blood."

Nichol felt her anger building, along with her fear for her children.

What if who planned this know where they are? What if they have been taken or hurt?

With her face flushed, she turned to the duke. "I must go to my children who are unguarded and make sure they have not been harmed. I will return as soon as I know they are safe."

Nichol turned and ran out of the castle. Surprising Victor at the gate, she shouted at him as she ran by, "I will be back."

She went to Zita's first. When she entered, Shadow was lying down and Athena was reading to Zita. The soft light Nichol recognized moved past her daughter's shoulders and into the street.

Both Zita and Athena saw that Nichol was rushed and out of breath. Athena rose and said, "Mama, we are well and safe here. And I know that Lucette and Aiden are as well."

Relieved with her daughter's words, Nichol crouched down so that her eyes met her daughter's steady gaze. She knew that Athena had spoken the truth.

Standing, she turned to Zita. "Only let in people you know. Secure the door when I leave. I will return to walk Athena home along with Lucette."

Before Zita could ask what had caused her to suddenly appear at her shop, Nichol turned and left. She ran a short distance to Hubert's shop.

When Nichol entered, Lucette, holding the bow she was working on, was surprised to see her. "Mama, I have more work on the shaft of this bow before I go. I am safe; do not worry."

Nichol pulled her up from the stool where she sat and held her for a moment. "Do not let anyone in before I return."

Feeling her mother quiver, Lucette asked in a broken voice, "Mama what is wrong?"

"Nothing that I cannot handle. I know that both of you are safe. I see that the light has been with both you and Athena. I will come back for you. Do not leave until then."

She left Lucette and began slowly walking back to the castle.

Looking back at the shop, she noticed a shaft of light flow in the window opening.

They are safe. I should have known that the Lady would not let harm come to them. I need to guide my children to be aware—always—of their surroundings. When we return to Harmonie, John and Otto will begin to train them on how to defend themselves when in danger.

Still in deep thought, her pace began to pick up along with her anger.

The assassins were after me, not my family. Robert and Aiden are safe, too. I was careless. Soon those responsible will feel my wrath.

Now at the castle's outer gate, she nodded to Victor as he waved for her to pass.

At the castle door, she lifted and dropped the knocker until there was an answer. Steward Thomas opened the door and told her that she was expected in the Great Hall.

When she entered the hall, all eyes turned to her. Walking down the center of the hall, her eyes did not leave the man lying on the floor, the dagger still in his shoulder. She stopped next to Otto and Richard.

Otto was kneeling next to the man. Duke Richard stood over him.

Nichol looked at Richard. "Is he dead?"

"Yes. We must go to the solar. There I will reveal what Otto and I heard him say."

Nichol bent over, pulled out the dagger, and wiped it on his tunic.

Richard then told Otto, "Take him outside but do not bury him. Tonight, you are going to visit the tavern where others like him gather."

When both were seated in the solar, Richard spoke first.

"You are a Lady Baron Nichol and an advisor to me. The people who brought this attack on you knew this. This was not just an attack on you but on my authority as duke. When questioned, the man's last words were that there was a bounty on you, not your family."

Nichol did not hesitate. "What if my children were with me?"

"I, too, live with the knowledge that one day I will be attacked. It is what we do here today that puts an end to the one behind the attack. My spies tell me that Lord Charles has many armed men and needs coin to pay for them. I know he has talked openly about rebellion to other nobles. One day I fear that he will challenge me with a surprise attack and that day may come soon. I must put an end to this now before an army is at my castle gate. You have made Harmonie desirable and he wants the taxes that Harmonie brings to my coffers."

Both sat in quiet contemplation.

Eight years have passed; it must end. I will find the evil Loupe. I know he is involved in what happened today. When I find him, I will put my dagger through his heart.

Richard broke the silence. "I heard that Lord Charles had a spy living in Harmonie. I did not give it much thought until now."

Nichol glared at him in disbelief. "What!? You have never told me this!"

"Nichol, we all have spies. That is how we know if there is tyranny at play. You are my spy when you see people and tell me what their true motives are. It has been years since I told Lord Charles that you were Lady Nichol Baron of Harmonie and I thought that he would obey my authority.

"I must now confront him. I will send a messenger to him that demands he come before me within ten days to explain his actions against you, or I will send men to bring him here. I want you to see and hear him from a hidden position."

That evening Otto put the man's corpse into a cart. Along with three other armed men, he visited the tavern where he knew the dead man and the two other men drank.

Otto opened the door and the dead man was brought in and propped up on a stool against a wall. Without a word said, Otto walked through the smoky tavern with a knife in hand. He stopped moving in front of a man with his head hanging down.

Looking at each person in turn, he began walking again until he was back at the door. With his knife, he pointed to the man where he stopped and gestured to the men with him.

"Take him."

Otto was the last to leave. He stopped at the door and turned around and pointed his knife to the dead man. "He will stay there for five days. If he is not there when I return in five days, another will take his place. Which one of you will it be?"

When they entered Ezra and Helene's home late that afternoon, all were quiet. Helene and Nichol's eyes met, and Nichol shook her head.

"We will talk when Ezra returns."

When Ezra returned from the warehouse, everyone, including the children, were sitting around the table. Nichol said, "Sit down and hear of my day."

Bewildered, Ezra moved to the table and sat down as instructed. The children were seated between Robert and Helene.

Nichol began her story from the moment the men approached her and Otto on the street. At the point where she threw the dagger and hit the man in the shoulder, Helene began to shake her head.

"Nichol, let us talk of this when they sleep …"

"No, Helene. They are old enough to know the world they live in. Not to tell them of these things will put them in danger."

Turning to her children, she said, "When you return to Harmonie, your training will become more intense. This training will help you flourish and grow strong with the demands that will be placed on you. Only then will you be ready for what is coming. Each of you has many of my skills. Your papa and I want to make sure you can use what you are best at whenever your skill is needed."

She took a deep breath.

"My children … my family. All will be well. You will thrive with your new skills. I want you to remember that the *Lady* has been with you since birth. The training that you will begin when we return to Harmonie is the same training that my papa had me begin when I was twelve years of age. It will make you stronger. You will learn how to defend yourself as a warrior would do. And you will learn how to anticipate threats. John and Otto will be your teachers.

"Your training will begin with this: everywhere you go, you will run. Your legs will get strong, stronger than most men's. As you run, your breathing will carry you further than before."

Nichol smiled as she felt their excitement and joy.

As she looked at her children, her eyes stopped on Aiden's young face.

I see him … this is what he has been waiting for.

"Now tell me what you did and learned today."

Excited, all three of them began to talk at once.

fifty-five

The Sword

Otto pulled his sword in one hand and a knife in the other.

The next morning Robert was the first up, lighting candles and stirring the embers of the night's fire before adding wood. A routine had been established to feed the children and prepare them for their apprenticeships.

A knock on the door was followed by a familiar voice. "It is me, Otto …"

Robert opened the door and let Otto in along with a gust of winter air.

"What brings you to our door this early, Otto?"

"The duke … last night I went to a tavern. The men who attacked us yesterday were there, drinking. One that I chased away yesterday was there. I cornered him and dragged him out. He will be taken to the duke this morning. I believe Nichol and I should be there when this man is brought before the duke."

Hearing Otto's voice, Nichol started down the stairs to the kitchen where he was speaking to Robert in a voice that carried alarm in it. Aiden got to the kitchen first. He, too, heard Otto's voice and was excited to see him.

First to the kitchen, he had a wooden sword in his hand. He gave a challenging look at Otto. Otto pulled his sword in one hand and a knife in the other. Aiden lunged and placed his sword on Otto's belly.

"Do you yield?"

"Yes. Let us eat first, then we fight."

"Otto, I want a real sword and knife like you have."

Nichol heard her son clearly and spoke directly to him. "When we get to Harmonie, you will get your sword."

Then she turned to Otto. "I told the children what happened yesterday."

The room was flooded with conversation when everyone had gathered in the kitchen.

Otto said, "Nichol, we found one of the men who attacked us as we walked to the castle. The duke wants us present when he questions him. On our way to the castle, I will tell you what I have learned about him."

"I told everyone about the attack. You may speak freely about it."

"Even the children?"

"They are old enough to know the world they live in … my world. It is one that I wished they did not have to deal with."

"That explains his challenge of me with his wooden sword." Otto relaxed, then smiled. "That boy is going to be a warrior. I will teach him."

Seeing that children were eating, Helene had joined them. Nichol asked her if she would make sure that their noon meal was ready for them to take.

Helene, too, was aware of the world that Nichol had brought to them and why Otto was here. Nodding to her, she said, "Go now, Nichol. I will take care of all their needs."

Aiden heard his mother's words. "Papa … I do not want to wait. Can we begin to make my sword here, before we return to Harmonie?"

Looking at his son, Robert placed his hand on his shoulder. "After we have finished our morning's work, we can select from the metal I have. Vilfred will assist me as it is made. Your job will be to make sure the coals are hot enough to hammer the metal."

fifty-six

The Duke

Why did he want the woman killed?

Entering the Great Hall, they sat down on one of the benches as they waited for Duke Richard to arrive. Moments later, Richard entered, consumed in thought.

He passed them without notice. They stood and bowed as he passed by.

The man that Otto had taken from the tavern was brought in and led up to the throne. His hands were bound behind his back and escorted by a guard on either side as he walked the length of the Great Hall. Stopping in front of the throne, the guards pushed the man to his knees.

Richard glared at the man dressed in rags. "Tell me why I should not take you to the gallows this morning."

Shaking and in a quivering voice, the man replied, "I needed coin and was not told what I was to do. When I saw Otto and that woman, I knew what was expected of me and I ran. I was not told of Otto. If I had, I would have known that we could not defeat him."

Still glaring at the man on his knees, Richard's eyes narrowed and both his hands clenched tight. "Look at me when I speak! You were sent to kill a woman. Her name is Nichol and she is standing by you. Look at her! Now tell me—who paid you?"

The man turned and looked up at Nichol. In tears, his voice shaking, he began to relate the story of the man who hired him.

"Speak up," Richard demanded. "I want his name and maybe I will spare your life."

"Ulric. He is the man that hired us, and when I returned to the tavern last night he was not there."

"Why did he want the woman killed?"

"Ulric was the messenger. The one who wanted her killed was a priest."

A priest? What priest is involved … could my brother be tangled in this?

Richard leaned forward, becoming increasingly annoyed. His neck veins tightened and his face became a ruddy red. He shouted, "I want the truth, which is the only way you can escape the gallows! Did you see this priest? Did he speak to you? Does this priest have a name? Does he frequent the taverns?"

The man was now trembling. In a shaky, lowered voice, he whimpered, "I do not know the priest's name. Ulric said that the priest pays him to do his bidding."

Furious with what he heard, Richard stood. "Take him away and put him in chains."

When the man had been removed from the Great Hall, he said to Otto, "You did well, Otto. Nichol's advice for me has been wise in the past and will be going forward as well. Her safety is important to me and to the duchess, who asked to see her before she leaves the castle.

"Given what happened yesterday, and on the ship to England, you can see why she needs added eyes and ears on her behalf, to keep her safe. I am aware of your family. It now makes sense for them to live in Harmonie as you have already done."

Otto could not believe what he just heard the duke say.

His wife Gabrielle and his boys all preferred to live in Harmonie now that they were there.

"Your Grace, the men in Harmonie will help to build a home for us since my travels with Nichol takes me away often when we are in Rouen."

Amused with the conversation of the two men and knowing that Otto and his family desired to live in Harmonie before the move was made, Nichol said, "You and your family will be welcomed in Harmonie, Otto. I think the duke was wise to encourage their move."

The duke was pleased with the idea of Otto staying closer to Nichol. Using Nichol's Joshua also as a messenger, he felt that he needed to do all he could to protect himself, and others in his circle, from possible betrayals.

"Remember, Otto, you cannot fail me in your protection of Nichol here and in Harmonie. Wait for her at the gate. I need to talk with her privately now and Judith wishes to see her."

Standing, he said, "Nichol, follow me to my solar."

The duke beckoned to the steward who stood close by. "Tell the duchess that Nichol will come to her in her chambers. I will bring her there after I end my meeting with her."

Nichol followed Richard to his solar and pulled the chair just in front of his desk. Richard sat down and stared at the documents in front of him.

She waited for him to speak first, his anger still apparent.

Richard looked up at Nichol. "I have been told by others, whose names I will not reveal, that you pose a danger to me and I must rid Normandy of you. At first I did not dispute that idea. They also said that you were a witch and that you have beguiled me."

He paused with a smile, though Nichol could see it was strained.

"Emma would have wanted me to send you away, to her. Then, I observed your power to see others' true desires. I also learned that you do not lust for power. It made me think they were envious of you. Others feared you.

"Now, Lord Charles wants the riches of Harmonie. He is a little man who will destroy anything in his path to get what he wants. The Priest Loupe is the perfect man to help him achieve his purpose. He thinks because he is a priest, he is without blame for his actions. He cannot hide behind the veil of the church, nor my brother, the archbishop. I will speak to my brother and make the bad priest his problem.

"I will also send men to find this Ulric and bring him before me. He will be reluctant to talk but we will discover who is behind this. I want to know who the spies are among us."

Richard laughed and added, "These are weak men who fear you as they should."

Nichol waited for the duke to pause. "You are right. Loupe is a bad priest and has chased and threatened me and my family for more than ten years. I will make him disappear."

Richard shook his head. "You cannot do that. I will tell you what the archbishop decides about him. I will send a dispatch to Charles through Joshua, which compels him to appear here in one week. If he does not, I will send armed men to bring him here.

"When he is here in front of me, I want you to observe him from a hidden position. Find Joshua and tell him to be ready today to leave and deliver a dispatch to Charles. He must also wait for Charles' reply."

Nichol was troubled. "What if he takes Joshua's life?"

"He will not. The dispatch states that if Joshua does not return in six days, I will send an army to bring him in front of me or destroy him. It will be his choice."

fifty-seven

Judith

Why do you ask? Do I look ill?

Leaving the duke's solar, Nichol let her mind drift to Duchess Judith.

A smile appeared on her face as an image appeared to her.

I know that she will have a baby girl before summer passes.

As she left the main castle, she felt the rays of the sun on her face. Voices of boys could be heard. Letting her eyes scan the winter garden, her gaze landed on two boys, both younger but one close to Aiden's height.

On a bench wrapped in a cloak of fine red wool from Harmonie was their mother—the duchess. Her smile broadening, Nichol raised her arm in greeting and said a loud hello.

The duchess turned toward the voice and her smile matched Nichol's in return.

Moving toward the seated figured, Nichol reached out her hand to her and said, "How are you feeling, Judith?"

Surprised by the question, she responded, "Why do you ask? Do I look ill?"

"No … I just know that when a woman is with child, there is sometimes a feeling of tiredness. I saw the glow on your face when I stepped out of the castle that told me …"

"With another child? Me?" The duchess was speechless.

"Yes. And now that I am near you, I believe you will have a daughter before summer ends, in August.

"A daughter?" Judith let her hand drop to her belly. "I had a different feeling this morning when I woke. I thought it was from

what we ate last night. Now, I know it is something wonderful …
a daughter I can hold in my arms."

"Yes, a daughter for you and the duke."

Nichol's face lit up. She said, "The activities in Harmonie
will be many as we start our harvesting for the coming fall after
your baby comes. Much of it will be brought to Rouen, but I have
a thought. The duke has told me that he goes to Fécamp often.
And he has mentioned coming to Harmonie to see what his land
is producing. Why don't you come as well? And why don't you
bring your children?"

As Nichol mentioned the word "children," she sensed the
boys moving toward her.

"Come, my sons. Give greetings to the Lady Baron Nichol and
give her your blessing. She is someone special to me and your papa."

With that invitation, the boys crowded closer to the two women.

Nichol turned to the tallest and said, "My son is as tall as you
are. You must be Richard, the third. And you must be Robert. That
is the same name of my husband and the father of my children:
Aiden, Lucette, and Athena.

"I come to the castle often to meet with your father. When I
am in Rouen, I bring my children and I stay with my uncle when
I am here. My home is in a hamlet called Harmonie. Much of
what we grow and produce comes to Rouen for people who live
here to buy and eat.

"You grow food for us to eat?" asked young Robert.

"Yes … and we bring fresh honey, too and some of the spices
that your cook uses. Do you remember having honey on your
bread?"

This time, young Richard responded. "I remember Papa saying
that it was made on land that he owns."

"What you heard your papa say is correct. We have many bees that make the honey in our hamlet. Then we bring it to Rouen so you can eat it on your bread."

When Nichol said that, Richard said to his mama, "I want to see how bees make honey. Can I?"

Smiling at her sons, Judith said, "We may do that this summer if your papa brings us all to Fécamp. Would you like that?"

When the boys heard their mother's words, they started running around the garden and shouting, "We are going to see the bees!"

Both women began laughing.

Judith turned to Nichol again, her hand over her belly. "Are you sure I am to have a daughter?" she asked.

Taking her friend's hand, Nichol responded, "Yes. I believe you will name her Adelais.

"Now I must leave, Duchess. I promised Ezra I would meet him at the warehouse at the dock to talk about the incoming shipments that will soon arrive. Are there any silks or spices you would like me to bring you after the ships are unloaded? I can arrange for you to see them with Ezra before they are taken out to the merchants here for selling. You can pick what you would like and he will make sure you get what you have selected.

"I will come to see the duke again before I leave for Harmonie. If the opportunity arises, I will mention bringing you and the boys to Harmonie with him."

As Nichol stood, Judith rose with her. She reached out to Nichol and hugged her. "You have made me very happy."

fifty-eight

Lord Charles' Threat

Bring them to the castle at once. We must prepare.

Six days had passed.

Joshua returned, riding past Rouen's outer wall and into Rouen, coming back after delivering Duke Richard's demands to Lord Charles. He went directly to Ezra's and pounded on the door. "It is Joshua …"

Helene opened the door immediately. "Is Nichol here?"

"No, Joshua, she walked with Lucette and Athena to their apprenticeships. She should be back soon. You look in need of food and rest."

"There is no time for that. I must go and deliver a message from Lord Charles to the duke."

As soon as he said that, he turned to see Nichol approaching the open door with Otto close behind. His clothes and his exhausted face told of the urgency of his message and his hard travel.

"I must deliver Lord Charles' reply to Duke Richard at once," was all that came out of his mouth.

Nichol heard his words and did not argue. Joshua mounted his horse and gave her his hand. Otto offered his closed hands for her to step on, lifting her up behind Joshua. Joshua turned his horse as Otto gave it a slap on its rear.

"I will meet you at the castle."

Joshua turned his head to Nichol, speaking over his shoulder. "I carry Lord Charles' response. I believe he will be at the castle before the week's end, mayhap sooner. I carry a word of warning to the duke that may not be in Charles' dispatch."

They rode through the gate and past Victor, who gestured them through, and dismounted at the castle door.

After knocking, Joshua turned to Nichol, "When I was handed the dispatch, at the same time, I saw many armed men gathering."

Thomas answered the door. He took one look and said, "Duke Richard is in the Great Hall."

Side by side, they approached Duke Richard and Duchess Judith eating at the table. Instantly, Richard and Judith turned their attention to Nichol and Joshua. The duke saw Joshua's state of dishevelment and the fatigue on his face.

With the parchment message in hand, Joshua stopped in front of the duke. He bowed, said "Your Grace," handed the parchment to the duke, and backed away.

Richard turned on his stool and yelled, "I need more candles to read this dispatch!" Then he turned to Joshua and Nichol, studied their faces, and said, "Sit down. I see the message still has the seal but your faces tell a story. What news do you bring to me that is not in this message?"

"Your Grace, I have delivered messages for many years and always have been asked the same question upon my return. When I told his steward that I had a dispatch from you, he tried to take it from me. I told him that I was to deliver it only to Lord Charles. They took my knife and I was escorted to him by two armed guards. I approached Lord Charles, knelt before him, and said, 'My Lord' as I handed the dispatch to him." Joshua paused in thought. "Do I have your permission to freely speak my mind?"

His impatience obvious, Richard gestured for him to continue.

"Your Grace, when I tried to stand, the guards pulled their knives and pushed me to my knees. I thought that they were going to kill me. Lord Charles read your message and raised his hand in the air—I think to keep them from killing me. I delivered this message wondering if I would survive. If luck blessed me, I wanted to observe the lands as I approached his heavily guarded castle.

"The condition of the farms and the people revealed to me that his taxes and the churches' tithes were more than his tenants could bear. When I entered his compound, his men were heavily armed, as though they were preparing for a battle. I was led back outside and was given his response … the parchment I have now given to you. I have a feeling that evil is in his heart and also with the men that surround him."

Candles were brought to the table and lit. After careful inspection of the wax seal, he then opened the parchment. His eyes moved back and forth as he read. Anticipation gripped those present, waiting for his reaction.

Richard put the parchment on the table, and calmly asked, "Joshua, how many armed men did you see when you left?"

"Many—maybe fifty, even more. I left as soon as I got his message."

The duke turned to Nichol. With urgency in his voice, he said, "Bring your family here … now."

Alarmed with his tone and response, she asked, "Are they going to Harmonie? Should I not be headed there?"

"No, he is coming here. It is Harmonie that he covets."

"I will gather many arrows and bows and bring them here as well. My daughter has learned to make them. My son will bring more swords that he and his father have made at the forge."

Otto was now standing next to Richard. "Otto, have Victor shut and secure the outer gate and alert the castle guard for what might come. You know of the men in Rouen that pledged fealty to me. Bring them to the castle at once. We must prepare."

Richard stood, as did everyone. "This man questions my authority over lands I own."

Turning to see Thomas standing next to him, he ordered, "Go to Archbishop William with what you have heard. I want him here with his guard when Charles arrives.

"His land was a gift from my father. If he continues to defy me, I will take the land away and put him in chains, ending his drive for power … and maybe him."

Next, he turned to his wife.

"Judith, find your finest clothes for Nichol. She will stand next to me as we look down on this greedy little man. We will be ready for whatever he brings. I want men posted far from the town walls to bring word of his approach, as soon as he is in sight."

fifty-nine

Preparing for Battle

We can send him home or to the gallows.
His actions will be his choice.

Robert and the children were brought to the castle. They came with a wagon filled with swords, bows, and many arrows.

Roger had weapons as well and stayed with Ezra and Helene in their home. Throughout the afternoon and into the night, Duke Richard's men at arms began to arrive, answering his call. Food was brought and preparation was made to repel any assault by Lord Charles.

With the first morning light, the castle door opened. Richard appeared and stood for a moment in the opening. More than one hundred men of Rouen answered his call, and more were coming. All turned to him and dropped, bending their knees. Calls of "Your Grace" were heard, followed by cheers and shouts of praise.

Richard raised his hand to silence the men. "I received a message from Lord Charles yesterday. He has challenged my authority, given to me by God. My father gave his father land and it seems he is not satisfied and wants more. He wants this castle and Rouen. Those of you who know him know that he treats the peasants poorly. None of you want this for you and your families.

"His threat is real. Soon, Charles will be here with many men. We can send him home or to the gallows. His actions will decide his fate."

Shouts of fealty were heard. Richard stepped down from the door landing and walked among them, exchanging words of praise.

Food and water were brought and placed on a table that had been stationed inside the castle's courtyard.

A galloping horse's hooves pounding the stone road got louder and louder as the horse and rider approached the gate. A man posted on the wall yelled, "Rider coming!"

The men quickly silenced their voices.

Richard yelled, "Open the gate!"

The rider was one of the sentry guards returning with word of Lord Charles' approach.

Entering the gate, he leaped off his horse and approached Richard.

"Men with arms are coming this way, Your Grace; twenty on horseback and maybe one hundred armed marching men. There are no supply wagons following. They are half a day away."

Duke Richard held his hand up again to silence his men. "Lord Charles is on his way and plans to lay waste to Rouen in support of his ruthless desires. He wants to destroy what we have … and to harm all of you and your families."

Turning to Otto standing next to him, he ordered, "Send men to warn the inns and taverns to stay vigilant. Be ready to bar their doors. We will use war horns to warn of the danger when the men approach. Tell the same message to all who live here in Rouen. With more men arriving, have them gather in a force concealed outside the castle walls that can attack and trap his men outside. Find as many archers as possible and position them on the wall; their arrows will be released on my command."

Richard turned back to those gathered in the courtyard. "Lord Charles wants what he cannot have. He ravages his land and now wants to do the same in Rouen. Today he will learn that he is not welcome here. Men, sharpen your swords, axes, and knives.

Prepare to defend your homes and families from the evil that is coming!"

Thunderous cheers and more shouts of fealty echoed within the walls of the courtyard. With one last wave Richard turned and entered the castle. He went to the Great Hall with Thomas next to him.

Once in the hall, Richard's demeanor of confidence changed to concern. "Thomas, have you heard from the archbishop?"

"No, Your Grace."

"Find him! It is his priest that has caused this."

"Your Grace, come and sit with me."

Richard looked toward the voice and saw Nichol, sitting in a darkened corner. A cautious smile appeared as he walked toward the familiar voice and sat across from her.

Nichol reached across the table and grasped his hands. She could feel him relax.

"Your Grace, he is nothing of consequence; a vassal who has pledged fealty to you, yet he brings a small army to your castle. He is but a wasp that flies in your face. His sting hurts but it is not deadly. When he arrives and enters this hall with all his arrogance, you will remove his stinger. I will make sure that happens."

Richard learned as Charles and his men moved toward Rouen, they pilfered food, injured peasants, and destroyed property.

Before the moon had risen, another report came to Richard that Lord Charles and his men had reached the outer walls of Rouen and appeared to be settling for the night.

sixty

The Confrontation

This woman is a witch.

When the stars began to disappear the next morning, the blood-red sun made its appearance over the horizon.

Three riders approached Lord Charles' encampment. In the center rode Joshua. They stopped just outside the camp, where the soldiers were readying to enter Rouen.

In a loud voice, he declared, "I have a message for Lord Charles."

Out of a group of men emerged an older man believed to be of some rank.

Joshua rode to him. He leaned down and handed him a wax-sealed parchment. "I will wait here for a reply."

The three waited and watched horses being saddled by men who were readied and assembled. It soon became evident that his reply was to march on Rouen.

Joshua looked to the men at his side. "I think we have our reply."

They turned and galloped back to the castle. Victor immediately opened the gate and they rode in.

With the gates closed behind him, Joshua was led to the Great Hall and approached the duke, who was in conference with his commander.

He bowed. "Your Grace, I delivered your message; I received no reply from Lord Charles. As we waited, men were preparing to enter Rouen. That was his answer; he gives you no respect."

The duke's eyes narrowed, his body tightened, and those near him took a step back. His roaring voice resounded in the hall.

"Has the archbishop arrived? If he is not here before Charles arrives, I will not let him in. Station the archers on the wall and prepare for battle. No one enters without my approval. Charles will rue the day he marched his men into Rouen."

Judith and Nichol entered the hall, and Joshua's expression changed as he watched them approach.

Richard turned to see what had distracted his messenger. A slight smile appeared on his lips; his approval was evident. Judith wore a blue gown with matching veil, while Nichol wore a red dress and white veil.

My women represent me well … and Nichol is wearing her dagger.

Richard kissed Judith on the lips. "You will be seated next to me when Charles is brought before me. Nichol, you will stand by me."

A loud voice came from the hall's entrance, echoing in the large hall.

"The Archbishop William has arrived."

Stepping aside for the archbishop, two priests and four armed men followed the man into the hall. William and Richard approached each other.

"William, we must go to my solar for a private conversation."

Outside the castle walls, loud shouts, yelling, and pounding could be heard as Charles, on horseback, led his men to the gate entrance.

In the solar, while Richard was conveying news of recent events to his brother, the archbishop, his steward Thomas burst into the room.

"Your Grace, Lord Charles is pounding on the gate, demanding entrance!"

The duke's response was immediate.

"Bring him and only two of his men with him to the Great Hall. I will listen to his demands there. Shout down from the wall to him and tell him I wish to speak with him there. Have at least ten men with you—for protection in numbers and strength—when the gate is opened."

After more shouting was heard, Lord Charles pointed to two of his guards to come with him through the gates. The duke's guards surrounded them as they were led to the Great Hall.

Entering the large doors that led into the hall, Charles was surprised to see the archbishop and two women elegantly dressed. His eyes stopped on Nichol, then dropped to the dagger at her side.

The duke beckoned to him and said loudly, "Charles—and only Charles—may approach."

Speaking in a whisper to his two guards, Charles stepped forward.

Duke Richard said, "You have brought angry men to my castle as if in battle. You have challenged me in my authority as duke. I will not tolerate it. You are not a lord and will no longer use that title. It was granted to your father as an honorary title for his services. It is not one to pass on to heirs. You have dishonored your father with your many actions."

Turning to Nichol, Charles' face took on a deep red hue. His rising anger was apparent. He pointed at her and shouted, "This woman is a witch!"

Richard waved his hand in dismissal. "What proof do you have that the woman known as Lady Baron Nichol is a witch?"

"The priest named Loupe told me of the strange birth of her daughter—and that she is possessed."

"You make these accusations when this priest is not here with you. Where is the proof of a strange birth and of being possessed?

"I am aware that you sent men to attack the villagers of the hamlet called Harmonie and Baroness Nichol, and that you sent men to attack her on the streets of Rouen. Do you deny that?

"Are you bringing these false accusations because Harmonie has thrived under her guidance? Do you have your eyes on the taxes she pays to the kingdom because of the success of Harmonie?"

While the duke spoke, Nichol watched Charles closely. She sensed that he would attack Richard with the intent to kill him. Leaning close, she spoke in a low voice for the duke's ears only. "His anger is out of control. He will attack you to kill."

Charles' neck veins were bulging and his face was bright red. He demanded, "What did the witch say to you?"

Richard became more alert after hearing Nichol's words. He mocked Charles as he turned to the archbishop. "What did the little man say?"

Immediately, Charles drew his knife and lunged toward Richard.

At the same time, Nichol pulled her dagger and threw it at her target: Charles' neck.

Charles fell at Richard's feet before his knife could penetrate the duke's chest. His blood gushed from his torn neck as he grasped his wound with his hands, attempting to stem the bleeding.

Gasping for breath, he at last fell silent, his life over.

Those present gasped at the events they witnessed.

Judith reached for Nichol's hand; the two women moved closer together.

Richard exchanged a glance with his brother, nodded his head, and stood.

Leaning over Charles, crumpled on the floor in a widening pool of blood, he removed the dagger and wiped it clean on the dead man's cloak. He then handed it to Nichol.

"Thank you for your fealty."

To all in the hall, Duke Richard announced in a loud voice, "I do not see a witch in this hall … I see a brave warrior who knows how to tell when danger is imminent, a warrior who is a woman."

sixty-one

The Rise

Sitting in his chair, Duke Richard begins to speak.
"Robert, come before me."

Shocked whispers and murmurs filled the Great Hall. All eyes were on Duke Richard.

Letting his steely gaze take them all in, he turned to Thomas. "Get buckets of water and rags to remove the blood. Move the body outside the hall door."

He continued to speak to the small group inside the hall.

"Archbishop William and I will speak to the men outside the gates as soon as you all hear what I have to say. First, Nichol, I want your husband Robert to be here. He is with your children in the castle. Would you bring him here now?"

As she left, he turned to his brother.

"William, I believe the best way to calm the men outside the gate is for you to speak to them. Tell them that Charles attacked me and was killed immediately. Do not say Nichol did it. They must leave their weapons and return to their homes. Charles was never a lord. He only called himself that because he was vain. I know that he knew that it was only an honorary title given to his father, one that would not be passed to any heirs. Will you tell them this?

"And William … this Priest Loupe is a bad man. He brings great dishonor to the church and to the kingdom. I have heard of much harm caused by him for many years. He needs to be dealt with."

"I will do as you wish, Richard. Once the gate is opened, I will be in front of you with your men behind you. I will say what you desire. Then you speak."

Richard turned back to those still there and saw that Nichol had Robert and with him were Lucette, Aiden, and Athena.

Surprised to see them all, he turned to Nichol. She nodded to him.

Sitting in his chair, Duke Richard spoke. "Robert, come before me."

Nichol had told her husband what happened in the hall and he was confused by the duke's request.

Stepping away from her and the children, he moved to stand in front of Duke Richard, who has now risen from his seat.

Addressing everyone in the hall, he continued. "Robert of Harmonie will now be known as Baron Robert of Harmonie in the valley and the forests surrounding it. Nichol will be known as Lady Baron Nichol of Harmonie. The land formerly under Charles' control will become a new hamlet, now under the guidance of Baron Robert and Lady Baron Nichol."

Robert's and Nichol's eyes met. Both were shocked with the duke's sudden pronouncement. The children moved closer to their mother.

"What does this mean, Mama?" Lucette asks in a low voice.

"I am not sure. I was not aware this would happen. It will mean great protection for all of us. And it means that Papa and I have a great amount of responsibility for those who live within Harmonie and the valley.

"I will know more when I speak with the duke. Now, there is much to do to settle down the angry men outside the castle wall."

Casting her eyes to the duchess, she saw a smile on her face.

As she glanced at the duke, he nodded at her.

Immediately, Robert and Nichol kneeled in front of the duke. In unity, they said, "I pledge my fealty to Duke Richard along with my loyalty and obedience."

Letting Archbishop William lead the way, Duke Richard strode directly behind him as they approached the main entry gate through the courtyard, still full of men ready to fight for the duke.

None of them knew what occurred in the hall … until the body of Charles appeared, being pulled on a cart. Loud gasps of disbelief resound in the courtyard.

Thomas gathered men to surround Duke Richard before the gate was opened.

A man positioned himself at the top of the wall and shouted down, "Make way and put down your weapons! Archbishop William and Duke Richard are coming out!"

Loud murmurs and talking started.

Again, the man shouted down, "Make way and put down your weapons! Archbishop William and Duke Richard are coming out!"

The loud talk and shouting stopped.

Men started moving away from the gate and wall. The man on the wall signaled down to open the gate.

As the gate opened, Archbishop William stepped out, dressed in his vestments as if he were within the church at Mass.

"God has spoken," were his first words. "The rebellious traitor Charles is dead. God has now chosen a replacement for Charles. You are commanded immediately to cease the feuding in your land."

Many voices were heard questioning what was happening … and then the archbishop stepped aside and Duke Richard strode forward.

sixty-two

The Duke Takes Control

Your fealty is to me, Duke Richard. Not to another.

Duke Richard raised both arms and cast his gaze throughout the crowd in front of him. Then, he slowly lowered them and took another step forward.

He began to speak.

"We have all been deceived by a traitorous man who called himself Lord Charles; a false title. Charles' father was granted a lordship for his services to my father—an honorary title that was not to be passed on. His son, the man you knew as Lord Charles, was never a lord, nor did he pay the rents and tithes that he took from you under my name to me. Charles only led you and your families into starvation and poverty. Now this man is dead, a just punishment for an evil man who rebelled against his true lord. As further punishment, I decree his lands and wealth are now forfeit.

"He stole from you. From me. From the church.

"That ends today. Robert from the hamlet of Harmonie has been chosen by God to be Baron Robert. He is supported by Archbishop William, and charged with the authority to lead Harmonie and the lands you now live within. Baron Robert and others will show you how to make your land produce more bountiful crops with greater yields. It is my command that you all turn away from fighting.

"Your fealty is to me, Duke Richard. Not to another. Any fealty to another will be seen as treason, and you will be hanged."

As he spoke, several of the men behind the front section dropped to their knee. Others followed. Those who were still standing looked around and knew the battle they came to fight was not to be. Slowly, they too, took to their knees.

Voices rose in unison. *I declare my fealty to Duke Richard along with my loyalty and obedience.*

Three men remained standing. They glared at Duke Richard in defiance.

Turning to Otto, the duke shouted the words, "Take those three and hang them" as he gestured at the men.

At the same time, Thomas roared, "Drop your weapons and make way for their capture!"

Over one hundred men regained their feet and quickly moved away from the three, who had swords ready in their hands.

Otto and two others moved aggressively toward them.

Hanging was not necessary. They were struck down as soon as the first dropped, with a sharp sword thrust through his belly by Otto. The other two were slain, one after the other, by the overwhelming strength of the men who came at them.

The remaining men once again dropped to one knee.

I declare my fealty to Duke Richard with loyalty and obedience echoed against the stone walls.

Looking out at them, Duke Richard said, "And I pledge to you my protection." He turned and departed through the gate, into the castle.

As the gate closed, Thomas spoke once more.

"Return to your homes. Take your weapons and do no harm or thievery to those along the way. Baron Robert will come to you in the spring to offer help. Harmonie is building a church and there you will be welcomed."

sixty-three

The Great Hall

Relief swept over her. Have I told too much?

When the gate closed behind Duke Richard, he stepped up a few steps to the main castle with the archbishop at his side. He turned to his men who had come to support him if the battle had commenced.

A thunderous cheer rose from them as they, too, dropped to their knees. Shouts of "I declare my fealty to Duke Richard with loyalty and obedience," resounded throughout the courtyard.

As Richard takes in their words, he turns to Thomas, who held a small chest filled with coins. "Give each man ten silver coins." He then turned to the men in front of him.

"For your service and loyalty, my steward will give each of you ten silver coins as you return to your homes." Raising his arm, he continued to speak. "Let those secured in homes, inns, taverns, and shops know that the danger has passed."

He raised his hand in benediction. "Now, go with God."

Duke Richard and Archbishop William entered the castle.

Moving forward, Richard was pleased with how the day ended.

Only four men died—all traitors. The day has gone well.

Proceeding into the Great Hall, he ordered the hall to be cleared of everyone except William, Robert, and Nichol. Those he asked to be seated at the table with him. His steward Thomas would join them in the room after the coins were distributed.

Gathering his thoughts, he turned to Robert and Nichol.

"My naming you Baron Robert is in name only, Robert. Your son Aiden will inherit the title, as eldest sons eventually do. You are aware that our laws and bestowed titles are for men only.

"If I could, I would have named Nichol as Baron Nichol. I could not and the archbishop agrees because women cannot carry that title.

"So, I have decided to create a special title. She is now Lady Baron Nichol, no longer a baroness. You both must travel with Otto to understand what the needs of the land may be. Charles claimed the land suffered from constant troubles, though his table was never empty. A decision will be made as to who will represent the two of you when you are not there, and who will collect the rents and tithes since you live between Harmonie and Rouen.

"Nichol, your advice is important to me. You killed Charles to save me. I know that you have been the leader around the creation and growth of Harmonie and its success. And, you have asked permission to have a priest and establish a church in Harmonie. I am also aware that each of your children has an apprenticeship with a Rouen merchant to learn a desired trade to support the Harmonie hamlet. Your charity to those in need here in Rouen has made you both admired and well known. For those who seek power, you are a threat to them.

"Your family is different from others in many ways and are all important to the kingdom of Normandy. For the kingdom, the archbishop and I have you all under our protection. With it, much good will come."

Archbishop William broke his silence. "I am pleased that you will have a priest, Lady Baron Nichol. I will no longer protect the priest known as Loupe. His actions and the harm he has done to many is offensive to the church and in direct opposition to our teachings."

Nichol had been listening closely to Richard's words, and now William's.

"Archbishop, Your Grace, I do not know if you are aware that Loupe has chased and threatened me from when I was a young girl. He was involved with the poisoning of my father Alexander, who was a merchant and, at that time, served as the port commander of Marseilles. My father always gave openly to the church but when Loupe came demanding coin for his own needs, my father refused. I saw Loupe's anger when I was in Papa's solar, hiding behind the tapestry on the wall. He also bedded my mother. Priest Loupe disrespects the church and God. With your permission, I will deal with him."

"You hid behind a tapestry?" asked the archbishop, his tone incredulous.

Robert and Nichol looked at each. He placed his hand on top of hers. "Tell them why you changed your name and ran, Nichol."

Feeling the dagger at her side, she sensed Papa was with her. Eyes connecting with the duke, she straightened her shoulders and began to relate her story.

"Before I was five, my father hired a woman to teach me to read and write. My name was Lisa then. I adored my father and he would play memory games with me.

"As the port commander, men would come to him with business ideas and requests for money loans. I wanted to learn what he did and I began to hide in his solar before he came in. I listened closely to the conversations and words that were said, and I heard how they changed in tones, ranging in loudness and softness. I wanted to know what the men looked like and removed stitches in the tapestry so I could see. Then I saw how men would shift their bodies and alter their facial expressions as well as the tone of their words when they spoke. Soon, I knew when a lie was being told.

"I remember when Papa discovered I was there." Her eyes were wet with memory. "He walked in front of the tapestry I was hiding behind. Then he said loudly, 'Lisa, what did you learn today?' I came out from the niche I was hiding in and I told him all I heard and saw.

"He was quiet. Then he asked, 'What else have you seen and heard?' And I told him about all the men who had been meeting with him in his solar for many days. I did not understand then that my father was training me to understand when someone was lying and someone was being truthful. He began to tell me when someone was coming to meet with him and I would hide behind the tapestry. He would later ask me about what I had heard and what I had observed."

While Nichol spoke, she observed the expressions of Richard and William.

Richard's slight smile revealed to her that he was now more fully understanding of the woman across from him.

William's look told her he was confused about the same woman. She was a contradiction in his long-held view of women.

Nichol hid a small smile.

"Papa was kind to the orphaned children who lived on the docks. He gave much coin to an old woman who sold herbs at her stall so she would get food for them. Her name was Rose. I later learned that she was his eyes and ears there and brought him valuable information of the happenings on the docks … both the good and the bad. When I was at the docks one day watching people, Rose saved me from my evil half-brother, who dragged me by my long hair to a tavern so that his drinking friends could attack me.

"Rose had one of the children run to Papa's port office. He found me in the tavern and pulled the men off me and beat them both soundly, along with my brother. He carried me to our villa and provided care all day and night for me. He wouldn't let my mother—who worshipped my brother—near me."

Nichol stopped. The duke raised his arm to Thomas, who had entered the hall while Nichol was speaking. "Bring us cups and a pitcher of water to the table."

Nichol nodded to him and continued.

"Eventually he made my brother watch as those who attacked me were hung as a lesson. Papa warned him that he would be next if harm came to me. One day Papa came into my sleeping chamber and said, 'You have gained strength. Tomorrow you are going to meet with Sir Roland. He trains all my men and he will train you as a soldier so your brother and anyone like him cannot harm you.'

Both the duke and the archbishop looked at each other.

A slight smile again appeared on the duke's face. *Her papa trained her well. If I have a daughter, I would want to protect her.*

Nichol saw the exchange and caught her breath. "I learned to run fast and how to use a bow and dagger. I began to wear boys' breeches so I could move faster and run more easily than when I dressed as a woman.

"Papa now asked me to be in his solar when he had visitors. He always asked me, 'What did you learn today?' We walked in our gardens and he revealed more about his business. Slowly, over time, I became his trusted apprentice. He learned that my brother was not his son and it upset him greatly that I could not inherit his wealth, at least then.

"It became clear to me that he did not trust my mother or my half-brother Fredric. He created a map for me and said, 'If my death comes, leave here at once, you must run to Paris and find a man called Ezra. Your mother and Fredric will come for you for the information you know about me and my business dealings. You know everything about what I do and where my money is—and that is what they want. Go to Rose; she will help you. Our house-keeper Margaux will prepare food and clothing for your journey.'

"Soon after that, Papa was poisoned. I hid his important papers and cut off my hair to appear like a boy. I called myself Nick. I was now running from my mother and Fredric, and the men they hired to find me.

"The dagger I wear now once hung in Papa's office. He never touched it, saying that it carried a curse and only the right person could touch it. Others who dared would die.

"I joined a merchant's caravan headed toward Paris and followed Papa's map from village to village. I knew I could run faster than the caravans could move and I decided to go forward on my own. I knew how to protect myself and I had the map. I slept in the tops of trees and tied myself to branches at night. I ran during the day, finding food at monasteries and sleeping in their longhouses. I had plenty of coin with me so I could buy food at taverns as well.

"One morning, I entered the road to begin running and I saw a monk and his donkey, named Moki. When I got closer to him, I recognized Brother Lemur, the monk I had met at a fair in the last town. His birth name was Timothy Lemur and said that I could call him by the name his sister called him—Timo.

"I have never met someone more devout with his devotion to God. This was also when the wolf pup found me, the one you know as Shadow. We walked many miles together until I decided I needed to hurry to Paris and find Ezra. I said goodbye to him and started running. Fate had our paths cross again later, and since then he has become my close friend, like a brother. Over time, I told him what had happened in my past and my true name."

Looking at Robert, she stopped and now reached out her hand to cover his.

"At one of the village fairs, I stopped for food and to watch people. I was dressed as a boy and I saw a young man at a table selling jewelry. I also saw someone stealing from his table."

Looking at Robert, she spoke to him, "I saw kindness and green eyes and wanted to warn him of the theft.

"Shadow and I approached his table and confronted the thief who threw the jewelry on the table and ran away. I picked up a bracelet, one that would sell for much coin in Marseilles. What I didn't know was that the young man selling the jewelry had noticed me, too. And he had figured out I was a girl.

"We talked and he asked why I was dressed as a boy. Then he showed me a silver braided chain. I decided to buy it, and he was surprised that I had the coin for it. Little did I know that I was talking to my future husband.

"We became inseparable. I reached Paris with my now-husband. He surprised me when I told him of Ezra and why I was looking for him. I was very surprised when Robert said, 'I know of Ezra … he is my father's brother.'

"Arriving in Paris, it reminded me of Marseilles. Robert led the way to the home of Ezra and Helene. Ezra was doubtful that I was Lisa, the little girl he had seen many years ago. As my story began, I put Papa's rings—the ones I took with me after his poisoning—on the table. Then, they all knew I was who I said I was.

"Many years have passed. I have survived many threats from my brother and Loupe and his men. I now have three children and have seen a community come alive. I am honored that the duke has placed trust in me—in us—to share what we know with him and those who live on his lands."

Nichol leaned back in her seat to signal that she was done. Silence filled the air. Relief swept over her.

Have I told too much?

Richard cleared his throat. "Just before I walked out the gate I looked to the arrow slit in the tower to make sure the archers were ready. I saw a flash of red. Am I to believe that was you with a bow?"

Nichol nodded. "Your eyes told the truth. I was there to protect you and William from harm if it was needed, Your Grace."

Again, those around the table were silent. Then Nichol began to speak again.

"The training my father had me receive as a girl gave me strength so I could outrun someone if I was in danger. I also learned how to protect myself with the bow and dagger. Both skills have been used over the years.

"I have looked forward to this day. I feel that I will be able to walk the streets in Rouen and live in Harmonie without fear of attack against me and my family."

Nichol leaned in and clasped her hands, pausing to obtain their full attention. She had more to say.

"There is something else you both should know about Timo. Robert and I arrived in Paris and were living with Ezra and his wife Helene. I was with child. When Lucette was born, it was after the Solstice. The sun was bright and I held her up to the light flowing through the opening in wall when the shutters were open. Her small body embraced it, almost as if seeking its light and warmth, just as I did. That is when the midwife acted strangely and suddenly left the room, telling Helene that my baby was cursed.

"A few weeks after her birth, we heard banging at the door. It was Timo and Moki in the middle of the night. He said that he heard that Priest Loupe was looking for a woman and her baby that was born of evil. When I heard the name Loupe, I knew that he used a rumor spoken by the midwife to justify his search of me. And I knew he was after the treasure he thought my father had and that I knew where it was hidden.

"That night, a decision was made for all of us to flee to Rouen. Timo went with us, Ezra stayed behind to see who would appear at his door. Within the next day, two men and Priest Loupe were at the door. They destroyed furniture and paintings, looking for coin and other treasures that had been promised to them by my mother and brother. Ezra then escaped to his brother's.

"I will pursue Loupe. I will confront him and bring him here for your justice. That I promise."

Now she was done. She had said more than she had told any-one but Robert and Ezra.

She directed her next words to the archbishop.

"Watching people, it is what I now do. I noticed that your body stiffened and your breathing quickened when I spoke of Loupe and that your eyebrows rose when I spoke of Timo. Do you have anything to ask of me?"

Taken aback with her directness, William said, "Nichol, I have nothing to ask for now. Give Timo a message from me. When he is in Rouen, I request a conversation with him upon his arrival."

Finally, Duke Richard spoke. Looking at Robert and then to Nichol, he said, "I believed you have been wronged. There is still much to talk about. Come to the castle in the morning. I want Robert here for part of our meeting as well. I know you plan to leave for Harmonie soon."

sixty-four

Priest Samuel

We have met before … you are not the same as the evil Loupe.

Throughout the winter, three times a week, Nichol purchased bread and dried or salted fish for her children to hand out to those in need. They did this when they weren't at their apprenticeships.

Nichol and the family attended Sunday Mass. When Timo was in Rouen, he would join them. Ezra and Helene compromised by attending Mass once a month. No one wanted to hear Ezra's critique after the service and all were glad it was only monthly. Ezra objected to the church's doctrine of absolute control over the thoughts and behaviors of all people and resented being the focus of their ire toward increasing demands and restrictions made on Jews and Muslims.

The hostility and persecution by the church toward Jews had become more evident. He would rant about the use of the tithes of the agriculture that went to the church and for the people who were treated cruelly by many members of the clergy.

For fear of what could happen, he paid a priest in Paris to baptize him and encouraged Helene to be baptized as well.

Two days later, Timo entered Rouen when the night shadows began to surround the homes in Rouen. He went directly to Ezra's and knocked on the door, announcing himself. An eye peered out from the hole in the door.

Timo put his eye to the door hole as a jest, and laughter was heard inside as the door opened. Out rushed Lucette, Aiden, and Athena,

Their destination wasn't Timo—it was to greet Moki.

Nichol embraced Timo as he entered, then stepped into the doorway and gave the children instructions. "Relieve Moki of his burden and bring it inside. Then, with Shadow, take Moki to the stables and make sure he is watered and fed."

Timo had a concerned look on his face. "Nichol, it will be dark by the time they return. Should the children be out when there is no light?"

"Shadow is with them, and no harm will come … not now. Timo, come sit down. We have much to talk about."

He went to the kitchen table and sat down as he let out a weary sigh.

"It has been a long day and I am grateful to be here with all of you. The good people of Harmonie are eagerly waiting for your return. I have many good stories to tell of Harmonie."

With his words, a sigh of relief spread around the table. Food and ale were brought to the table.

Timo took a long drink of ale and a bite of bread as Nichol, Robert, Helene, and Ezra sat across from him. "Tonight you will tell us of Harmonie when the children return and after they are in bed, we will talk of Rouen."

Timo stopped chewing, and his eyes got big. "Is there danger? Do we need to leave at once, as we did in Paris?"

Nichol reached for Timo's hand. "Not this time—we are not in danger. Much has happened. The man you know as Lord Charles is dead and Priest Loupe will no longer be a threat to us or to Harmonie. We are all eager to return to Harmonie in a few days.

The children are longing to be back home near the lake and forests. They want to climb the hill as soon as we cross the stream, before we reach our home.

"And Timo, they need your teaching and guidance."

"I need them as well. They inspire and challenge me." Timo paused, then he looked around the table. "I know they are not like other children."

Just then, the door opened and the three children burst in. They went directly to Timo for his attention.

After handing out hugs and greetings, Timo told the children to fetch a leather satchel he had brought with him. When he opened it, he pulled out new shoes for each of the children. Made with a heavy leather sole, he had lined them with rabbit fur covered with thinner, tanned leather.

Excited, Aiden immediately removed his old shoes and let his feet slip into the new ones as his sisters watched him. Wiggling his toes against the soft fur, he walked to the door and returned to the table.

"These are wonderful," he exclaimed with a big grin. To his sisters, he said, "You put them on, too!"

As they did, laughter resounded through the house as their toes first felt the fur. Timo was pleased that they liked his gift. He added, "They are for your walk back to Harmonie."

Talk of Harmonie filled the room—happenings, events, the longhouse, and tales of people impatient for their return.

After the children went to bed, Nichol and Robert told Timo about Lord Charles and the confrontation at the gates of the castle when he arrived. Nichol also told him about the duke's meeting that followed.

By now, it was late and all of them needed rest. Nichol told Timo that the archbishop wanted him to come before him when he returned to Rouen.

Her friend took a deep breath, sighed, and nodded in understanding. Before they went to bed, Nichol looked at Timo.

"It appears you want to say something."

"There is a person in Harmonie that does not belong there. I will let you … no, when you arrive, you will see him and know."

As Timo got up, he said, "Must I bow and call you Baron Robert and Lady Baron Nichol?"

Both laughed heartily. "After what we have all been through? We are always Robert and Nichol to you. You are family."

The following day was Sunday.

After Mass, Timo was speaking with one of the priests outside the church. He waved to Nichol and Robert and their children to come join them. Nichol and the young priest immediately made eye contact.

Timo knew they had seen each other before. "Nichol, you need to know more of Samuel."

Nichol looked directly at the priest named Samuel; her head tilted in thought. A small smile was evident on her face. "I know you want to talk to me about that day in church years ago."

You are not the same as the evil Loupe.

Samuel responded, letting his face reflect a smile as well. "You know my mind … We have much to talk about."

"We cannot talk here. There are too many ears listening and people watching us. Tonight, can you come to Ezra's?" Samuel nodded and they left.

That evening, Samuel came to Ezra's door. The children were already in bed and the adults gathered in the room adjacent to the kitchen.

Robert had built two benches with long seats and arms at each end like the one he had made to surprise Nichol years ago in Harmonie. Helene had added cushions that were stuffed with feathers. Several stools were added for the growing family and anyone who visited.

Ezra and Helene welcomed Samuel as Nichol, Robert, and Timo did. Nichol watched Samuel as Timo introduced him to Helene and Robert.

I see him. The Lady is with all of us tonight.

Timo spoke first. "Samuel and I have had conversations over the years and we talked about our lives and found out we are not that different. A month ago, he asked me about you. Without thinking, my first words were that you were a gift from God.

Without pause, Samuel told me that only a pope could decree such a gift. Then I said, 'See for your own eyes.' After that conversation, something happened to Samuel. He can tell you himself what changed his mind."

Before speaking, Samuel cast his eyes around the room, pausing on each person's face.

"A month ago, when I was lying on my sleeping palette, saying prayers, a light suddenly appeared in my room. An angelic voice came from the light. I was awake when I heard the voice, but then I woke up the next morning without clear memory of what the angel said to me. I know my brothers. If I told them what I saw and heard, it would bring looks and laughter, and possibly the accusation of heresy would follow.

"A day passed. I felt the need to find Timo and to pray for your family."

Samuel paused. "Now that I am here, can you tell me why? I seek answers, and I know they are here." Looking directly at Nichol, he continued. "Can you tell me about the light and angel's voice?"

As Samuel spoke, Nichol's heart skipped a beat. Warmth flowed through her body.

Yes, the Lady is here with us … and now one more. She brought him to us.

Ezra stood and spoke first. "It is going to be a long night. I will pour wine for all." The cautious mood was now replaced with laughter.

"Before you give me the knowledge that I seek, Nichol, I need to explain further. For reasons that will come later and may not be revealed tonight, none of you here are held in great esteem with the church hierarchy. You probably know that. Eight years ago, at Mass, you accused Priest Loupe of trying to kill you and your family.

"In doing so, you embarrassed Archbishop William in front of the congregation. He was angry afterward. I was a novice; my innocence changed that day.

"In the past, I have overheard conversations that have made me question the church and its absolute authority over those it serves. The church hierarchy is as imperfect as the people it serves, but I do not think the hierarchy believes this. I do believe the church itself good, but there are people in the church that are not. They do not belong."

Pausing for a moment, Samuel was aware he had crossed over a line. Taking a deep breath, he continued.

"Priest Loupe is one of the bad ones. He is ruthless and evil. I do not know what secrets he holds over the archbishop and others that allows him to still be a priest. The man should have been excommunicated soon after that day at Mass. I do not know where he is, but I do know he was protected by Lord Charles. Since that time, many good people have come to me and are frightened by things they do not understand. That does not stop them from being quick to judge—and possibly condemn—what they have seen."

Pausing in thought, he continued timidly, "Over the years, I have had short conversations with your children. They are now older and different from others. For their own protection, they must learn the right words to use when they are not with you. With your blessing, I can teach them what to say and not to say when around religious people. If you like, I will only have conversations with them when you are present."

Nichol and Robert exchanged glances; their faces full of concern.

Samuel knew his words bothered them. Looking directly at them, he said, "I became a priest to do God's work on earth. When I see your children, I see that they are pure of heart. I feel that calling once again. It has been missing from me for some time."

Samuel's last words broke the rising tension around the table. Ezra quickly stood and poured more wine.

Once the wine was poured, everyone waited for Nichol to speak, as they knew she would.

"We are leaving soon for Harmonie and won't return as a family until the next winter comes. Timo and I will make trips to Rouen with the goods the Harmonie community makes. During those times, I will also meet with the duke. Robert and I will have new duties with our titles.

"Samuel, our hamlet of Harmonie would welcome a priest. If the duke and archbishop agree and you wish to assume the responsibility, I will talk to the duke and archbishop about you becoming the valley's priest. I know that Timo would welcome it, as we would. Would you be willing to move from here?"

Samuel's smile and nod of assent was what Nichol was hoping for. She saw him that morning at Mass eight years ago and now his description of the *Lady's* visit confirmed he would be a protector of the valley.

Her final words answered his question.

"When you came here tonight, you said, 'Now that I am here, can you tell me why?' I think you found the answer. You are here for the same reason we all are. We all know of the voice and the light you experienced. Since I first heard it, I have called it the *Lady*. She has been with me since I was a young girl—at times warning me and protecting me. She guided me to Timo, then to Robert, and finally to Ezra and Helene.

"When I was threatened, along with my entire family after Lucette's birth, the *Lady* brought a vision to me that led us to the valley and the creation of the hamlet known as Harmonie. You will understand more the first moment when you see the valley for yourself."

The conversation continued long into the night.

Finally, Helene said, "We all must get sleep. There is much to do before we leave."

The next morning, Nichol's first thought was of thankfulness.

Soon, the children would leave for Harmonie, a safer place for them.

But first, I must meet with the duke.

sixty-five

Helene's Decision

I want to be with the children.

As Helene lay her head down, she turned on her side and reached out to touch Ezra's chest. "We must talk … just you and I."

Ezra's drooping eyes opened fully. Sitting up, he asked, "Do we need more wine?"

Laughing, she pulled at him to lie down again. "No more wine. I want to talk about us. What I want is to go with Nichol and the children … to live with them all the time. When they return before winter begins again, I will return with them.

"I want to be with the children. When they leave Rouen, I want to go with them. And they need me, as Nichol does. With Robert as the Baron and her as Lady Baron Nichol, I am sure the duke has plans for them. If Nichol was a man, you and I know that he would have named her as a count.

"Timo told me that many families have come to live in Harmonie. It is where I want to be …"

Ezra's words that interrupted hers were a surprise. "… And it is where I want to be. There … with them … and with you."

Both were wide awake now.

Ezra continued, "I have much to do here before I can move to live there with you. Right now, I am planning to move the winter after this one. You go ahead and make our home. My brother and Dinah may want to move at some time as well, as they followed us to Rouen. Olaf and Marie have grown in the business and now have a family here."

Helene was delighted and immediately began planning in her organized way.

"I think Dinah will want to come bring Raisa so she can be with her big brother. The idea of Timo teaching the children will be good for them. I can be part of that. And I can make items for the merchants as the other women do when they gather in the longhouse."

Ezra chuckled. "Helene. All of this can come to you … to us. We have much to talk about and plan. Tomorrow, we will tell Nichol of our decision. Now, we need sleep. Tomorrow, you must prepare for your journey. There are things you will need …"

Yawning, he murmured, "… oh, and a cart to transport them. I know a merchant who can arrange it … "

Then he drifted off.

The next morning, Ezra woke, almost with a spring to his feet.

Helene woke to his movement. "Ezra, I see a change in you …"

"My dear, I had a thought in my sleep. I see a new longhouse being built. I see myself and new families in Harmonie that will bring more trade and men with skills.

"It will become our main home, with this one used by us and Nichol when we travel back and forth.

"And I see our niece Raisa becoming involved in E & N. She is learning the trade side working with Marie and Olaf and desires to be here in Rouen. The three of them will all watch over our interests, allowing me to spend more time with you in Harmonie."

"Ezra …" She laughed with delight, almost clapping her hands. "We have the large family we always wanted."

sixty-six

Timo and Archbishop William

I'm a farmer at heart and best at blessing the land as it is laid.

Timo was deep in thought as he approached the Rouen cathedral where he, Nichol, and her family attended Mass and prayed when in Rouen. He stopped just before entering and realized belatedly that he was at the wrong door. The archbishop's dwelling was next to the cathedral and that was where he was to meet with Archbishop William.

Still, he felt the need to enter the cathedral. Memories of his structured life as a monk returned as he entered.

Pausing, he pushed back the hood of his cloak and saw others in the cathedral who were there with heads down in prayer. Moving down the aisle, he found a pew that was away from the others and sat down. He looked at the altar, but his thoughts were elsewhere. Closing his eyes, it was not a monastery or church that consumed his thoughts.

God is not here. God is in the valley, the forests, the lakes, and rivers, and all living things. Harmonie is my true home—no longer is my place in a monastery. This cathedral is made by man, but the valley is made by God and it is the true cathedral. I have found it to be the true place to worship God. I have known this for a long time.

Timo continued staring at the altar. In his mind, he was now on top of the hill looking down upon the valley. Closing his eyes, he saw Harmonie.

In the distance, Athena was slowly walking toward him, covered with bees. A smile and then a deep breath as a warm feeling came over him.

Someone sat next to him and ended the serene trance that had completely captivated him. Opening his eyes, he turned to the intruder who had breached his inner sanctuary.

Speaking in a soft voice, Timo said, "Samuel, what brings you to my side this morning?"

"I looked for you at Ezra's this morning and was told that you went to see Archbishop William. I walked into the cathedral and saw you sitting here."

"I have been told that the archbishop wants to see me. It is his wish, not mine."

"Do you feel threatened by him?"

Timo shook his head. "I'm a farmer at heart and best at blessing the land as it is laid. No, I do not feel threatened. I do not feel anything toward him. I do not need him to be between me and God. For me, he is not necessary."

Samuel's voice and demeanor turned defensive. "What do you mean?"

"When I was a monk and prayed, it was between me and God. I believe that it was God who directed me to Nichol and to Harmonie. When I think of the valley and its abundance, to me it is more beautiful than this cathedral. When I am there, I feel that God has nourished me and those who live there.

"There is a hill that looks down on the valley. When you come, I will take you to the top. You can pray there, and then you will understand." Timo stood. "I must go to see Archbishop William. When I am done, I will find you and tell you of our conversation."

Just before Timo left the cathedral, he turned back and saw Samuel looking at him. Their eyes met, and they nodded to each other. He then turned and walked the short distance to the large adjacent dwelling.

Knocking on the outer gate, a priest opened it. Timo introduced himself and was told he was expected.

As the priest led the way to the archbishop, Timo noted the opulence of his surroundings, a place of luxury created for one man.

Is this what God wants when so many are poorly clothed and have little to eat? I think not.

Timo was led to a large room where Archbishop William was seated behind an ornate table, the centerpiece of the room. The priest who escorted him stood next to Timo.

An opening in the wall brought light to aid the many lit candles in the cold room. Timo stood in front of the archbishop's table and was purposely ignored.

Timo had time to observe the man seated in front of him.

I see a family resemblance to the duke. The archbishop is adorned in a purple cape and a gold pectoral cross; underneath the cross is a white silk vestment. I wonder if the white silk came from one of Diego's shipments.

Without looking up, William held his right hand up. His index finger was adorned with a large ring with dark blue gems embedded around the cross insignia on its crest.

Timo approached, bowed, and said, "Your Grace," then kissed the ring. He stepped back and waited for the archbishop to speak.

William looked up and sat back in his chair. His eyes narrowed as he glared at Timo. The cold room matched his icy stare; he appeared to be annoyed at the man standing in front of him. In the uneasy silence, Timo observed his facial expressions and body movements.

Nichol taught me well. I will reserve judgment of him later.

Timo waited.

William cleared his throat. "Do you know why you are here?"

"No, Your Grace."

"What can you tell me about Nichol and her daughter—the one that was born of the devil?"

"The child is not of the devil. That was a rumor that Priest Loupe used as a pretext to enter Ezra's home in Paris, to steal his coin and possessions."

Now I know why I am here.

William's anger grew with his response. It was clear to Timo that the archbishop had determined who Nichol was before he entered, contrary to what his brother, the duke, told him. Timo realized that the man in front of him was taken in by Loupe's lies.

Sensing the archbishop's anger, Timo decided to be bold.

"I was at the monastery in Paris when I heard of the priest's accusations. I must tell you the story of how we met and the reason I left the brotherhood. Only then will you know Nichol."

Without saying a word, William appeared irritated and waved his hand to continue.

Timo knew he needed to make the story short yet truthful to confront and disprove the lies told by others.

Loupe lies, using fear and hate to capture his victims. Is the archbishop one of his victims?

"I met Nichol in Vienne and I knew her as Nick. We had a tent where I was one of the brothers selling the bounty from our gardens. Nichol bought food for her trip from me and later when I was taking seeds and cuttings to other monasteries on my way to Paris, I met Nichol on the road. She was running from her mother—who poisoned her father—and her half-brother Fredric who chased her all the way to Paris. Loupe was the one who gave coin to Fredric to continue the chase."

William was showing frustration with Timo's story. He asked, "How do you know it was Priest Loupe helping Fredric and the mother?"

"The mother's name was Astrid. It was she who poisoned Alexander, Nichol's father, for his fortune. Priest Loupe bragged about bedding the mother to others. After Alexander's death, his fortune disappeared and the mother and Priest Loupe believed that Nichol had taken it or knew where it was.

"She had no treasure, traveling to Paris with the clothes on her back and her dagger. Her father had left her a map with his instructions that if he was to die, she would need to reach Paris and find Ezra, his trusted partner in the merchant business. Others would cause her harm with the knowledge she had learned from him. She slept in barns and monasteries along the way and found Ezra.

"This is what I know. I have been with Nichol and her family for years now. There is nothing in her spiritual being other than her devotion to God and family. Her father gave her strength and wisdom … I honor my vows to God and found my calling in Harmonie with the good people living there.

"Your Grace, Nichol was baptized as a baby shortly after her birth. You baptized her children and husband. She does not hide herself from others. She is who you see before you, not of the lies of the Priest Loupe.

"Her father gave to the church and to people in need. Nichol learned from him to do the same. Nichol told me that Loupe went to her father and demanded more than the church tithes. Her father refused to give more, knowing it would not go to the church. Loupe then threatened him. Not long after this, her father was murdered. She knew this because she was in her father's solar listening and watching Loupe behind the tapestry on the wall."

Timo revealed more about Nichol as he talked and noticed William's face began to change. At first, he slumped in his chair and looked away in thought.

Timo finished talking and waited for William's response. The silence was deafening. He turned slightly and let his eyes connect with the priest standing next to him. He noted a slight smile and a nod.

Then turning back to the archbishop, Timo waited.

Archbishop William raised his eyes from the desk. His facial expression had changed. His questions now moved away from the midwife's accusation and Priest Loupe's expanding lies and rumors and focused on Harmonie.

Enthusiastically, Timo told him of the creation of Harmonie and how its productivity supported Duke Richard and gave tithes to the church. "With its growth, we plan to build a church this summer and request your support of having the man you have influenced and trained become our priest. We would welcome Priest Samuel if you would allow it.

"Your Grace, after all these years, after all the false accusations and cruel rumors it was always about Alexander's perceived treasure. The treasure was his daughter. She was then known as Lisa, and then became Nichol to escape the death traps Fredric and Priest Loupe were devising for her. It was her knowledge of his merchant trade that she carried and shared with Ezra when she arrived in Paris many years ago."

Timo paused, then continued. "God has purposes for all men and women. We are all seen as equal in his eyes. Nichol has always been generous in her charity to those who live in Rouen. Nichol has purpose as we all do. I always add her to my prayers because

God sent her to us. This I am sure of. And I would encourage you to do so as well."

His movements abrupt, Archbishop William stood. "Samuel may go to this place you call Harmonie. I will tell him. You may go now."

Timo bowed, turned, and left immediately.

Nichol was his next destination—to tell her of his meeting with Archbishop William.

sixty-seven

Timo's Reveal

There was something about him that worried me,
telling me to be cautious with any dealings we have with him.

Hopeful of locating Nichol, Ezra's home was Timo's destination. No one was there. Then he remembered that Nichol said she would be at the warehouse in the afternoon. He redirected his path and quickened his step.

At the warehouse entrance, he was greeted by Marie, holding her youngest. Entering, he found not only Nichol but Helene. He could hear Marie and Olaf's other two young children playing somewhere nearby.

Nichol took the child Marie was holding and walked with Timo further into the warehouse, where they encountered Ezra and Olaf. Timo was immediately the center of attention. Without asking one question, he knew what they wanted.

Timo grinned, then spoke. "Samuel will come with us to Harmonie. For now, I do not believe the archbishop will pursue any grievances against you. His anger was toward Priest Loupe. Nichol, we will talk more tonight when the children are asleep.

"There was something about him that worried me, telling me to be cautious with any dealings we have with him. When I explain later, you will understand.

"Now that I am here, Olaf, show me the warehouse and I will tell you what is ready to be brought from Harmonie. The valley has produced much to move here."

Listening to Timo's words, Ezra added, "Diego is due to arrive with another shipment very soon."

Timo left the warehouse promising to return that night to Ezra's, to tell of his meeting with the archbishop. He walked with no destination in mind; his thoughts were on his meeting with Archbishop William.

The archbishop never showed concern about the poor or the many orphaned children that both hid and ran in Rouen. All he did was complain about them.

When Timo told of how Nichol walked with streets and gave bread out, the archbishop glared at him. When he suggested that a stall be created in Rouen to dispense broth and bread to those hungary or give cloth to those that needed it, he was met with silence. The archbishop's face was filled with disbelief and he responded, "Why would we waste coin or food on them? They are worthless to the church."

There is something amiss about him. The man is not a man of God … he is a man for himself.

A short time later, he found himself standing at the docks and did not remember how he got there. His mind was intensely focused on every word, every movement, every facial expression of William's.

There are meanings behind his words and actions that I do not completely understand but if I describe them to Nichol, she will know.

Timo put his hand up to shade his eyes and looked up at the sun's position in the sky. A smile spread across his face.

I have time to visit the children in their apprenticeships.

Timo's first stop was Vilfred's blacksmith shop, where Robert and Vilfred were heating a piece of iron. Aiden was busy on the bellows. He turned toward him and without stopping, Timo heard the rush of air keeping the coals red hot. His white smile, surrounded by a blackened face, welcomed him without a word spoken.

Smiling back with an approving nod, Timo spoke with Robert and Vilfred. Aiden had done his job well, and soon the men were interrupted with Aiden's words, "They are ready." The iron in the coals had reached the right temperature for them to work the metal.

Timo's next stop was the bowyer. When he entered, Lucette was working, shaping a bow under Hubert's direction. Again, Timo received a smile as he entered. As Lucette introduced him to Hubert, Timo could see that there was great concern on her face.

Timo understood her concern. Hubert was not well. He had seen much illness and death as a monk, and it was obvious Hubert was close to the end of his life.

Lucette was the only one who came to see him and cared for him. She did her best to take care of his needs and feed him and make him comfortable when she was with him. Taking the old man's hand, she said, "Hubert, Timo is a monk …"

As her words left her lips, she felt Hubert's life slowly slipping away.

Timo kneeled next to him and took his hands. Lucette did the same and they prayed together within their circle of six hands. When his prayer was done, he looked at Lucette. Tears were dripping down her face.

Rising, Timo placed his hand on Lucette's shoulder.

"I will see you tonight. His time is coming soon. I know of your gift, Lucette, and we will talk of it tonight with your mama."

His eyes were wet with sorrow for Lucette. He sensed her feelings for Hubert. It was her devotion to him in his final days and her concern for another.

She is her mother's daughter. She knows that he will meet death within days.

He then left to see Athena at Zita's shop.

Entering the healer's shop, he was immediately greeted with a hug from Athena and was introduced to Zita. "Meet my friend, Timo the monk." Zita took Timo's hand and encouraged him to sit on a stool.

When he did, she and Zita moved to the table they had been working at when Timo entered the shop. Zita gathered several herbs together and cut them into piles. Athena moved each pile onto a square cloth, wrapping each and moving them to the left side of the table.

Turning to Timo, Zita said, "One day I will be her student as well."

Zita noticed that Athena became anxious by the sudden praise bestowed upon her. She put her arm around the girl and a hand on her chest. "Athena, in your heart, you know who you are."

Timo changed the conversation. "Have you told Zita that soon you are returning to Harmonie?"

"Yes, and I want her to return with me. Harmonie needs a healer." Athena turned from Timo to Zita, and added in a soft voice, "But she told me that she is too old to travel."

"Athena, my child, I am needed here in Rouen. One more winter with me in Rouen and you will know more than I. You are meant to be the healer of Harmonie. Now it is getting late, and you must go home with Timo. I will see you tomorrow."

Zita leaned toward her and kissed Athena on the cheek. "Go now, child."

On their way to Ezra's, no words were spoken until they reached the door.

Athena turned to Timo and put her arms around him and sobbed. Timo held her, allowing her to speak when she was ready.

"Timo, I may never see her again."

"Athena, she will always be with you." He patted her on the shoulder.

"I am going to feed Moki. Tell your mama that I will help serve the evening meal at the monastery and then I will return here later tonight." He knocked on the door and it was opened by Roger, and they exchanged greetings as Athena entered.

Timo slowly walked to the stables where Moki was kept. He took straw and hay to his four-footed friend and filled a water bucket. While he wiped him down with woolen cloth, Timo talked to him of his day, as he had done so many times before.

Speaking to Moki as if he was a brother, he murmured in a low voice to his trusted companion of many years.

"My friend, we will soon go back to Harmonie. Today has been a day that I may never be able to explain. This morning, I was questioned by Archbishop William and after that, I had the pleasure of being with the most remarkable children.

"The archbishop is a petty, selfish, ordinary man, and the children are loving and caring. We are most fortunate that Nichol found us on the road that day. My God has come in the form of a *Lady*. She is a spirit that has brought much meaning and guidance to me, to all of us."

Timo bid goodnight to Moki and went to the monastery that was not far from the archbishop's palace. As he approached it, his thoughts remembered the countless monasteries when he worked and guided his brothers in their plantings for greater productivity. He cherished the mission of many, where they helped serve travelers and those less fortunate.

If I hadn't traveled from monastery to monastery, I would never have met Nichol.

Then his mind turned to his day. It gratified his spirit to see that the children had created their own missions of helping others. One thought kept resurfacing in his mind: *How can these young children see and do what the church should be doing and yet is not?*

As he recalled his meeting with Archbishop William, a sour taste filled his mouth.

I do not trust that man.

Timo knew he would better understand his thoughts after reliving his day with Nichol and the family that night.

Leaving the monastery, something captured his attention. He paused in the middle of the street and looked up to a clear moonless sky. The stars were bright and stood out from the dark sky that surrounded them.

Are they trying to escape the darkness that surrounds them? Is that a message for us? Can we escape the darkness that is in men's hearts?

With those thoughts, he told himself, *I must return to Ezra's quickly.* He began to walk faster, following the cobblestone street beneath his feet to Ezra's door.

Timo knocked on the door and was let in by Robert. Nichol, Helene, Roger, and Ezra were seated at the table. Once he was seated and a cup of wine placed in front of him, he turned to Roger and said, 'We have missed seeing you."

Nodding at Timo, then to the others, Roger replied, "Ezra has kept me busy traveling to Paris to maintain the merchant presence there. I will tell more of that later … but, what we all want to hear is of your meeting with the archbishop."

With his words, Shadow came down the stairs and lay by Timo's stool. Nichol turned her ear upward, knowing that the three were huddled at the top of the stairs to listen to what was being said.

All eyes turned toward Timo. He took a large swallow of wine and began describing the day's events, from the time he arrived at the cathedral and his conversation with Samuel to the archbishop's palace.

With his recollection of the words, he spoke in detail of the archbishop's negative reactions to much of his life as a monk and why he no longer served in a monastery.

He ended by saying, "If it wasn't for the time I spent visiting each of the children's apprenticeships, I would have been in a foul mood after my interaction with the archbishop … He is a man I do not trust."

Before Timo could continue, Nichol interrupted, "We need to hear your thoughts, Timo. You looked into his eyes and watched him as your story unfolded. What are the first words that come to you?"

"Fear. He is to be feared."

"Why?"

"He cares for no one; he can see their pain but does not care."

"What makes you say that?"

"I cannot explain, but his eyes were as cold as the room he sat in. When I walked out from the palace, I had the feeling that he did not want to hear what I had to say. Truth is only what he wants it to be."

Those at the table remained silent.

Timo continued, "I still do not know enough about Samuel to tell him all of today's meeting. One day perhaps … maybe on the road to Harmonie."

"Did the children tell you that I visited with them today at their apprenticeships?" Timo asked with a smile.

Helene said, "They were so excited that you came to see them. It was all they could talk about when they walked in the door."

Timo said, "This I know. I want to return to Harmonie with the children, which is where they should be. That is where they are safe from those who do not understand them."

Ezra had been silent as Timo expanded on his experience at the palace.

"I agree with Timo. The archbishop is not like the duke: someone who can be reasoned with and who can see beyond his castle walls. The archbishop is cunning and greedy. He turns a blind eye to the evils that have infiltrated his church and practices. It is the archbishop that has allowed for men like Loupe to prosper, using them as a weapon against the people to keep his hands clean.

"It is important that we know of him and understand his ways." Turning to Nichol, Ezra continued, "When will you see the duke again?"

"In the morning. I will ask Otto to join me." She turned to Timo. "It's time to prepare to leave for Harmonie before another week passes. Helene will be coming with us to live there and eventually Ezra will join her. The children have things to do as they finish their apprenticeships here in Rouen. Lucette knows that Hubert has very few days left. We won't leave until he dies."

Turning her head to the stairs, she said in a loud voice, "I know you three are up there. Go to bed now. In the morning, you will tell me what you have learned."

With her words, all the adults' eyes turned to the stairs. Movement could be heard, and smiles escaped from the lips of each at the table.

Shadow left Timo's side and moved to the stairway. Giving Nichol a soft *woof*, she moved up the stairs to the children's room.

Timo stood. "It is late and I will stay at the monastery tonight.

Much has been said and there is much to think of and do to prepare. I would like to see Hubert with Lucette again before I leave."

Roger stood and followed him to the door. "I will be at Amos' Inn. I suggest that we meet again at the warehouse in the afternoon when we can include the others."

Saying goodnight to Ezra and Helene, Nichol and Robert went to their room.

Once abed, Nichol tossed and turned until Robert said, "Tell me what troubles you so you can sleep."

"I cannot get over Timo telling us about the archbishop. I have had the same feeling from the first time I met him. Then he said that the children need to be in Harmonie to be safe. Is there no end to the danger? Must we be aware of everyone we meet? I do not want to live in fear—not just for us but for our children as well."

Her mouth tightened in determination. "When we are in Harmonie, their training will begin. They will not only learn to defend themselves but to pursue those who threaten them."

Robert pulled Nichol to him; her body was tense. He could feel the anger within her. His warmth flowed to her as he whispered in her ear, "Remember what Lucette said to us when she came home today?"

Slowly he felt the tension beginning to ease from her body. Nichol now turned fully to him, pressing her body to his.

"Yes. Lucette said when she and Timo held hands with Hubert, they prayed for him. She then prayed to the *Lady*. Still holding Timo's hand, she felt that he had, too."

Robert pulled her on top of him, and she came willingly as she nuzzled her face to his neck.

sixty-eight

The Duke's Solar

You and Robert are going to come to the castle this morning.

The next morning, a man arrived at Ezra's.

Helene was alone. Without opening the door, she stood behind it and spoke through the peephole.

"What do you want?"

The man said, "I have a message for Lady Baron Nichol. It is from the duke."

Helene was now on her toes, peeking out through the hole in the door. She recognized the man as one of the duke's couriers. Opening the door, she said, "Nichol is not here but she will be back soon. Can I give the duke's message to her?"

He abruptly shook his head. "I must deliver the message to her."

"Then you must come in and wait."

As soon as he sat down, Nichol came through the door. She recognized the man. "Do you have word from the duke for me?"

"Yes … you and Robert are to come to the castle this morning."

"Was that all he said?" Her brow wrinkled.

"Yes. Knowing the duke as I do, it was a demand to be present, Lady Nichol Baron. You should come soon, as it is wise not to make him wait for your arrival."

"Tell the duke that I will be there as soon as I find Robert and Otto."

Just as the courier shut the door behind him, Helene voiced her concern. "Now, what has happened that it is so urgent for you and Robert to appear before him?"

Nichol was quick to soothe her friend. "Do not worry, Helene. So much has happened in just a few days and we are leaving soon. I know that he needs to meet with us. When I return, I will tell you what he said. The children are settled with their jobs. I will go to the forge for Robert and then find Otto. The three of us will go to the castle."

Announcing their arrival at the castle, Nichol and Robert were escorted immediately to Duke Richard's solar. Otto waited at the door to the duke's solar so they could speak privately.

As they entered, they bowed and said, "Your Grace."

Today, there were two chairs in front of his desk. The duke nodded his head toward Otto, then turned his attention to Nichol and Robert.

Richard smiled and motioned for them to sit down. Nichol returned the smile and said, "Robert, our children, Helene, Timo, and Samuel will leave for Harmonie before the week's end. If needed, I will stay until you do not need me."

Richard's gaze turned to Robert. "Nichol is needed here as well as in Harmonie and soon in the new land as Lady Baron Nichol. She will join you in Harmonie within a week. She will not be delayed here by me."

His next words were directed to them both.

"From now on, Joshua, Otto, or Timo will be the only messengers I trust to deliver messages between us, whether you are here or at a distance. Soon I will send armed men with you to escort you to your new lands that were once Charles'. You and Robert are the only ones I can trust to oversee these lands. I will find a lord for you but now, you must oversee the lands that Charles neglected."

An idea struck Nichol.

Garlyn … Garlyn would be ideal as the lord.

"Your Grace, I have someone who knows the valley and its people well. He has been the mayor of Harmonie and kept order and communicated with me when I am away. He has worked closely with me to combine his hamlet with ours; the one we used to call No Name. Garlyn may be the ideal lord for you to collect taxes and help keep order, and he is someone you can trust. If you choose to honor him, I encourage you to grant the lordship for his lifetime only. He has no heirs to assume the title."

Taking in her words, she could tell that he would approve her recommendation.

Nodding, the duke continued, "I am aware that Leiv will soon sail to England and back, docking at Fécamp. I will send a message with him to Queen Emma. If you have a message for her, you may choose to do the same.

"Diego now has four ships. When he does not dock in Rouen, I want him to dock his ships at Fécamp as well. Your E & N warehouse with Ezra has become very successful. Other merchants and shop owners in Rouen have gained in wealth.

"There are some, though, who have become jealous of your success and your access to me. Envy breeds ill feeling, and I want to put a stop to these rumors. You and Ezra have dealt in good faith with me. That is why you must always dock here or in Fécamp. I will be in Fécamp this summer with the duchess and our children. I will arrange to visit Harmonie at that time.

"That is all I have to say today, Nichol. After Robert and others have left for Harmonie, you must come here. We have much to discuss before you leave for the spring planting."

Nichol and Robert rose to their feet.

"You must promise me that this summer when you leave Fécamp, you bring Duchess Judith to Harmonie with you. The good people of Harmonie would be overjoyed." Nichol's words were delivered with a smile.

Richard stood and smiled as well. "I promise," he said as he led the way to the door and Otto.

Nichol said, "Please tell the duchess that I wish to see her before I leave."

Nichol and Robert went directly to the warehouse. There they found Ezra, Achim, Raisa, Olaf, and Marie.

Otto left after telling Nichol he would meet her back at Ezra's that afternoon.

Nichol told them about the conversation with Duke Richard and a surge of energy could be felt by all.

Ezra could not wait to boast. "These merchants the duke spoke of should be jealous. The duke told you what I have known for a long time."

Olaf was pleased with what he heard. "Tomorrow we must begin to load the carts and then the day you leave, we will load the pack animals. Marie, tell Nichol about the list."

"Timo gave a list to Raisa of what they need at the longhouse," Marie said. "She can read and write now and will help Achim and Ezra with the list of goods that will be sent on each trip back to Harmonie. I will arrange for a few people to travel with you."

sixty-nine

Goodbye Rouen, for Now

Stay close to them; they need you.

I t was a cloudy morning on the last day of February as all gathered at the warehouse. Horses were hitched to the carts, and the last of the packs were secured on the mules. The cold weather would not dampen the spirits for those returning to Harmonie. Warm weather would soon arrive and all wanted to be in the valley to enjoy it.

The day before, the children each said their goodbyes. Vilfred the blacksmith gave Aiden a knife he made for him as payment for his work. Zita embraced Athena and gave her the parchments telling the story of Athena the Greek goddess that they read together. A tearful Athena embraced Zita and promised that she would return.

Lucette was not herself; she did not want to leave Hubert, who still clung to life. Nichol noticed her melancholy as she loaded the bows, arrows, and tools onto a wagon.

Nichol hugged her daughter's shoulders. "I know you do not want to leave him. I promise I will take care of him in his last days. Zita has given me a drink to ease his suffering. Lucette, know this … he did not want to die before you left. He wanted to give you his knowledge and the tools to carry on his life's work."

"How do you know this?"

"He told me. After you left yesterday, I went to see him. And I promised that I would be with him when he took his last breath."

Nichol gathered Robert and her children in a huge embrace. She said, "I will soon follow. You listen to and mind Granmama Helene."

At Helene's side in the cart was Dinah, Gideon's mother. Her desire to be with Gideon's and Gunvor's children was all she needed to make the move with her sister-in-law Helene.

Shadow nuzzled Nichol's leg. She kneeled down and pulled her close and whispered in her ear. *Stay close to them; they need you.* She then scratched Shadow's ear, and murmured softly, "It is time to go home, Shadow. Take care of Lucette, Aiden, and Athena."

His shoulders straight, Robert walked tall as he led his children away. They started north toward the gate in the outer wall surrounding Rouen. With Timo at his side, Moki moved forward with his burden, followed by several carts loaded with goods. Each of the children were in charge of making sure the carts stayed with the group. Samuel walked alongside Timo with a watchful eye on the children.

Nichol watched as they walked away, wishing she was with them.

Memories came to her of the moments when she turned around and looked back upon Marseilles. A smile appeared upon her face while she gazed at her children walking together. Aiden bumped Lucette off her stride. Lucette pushed him back and Athena pushed Aiden but failed to move him at all.

Something familiar about them caught her attention then.

Lucette and Athena are dressed as boys, from their wool hats to their breeches and cloaks. They are my children.

Nichol returned to Ezra's from the warehouse. As she entered the house, it felt empty to her. *I miss them already.*

There was much she needed to do to prepare for her next meeting with the duke and her departure in a few days. *I promised Lucette that I would see Hubert. I will take him some warm broth and sit with him before Ezra returns.*

Arriving at Hubert's, Nichol knocked on the door. There was no response.

There was no lock on the door and she entered, announcing herself by saying her name aloud. She could see Hubert's frail body lying on his bed. His eyes were turned toward her.

Closing the door, she removed her cloak. Seeing the small lit candle, she searched the room for more and lit two to radiate more light so she could see the old man.

As she did, she could see him try to sit up, then slump back. Going to his side, she could hear a rattle in his breathing. Taking his hand, his skin was cold to the touch. She looked at his feet. They felt icy. She knew his time was near.

Looking him in the eye and leaning close, she said, "I promised Lucette I would come and be with you. I have brought you some broth. Would you like to drink?"

His lips barely moved as he struggled to speak. "No. It is time for me to close my eyes. Give the coins in my purse to Lucette. She will take care of your needs and make all your bows and arrows."

Those were his final words.

Nichol held his hand with each breath he took until there was no more.

Gathering her cloak, she saw the purse in his other hand. She was unsure if Hubert had made any plans for what to do with his belongings or his body. She took the purse for her daughter and closed the door behind her.

After some thought, she decided to tell the duke of Hubert's death and ask if his men could take care of it.

When she returned to Ezra's, she could hear his voice behind the door. Opening it, she discovered Achim and Raisa were there as well. The men were seated at the table with a cup of ale in front of them.

Raisa was stirring something in the pot. The aroma of rabbit stew laced with vegetables filled the air, while the small fire beneath the pot warmed the room.

Ezra watched his niece as she removed her cloak and hung it. Her quietness was unexpected. "Nichol, is all well?"

Turning to him, tears welled in her eyes.

"Yes and no. I miss my children and Robert. I know that they will be well on their journey. I've just come from Hubert the bowyer. He has been teaching Lucette his craft and I promised her I would see him. This afternoon, I held his hand as he said his last words and closed his eyes."

Silence filled the air. Raisa put down the large spoon she was stirring the pot with and hugged Nichol.

Ezra said, "I will take care of this in the morning. Hubert had no family. You and Lucette became the family for him. I will distribute his goods to his neighbors and get a priest to do a burial for him.

"Your task is to work with the duke on your remaining days here. Tomorrow we can talk about what you and I need to do before you leave."

"Thank you, Ezra—from me and Lucette."

Relieved with his words, she sat down.

Raisa placed bread and bowls of stew on the table. All were hungry.

Going Forward

*I think we should open our own shop
in the middle of all the merchants.*

Patting his belly, Ezra let out a large belch and chuckled. The And tise broke the silence around the table that evening. Ezra lifted his cup and said, "Raisa, I think we should have wine now. We must make plans for Nichol's meeting with the duke tomorrow."

"Ezra, before you start, I want to get a piece of the parchment that Timo gave me so I can write down what our needs are." Standing up, Nichol moved toward a chest in the side room. Opening it, she removed the paper, a quill, and a small inkwell. Moving back to the table, she sat down and laid them out.

Removing the stopper from the inkwell, she picked up the quill. "We need to think about the needs for the coming year, for E & N and for Harmonie.

"I know that Harmonie needs more labor to meet the cloth demand of Rouen and surrounding areas," she said as she began to write. "Rose and Amos want us to produce a higher quality of cloth than the competition. They want colors of cloth that catch the eyes of the buyers.

"Achim told me that he and Gideon can make farm tools, knives, and swords for us and to resell in Rouen.

"Timo wants more leather for products that he can make, and he wants to teach others to craft things as well. He says that we can make many items in Harmonie and sell them in Rouen—

things like shoes and body protection for the hands, arms, and shoulders."

As she spoke, she continued to add words to her parchment. Raisa watched every letter as Nichol added them to make words.

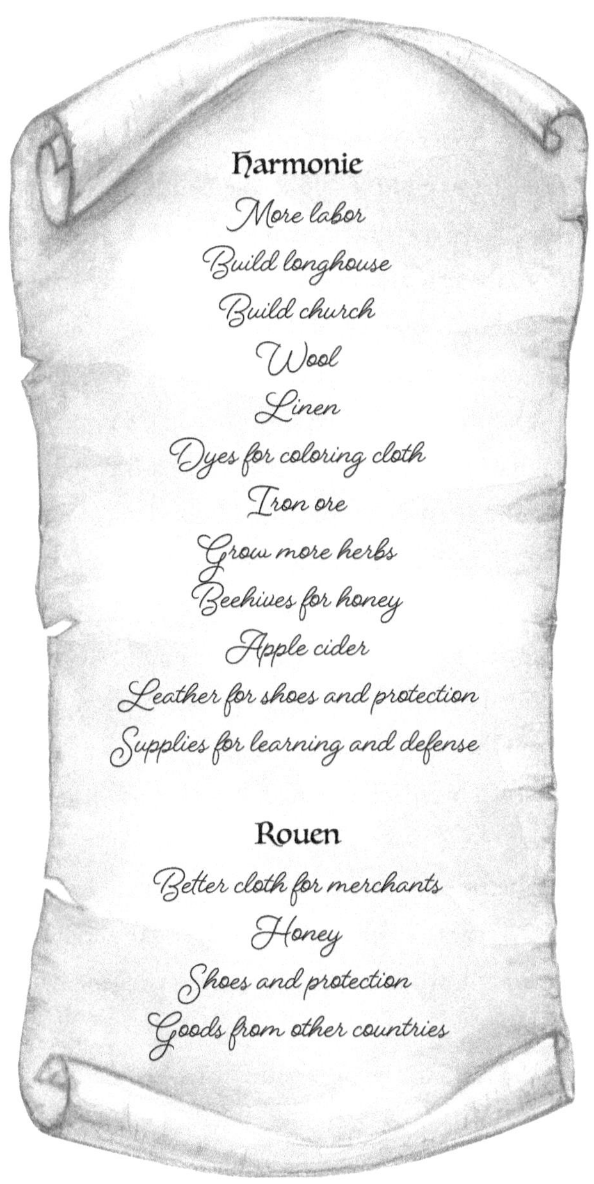

Ezra offered his thoughts. "I think that we should look at what the Paris merchants are offering. Since Diego and Leiv are both docking in different ports, they should be able to tell us the latest news about what is happening with the merchant trade and ideas that arrive with every shipment that they bring in.

"They have given us an edge over other merchants. We need to think of selling our goods outside Rouen to create new markets and bring in merchandise that is desired.

"We have had a good year, Nichol," he added.

Raisa had been listening closely. Her merchandising skills had grown to match Ezra's over the past year. "I can help to find out what the shop owners want. I will visit them all and find out their needs. That way we can lessen what's in the warehouse.

"I think we should open our own shop in the middle of all the merchants that will allow them to buy there as well as at the main warehouse. The gems and jewelry that Robert makes can be displayed in our shop. We won't be competing with them, just making it easier to get merchandise for them to resell in their stores.

No one left Ezra's that evening. The planning and sharing of ideas continued over into the next morning. Everyone was short on sleep from the exhilarating conversation.

Raisa served bread, cheese, and dried fish as the conversation continued.

Nichol finally said, "We are now in agreement with our plan for E & N Merchants. I will speak with the duke about renting another space in town that would become a convenience for the other merchants.

"Our needs will likely grow with the expansion of Charles' land if it is to be added to Harmonie. Plus, using the Fécamp dock will have added costs to it with transportation to Harmonie."

seventy-one

A New Direction

The air in the room had changed.
Nichol could feel his attitude shift.

Otto arrived later that morning and pounded on the door, announcing himself. He was in a foul mood. "It is a cold day." He had more to say until he looked at those present and stopped the words from leaving his mouth.

Raisa took a piece of cheese and bread to him.

Nichol put on her wool cloak and placed the hood over her head. They stepped out into the cold damp air and began walking with purpose to the castle.

Nichol stopped and turned to him. "You seem angry this morning. Tell me what troubles you."

"I miss Gabrielle and our sons. They have been in Harmonie all winter. I miss my wife and my boys need me." His voice was strained and hoarse with emotion.

Nichol took his arm and they continued walking.

"I must see the duke this morning, and then we will leave for Harmonie within a week's time. We need to plan what we will take and what labor we need to hire to come with us." She sensed that Otto was relaxing.

The duke might not be as easy to please this morning.

Nichol knew that the duke did not want her to leave, even though he had said he was aware she would be. She needed to reaffirm her loyalty to him and that she wanted to make sure the new land next to Harmonie would be protected.

When they arrived, Thomas escorted them to the Great Hall where Duke Richard was eating by himself. Nichol sat down across from him while Otto stood next to her. Waiting for the duke to speak first, she stayed silent while he continued to consume his food without looking up or acknowledging her.

Otto excused himself and went to the kitchen to wait for her.

"Your Grace, what troubles you today?"

"You are here to tell me you are going back to Harmonie." His tone was abrupt.

"Yes, Robert and the children left yesterday. However, that is not what troubles you. You already knew I would be leaving. You told me you had much to discuss with me."

The duke looked up and gave a heavy sigh. With sadness in his voice, he said, "I will not burden you with my problems today. Your counsel through the years far exceeds that of others, and you are the only counselor that has advised me without prejudice."

Richard reached across the table and took Nichol's hand.

Nichol saw what he wanted: He desired what Nichol could not provide. "When I send a messenger, you will respond or return when you are needed."

"Yes, Your Grace, I will. Send Joshua when I am needed. In the summer, you must come and leave what troubles you have behind. Bring the duchess and your children."

She smiled. "There is something I want to show you that Timo has created for the many children of Harmonie. He has taught them how to make tablets. Now they are writing words and can read them. At first, only my children were there. Now I am told that there are more than thirty boys and girls."

Nichol squeezed his hand. "Duke Richard, you know that I will always be here when you need me."

Duke Richard leaned back in his chair and took a swallow of his wine. He had an amused grin on his face. "The duchess tells me you and my sons met in the gardens before you left the castle the last time you saw her. Do I understand that you have invited them to Harmonie to see how bees make honey?"

"Yes, Your Grace, I met them. I told them about what we did in Harmonie and asked if they ever had honey on their bread. Both boys responded they liked honey.

"Then I told them that where I lived, we had bees that made the honey on land that you own. Your son then asked if they could see the bees and the duchess mentioned that it could be possible if they were brought to Fécamp during the summer visit.

"And that's where we left it. Of course, whether they come is up to you. Then you would see firsthand what we are growing and doing and see the training we are do with our children."

"Training?" the duke asked, surprised by her statement.

No wonder she can handle a dagger and the bow as she does.

Then he said, "If I have a daughter, I will want her to know how to defend herself as your papa did for you."

"I know you would, Your Grace. In Harmonie, girls and boys are being taught these skills by John. I know Otto wants to help as well. And Timo will be teaching them how to live off the land by knowing which plants are safe to eat.

"Your boys might be interested to see what they do. Our children are also learning how to read and write with Timo's and my help, as I did with the scriptures."

"What you have proposed is possible. The duchess has not been feeling well since winter started ..."

"I know. She told me. It will pass." Nichol smiled and looked kindly at him. "Your wife is with child again. This time, she will bring you a beautiful daughter."

The air in the room had changed. Nichol could feel his attitude shift. Startled with what she had just said, his mouth dropped open. "A daughter …"

"Yes, a beautiful daughter. Your Grace, could we talk of what you desire Robert and I do when we all meet again? I do not know the widow of Charles, but I feel that it would be wise if you befriend her so that her loyalty will be to you. And we should talk more of Garlyn, the man who is now mayor of Harmonie. He is the same man I suggested to you as a possible lord of the new land."

Nichol then stood, saying, "I will see Judith as I leave and return tomorrow if you desire."

Nichol found Judith in the garden wrapped in a cloak. "I hoped to see you before you left the castle, Nichol."

Taking a seat close to her on the bench, she replied, "I will be here for a few more days. When I come tomorrow, I will bring you some of the herbs I drank in hot water that eased my belly unrest when I was pregnant. It should help you feel better."

The two women talked of children and the desire for warm weather once again.

Nichol stood and reached her hand out to take Judith's in hers.

"With the passing of the Solstice, we will rid ourselves of our cloaks for many months. I will see you tomorrow with the herbs. Ask your woman to make hot water when I am here and I will share a cup with you. Though I am not with child, I enjoy the taste.

"Now, go inside and warm yourself."

Leaving the duchess, she went to find Otto in the kitchen where he usually went to wait for her.

When they cleared the gate on the way back to Ezra's, Nichol said, "The duke will visit Harmonie this summer. I have invited him along with his family. He will see firsthand what we are doing —and see the defense training Timo and John have created for the children."

Otto's smile was all that Nichol needed on that cold morning.

seventy-two

Che Next Day

Many greeted her with a Good morrow and Bonjour.

Otto arrived at Ezra's as the sun was peeking over the horizon. He knocked on the door and announced himself as usual.

Nichol answered the door and smiled at him. "You are early this morning. If you feel like I do, you will be as pleased as I will be to leave Rouen for Harmonie." She stepped past Otto into the street. As she looked up, she could see that the sky was a kaleidoscope of brilliant oranges, reds, and golden colors.

Turning her head to take them in, she called to Raisa in the kitchen, "Bring your cloak and walk with us to the end of the street to see the sky change its colors. The beauty of the sky this morning fills me with joy."

The three walked side by side in the morning's early hour. As they moved down the street, others noticed them. Knowing Nichol and what she could do, people observing them were eager to know why the three were moving swiftly toward the end of the street. Curious, they followed them. Many greeted her with a *Good morrow* and *Bonjour*, nodding their heads and then walking behind the threesome.

When the shops and homes were no more, Nichol stopped. Silence surrounded everyone as they all gazed toward the sunrise unfolding and rising with each moment. The reds and oranges blended with the yellows, blues, and purples.

Nichol took in a deep breath and then relaxed. She felt joy flow through her body, knowing that her return to Harmonie would be soon.

She took Otto and Raisa's arm and pointed at the sky.

"In Harmonie, they are watching the same sunrise as we are." She then turned to the town people and said, "Good morrow to all of you. The sky you see is a gift to you each morning. Promise yourself that you will remember to come out and let your eyes and mind receive it at daybreak."

Otto turned to Nichol, "After your meeting with the duke, we will begin our preparations to leave for Harmonie within a day."

As they turned, they again wished those who followed them a good morrow.

After returning to Ezra's, they consumed their morning meal before setting out for the castle.

Gathering her cloak, Nichol said to Ezra, Achim, and Raisa, "We will come to the warehouse after meeting with the duke to plan for our departure tomorrow."

seventy-three

The Duke

Your Grace ... what did he mean 'It is not over'?

Arriving at the castle, Nichol greeted Victor at the outer gate. "My family has returned to Harmonie. Otto and I will follow tomorrow." As she spoke, she gave him two silver coins.

"When Duke Richard needs to see me, he will send his messenger and I will return. Keep a watchful eye. You and I both know that there are some who would cause the duke and his family harm. Let the steward know when you hear words of unrest in the streets."

"You have been good for the castle, my lady. We all know that you kept Lord Charles from harming the duke." He stepped aside for her and Otto to enter, bowing his head as he did.

Thomas then greeted her, also bowing his head slightly. "The duke expects you in the Great Hall."

Leading the way to the entry, the duke saw her and Otto and quickly dismissed the lord he was talking to. As the lord walked toward her to leave, he shot her an angry look. As he passed her, he mutters, "It is not over ..."

Nichol says to his back, "And good morrow to you as well ..."

Otto's eyes widened with her response. Duke Richard heard it, too. He laughed out loud, then beckoned the two forward. Moving forward, she and Otto bowed to the seated duke.

"Your Grace ... what did he mean 'It is not over'?"

"Welcome to my world ... it is never over. You will always have someone after your head and what you have created in Harmonie.

Charles would never think to build his land for the people who lived there. He could only think to take yours.

"You must stay alert at all times, Nichol. That reason is why Otto accompanies you everywhere. He keeps you safe from those who would harm you."

Taking in his warning, she reminded him she and Otto would begin their journey to Harmonie, planning to depart the next day. "Before we leave, you said that you had much to discuss with me. Can we do it now?"

As she spoke, Richard thought, *I do not want her away from here. I need her here to learn of others' intentions and motives.*

What he said was, "I will send messages to you through Joshua and John as before. If you have a need to message me, Otto can deliver it and return with my response.

"Charles is no longer a threat, but I do know that there are others who were loyal to him and who also want what you have. You will need to be aware outside the borders of Harmonie.

"When I message you with a map to meet me on the road leading to the land that Charles oversaw, be there two days from the time you receive the message. You will need to bring Robert and Otto with you. I have no idea what we will find and what resistance is still there. I just know that there will be some.

"What is important is to put you and Robert in charge and persuade whoever is in residence there to support me. I know that you will be able to see who they are when we arrive with your skills."

"Your Grace, I would like Garlyn to go with us. He is the one that I propose be the collector of taxes for you. He knows how to see the land and people through our eyes. Have you thought of my recommendation to have him as the overseer? And, did the land Charles claimed ever have a name?"

The duke paused to consider her question. "I know of none. I suggest you and Robert call it something that will fit with Harmonie."

He continued.

"Dealing with the collection of taxes from Harmonie—and now Charles' land—will require a strong manager. If you believe that Garlyn would be the right person for this position, then I will support your decision. I want ten percent of the tax collections that are made from those living in the valley and for the use of my lands that you are now going to manage."

Duke Richard was silent for a moment. "You should also be paid for your services and your fealty to me. The land of Harmonie and now of Charles are under Robert's and your management. You may give another name to what Charles had or call the entire valley Harmonie.

"You have been paying rent to me for many years for the land use. With Ezra's knowledge as a moneylender, involve him on taxes and the managing of the properties. With your expansion into trade, I will also impose a tax on the growth within Rouen and on the growth you will see in Harmonie and what comes from Harmonie's expansion.

"Above all else, everyone who lives in Harmonie must pledge fealty to me."

Nichol listened carefully to his words.

Robert and I have a responsibility now to so many. I know that Ezra will help us. And we must speak to the men in the valley. If there is a conflict, they may have to fight for the duke.

"Your Grace, I will honor your requests and speak with Ezra tonight of what you propose. He knows he must support what you desire. And when I return to Harmonie, I will gather all in the valley and tell them that in order to remain in Harmonie, they must pledge fealty to you.

"Your presence in the valley this summer will be important. Few have seen you. I will await your message that you are coming and we will plan a celebration. And Robert and I will also await your message to meet on the road to Charles' land, which I hope will come soon after the weather turns.

"I have one thing to ask you. Ezra desires to rent a store on the main street of Rouen. We felt it would assist the merchants in picking up goods that Leiv has brought in and what is sent down from Harmonie for sale.

"It would provide some ease for the merchants of Rouen. They could go to either the warehouse or the one in middle Rouen. Ezra's granddaughter Raisa and he would manage it. Olaf and Marie would oversee the main warehouse. Rouen merchants can get goods from either location at their convenience."

Listening to her request, he felt that it would benefit all the merchants. "A middle warehouse would satisfy many of the merchants to access the goods that you bring in. They will then resell what is purchased in their shops at a higher price. The rent to you would be what other merchants on the street now pay. My steward will make the arrangements with Ezra."

Nichol was relieved that the plans she and Ezra made were well received.

"I have a small gift for the duchess. I promised her some special herbs and a brew to make to help her with her discomfort during these months. With your permission, I will seek her out and then wait for Otto at the gate."

Duke Richard stood.

"Lady Baron Nichol … I will see you again in a month's time when I come. Joshua will carry a message to you of when and where to meet. Go with God."

He offered his hand to her. She took it, and he said, his tone serious, "Stay alert at all times. You are a strong woman—one who many men wish to destroy. I do not want harm to come to you."

She smiled at him. "I have been aware of the feelings of others toward me all of my life. I will be on alert. Be well, Your Grace."

Letting go of his hand, she nodded and turned to Otto. "I will not be long with the duchess," and left the Great Hall.

The two men stood.

The duke said, "Walk with me, Otto," as he moved toward the door.

"There will be more threats to her as it becomes known that she and Robert, and now Garlyn, will be overseeing the new land. She has risen far in her position and now wealth and great jealousies will arise against her. Stay close. If you hear of threats, send word to me at once."

Otto bowed his head. "I will stay close to Lady Baron Nichol. I will protect her with my life. I will carry out your wishes, as my oath of fealty to you is as strong as the day I first swore it."

seventy-four

The Last Day

She has carried me and others
further than I thought possible.

Giving the duchess the herbs she brought, Nichol asked, "Is there warmed or hot water ready so that we could brew a cup and enjoy it as we talk?"

The duchess' eyes widened when she heard Nichol's suggestion. "Oh, I would like that very much."

Turning to the attendant closest to her, she asked for a water-skin of warmed water and two cups. The woman brought the bag and cups and placed them on the small table close to the duchess.

Nichol stood and poured the liquid into each cup and then added a small pinch of the herbs, now settling to the bottom of each cup. "We will wait for a short time before we drink anything."

Then Nichol added, "This is what Helene would make for me each morning and night when I was with child. It helped me feel better. My daughter Athena has added a few of the herbs she has been growing in our gardens. Now, I like having it instead of ale or wine."

While the herbs steeped in the warm water, Judith said to her, "I will miss seeing you when you return to Harmonie." She looked down at her hands, now clasped in her lap. "There are so few that I can trust and talk openly with."

Nichol thought about the duchess' words. "Here is my promise to you. When I am in Rouen, I will come to see you each week. We can just sit together and enjoy your gardens. We can talk of children. We can talk of things that are of concern only to you. I will listen and if you want my advice, you can ask me. Anything you share with me will always stay only with me."

The duchess could feel her body relax as she heard Nichol's last words. "Thank you, Nichol. I know that I can trust you, just as Richard trusts you."

"You can ... and I will share with you any new herb mixes that my Athena creates for drinks and foods. When we have honey, I will bring it to you as well."

Finishing their drinks and after much talk, Nichol stood, as Judith did. Saying their goodbyes, Nichol moved toward the gate.

Seeing Otto waiting for her, she picked up her walking pace.

Victor watched them approach with a smile on his face. "You will be missed, Lady Baron Nichol. When you come, you cheer me. Give Shadow a scratch on her ear from me."

"I will return, Victor ... I promise."

There was much to tell Ezra, Olaf, and Marie this evening.

As Nichol and Otto approached the warehouse, they could see that there was a lot of activity around the dock area. Diego had brought in another shipload of goods and crates, sacks, and barrels were being offloaded to transfer into the building. The cool air was warmed by the movement of the workers.

Laughter boomed amid the noise of the busy men and Nichol's attention was pulled to a familiar voice. Olaf's deep tones filled the air as he shouted out directions to the men unloading the crates.

Turning to Otto, she said, "I will meet with Ezra and tell him of my discussion with Duke Richard. While I do that, prepare for us to leave at daylight with horses and food for the trip. Stop by Amos' Inn on the way back from the warehouse today and ask him to pack food for two days for us. Tell him we will pick it up at daybreak tomorrow. If you see anything here that we should take with us, include that as well."

Greeting Olaf, she passed through the warehouse door and smelled the familiar odors of sawdust and newly sawn wood. Large beams supported the massive roof overhead.

Shelving had been assembled with multiple levels inside and placed in rows so that anyone could walk easily between the rows and select what they desired to purchase. When merchants or shop owners visited the warehouse, they were individually escorted through the shelves of goods to make their selections by either Olaf, Marie, Ezra, or Raisa.

Nichol knew Ezra had trained all of them in how to get the best price for the types of items carried. Olaf and Marie were experienced and knew all the shop owners in Rouen. Recently, even a few merchants from Paris had visited the warehouse, making purchases of the rarer items in stock for their own shops.

When the talk first started about returning to Harmonie, Ezra confided to Nichol that he knew he would soon be able to spend more time in Harmonie with Helene and the children. Much of his knowledge had been already been passed down to Raisa who had become his apprentice, shadowing him everywhere.

"I tell you, Raisa has the eye and ear for business. The merchants complained about you because you were a woman … but they soon learned that you were fair to them. Raisa will be the same. Soon, they will not be surprised to see a woman handling business at the warehouse."

Nichol could hear Ezra's voice, but she could not yet see him. Heading toward the sound, she found herself between the shelves that contained many types and colors of cloth, silk, and heavier leather pieces for shoe soles. She smiled at the careful organization of the goods, knowing that it had to be Marie who was behind it.

Finally locating Ezra, Nichol spoke loudly, to catch his attention. "I have come from the duke and there is much to tell you."

Hearing her words, he looked up.

With a tilt of her head toward the rear of the warehouse, she added, "We should speak where others cannot hear. Let us go where it is quieter."

Telling Raisa he would come back soon, Ezra led Nichol to the doorway of Olaf's and Marie's home, entered, and sat on the stools at the kitchen table.

"The duke had much to say. He confirmed that he would meet us on the road to Charles' old land and that he will inform all who live there that it is now part of Harmonie. He will also tell the tenants that Robert and I are now Baron and Lady Nichol Baron and Garlyn will oversee collecting taxes from this property, acting as a lord.

"Otto and I will leave in the morning and ride hard to Harmonie to get there by the following night. We will ring the Great Bell the next morning and call everyone together, to tell them the news we bring.

"Ezra, we are under the duke's protection. But he insists that all who live in Harmonie pledge fealty to him. Robert and I pledged ours to him after Charles was taken down. Now it is time for the others to pledge as well, so that we may be truly under his protection.

"He said he will send a map by messenger, telling us when and where to meet him to inspect Charles' former land. He wants Robert and Otto to come with us and he will have other men as well.

"I told him of your desire to add a middle warehouse in Rouen. He welcomed the ideal and said that it would benefit the other merchants and shop owners. He then added, 'With Ezra's knowledge as a moneylender, involve him on taxes and the managing of the properties.' Then he said, 'I will add a tax on the growth within Rouen and on the growth you will see in Harmonie and what comes from Harmonie's expansion.'

"So, Ezra, he has agreed to your proposal for the middle warehouse in Rouen. Do you have a space in mind that would be available? If you do, I would go to the castle and propose it, either meet with his steward or meet with Duke Richard first. I reminded the duke that you are clever with coin. Think about how we are to pay taxes and when we do it to him. I have been renting the land for many years and paying with coins and products from our shipping."

Ezra listened closely to her words. *She has carried me and others further than I thought possible. She has become the protector of many.*

Clearing his throat, Ezra reached out his hand to cover hers. "I know of adversity as a Jew and the need to be on alert. We will all stay vigilant. What you, Robert, and your children have brought in happiness to Helene and me is far above anything we have ever valued. You are the daughter we longed for."

Tears welled in Ezra's eyes as he said, "You will be missed here, my Nichol."

Blinking back her own tears and placing her other hand on top of his as he spoke, she said, "And I will miss you, too. You have become as a father to me and a partner in business. Papa was wise in directing me to you if something happened to him."

Nichol then stood, leaned over, and hugged the man she loved like a father.

"Otto and I leave at daybreak. There is no need to have Raisa fix a meal for us. If I do not see her before I leave, tell her to seek out Rose. There is something there for her from me.

"We will pick up food from Amos' Inn and then ride to Harmonie. As I walk back to your home, I will stop at several of the shops along the way, including Joseph's and Rose's."

Speaking with Marie and Olaf, she ended with, "Be well."

As she left the warehouse, she saw Otto drawing near.

Approaching him, she said, "I will walk back through town and stop at several of the merchants to bid them farewell, Otto. I know you have much to do. I will be ready before you arrive with the horses at daybreak tomorrow."

As she began to walk toward the main street to town, she heard a loud shriek from the sky behind her. Looking back at the warehouse, the red-tailed hawk was perched at the peak of the roof.

A smile spread across her face. *I knew you were here, Papa.*

Stopping into several of the shops, she greeted the merchants inside with a cheerful "good morrow." She also let them know Ezra would be explaining the location changes with the warehouse.

Nichol always carried coin with her. If she saw something in a shop that she desired or that could be used at Ezra's, she bought it. By the time she arrived at Joseph's and Rose's shop, she had several small packages in a basket she had also purchased.

Joseph looked up from behind the counter in his shop. His eyes lit up when Nichol entered. Standing, he said, "Good morrow, Lady Baron Nichol."

At the same time, he shouted over his shoulder to the back of the shop, "Rose, come … Lady Baron Nichol is here."

"Good morrow to you both," Nichol said warmly. To Rose, she added, "Do you remember when I first came to your store and I was in rags? You showed me beautiful cloth that I bought from you and made into new garments. Now I would like to have three new dresses and head coverings for Raisa with some of your lovely cloth. I will ask her to come to your store to talk with you about making them for her.

"I leave for Harmonie in the morning for our spring planting. Will you help me select the cloth now for the dresses? I will pay you for the cloth and the time you spend sewing."

"Come with me, Lady Baron Nichol. I have new cloth in the back that should be right for young Raisa."

Following Rose to the back area where she sat when she sewed, her eyes immediately landed on numerous different colored bundles of cloth, stacked on a table. Putting the basket down, she picked up several lengths of assorted colors of cloth and handed them to Rose. "I believe Raisa will like these best. Thank you, Rose."

Gathering her basket as she turned to leave, her gaze fell on a length of beautiful vibrant silk. She caressed it gently, enjoying the smooth feel of it under her hand.

Handing it to Rose, she added, "I will purchase this for me. Make me a dress like the one I am now wearing. Remember to add the hidden slits on the sides where I can carry things. I will return to see you both when I return from Harmonie before winter."

Paying with coin, she bid them both farewell and continued on her walk to Ezra's.

seventy-five

Return to Harmonie

I close my eyes and the valley comes to me … I am home.

Once they departed Rouen on their way to Harmonie, Nichol and Otto rode from sunup to sunset for two days. On the first day, they picked up food at Amos' Inn just after sunup. As the second day drew to a close, they crossed the stream at twilight and rode around the hill until the valley came into view.

Nichol stopped for a moment and Otto rode up next to her. She looked down into the valley, then tilted her head back and closed her eyes. Taking a deep breath through her nose, she paused. A huge smile lit up her face.

Otto watched with curiosity. "What do you smell?"

"I smell the sweet grass and the trees in the forests, the scent of food cooking over fires. When I open my eyes, I see whispers of smoke from the houses in Harmonie curling into the sky, telling me people are safe and tending their hearths. When I am far from Harmonie, I carry its sight and smells with me. When I need comfort, I close my eyes and the valley comes to me … I am home."

Otto closed his eyes and breathed through his nose. "It is much better than the stench of Rouen on a hot summer day."

Nichol laughed and agreed. "Let us finish this day with our families. Gabrielle and your sons will be pleased you are finally home."

In the village, Robert and the children heard the sound of approaching hooves. They knew … Mama was back!

Lucette, Aiden, and Athena ran out to greet them.

After dismounting, Aiden took the horses to be watered and fed. Helene was at the door, watching her young family as they reunited. A sense of peace surrounded her.

Nichol was exhausted from the trip. After greeting all and scratching Shadow's ear, she moved into the house. Helene had a bowl of rabbit stew on the table.

"Eat a little, Nichol. I am warming water for a bath for you now. Sleep will come fast and we can all talk in the morning."

Nichol heard her words and ate with her daughters cuddled close by her side. The stew warmed her and she could feel the numbness that had taken over her body from the long ride begin to subside.

Finally, she said, "Tomorrow we will bring everyone to the longhouse. There is much news to share."

And then her mind thought of Shadow.

Where is she? Why wasn't she the first to greet me?

Did something happen?

Looking at the faces around the table, Nichol asked, "Where is Shadow? Has something happened to her and no one will say?"

"Mama … we were close to the woods with her and she suddenly stopped. She looked at us and then she ran toward a cluster of trees that had rocks … I … I don't know where she went …" Lucette murmured, with a catch in her throat.

"I think I know, Mama …" Athena volunteered. "I saw the face of another wolf in the trees. It was white. I think Shadow just wanted to play with a friend like her."

With Athena's words, Nichol knew.

Shadow has found a mate. She will be back.

She reassured the anxious faces of her children. "Shadow will be back soon. Maybe with a surprise for all of us."

She turned to Helene. "I am ready for the bath you have prepared, Helene, and a long sleep."

Hearing her words, Robert went to her and gently took her elbow to assist her in rising from her seat. "A warm soak will do you good. Come, I will make sure you are steady enough to get into the bath and afterward … to bed you go."

In the morning, Nichol felt like a new person.

She sent the children out to all the homes in the valley with a message telling of her and Otto's return, and that there would be a meeting today at the longhouse for all in Harmonie. The time would be announced by the ringing of the Great Bell.

To Lucette, she added, "Tell Garlyn to come to me soon so that I can speak with him before the meeting."

With the children out performing their messenger tasks, she turned to Robert. "Walk with me. I need to feel our valley once again and I will tell you of my meetings with the duke. Much has happened since you left a few days ago."

She spoke to Helene as well. "Ezra is well and looking forward to coming here in the summer to be with you … and with all of us. He is ready to make this his home. When we get back from our walk, I will tell you of Raisa, the warehouse, and new plans."

Helene sensed that all would be well; her Ezra would soon be present in Harmonie. She held Nichol's cloak out to the woman she considered as her daughter.

Cuddling the garment's added warmth closely around her, Nichol and Robert set out. As Helene watched, a smile crossed her face as she saw Robert stretch his long arm around his wife's shoulders and Nichol slip hers around his lower back.

Later that afternoon, Nichol, Robert, Helene, and Dinah brought Timo, Samuel, Garlyn, Otto, John, Gabrielle, and Cara to the longhouse before the ringing of the bell. Sitting together at one of the long tables, Nichol told them of the duke's decision to make Robert lord of the valley, and what the duke had decreed for Charles' land.

"To outsiders and when we are in Rouen, we are now Baron Robert and Lady Baron Nichol." And then she laughed. "When I am in the valley, do not call me 'lady' and Robert 'my lord.' To all of you, we are no different now than we have always been."

She told them of her meetings with the duke, then stopped.

Everyone at the table waited for what they had become accustomed to from Nichol—searching for what to say next and then speaking.

Turning to Garlyn, she announced, "Meet the new overseer and Lord of Harmonie!"

Words of praise were bestowed on him, followed by clapping and celebration for their trusted friend and ally.

The small group was anxious for words from Rouen that only Nichol could provide. She spoke openly, knowing she could reveal more details at the community gathering that would arise with their questions when the Great Bell rang to call everyone together.

Timo spoke up. "Well deserved praise to you, Lady Nichol Baron; you have done well for the people of Harmonie and also the new lands of Baron Robert."

Nichol continued, "I have not seen a hamlet that has prospered like Harmonie. The duke said the same to me the day before we set out to return. We not only produce all our food, we spin yarn and make cloth, shoes, and other goods for Rouen and the villages that surround it. With more land to manage, we can continue to thrive and prosper.

"We must stop thinking of it as Charles' land; the land is now part of Harmonie. My question for all of you: Do we give it a new name or just call it Harmonie?

"I believe the land can become as successful as we are. The duke knows this and that is why we were given this land to manage. The way we continue to gain his favor is if we fill his chests with coin, goods, and produce ... and that is what we will do.

When Aiden rang the Great Bell, the road to the longhouse quickly filled with people. Soon they were standing shoulder to shoulder inside. Shutters were opened and people mingled together, filling the longhouse to capacity. Inside, excitement grew and conversations became louder.

Nichol moved among them, listening to their concerns. It was now time for her to answer them. She stood on a stool and asked for quiet. As she looked around the room, she saw Samuel and extended her hand to him.

"Everyone ... I want you to meet Priest Samuel. I know that some of you have seen him about and already met him. He is to be the valley's priest and was sent to us with Archbishop William's blessing. You should know that Samuel came to Timo and me and told us of his desire to come to Harmonie once he learned about what we were doing here in the valley to make it a better home. He believed that God had blessed us and wanted to become part of it. Soon we will build a church. Until then, Mass will be held here in the longhouse."

With her words, excited conversations again filled the air.

"Some of you have heard that Duke Richard has titled us as Baron Robert and Lady Baron Nichol of this valley. He has also granted us the lands that Lord Charles once held. Some of you know that Charles is dead.

"This morning, I told Garlyn that Duke Richard named him Lord Garlyn and official overseer of the valley. He has accepted this. Soon the duke, Robert, and I will go to inspect the lands that Lord Charles once claimed. We must welcome into our fold those who lived under Charles' cruel reign. With the new lands, we will become more profitable and make the new lands profitable as well.

"During the summer, Duke Richard will come here. He is curious about why Harmonie is far more successful than other places within the kingdom of Normandy. He knows that many children are learning to read and write, and that we are teaching them how to protect and defend themselves. No other hamlet or town does that.

"We are now officially under Duke Richard's protection. To maintain that, each of you will need to pledge your fealty to him when he is here. Will you do that?"

With her words, the crowd started talking.

Loud shouts of "Yes!" were heard, followed by many voices talking all at once. One farmer asked Garlyn to speak.

Standing on a stool as Nichol had, he said, "You have all prospered with my and Nichol's guidance. We will be here with you. To have the duke's protection is good; I will pledge my fealty to him when he comes. I think you should, too."

Nichol was pleased with the words she heard being spoken from others.

Once again, she stood on her stool. The crowd saw her and the noise level dropped.

Pointing her hand to a table in the back near where Helene stood, she said, "To end our gathering tonight, let us drink to our success. There is plenty of ale for all."

With Robert at her side, she stepped down.

He beamed with pride. "You did it, Nichol. The valley is one."

seventy-six

Winter Is Ending

*Shadow will need much food and water
for the next two months.*

Eight years ago, Nichol's children were the only children living in Harmonie.

Now many families with children lived in houses lining the main road leading to the Harmonie House. Nichol's home had been the first house. Now, as her eyes scanned the valley, she felt that they were all blessed to be together in this valley of peace.

Harmonie House was now a weekly gathering place where wool and linen were woven into cloth. Bread was baked, and fish from the lake or ponds were dried or salted. The longhouse had been transformed into a community center to keep villagers informed and share ideas. No one felt isolated, as they could have felt during the winter months.

With the added growth of additional residents, building of more homes could be seen. It was common to see men gathering to help a new family with a house-raising. With Nichol's news of a church in the future, many were excited about when the building would start.

With over thirty children in Harmonie, Timo, Otto, and John had created a plan to keep them busy in the months leading up to harvest. Everyone, including the children, helped in harvesting the winter wheat and preparing the land for the first planting of spring.

As the winter months came to an end in March, Timo led the children in storytelling, teaching them to read and to begin writing their letters. Timo's storytelling was always a favorite with them.

With his guidance during the late fall and winter months, Harmonie House was used for daily lessons in reading and writing, lasting from the end of harvest to the beginning of the next spring seeding. Not only did the children of Harmonie know their letters and numbers, some also learned how to read and write.

Every time Diego returned to the ports in Rouen and Fécamp, he brought books back from his travels to lands bordering the Mediterranean Sea and Cordova in Spain. Reading from them—and Timo's storytelling—kept the children captivated.

John and Otto had the children running everywhere, just as Nichol had been taught by Sir Roland when she was young. Aiden had become skilled in making swords and daggers under Robert's guidance before leaving Rouen. For the lessons in defense, Otto had the children gather wood and bring it to Aiden. He and Gideon would carve it into swords for them to use in their sessions.

Otto's boys were a few years older than Nichol's children. The five of them had become friends, working together. One of the boys wanted to make bows with Lucette and the other, on waking, headed to the forge to help Aiden and Gideon.

As the mayor—and now the lord of Harmonie—Garlyn took his duties seriously.

He began ringing the Great Bell before the sun set on Friday to announce the community gathering at Harmonie House with two short rings, a pause, then two more. That sound told everyone it was a safe announcement and did not mean danger. The women brought food to share. Timo's storytelling had grown to include singing. Both the adults and children looked forward to those shared times of community.

All of Harmonie's children were different from those in the other hamlets and towns, where children did not learn reading, writing, and numbers. In Harmonie, they were expected to learn. And they were taught how to protect themselves if danger arises.

A few weeks later, Nichol was talking with Garlyn and Robert.

"We need more people to work in the fields, but also craftspeople to help fill the shops in Rouen with goods made in Harmonie. And then, we should be building a sturdier, wider road to connect us to the new Harmonie that was once Lord Charles' land. We know we need more workers to help us with all this. Why not ask those who live here if they have any thoughts on how to get more workers and expand what we do here?"

Garlyn nodded upon hearing her words. "Yes, we need many more, especially more like Olaf's father, Harald. The Norsemen are skilled workers in wood, but they are not good farmers. If we could welcome them here, with Timo's help they will become both—good at building homes, plus building carts and tools. I have never met a Norseman who didn't have a good axe with him."

"You are right. In Rouen, there are many Norsemen. Some have families, and those would be ideal. We could offer them land if they would move to Harmonie. Winter will come to an end soon. We need to plan for getting more labor here.

"We should prepare to go and see the land that Charles controlled. I expect to receive a message any day from the duke to meet him and his men as they ride to the north. Garlyn, I would like you and Robert to go with us."

As Nichol spoke with Garlyn, she could hear her children's voices, then shouts. "Mama … Mama … Shadow has come home …"

Standing, Nichol said, "There might be away to get a message to Rouen with Otto. He could talk to Olaf. Perhaps he knows of some Norse families in Rouen agreeable to moving to Harmonie. Let us talk more of this in the morning."

As she began walking toward the children, she saw Shadow moving toward her.

At the sight of her beloved pet, Nichol broke into a run and crouched down to receive her, arms out. Shadow nestled close as Nichol scratched her ear, while dropping her other hand gently onto her pet's belly.

"Where have you been?" she murmured softly. "And what have you been doing?" Shadow nuzzled her head under her chin and Nichol laughed out loud. "So … we are going to have pups, are we?"

Hugging Shadow once more, Nichol stood and called to the children to come to her. "Shadow will need much food and water for the next two months. She will have pups then. There may be a pup for each of you."

With her words, the three children started jumping up and down in their excitement. Aiden immediately declared, "Mine will be called Hunter."

Athena could hardly contain herself. She remembered seeing the face of the white wolf that Shadow had run toward and then recalled an illustrated parchment she looked at while in Zita's shop in Rouen. "Mine will be called Zita."

While her sister and brother spoke as though the pups were already here, Lucette was silent. Finally, she said, "I will wait until they are born. Mine will tell me what the name is to be."

Nichol was pleased with their enthusiasm.

All of us will learn from them. The pups will bring joy to them … and their own protection as Shadow has done for me many times. They will teach them much as they grow.

"Come, let us take her to the house and feed her. I know she is wanting food."

As Nichol spoke, Shadow nuzzled her leg and then started walking to the house.

Athena looked up at her mother as she walked beside her. "I will make a special brew to add to Shadow's water to keep her strong."

seventy-seven

Rurik the Norseman

With his sunken cheeks, Lucette thought, he is starving.

nichol opened the door and stepped out into a warm spring morning and took a deep breath, quietly enjoying the sun's warmth.

Suddenly, Shadow bolted past her, with Lucette and Aiden close behind. The two wanted to avoid last-minute questions from their mother and there was no time to waste. They were on a mission.

Watching the two sprint away, Nichol glanced at her youngest in the doorway, noticing the tears streaking down her cheeks. With two fingers in her mouth, she lets loose the special whistle she used to call the children to her. It was a piercing sound that on a calm day could be heard throughout the valley.

Neither child stopped.

"Aiden!" she yelled in a bellowing voice that was a demand, not a request.

He heard, stopped, and turned around.

"Take Athena with you." She could see him turn to Lucette. He received a slight nod from the head of her daughter.

Aiden turned and beckoned to his younger sister, yelling out at the same time, "Run fast to catch up with us!" Athena's legs carried her quickly to where Lucette and Aiden waited.

Before they could continue, Nichol shouted, "Where are you going in such a hurry?"

What are they up to?

"To the forest," yelled Aiden and turned to Athena. "I thought you were behind us." And then to Lucette he said, "Did you see how fast she ran to catch up with us? If there is trouble and we must escape from anywhere, she can run faster than we can. If we ever need help, Athena needs to be the one to fetch it!"

They ran across the road past the chicken coop and longhouse to where the grass meets the trees, with Aiden in the lead. "Shadow, come here," he called out. Aiden kneeled when Shadow approached. He rubbed her head and neck while pointing to the ground and broken grass leading into the forest.

Lucette kneeled on Shadow's other side and pointed to the ground, then to the forest. She whispered in her ear, "Shadow, hunt."

The animal continued sniffing, then looked to Aiden and back to Lucette. All at once, she darted into the forest, nose to the ground, with the three children following.

Unsure of what they might find, the eager chase began.

Robert heard Nichol's whistle and moved away from his workshop. Joining Nichol outside their Harmonie home, he asked, "Is something wrong? Where are the children?"

"They went into the forest. They have Shadow with them; they are just being adventurous. I told Aiden to take Athena with them. I have a feeling that the two wanted to leave her behind."

Moving closer to Nichol and lowering his voice, he murmured, "So, we are all alone?"

Smiling, she took his arm and they both went inside.

A moment later, the door was no longer open.

The previous day, Aiden had been collecting eggs for the morning meal. Instantly, he noticed another hen had gone missing. Not seeing animal tracks, he looked past their enclosure and discovered footprints in the wet grass leading to the forest.

Solving the mystery of the missing hens was the goal he and Lucette had decided on the day before and were now ready to undertake. They hadn't planned on including Athena. Lucette was worried that if they got into trouble, she might not be able to react as fast as they could. Her mother's whistle and the speed of how fast he saw Athena run changed his mind. If it was needed, he would be the protector of his younger sister.

Unaware of how long they had been following Shadow or where they were in the forest, Shadow suddenly stopped. They had come to the end of the forest where it met a tall grassy meadow. She looked straight ahead to a growth of trees in the distance, lifting her right front foot off the ground.

Lucette sniffed the air. "I smell smoke."

"I do not smell smoke," Aiden scoffed.

Athena looked at her sister. "I can smell it ... and I see it. There ... I see a wisp of smoke coming from over there."

Aiden's and Lucette's eyes met. "You have the nose of a dog, Lucette. It seems Athena does as well. And Athena's eyes see things before we do."

Lucette slapped Aiden's arm. She raised her finger to her mouth and whispered, "Quiet," then Athena giggled and grabbed Aiden's hand.

Looking down, he gently put his hands on Athena's cheeks. "Stay behind me."

Lucette placed her hand on Shadow and felt the tension under the dog's fur. She crouched and slowly moved alongside Shadow, grasping her fur in her hand to hold her back.

The smoke came from a cluster of trees and shrubs in the center of a meadow. Whoever started the fire was in a perfect place to see who approached while avoiding being seen.

Lucette whispered, "Let's stay here and observe to see how many there are. I know the thief is in there; I can smell chicken cooking now."

Aiden rolls his eyes. "Can you tell if it is done?"

Impulsively, Lucette jumped up. "I will prove it to you." She started walking across the open field to the trees. Immediately, Aiden and Athena followed her, passing through several clumps of trees and coming within sight of the fire. No one was tending it.

"Chicken, just like I said," Lucette declared.

Athena spoke softly while pointing at a group of trees. "I can see him; he is hiding there."

With Shadow at her side and alert, Lucette raised her voice and yelled, "Come out!"

The three nervously scanned the area.

Shadow approached slowly, giving off a low, snarling growl and showing her teeth.

A man abruptly emerged from behind a tree.

"Shadow, stop!" Lucette commanded.

The man was small in stature, but his arms and back were broad and powerfully built. His clothes were torn, barely covering his body.

Her eyes dropped to the knife in his belt and she was aware he made no attempt to remove it. She knew that he was not threatened by them, but he was alarmed by Shadow. Seeing his sunken cheeks, Lucette thought, *he is starving*.

Aiden spoke first, saying, "I am not afraid of him."

Approaching the fire, he added, "This chicken looks done to me," and gestured to the stranger to sit and eat. Aiden pulled out bread he had brought and offered it to the stranger.

The girls approached the fire, each taking a seat on the ground around the fire, opposite the man. Lucette sat closest to him.

Taking the bread Aiden offered, the stranger began breaking it apart into small pieces he could chew. Without eye contact, Lucette studies his features more closely: braided golden hair; light skin under the accumulated dirt; a full blond beard; and maybe younger than his scary appearance.

We do not want him as a foe.

Aiden, overcome with hunger himself, took out his knife and began to carve the chicken. The stranger looked up, grabbed Aiden's arm and studied his face.

"*Berserker,*" he declared, then gestured for Aiden to continue carving the chicken.

Overcome with curiosity, Lucette pointed to herself and said, "Lucette."

Then she pointed to him, a questioning look on her face.

No response.

She repeated herself, again holding her hand to her chest: "Lucette."

He looked at her and then responded with his hand to his chest: "Rurik."

She then pointed to Athena and Aiden, saying their names.

No answer.

Pointing to her brother and then her sister, touching each on the arm, she repeated their names. Looking at Rurik for his response, he hesitated, and then spoke each of their names, pointing to each of them in turn.

Lucette moved closer to him and they all began to eat. She decided Rurik was a man of few words.

How do I get him to talk?

She touched his arm to get his attention. She then started by pointing to the bread and said, "Bread," and pointed to him.

Rurik responded with "*Brød*"—or at least that was what she thought he said. Then she repeated it back to him, holding up a piece of bread and repeating, "Bread ... *Brød,*" holding her piece of bread up as she said it.

I think I understand him. His words are similar to the language of Olaf and his family. I know them from being with Gunvor and Tova.

His eyes widened and his expression softened when Lucette responded with the exact pronunciation of the word in his language.

"I know that Mama is wondering where we are. We should start home," Athena said to her sister and brother.

"Wait ... I don't think we should leave him here. He needs food and shelter ... and something to wear for warmth. He will keep stealing our chickens and eggs to eat," Aiden added. The girls nodded in agreement.

As Lucette stood, she said, "Let us encourage him to follow us. When we get home, Papa will know what to do." Telling the others to slowly stand, Lucette then motioned for him to follow them, saying, "*Komme.*"

Rurik watched them as they began to leave. Hesitant at first, he rose ... and followed. He seemed to know the path to where the houses were.

On the way home to their hamlet, Lucette would point to an object and say what it was. Rurik responded with the word in his language. In turn, she would repeat them back to him.

An alliance had been born.

Shadow walked among them. Her neck fur was no longer standing up.

They exited the dark forest close to the longhouse and approached their home.

Aiden and Lucette had heard the stories about people called Norsemen that struck fear in people. Since Aiden could remember, he believed that all Norsemen were dangerous.

Their whole plan to bring Rurik home was not well thought out.

Nichol was on her hands and knees, working in the garden next to their home. Hearing the distant chatter, she looked up and saw them coming across from the longhouse.

Why are they walking so strangely?

As the three approached, they huddled closer together as if they were hiding something. Still, Shadow was acting normally.

What are they up to?

Being curious, Nichol asked, "Where have you been? What did you bring home? And what did you learn today?"

They all separated at once, revealing Rurik standing just behind them.

Nichol quickly stood, alarmed at the sight of a stranger.

She beckoned to Athena. "Papa is in the blacksmith shop. Go tell him we have a guest and to hurry home. Come home right away after you tell him and don't speak a word about this man to anyone. Everyone will know soon enough."

Nichol walked up to Lucette. "Does he have a name?"

"Yes, it is Rurik. I think he is a Norse raider. He speaks the language of Gunvor and Tova, but a bit differently. We could understand him."

"Yes, but what is he doing here?"

"He has been stealing our chickens and eggs to eat. I can talk with him and we thought—"

Before she could finish, Robert arrived, holding a hammer. From his expression, Nichol could tell his concern matched hers.

"Everyone inside. We need to discuss what to do before everyone in Harmonie knows about this."

Lucette turned to Rurik and pointed at the forge building.

"*Gā.*" Then she and ther other siblings followed their parents inside.

Looking at her daughter, Nichol thought, *She is just like me.*

Once inside, Nichol took her dagger and slipped it inside her tunic before putting bread on the table.

In a scolding voice, coupled with a fierce stare, Robert demanded, "Aiden, you are first. Tell your mother and me why this man is now in Harmonie."

"Something has been stealing our chickens and eggs. The other morning when I went out to get eggs, I saw footprints on the wet grass. The steps were human, not animal prints. The steps went into the forest and they began from where the chickens lay their eggs. I told Lucette and we decided that we would follow them.

"Today we followed his footprints into the forest and Shadow picked up his scent. Athena saw his campfire smoke before we did and Lucette smelled the chicken roasting. When we found him, he did not look dangerous. We shared our bread with him and brought him home. We can talk to him."

Robert looked at Nichol. Moments passed, then he turned to Aiden. "Aiden, what should we do with him?"

"Let him stay, Papa. He could help around here."

Lucette then explained why she led the Norseman to their home. "I want to know where he comes from, how he got here, about his people and more of his language. I touched his arm and saw him. He will not harm us and he can help us."

Aiden stood next to Athena, and proudly stated, "Athena saw the fire at the same time Shadow and Lucette smelled the smoke. Then when we came to the fire, Athena pointed to where Rurik was hiding before we could see him. Only then did Shadow get his scent and growled in his direction." Aiden tickled her. "You see things we do not. I want you to come to the forest with us when we go again."

Athena giggled and gave her brother a hug, knowing that she would be included in their adventures from now on.

"Lucette," Papa said, "Go bring Rurik back from the forge."

So much had just happened and a decision was needed.

Robert turned to Nichol for her reaction. Their eyes met and both were silent in thought. Nichol and Robert moved away where they could talk in low voices and not be heard by Aiden and Athena.

"Lucette senses things differently than what I do. She is who I was at her age. We can't send this man away." Nichol paused in thought, then turned her head to her youngest.

And what does this young one sense that I am not aware of yet?

Everyone turned to look at Rurik as he came in. His head was tilted downward, though a narrowed stare upward appeared from his eyes, almost buried behind his heavy beard and bushy eyebrows.

With intense concentration on Aiden, the man slightly bowed with respect and he again said, "*Berserker.*"

With a heavy sigh, Robert nodded his understanding. "He can sleep in the barn if Timo approves," he said to the children. "Mama and I will let others in Harmonie know he is staying here and calm any fears that arise."

Turning to Aiden, he continued. "I am angry that you did not tell us about the missing chickens and eggs. But I am pleased you are all home safe."

Robert motioned to the group that they should go outside. Rurik was watching the parents and then Lucette spoke, "*Sove dyrehuse.*"

Nichol realized that her daughter had just told him where he was to sleep.

Lucette spoke. "Papa, he can help us work in the fields and I want to learn about him."

Robert looked at her and smiled ruefully. "You are just like your mother."

She, too, casts a spell on me just like her mother does.

Later, with the house settled and the children asleep, Nichol whispered to Robert in their bedchamber later that night.

"I do not want to let Lucette, Athena, and Aiden out of my sight but that is not possible. I must accept that their destiny is their own. And my destiny is to watch over them."

"Nichol, Rurik looked directly at Aiden and said the word *berserker*. Do you know what it means?"

"I heard it used once before in Rouen, describing a Norseman who could not be defeated. It seems that our Aiden might have some warrior in him."

Silence filled the air and then she added, "The *Lady's* voice came to me after we ate. She said, 'Your children are different. They have gifts that will carry them through their lives as their purpose beyond Harmonie is revealed. They are safe with this man and he will train them as your papa had Sir Roland train you.'

"The *Lady* guided and prepared me with knowledge and wisdom. I will pass on her lessons to our children. She has given them abilities far above what I was given. Her purpose in doing so, only time will tell. All I know is they are in her hands and under her guidance."

Her words floated above the two of them.   snuggled closer to Robert as she spoke. His arms gently enveloped her as they drifted off to sleep.

Their children were safe.

Sitting at their table the next morning, Robert smiled at Nichol as he said to the children, "Do you think Rurik will be gone?"

The children were silent, but he knew from their reaction they wanted Rurik to stay. "Aiden will help me and Gideon at the forge today."

Robert knew in his heart that Rurik would not be gone. Then he added, "I am glad that he is here. I believe he can help with the building of homes, the new longhouse, and the church that is needed."

Looking at the immediate smiles from Athena, Lucette, and Aiden, they approved as well.

Silently agreeing with Robert, Nichol thought, *now we have another set of hands to help and he will have an eye out for my children.*

After a few moments, Robert continued to speak. "He must not look frightening. I will gather clothes for him and speak to Harald this morning and ask him to come immediately. He can talk to him and reveal more of who he is and how he came to be here.

"Aiden, take this bowl of pottage and bread to Rurik. When you return, we have things to discuss while we eat."

Listening to her father, Lucette asked, "Can I be with Harald when he talks to Rurik? I want to learn more about his land and how he got here."

Aiden returned from the forge and sat down and began to eat. Calmly, he said, "Rurik was not in the barn. I found him already at the forge. Papa, he started the forge coal; it is ready for our work." Smiling, he added, "I think he knows what you were making."

Nichol sensed the *Lady* was close by. *I now understand the reason he is here.*

"Did you touch him, Lucette?"

"Yes."

"What did you see?"

"He has not been a good man, but he seeks peace. That is why he is alone. He wants to leave his old ways."

Lucette will master his language quickly. She has my gift.

To all of her children, she asked, "What have each of you learned about Rurik?"

seventy-eight

Timo's School

*You are welcome to come and
learn letters and reading, too.*

As soon as Timo arrived in Harmonie, he wanted to teach the children about the land, and to read and write.

When he first became a monk, he could not read or write. He saw that most of his brothers did and that they all shared duties. Some spent more time in the fields tending the land; others prepared meals; and some were scribes, writing and reading.

His interests had been in the lands. He could see that he had many skills that would help the monastery be more productive in its crop-growing. Going to Abbot Sebastos, he told him of his knowledge and that he desired to learn to read and write so that he could share what he knew with others.

Timo learned to read and write, eventually making many pages of his instructions for growing and cultivating, rewriting them over and over so he could give small parchments to the monastery's brothers who worked in the fields. Within one year, all saw that the crop production was far greater than it had ever been. Now the brothers could feed more people.

One day, Abbot Sebastos came to him. "Brother Lemur, other monasteries should know what you have taught us. I have decided to send you on a mission to share what you know. With your writing and the drawings you include on your pages, the knowledge you have would be welcomed. With your donkey, you could carry your parchments and seeds to show them what to do."

Then the abbot gave him a parchment with a map on it that identified the locations of many of the monasteries along the road to Paris.

Timo was honored with the request of his abbot. "I will, Abbot Sebastos. I will begin my new journey before month's end. There is much to write so that I can leave a parchment with each monastery where I stop."

Little did Brother Lemur know that he would encounter a young girl—disguised as a boy—running for her life. And that when he revealed his true name, a name his younger sister could not pronounce, and the name she called her older brother, it would be the name that stuck going forward.

Timo.

The young girl was Lisa, then calling herself Nick—and now Nichol.

Timo began by sectioning off space in the longhouse. He had visited the homes and told the parents that he would do storytelling for their children and teach them how to read and write letters each day during the winter months. It was decided that the children would come to the longhouse every day at midday.

He told the parents before he left each home, "You are welcome to come and learn letters and reading, too."

Soon, the longhouse at midday had both children and parents learning.

On the first day, Timo said, "This is your writing tool for your wax tablet," as he handed it to each child and adult. "Gideon made these short iron sticks that are pointed on one end and flat on the other for you."

"What is a writing tablet?" asked one of the children.

Timo then picked up what look like a small piece of wood. He held it up so all could see what was in his hands. "This is a wax tablet. The writing tool I gave you will make marks in it with the sharp point. Those will be letters. The flat end will be rubbed over the letters to remove them when you are done."

His words created chatter and excitement. Then he added, "Each of you will make a wax tablet today. Then you will begin to learn letters and words."

With all eyes on him, he moved to a table that was filled with pieces of wood. Some pieces were flat; others were long thin pieces. There were also torn rags on the table.

"Watch how I make the base for the wax tablet." Timo then picked up a flat piece of wood and four pieces of the thin wood. There was a small bowl of hide glue. As he picked up each piece, he described what it was.

He then reached for a separate stick and dipped it in the glue bowl, spreading the glue on one side of the thin wood. He placed the stick on the flat wood edge and pressed it so it would adhere. He did the same thing with the remaining three pieces.

Holding it up at a slight angle to show them what it will look like, he added, "The glue needs to set and dry until tomorrow. I will leave it here."

Taking one of the rags, he rubbed the excess glue from his tablet and put it down.

"It is your turn now. Each of you will come to the table and get a flat piece and four pieces of the thin wood—two long and two short. And you will make the tablet base. Make sure you press on the sides so the glue sticks to the base wood."

Noise erupted as kids and adults moved to the table. Several could work at the same time while those waiting eagerly offered encouragement and advice.

Overseeing them, Timo reminded them to clean where they were working with the rags and to leave the drying tablets on another table for the next day. One by one, they finished.

Then Timo clapped his hands three times, and said, "Come and sit here with me. I have a story I want to tell you of how the bees decided to come to Harmonie …"

The next day, everyone returned and he could see that others had joined in to watch what would happen next. There was a pot of warmed wax on the table that held the pieces of wood.

"Come closer so you can see what I will do next," Timo said.

He then picked up a glued tablet base he had made the day before and poured in a thin layer of the wax from the bowl. He tilted the tablet gently from side to side on the table so the wax would spread evenly over the surface.

"Now you will wait until the wax begins to harden. It will happen quickly." He could hear the excitement in their voices as they talked amongst themselves.

Within a few minutes, he picked the tablet up and turned it upside down. The glue stayed in place and did not run out.

"You can now write on your tablet with the sharp point of the stick I gave you yesterday. When you gently use the flat edge, your marks will be removed."

One by one, they were called forward to claim their glued piece and then pour the wax. When all had finished, Timo clapped his hands three times. They knew a story would follow … and it did.

When he was done, he told them that they were now responsible for their tablets, and they should always bring them and their writing tool whenever they assembled to practice writing at the longhouse.

Telling them that he would see them the next day to begin learning the letters of their names, he was delighted to hear the happy sounds as the children left.

seventy-nine

Training Begins

*Stopping, she took in the young faces
that were eager to hear more.*

The tilling of the land and planting of the new crops would begin in a few weeks. That left a space of time for Otto and John to start their training of the older children on how to protect themselves. They would begin to teach the skills that one day could save their lives.

At ages nine and ten, Lucette, Aiden, Athena, and other children in Harmonie were old enough to learn basic fighting skills. The plan that Otto and John had was to teach the children of Harmonie, much like Nichol had been trained by Sir Roland when she was a young girl.

Now with Rurik's help, more tactics on how to defend themselves if they were attacked were added. The children were also taught how to find food in the forest to survive on.

Otto and John had the children sit on the ground, talking amongst themselves. Showing children how to protect themselves was something they had never thought of.

Then Nichol appeared. They knew she would be present to assist in the teaching. Her feats with a bow and dagger had been seen by many in the valley. If someone hadn't witnessed her talents personally, they heard about her abilities from others.

The young girls were in awe when they heard the adults talk about her. And now with Lucette showing such talent in making bows and arrows, some even wanted to learn how to use a bow.

When she stood in front of them and greeted them, one girl spoke up. "Are you going to show us how to use a dagger like you do?"

Laughing, she said, "I will be teaching you about the bow and sometimes the dagger. This morning, I come to tell you why you are here. When I was a young girl, my papa took me to a teacher to learn how to protect myself and survive if I was suddenly alone in the world. I went to his class every day. Otto, John, and Rurik will teach you as I was taught.

"From the beginning, I was told I must run everywhere to strengthen my legs. I ran to class. I ran home. I ran down to the port from my home. I ran everywhere. Later, my ability to run kept me alive when bad men tried to harm me.

"You will be encouraged to run, not walk, when moving about Harmonie and in the forest. Rurik will teach you how to track animals while observing their surroundings.

"Otto and John will teach you fighting and defensive moves to use when you have no weapons."

Stopping, she took in the young faces that were eager to hear more. She could tell they were excited. She then asked, "Are you ready to start?"

Several of the boys jumped up. They were ready. The girl who asked about the dagger was up as well.

Yes, they are ready.

Nichol motioned to Otto to come forward.

As Nichol spoke, Otto had been looking at the children and had begun assessing them.

When he stepped forward, he said, "As I point to each of you, I want you to move where I direct you to stand. Then go there and wait until everyone is in a group. There will be three groups in all." As he pointed at each child, he moved his arm to a section until all were placed.

The first group had the tallest children in it. Otto told them, "I want this group to run to the top of the hill and return, running back to here. Then stop. Ready … Go!"

To the second group, he directed them to a tree and back. The third group was instructed to run to the bottom of the hill and back.

He waited and watched.

When his session with the children ended, he knew that they had work to do around their homes and to help in the fields. Telling them that the morning time with him and John was over, he asked them what they would do next.

One boy said, "I am going to run home … all the way."

Otto laughed and said, "Yes … all of you will run to your homes, and then you will run to the field or to where your next destination is."

He stopped, looked over all their faces and added, "Whenever the bell is rung for us to gather, stop what you are doing and run to the longhouse. John and I will be there to give you your next lesson. Now *go* …"

Through the spring, the children were taught how to use a dagger and the correct use of the bow to hunt, just as Nichol had been taught. They practiced in pairs with wooden swords. All were thrilled to learn how to use a shepherd's sling for hunting.

For Aiden, the sword was his weapon of choice. For Lucette and Athena, there was no single choice; they took well to all weapons that were taught. They would ask questions about how to fight in combat, and various strategies of battle and warfare.

Although Aiden and Lucette were just a month apart in age, he now stood a full head taller than she did. His days were often spent in Robert's blacksmith forge that Gideon had mastered. His arms were already starting to show curves of developing muscle.

Aiden's dark hair had shades of auburn and was now a curly Mass that Nichol kept trimmed close to his head. "I want to make a dagger just like Mama's," he told his papa after one of his runs.

Robert laughed. "We will make the dagger together and add gems to the handle, just like hers."

Aiden ran to Robert and embraced him. Enjoying the enthusiastic burst of emotion from his son, Robert immediately felt his strength—and something else he could not explain.

My son has the physical presence and strength of a grown man.

When Lucette was next to Nichol, she displayed a similar appearance and many of her mother's mannerisms. She loved to draw and the images she drew reminded Nichol of her wall drawings in the villa when she was young. There was a quiet side to her that reminded her mother of how—long ago—she had listened to others, pulling out meaning to the words expressed.

Her eyes were a chocolate brown and when she focused them on someone, it was as if she could see through them. Her hair was deep brown, almost black.

Lucette was an observer and she did it as her mother did: with her eyes, ears, and feelings. She also could duplicate her mother's whistle—a loud, penetrating shrill tone.

Athena was blessed with the features of a child born around the eastern Mediterranean Sea. Black hair and deep-set green eyes of a color that challenged description. The contrast of lustrous black hair and her olive skin brought stares from those who first saw her—truly an emerging beauty.

One early evening, Nichol and Robert sat on the bench outside their home, watching the children play. He turned to Nichol and said in a soft voice, "She does not seem to be fully of me or you."

"I have wondered that myself. I see my eyes in her, but nothing else of your or my features in her. And she is quite tall for her age."

Nichol covered her eyes and looked up at the red-tailed hawk that was circling overhead, screeching. The children stopped and noticed the hawk coming closer.

Athena mimicked the hawk's screech and it flew down and perched on her outstretched arm.

Lucette turned to Nichol and Robert. "You know who it is, Mama. He is from your papa. He visits us when we are on top of the hill."

Robert turned to her and laughed. "I wonder, is there another father?"

Nichol's eyes got big and with a serious look on her face said, "Definitely not another father … but there is the Greek god Zeus. I think her reading about him could be the influence.

"After you had left for Harmonie, I stopped to buy some herbs from Zita. When Zita was a child, she heard stories from her father and mother that had been handed down over time. One story told of a Greek goddess named Athena. Then she took me to her back room where she kept part of a parchment manuscript that was written in Latin. The manuscript told part of that story.

"After I read it, I looked up at Zita and with an earnest look, she said to me, 'That is your Athena.' Zita said, 'Until Athena walked into my store, I thought that the Greek legends were just myths. I do not think that any longer. Your Athena is special.'"

Both sat in silence. Neither knew how to further respond.

Then Robert took Nichol's hand. "Athena is our daughter and her mysteries will be revealed to us as she grows."

Nichol remained silent and just squeezed his hand.

This child is a riddle; perhaps she is the Lady's child. Only time will tell—a curious child, a child of the earth. Who are Lucette and Athena, if they are not ours?

Robert pointed to Aiden. "He is a joyful child, gentle with his sisters and protective like Shadow. One day we must tell him that we love him, but Marie is his birth mother and his father is not known personally to us. From what Marie told us shortly after we found her, she was raped by the son of a nobleman. One day, Aiden may choose to claim his rights."

eighty

Joshua Arrives

Duke Richard will meet with you and Baron Robert where the road turns through the forest toward Harmonie in three days.

One month had passed since Nichol's and Otto's return to Harmonie.

Fields were being plowed, home gardens were being planted, and longer daylight and warmth was enjoyed by all. Harmonie was full of activity and spirits were high.

A lone rider appeared in the valley and was recognized by those in the fields. Joshua waved as he passed the workers.

A loud whistle came from Lucette's lips and resounded across the field.

The three children began to run in the direction of the longhouse. Otto's boys followed them.

Joshua smiled. *They are running to the longhouse, trying to get there before I do.* A slight kick brought his horse to a trot.

The children ran as fast as they could. Soon they were being cheered on by those still in the fields. Some waved their arms, yelling out, "Run faster …"

Joshua was amazed at what he saw. *Those children can run faster than I can.*

Hearing the commotion, Shadow quickly moved to the door of the longhouse, alerting Nichol. She went to the door and saw the children running across the field toward her. Then she saw Joshua, coming closer on horseback.

John and Otto saw the children running and shouted at them to run faster.

Now Joshua was surprised to see that they were ahead of him and urged still more speed from his horse. Neither Joshua nor the children wanted to be the last to reach the longhouse.

The children arrived just before Joshua to cheers from those watching the race. His horse was spent; it could go no faster after the long trip from Rouen.

Everyone surrounded him as he dismounted. Handing the reins to the children, he said, "Take him to the pasture and provide water, then come back to the longhouse."

Joshua stood, stretching his tired muscles while he talked to those gathered around him.

Looking at Nichol, he said, "Duke Richard will meet with you and Baron Robert where the road turns through the forest toward Harmonie in three days. We will stay on that road to the new land. There is more to tell, but first, I must eat. We must leave in the morning and wait for the duke's arrival."

As he said his words, Helene was already at his side with a plate of bread, cheese, and cooked rabbit. She was eager to hear words about Ezra and if Joshua had anything to tell her.

In between bites as he devoured the food, he continued to speak.

"It is not wise for us to make the duke wait at the meeting place. He is bringing many soldiers with him to move on to the new land."

As Nichol heard his words, she decided she should ring the Great Bell to bring people together in the valley to the longhouse. She knew that the valley should also have men to accompany them and the duke's soldiers to show Harmonie's support.

As the workers in the fields started toward the longhouse, Joshua continued, "I spoke with Ezra before I left and he sees a larger market for the warehouse products. He also believes that he will find skilled workers from Rouen to help with building homes."

Turning to Helene, he added, "He will travel here soon. He is looking forward to seeing the new growth and eventually coming here to be with you."

Nichol could see Helene's shoulders relax and a smile spread across her face upon hearing his words.

Speaking to Nichol, now with Robert and Garlyn at her side, Joshua continued, "The duke told me that Charles was a poor manager of the duke's land and treated those who lived there badly."

She knew Joshua had an excellent memory; his words were true as the duke had said the same to her.

"What I do know is that we cannot plan for the new land until we see it and meet those who now live there. We need to determine what their needs are and what they can do and contribute. Most likely, we will be away for a week," stated Nichol.

Turning back to Joshua, she said, "Joshua, we welcome your words and have been waiting for your arrival. We have been referring to the new land as New Harmonie amongst ourselves. Whatever it should be called, the right name will surface."

She directed her next words to her inner, trusted circle.

"There is much we need to do to prepare now and we must do it quickly."

Individually, she began telling what she needed, from food to transport and to the weapons she would like to have with her small group when they met with the duke. It was not out of the question that they might have to act defensively if there was an attack when they reached Charles' land.

As they listened, heads nodded. The new adventure seemed to create an air of excitement.

The Great Bell was rung, calling all in the valley together. Robert and Nichol stood outside the door, greeting everyone who had come to the longhouse. Soon, the longhouse was crowded with residents and alive with activity.

Garlyn stood on a stool and held his hands up, waving them to get everyone's attention. He then spoke in a loud voice, saying, "Nichol and Robert have returned from Rouen. They have much to share. As your mayor, I will reveal the first before I step down and bring Nichol up."

Murmurs buzzed throughout the hall. *What words? Good? Or bad?* could be heard.

Garlyn smiled at the questioning crowd. "The first is that Baroness Nichol is no longer Baroness Nichol …"

The crowd gasped, taken aback. Shouts of "NO!" came from the back of the room.

"She and Robert have new titles … let us hear from Lady Baron Nichol and Baron Robert."

Silence, then the noise erupted with loud banging on the tables, clapping hands, boisterous cheering, and chanting, "Nichol … Robert … Robert … Nichol …"

Garlyn stepped down and Robert took his place on the stool. "I know you do not want to hear from me … yet … but it is Nichol who carries the words of Duke Richard to you. Welcome the Lady Baron Nichol …"

Thunderous voices rose in the air as Robert stepped off the stool, offered his hand to his wife as she stepped up to speak.

As the crowd settled down, she spoke.

"First, let me thank all for the hard work you have done in our fields where our harvest has been taken to Rouen and enjoyed by those living there … harvest that is paid for. The duke is aware of the taxes that we pay for use of his land. Thank you to those of you who create the crafts and cloth that are sought after now, even in Paris. And thank you to all of you who have made Harmonie a desirable village to live.

"Those of you there at the time remember when Lord Charles attempted to attack me and you joined in to repel his men. Lord Charles is no more and was defeated in Rouen when he attempted to kill the duke."

Now, the noise level rose … and clapping of hands in the long-house grew loud enough to shake the rafters. One man stood and yelled out, "He belongs in hell."

Looking at the man, Nichol raised her arm. "Yes, he does."

Then she continued, "Next, our Garlyn will no longer be mayor here. A new mayor will be selected. The duke has named him Lord Garlyn, to replace the evil Charles."

Now the crowd stood and cheered as a huge smile spread across Garlyn's face.

"Not only will Lord Garlyn be the overseer of the valley of Harmonie … but he will be the overseer of the land that was Charles' … land that will be joined with ours. We have called it New Harmonie.

"Joshua brought a message from the duke; we have been told to meet him on the road to New Harmonie. Soon, Robert, Timo, Otto, Garlyn, Priest Samuel, and I will ride there with Duke Richard and his soldiers to take control of the duke's land and the people.

"None of us know what we are likely to encounter, or if those who live there will welcome us or be hostile. There is much we must do to prepare over the next few days for our travel. I believe that the combined Harmonies will bring power to all of us and favor of the duke."

Nichol gave a last wave and stepped down from the stool, supported by Robert's hand. The air and energy in the longhouse was something no one had felt before.

Harmonie was a success.

Garlyn jumped up on the stool and yelled out, "It is time to celebrate! Helene has created a feast for all to partake. Enjoy!"

Then he stepped away to be with his community.

Garlyn took charge of which men would accompany Robert and Nichol. Timo and Samuel were asked to travel with them as well, along with Joshua.

Helene began preparing and packing food for the trip. Lucette brought over extra bows and Aiden delivered many swords that had been made at the forge. One of the carts from the barn was brought forward to carry supplies and the weapons that Otto and Joshua assembled.

As Nichol looked over the cart as it was filled, she said, "I think it is best that we don't look like we are taking them over. We are their neighbors and want to be welcomed by them."

By late morning the next day, they were ready to leave. When Robert finished loading the cart, he noticed a lone figure on the road coming toward the longhouse.

It was Leiv.

He had made the first voyage of the year from England to where the Harmonie stream entered the channel. From there, he needed help to unload his cargo for the overland transport to Harmonie.

Nichol looked at Otto. "Your boys and our children must help him move his cargo to Harmonie." Helene, Dinah, and Gabrielle were all there to see them off and heard Nichol telling Otto about the cargo.

Otto's wife, Gabrielle, said, "Nichol, our sons can help lead the way and return with the cargo to unload it here in the storage warehouse by the longhouse."

Turning to Leiv, she asked, "When do you want to return to unload?"

"All I need is a break from the long walk and some food. It is not a full day's walk. We can start out early tomorrow morning. It will take at least one day to unload the ship and then start the journey back to Harmonie. I believe it will take two trips to unload and return here for storage."

Nichol knew that the number of horses that were planned for meeting the duke needed to be reduced so that some could be used to transport cargo in carts back to the Harmonie warehouse.

Nichol and Robert's eyes met. They both knew that the quiet days for them in Harmonie were over. With Leiv's sudden appearance, more responsibility would be placed on their children.

Calling their children to them, they lowered their voices. Nichol spoke first.

"We are counting on you to use your skills to keep everyone safe on this journey. Lucette, you told me you remember the bad men attacking us when we went to see Queen Emma many years ago. Leiv and his men fought them by my side. He will be there for all of you if you need help."

Then Robert spoke up. "Leiv can be trusted. And we trust you to look out for each other and Otto's sons and to bring all the goods back. Aiden, I know that you have the strength of a grown man. It will be needed."

"Girls, Shadow will be with you at all times. Keep her close. You know she is hungry with the pups growing within her," Nichol added. "You will leave tomorrow for the ship. Be ready for Leiv."

With everything ready, all were mounted on their horses except Nichol.

Helene and Gabrielle went to Nichol's side when she motioned them close. She cleared her throat before beginning to speak.

"Tell the children when they are not needed by Leiv to return here immediately. My fear is that once they stand by the sea, it will speak to them, luring them to the adventures it can offer. The sea will beckon them to explore further, and I want them back before we return from New Harmonie. I do not want to lose them … not yet."

Helene put her hand on Nichol's. "You and I know it is not for us to decide. We are just their guides; their destiny belongs to another."

With her words, Nichol held her breath and then let out a sigh of relief. *She is right. The Lady will be with them, too.*

Shadow was already at Nichol's side, ready for her next adventure. It was not to be the one she thought.

Nichol crouched down and rubbed Shadow's left ear, speaking softly into it at the same time. "You must stay with the children while I am gone. Protect them. Go with them when they start walking. Do not leave their side and bring them back safe to me. I will return."

Scratching her pet's head, she hugged the great wolf dog and rose to her feet.

Shadow turned and moved to sit by Lucette.

Nichol turned, mounted her horse, and rode with the others down the road.

eighty-one

New Harmonie

Duke Richard will know what to do.
These men must not remain in New Harmonie.

Riding out of the forest, they stopped at the main road that led to New Harmonie. Finding a small meadow for the horses to graze and to rest until the duke and his soldiers arrived, their wait began.

Nichol seemed preoccupied with her thoughts.

Robert and Timo noticed. They had seen her in this mood many times before. Timo looked at Robert, "Soon she will reveal her thoughts to us."

Robert looked at Timo. "I will go to her and wait for her to speak. When she is ready to speak, we should both listen to her words."

Nichol walked to the middle of the road and stopped. Motionless, she stood looking down the road toward New Harmonie. Her eyes were fixed on something in the distance. Robert approached and stood silently next to her. He knew that she was seeing more than the road.

Timo had now come to her other side. Garlyn, Otto, and Priest Samuel were now watching as well.

Nichol began to blink and slowly turned to Robert with a solemn look. "There is a woman who needs me and a village that needs us. Let us return to the others. I will tell everyone what I saw."

Timo went to Samuel. Quietly, he said, "Do not judge her from what you see or hear. Your silence of her and her actions will protect all of us. Just remember and watch her … she is the mother of all of us. She has received a spiritual vision, and I believe it is from God. Nichol has been sent to us and is *His* emissary."

Standing close together, Nichol looked into their eyes. As they eagerly waited for her vision, she began to speak.

"I have traveled many roads. Yet just a few where I saw the destination. Some of you here followed that vision with me that led us to the creation of Harmonie. As I was standing on the road, a vision came to me of a small village that leads to a hill surrounded with timber walls. Within those walls is a small stone castle. Also, inside those walls, it appears much like Rouen. There are shops and stalls that are supported by the many people living nearby.

"There is a man inside the wall who assumed Charles' place. He has support from others. I will point him out to the duke. He will challenge Robert for the control of the New Harmonie, but only when we leave. He is a coward. I remember him as he stood silently next to Charles while he died in the Great Hall. Charles' widow Katharine and her children are being held captive and they live in fear."

Nichol paused as her eyes narrowed and her jaw tightened.

Robert put his arm around her and said, "Duke Richard will know what to do. These men must not remain in New Harmonie."

Early afternoon the next day, Duke Richard arrived with forty soldiers.

Otto was down the road waiting. When he heard them approaching, he rode back to tell of the duke's arrival.

Nichol, Robert, and the others led their horses to the side of the road. Timo brought the cart into position. They were ready to continue.

The duke had a large grin as they all bowed to him. In a loud voice he said, "Nichol, I see you are again in breeches. Are you ready for battle?"

That brought laughter from the soldiers. Many knew her as the lady with the wolf and had heard tales of her past.

The duke motioned them closer. "Let us ride until dark—you and Robert next to me. Otto, you take four men and ride ahead."

As they rode, Nichol told him of her vision. Duke Richard stayed silent. He had been on the land there years ago and she described it much like he remembered.

Robert noticed she did not speak to him of Charles' widow being held captive but asked about Judith and the children. The duke seemed of good cheer. Being away from the problems of Rouen and Normandy appeared to be beneficial.

With the dimming of daylight, a meadow appeared that would be ideal for the night. The duke's tent was raised and a fire was made to cook the evening meal. The duke had brought a wagon with weapons, food for many days, and plenty of ale.

While there was still light, Duke Richard, Nichol, and Robert walked among the soldiers. Many knew of her and she of them. As she spoke with the men, her questions were about their lives and their wives, children, or the girls in their lives.

When the sky went dark, several large fires cast shadows among those now resting on the ground. After cups of ale were consumed, a young soldier Nichol knew by the name of Daniel stood and said, "Lady Baron Nichol, show us your dagger. Where did you get it?"

All eyes turned to the duke, who lifted his cup of ale toward her. "Nichol, tell these men the story of the dagger."

Nichol stood and slowly removed the dagger from its sheath, allowing the beautiful jewels adorning it to be reflected in the fire's light. The men were focused on her every move. Slowly, she turned around and held the dagger high, displaying its beauty. The firelight flickered off the blade. The only sound was the firewood sap popping with heat.

Nichol knew the whole camp's attention was on her and every word she spoke.

She began, "A long time ago a Persian nomad awoke when a fireball fell from the heavens. The fireball was coming toward him yet missing him when it struck the ground. The sound it made hurt his ears. When he went to where it landed, the heat coming from it was as hot as any fire he had felt. He moved away from it. The heat it generated was hotter than any forge he had been around. Knowing he couldn't touch it until it cooled, he slept again.

"The next morning, he thought it was a rock until he picked it up."

Nichol put the dagger in its sheath and walked to Daniel.

"Pass it around for all to see." To all the men, she warned, "Do not hold it too long. Quickly pass it to the next soldier. When it is returned to me, I will tell you the rest of the story and then you will know why. Remember, you must pass it quickly."

When the dagger had returned to her, she continued relating in great detail the rest of the dagger's story and how she came into its possession, not realizing that as she spoke, her shadow from the large fires cast an immense image of her on the surrounding forest. Within her story, she revealed the dagger's curse, and how too many men had been beguiled by its beauty.

Murmurs were heard when Nichol said, "If the dagger lands in the wrong hands, the possessor of it will die a horrid death. My papa was given the dagger out of spite when he was the port commander of Marseilles. He felt its importance and displayed it on a wall in his solar. Before he was murdered, he had made a map to show me how to escape from Marseilles if he was attacked. After his death, I took the dagger from the wall and have kept it at my side since that day."

Her last words ending the story would reveal who she was.

"There are many questions about the curse with few answers. Sometimes we must accept what we do not understand. I do not know why this gift from the heavens came to me—all I know is that it repels evil and I am the rightful owner of it."

Nichol put her hand to her heart and paused with a smile. "When we arrive at New Harmonie, we must come not as conquerors but to bring help and the offer of prosperity to those who lived under the evil of Charles."

Richard came forward. "What she has said is true. I have seen it for myself. We have a long ride tomorrow, get some rest."

He turned and entered his tent with guards posted outside throughout the night.

The next morning, they entered the road and only stopped for the noon meal.

Nichol rode next to Richard; they separated themselves from the scouts in front and the rest to talk privately. Starting with talk of Fécamp, family, and Queen Emma, Nichol tried to keep him focused. She talked of trade, from the lands surrounding the Mediterranean Sea, and even briefly about his brother, Archbishop William.

She also saw him and his desire for her.

He could endanger our future.

He became quiet, then said, "When I am in bed with Judith and having pleasure with her, I imagine she is you."

"You know we can never be together."

"You could be my mistress."

"There are many people's lives in our hands. We must not let our lives interfere."

"Does that mean you have no wish to be closer?"

"No, Richard. It means we are observed by many in your castle and by your soldiers. I will never lie to you or deceive you. My value to you and your lands is far greater than of me being a mistress. I will not put you in danger."

She smiled. "Let us stop and wait for the others to catch up. When I return to Rouen, we will talk in your solar."

Nichol saw his face … her reply was not what he wanted.

Duke Richard is the most powerful man in Normandy, and maybe the most dangerous to me. Still, so long as I serve a purpose to him, Harmonie, my family, and I are safe.

That night after they had their evening meal, only one cup of ale was given to each soldier. The same young man who asked about the dagger the night before asked, "Lady Baron Nichol, do you have another story?"

Nichol stood with most of the men sitting in front of her. "I have many stories but Daniel, you are too young to hear them."

Laughter rang out into the dark forest that surrounded them, followed by complete silence. Again, she had their complete attention. And then she began.

She started telling her story of growing up in Marseilles and the love of her father. She paused, looking down. As tears filled her eyes, she struggled to talk.

Taking a deep breath, she then looked up. "My mother poisoned my father. As he was being buried, I left Marseilles for Paris to find my papa's partner. You may know him; his name is Ezra."

Extending her arms, she gestured at her clothing. "I cut my hair short and put on breeches to disguise myself as a boy, much like the clothes I wear now."

She pointed to Timo. "I had been taught to run and to defend myself. This is where I met a monk that all of you know as Timo and his donkey Moki as I ran to seek Ezra in Paris.

"One morning I woke up to a small pup licking my face. I believe all of you know Shadow." She smiled as she looked at Robert. "At a monastery fair, I met my husband, Robert. My papa had considerable wealth and that is why he was murdered. His strong box was empty, and my mother thought that I knew where his gold, silver, and coin were hidden.

"I was chased by my evil brother all the way to Paris and then on to Rouen. I did not know that a priest had given him coin to continue pursuing me. He, too, thought that I knew where my father's treasure was. It was a fool's errand. Parts of my brother were found in the river and his head was found at the door of the miscreant priest."

Scanning those seated on the ground in front of her, she saw their eyes were wide open and no one moved.

She added, "Some of you may know the priest; he goes by the name of Loupe. He is nowhere to be found and Charles is dead. The rest of the story is ours in the making as all of us enter the village and fortress of the late Lord Charles and introduce Duke Richard and Baron Robert to those who live there."

Daniel said, "I have heard stories of you and your bow killing many men."

Not answering or denying his question, she just said, "It is true … I am skilled with the bow. But those stories will have to wait for another day."

Looking at the young man watching her, she said to him, "One cold night when I was alone on my way to Paris, I fell asleep hidden from those who chased me under a large pine. I was too tired to climb it and tie myself to a limb. I slept on the cold ground and woke with a cloak of warmth covering me.

"I heard a soft voice whisper in my ear. Instead of being afraid, the voice gave me courage. Her words to me were, 'You are your father's treasure.' I knew I was not alone and dreamed of my father as I fell back to sleep."

The camp fell silent as guards were posted and the fire burned down.

Nichol touched everyone that night, even Duke Richard.

She entered his thoughts as he sought sleep in his tent.

Nichol is right. I do desire her … but her strength and her wisdom will make me more powerful. She will remain my trusted advisor and is not a threat to me.

As the sun rose the next morning, Nichol went into Richard's empty tent.

She changed into the one dress she had brought with her, one of the new ones that Rose had made for her, rich with shades of blue. Over it was a cloak to keep out the morning cold. Braiding her hair, she let it flow over her right shoulder.

Approaching Robert, he smiled at her with approval. "Are you ready to meet the people as Lady Baron Nichol?"

Everyone had either mounted up or started walking. Soon, farms began to appear on either side of the road. When people saw them approach, they ran inside their homes or hid out of fright.

Duke Richard saw their fear and sent Joshua and Garlyn ahead to announce their arrival.

Charles' fortress could be seen, perched above a large village that led to the fortress.

Richard was riding just behind soldiers in front. Robert, Nichol, and Priest Samuel followed behind Richard. When they entered the fortress, people stopped what they were doing and stood, lining the streets on both sides and bowing as he rode by.

Nichol watched their faces and reactions. She was the only witness to their carefully concealed fear and hate.

I see them. I know what they feel.

At the stone castle, they dismounted. Richard entered with Otto and two other soldiers. Nichol stopped at the top step before entering and turned to see a crowd forming around Richard's men.

It was not curiosity she saw on their faces. Instead, she perceived a fear of strangers that could erupt in violence at any moment. Nichol turned to Samuel, dressed as a priest in a dark robe.

"Walk among them. They will listen to you. Tell them we come in peace and are here as one of them."

As Samuel walked down the steps and into the crowd, Nichol followed the duke and Robert into the castle. The dwelling appeared much the same as Richard's in Rouen, but much smaller.

Entering the hall, there was a chair two steps above the main floor. The man seated in the chair stepped down and bowed when Richard approached him.

Motioning to the man to rise, Richard took his place and sat down. The duke commanded everyone's attention except Nichol.

Nichol went to the steward who was present when they entered.

"Where is the widow of Charles?" she demanded.

His face went blank. In a loud voice heard by all, she spoke again.

"Where is the widow of Charles?" With his hand, the steward gestured and said, "This way."

The steward led her to a door on the second floor, and Nichol tried to enter but could not. It was locked. Behind the door, she could hear a child crying.

"Open this door."

A smirk appeared on the steward's face. "Who are you to order me to open this door?"

She drew herself up and put her hand on her dagger. "I am Lady Baron Nichol. By order of Duke Richard, my husband is now the Baron of this castle and lands and I am his wife."

Fumbling with his keys, he quickly unlocked the door.

"Leave now," were the only words she said to him.

Nichol slowly opened the door and saw two women trying to shield three children.

"I am Lady Baron Nichol," she announced, and then looked at those inside the room. She directed her words to the more richly dressed woman of the two.

"You must be Katharine, the widow of Charles."

Her gaze dropped to the children. "And, of course, these are your children. Tell me, Katharine, who locked you in here? Why is there only one candle in this room? Why is there no firewood for a fire?"

Katharine did not answer.

Nichol approached her and held out her hand for her to take. Slowly, Katharine extended hers. Nichol gently took it, covering her own hand over Katharine's. Both women closed their eyes.

Nichol could feel Katharine's fear and then sensed it ease away, eventually disappearing.

Opening her eyes, Nichol said, "Come with me and bring your children. I want you to meet Duke Richard and my husband Baron Robert."

Nichol offered her arm and the two women walked side by side to the Great Hall. Entering the hall, Nichol saw men standing in front of Richard.

The duke was unhappy; his anger was apparent. Robert and Garlyn were standing on either side.

Nichol whispered to Katharine, "Have your attendant take the children outside where the village people can see they are not harmed. I want you to tell me of these men."

Her first words tumbled out, so soft Nichol had to strain to hear them. "They will kill me if I talk about them."

Speaking softly, Nichol patted her hand. "Do not worry; they will not harm you. Stay here, we will talk later. We are here to help you and your children, not harm you. I, too, have three children."

Meanwhile, Richard asked several questions of the two men that they appeared unable to answer. He, Robert, and Garlyn watched as Nichol approached. Robert had seen the look she wore on her face before and knew not to say anything. They all remained silent.

The two men standing before the duke turned and saw her approach.

She now stood on the floor in front of Richard and pointed at the two men.

"These men came to Rouen to kill you, Your Grace. They are both cowards. Before we arrived, they had been keeping Charles' widow Katharine and her children locked in a damp, cold room with no fire and only a small candle."

Richard said, "What should we do with them?" His fingers began to drum impatiently on the arm of his chair, a sign of his growing anger.

"Let the people decide. We must hear their grievances, and then these evil men need to be dealt with. They are not good men, and they have mistreated the people of this place in many ways.

"There are many good people here, and Katharine is one of them. Without Charles' presence here, I believe she will have a strong loyalty to you and can also influence those who had been mistreated by Charles.

"It would be wise for you to walk among the people, to allow them to pledge their fealty to you. In turn, you have an opportunity to tell them that Harmonie is supportive of them. We will aid them by showing them how to grow better crops to feed their families and that Harmonie is a good community to have as a neighbor.

"Charles had many men come to Rouen with an aim to cause you harm. It is not yet clear whether they were loyal to him or whether to come. Katharine will know who creates trouble. Some of them are still here. I believe that she could work with Garlyn. And if she desires, she should reside within the castle."

For all to hear, she added, "Your Grace, Baron Robert and I do not want to continue the reign of fear that has lived too long in Charles' name. As the weather warms, we invite a group of men and women to come to Harmonie so they can see what we have done. They can learn much, and with their increased pro-duction, Harmonie—and now New Harmonie—will enrich your lands and you.

"We desire to stay here for a week so we can know of the skills of those who live here … and to learn who we can trust … and who you can trust as well. I believe Katharine will be of help to me."

The duke agreed, giving approval with a single short nod.

Turning his head toward one of the men who was with Charles in Rouen, he spoke, "You and the other who was with you will come with me now."

Otto bound the men's hands and led them outside to the courtyard. Immediately, the villagers moved away from them, knowing that the men were being led to a single post that had been placed there and used often by Charles. Jeers were heard as they passed. A man came forth from the crowd and spit on them.

These actions did not go unnoticed by Duke Richard, who then spoke to the crowd standing shoulder to shoulder in the courtyard.

"Charles and these men led an army to threaten me and Rouen, but they were not successful. As they traveled there and back, they stole from many on their way. The strong box in the castle is empty. These men and others stole from you and me, and they cannot go unpunished."

As he talked, the men were tied to the post. Standing by Richard was Robert, Nichol, and Garlyn. Richard put his hand on Robert's shoulder. "Robert is now Baron of these lands."

Next, he placed his hand on Nichol's shoulder. "His wife is Lady Baron Nichol." Last, he lay a hand on Garlyn's back. "This is Lord Garlyn."

Richard turned to Robert. "You must speak to them."

Robert stepped forward to silence, knowing his every word would be measured. In a soft voice, he began.

"I am the son of a blacksmith, and my wife Nichol is the daughter of a merchant. We call the valley where we live Harmonie. When we first arrived in the valley, there were few people living there. We learned that most were not there by choice. Instead, they were hiding from men like Charles.

"God and Duke Richard gave us the valley to live in and we have prospered. A few of us have called your land *New Harmonie* as we are neighbors. Duke Richard is here today to give you what he gave to us: a chance to make this New Harmonie a new, better beginning. In the days ahead, we will walk among you and speak with you all. May God bless each of you."

Robert stepped back to Nichol. The crowd stayed in the courtyard. There were no shouts of anger or praise, just the steady murmur of conversation.

They stepped down from the stairs into the crowd with Katharine and her children between them.

Otto's concern about her safety was evident but Nichol knew at that time she wanted no escort. Nichol sensed that Katharine was more at peace with the transition.

Nichol smiled at her, and Katharine offered a smile in return.

Then Katharine said, loud enough for others to hear, "Lady Baron Nichol, I welcome you here to New Harmonie."

Nichol was pleased with what she heard.

Katharine will be important for this village.

She then watched the crowd still milling about in the courtyard. A few men stood out from the others to her.

In the next few days, she would find them and learn their names.

It was possible there would be more residents that New Harmonie needed to be rid of.

eighty-two

New Beginnings

You can rely on me to support you;
to be an advisor as I am to the duke.

As the duke readied to depart four days later, he identified fifteen of his men to stay behind with Garlyn. At Nichol's request, one was the young soldier Daniel who asked so many questions of her at the campfire.

With the duke's approval, Nichol and Otto decided together that he would also remain in the castle and bring his family to live there with the rebuilding of New Harmonie.

If she needed any protection when she traveled, John and Joshua would handle it. One of them would travel with her to and from Rouen and when she was away from Harmonie.

Nichol knew that the duke was impatient to return to Rouen.

To him, she suggested, "As you depart, would you walk with Robert and I through the streets in the village? Do this to show the people you are not like Charles and that you have concern for their living. There are good people here. I have felt it as I have talked with many of them. Their fear is easing, Your Grace. As fear leaves, fealty to you will arise."

She added, "I have the trust of Katharine. She knows much about the people here, and the harm and fear Charles had created. She will become a strong ally for us … and for you."

Absorbing her words, he said, "I believe you are correct. With Otto here, we will always have eyes and ears to our benefit. I am confident that you and Robert will bring these people together as one with a common purpose.

"Everything that Charles had accused you of was untrue. You and the people of Harmonie have taken no advantage of anyone. The only fraud and liar was Charles himself."

As they walked, villagers joined in. As the duke spoke to one man, the man dropped to his knee, pledging his loyalty and faith to the duke. Others followed. Soon, all those present had pledged fealty to Duke Richard.

As he mounted his horse to depart, he said to Nichol, "You have done well."

Nodding her head, she said, "Your Grace … you know we are here to serve you."

The next morning after Richard's departure, Nichol decided that Robert, Garland, Samuel and Otto would all walk New Harmonie together. She asked Katharine to leave her children with her attendant and to join them.

When they were about to set out, Timo arrived with the cart they had brought with them from Harmonie. Within the wood walls surrounding the castle, they started to mingle with the stalls and shops.

Following the smell of bread baking was their first stop. Robert exchanged a large sack of flour from the mills of Duke Richard in Rouen for loaves of bread. They continued on their way, paying for dried meat and cheese.

At the leather shop, Timo handed a leatherworker some tanned leather from Cordoba. Awed by the quality, the man proclaimed it was the finest leather he had ever seen.

Conversations of families and children were exchanged at each place they stopped. People began to gather and walk with them. Bread was shared as they walked.

Next to the leather in the cart was a wrapped package. Within it was a blanket covering brightly colored cloth. Nichol noticed Katharine's eyes were fixed on it as it was uncovered.

"Do you have a cloth shop here?" Nichol asked.

Still staring, Katharine picked up a bolt of blue linen. "Yes, but not with the type of cloth and the beautiful colors you have here."

Nichol smiled. "Take me to the shop."

As they entered the shop, Katharine greeted the woman who owned it. She then introduced Lady Baron Nichol to her.

Nichol smiled. "Hello. I have some cloth I would like you to use to make Katharine a new dress." As she spoke, she gave the woman the cloth that Katharine had admired. "I know that you have the skills to make something special for her."

Then Nichol began to look over the cloth the woman had in her shop. "Would you like to have more cloth with additional colors for sale? I can arrange for cloth to be brought up from Harmonie so you have more to offer the women here."

The shop owner had never had such an offer. "Your Grace, I would welcome anything new here."

"The next time I am here, I look forward to seeing the beautiful dress you will make for Katharine. The blues in it will match her eyes."

With that said, Nichol and Katharine left the shop and continued their walk. "No one has ever done anything this nice for me, my lady. I thank you. Already I know that life will be better for many here."

She hesitated a moment and then continued to speak. "Lady Nichol Baron, I have noticed that you seem to speak for Baron Robert and others. Why is that?"

After thinking for a moment, Nichol replied, "Our marriage has always been equal with the two of us. We each have different strengths. I was taught as a young girl how to read and write.

I was also taught how to fight and to defend myself. With my strengths, I can often fight better than most men.

"This is why I am one of the duke's advisors. I see you as the main leader in New Harmonie. You can rely on me to support you, to be an advisor as I am to the duke. You can trust those that arrived with me as well. Bring any concerns or needs to Garlyn and Otto. Both are to be trusted, as well as Timo, who is here when he is working in the fields. Otto and his family will move here to make this their new home.

"Katharine, I will leave you with coin. When I am in Rouen, I often walk the streets and share bread with children who are hungry. Use this coin to get bread to share with others who are in need."

Timo later returned to the leather shop and shared his ideas about shoes that the villagers could use. He also inspected the farmland outside of the village. He told Nichol later, "I see why their crops are poor. I would like to stay longer so I can help them in their replanting so they will have more food. That is, if you agree."

"As long as there are men we can trust to protect you, it will help them all. And it will further unite the two lands. Otto will he here as well and he will keep his eyes on you."

Robert went to a blacksmith shop. He was curious about what goods had been made and to see if he could explain what was being made and used in Harmonie that could also be made in New Harmonie.

He had a few of the nails with him that he had made and gave them to the blacksmith. When the blacksmith saw them, and then examined them, he exclaimed, "These are stronger than my nails! Why?"

"It's all in the fire and technique. I will show you how to make yours stronger," was Robert's response.

The Harmonie visitors retained their caution. Whenever they went out into the village, they would always take a soldier with them, knowing that there were dissidents in the village who resented their presence.

Robert, Nichol, Garlyn, Otto, and Samuel walked through the village everyday, and the crowds following them kept growing. And the villagers would ask questions and get answers.

They could see a shift in the attitude of the villagers toward them. Many had questions. Many also shared stories of Charles' cruelty and the privations they suffered under his rule.

Nichol and Otto quickly identified those who remained loyal to Charles and could create trouble.

The week had come to an end, and Nichol and Robert felt they could return to Harmonie. Gathering Garlyn, Samuel, Timo, and Otto together, they made their final plans.

Otto and Samuel would return with them. Samuel wanted to oversee the building of the Harmonie church and Otto intended to gather his family and return. Then Otto and his family would live in the castle, along with Katharine and her family.

Garlyn decided to remain to oversee the duke's soldiers, and he would also stay in the castle, using it as his home when he was away from Harmonie.

Turning to Timo, Nichol said, "I see you … you are as excited as when you first saw the valley that would become our hamlet of Harmonie and now has turned into the village of Harmonie."

"I am, Nichol. I am needed here now. I will come back and forth as Garlyn does." Then Timo said to Otto, "When you return, will you bring Moki with you?"

"My boys will be happy to bring him. Tell me what else we should pack on Moki to help you with your planning. I know you will need seed. What else?"

eighty-three

Back to Harmonie

Come, Samuel, we can travel safely now.

The next morning, Nichol went to Katharine's room to tell her that she would be departing for Harmonie that day.

Dressed in her riding breeches, she explained, "Garlyn and Timo will stay behind with the soldiers. Timo is excited to share his ideas to increase yield in your fields. He is very happy living with the famers and within the fields and has found a place where he can stay. Garlyn will be available to you if you need help. Do not be afraid to ask. He will be working on rebuilding your village, sweeping away the fear and chaos that Charles had created.

"Otto will be with me and return soon with his family and Timo's donkey Moki. I think it would be a good idea if he and his family live in the castle with you for your own protection … and that Garlyn does as well. The soldiers will be under Garlyn's direction. They will stay until the duke wants them to return to Rouen."

Moving her head in agreement, Katharine said, "Lady Baron Nichol, I will miss your presence. For the first time ever, I have felt safe within these walls. When I heard of Charles' death, I became more afraid. I was attacked the night they returned and then locked in my room with my children.

"The men tied to the post are not all of the bad men; there are others who will take their place. I think they are just waiting for you and the soldiers to leave. When you return, I might not be here or alive."

Reaching out her hand, Nichol reassured her friend, "You will be protected from these men. I am Nichol to you, Katharine.

I know my children are older, but they will want to meet yours—and you. I will bring at least one with me the next time I come. Now I have a gift for you. It is from the dressmaker."

Nichol handed her a wrapped package, and Katharine was quick to open it. She gasped in surprise, and her eyes widened with tears. In the package was the cloth woven with blue colors Nichol had brought and now was a beautiful dress.

"I was right; the color is lovely on you."

Speechless, all Katharine could say was, "Thank you, my friend."

As she turned to leave, Katharine walked next to her. Reaching for Nichol's hand, she squeezed it gently. As the two women left the castle gate, Robert, Otto, and Samuel were mounted on horses. Otto held the reins of Nichol's horse. As Nichol mounted, several villagers had gathered.

"We will be back soon," Baron Robert declared. "Garlyn and Timo will remain to help you, and Otto and his family will be here next week."

Nichol edged her horse next to Garlyn, leaned down, and spoke softly.

"Katharine told me there are others in the village that are a danger to her and to you. Alert the soldiers, and do not leave her, Timo, or yourself without protection. If someone challenges you, execute him for all to see."

Otto had left instructions with the soldiers. "Cut the men on the post down and drag them out of town after we leave. Let the animals deal with them."

As the four left New Harmonie, many of the villagers removed their caps. They waved in return. New Harmonie was well on its way to a new beginning.

Nichol wore her bow on her back with a quiver of arrows. Her dagger was at her side.

Robert noticed.

Why the bow?

Riding a short distance away, just before a bend in the road, Nichol stopped and looked back at New Harmonie. Thoughts of the last week could not be easily left behind.

All in the party remained quiet, mulling over their own thoughts of the week's events. Robert and Otto knew that Nichol would eventually reveal hers to them. She turned to proceed and they continued riding away.

Samuel was uneasy with the silence and began to silently pray as they rode.

Nichol moved her horse next to Samuel. "This road we are traveling on was built long before we arrived and will be here after we are gone. Slaves made this road for the men that conquered this land. They left long ago and went back to where they came from. This road is now ours, and how we use it depends on us. Did we bring peace or conquest to New Harmonie? I think we have bought both. They are good people and we will bring to them the same things we brought to the valley of Harmonie."

Samuel said, "I prayed for you and for God to keep you safe." He thought for a moment, then continued, "You are truly noble in your words and deeds. God is with you, Nichol."

Nichol reached and placed her hand on his arm and smiled, not for his compliment but for his understanding of her.

I know the Lady is smiling, too.

Nichol spied her red-tailed hawk flying above.

Papa … I knew you would be here.

She had another feeling. The three villagers that she had identified as Charles' loyalists were out of sight, even though she sensed the evil men were not far behind them.

We must be prepared.

It was late morning now. Glancing up, she saw the red-tailed hawk making circles to the right side of the road.

This must be a signal to leave the trail here to reach Harmonie.

Calling out to the men, she gestured to the right side of the trail. "We will stop. The way back to Harmonie starts here. There were three men I saw in New Harmonie who I sensed wanted to cause us harm. I believe we are being followed. Let us rest the horses behind these trees and wait. Soon we will know."

Heeding her words, everyone dismounted. Otto raised his eyebrows when he saw Nichol stringing her bow and nocking an arrow.

"Are you sure?" Otto asked.

"Yes. They are coming. Samuel, stay back. Otto, Robert, and I will handle this."

As she heard the sound of hooves fast approaching, Nichol signaled Otto and Robert to mount and stay out of sight.

Nichol stepped out on the road with an arrow nocked and her bow at her side. Seeing her alone on the road, the men charged at her.

She yelled "Otto!" and raised her bow. Immediately, her arrow released and found its target. The riderless horse continued forward, slamming her to the ground and spilling the arrows out of her quiver.

Seeing Nichol dazed and lying on the ground, Samuel ran to her and helped her up. She yelled, "Arrow!"

Samuel picked up an arrow and handed it to her as Otto and Robert charged the other two men.

Otto, wielding his sword over his head, brought it down with great force, slicing one of the men open from his neck to mid-belly.

The third man was now in fierce combat with Robert who was blocking Nichol from her target. She started running, positioning herself to have a clear shot at him, while Otto tried to maneuver himself to help Robert.

Still on the run, Nichol drew back on the string and released an arrow that grazed Robert's arm before continuing to its target.

The man slumped in his saddle and then fell to the ground.

Nichol went to Robert as he dismounted. They embraced as no words were spoken. Samuel and Otto joined them as the sound of moans were heard from the last one, who was still alive.

Removing her dagger from her hip, she placed it in his hand. *What will he tell us?*

She began to ask questions. "I will let you live if you tell me if there are more who followed Charles and want to do harm to me."

He shook his head and whispered, "No."

Then she said, "I saw you first in the village, lusting for my dagger. You know you want to rob me of it. Do you not know of its curse? That only the rightful owner can touch it and if another does, he will die a painful death."

Suddenly, he began to feel pain in his legs and in his belly. His throat was closing and his breathing shortened. Gasping for air, his life was over.

Nichol removed her dagger from his hands and inserted it back in its sheath on her belt. Hearing the screech of the hawk, she turned to Otto.

He had already removed the arrow from the first man. Cleaning the blood off it and his sword with the dead man's clothes, he returned the arrow to her quiver.

Samuel led Nichol to rest against a tree while Otto cleaned Robert's wound and wrapped it with cloth. The young priest had never seen Nichol fight before and was stunned by what had just unfolded in front of him.

Robert gathered the swords from the men, noting the inferior quality of them.

"Otto, where we stopped with the horses is a pathway that will lead us home and shorten our ride by more than one day back to Harmonie," said Nichol.

With Samuel's help, and holding her right arm against her chest, Nichol slowly mounted her horse. She looked up to the sky again.

"The hawk will guide us to Harmonie. A new, shorter road between the two villages will save us time and effort."

Otto had his sword out, prepared to mark trees as they moved forward so they would easily see them when they returned. "Harmonie can use the horses. We will take them with us," he said, as he gave Robert and Samuel each the reins of a horse. He planned to guide the third one himself.

Looking at Samuel, Nichol urged, "Come, Samuel, we can travel safely now."

As they rode, the red-tailed hawk showed the way. When there was a shift in its flight, Nichol would call out a new direction.

Thank you, Papa.

eighty-four

The Longhouse

I knew there would be. We will talk tonight.

Returning to Harmonie, they rode in from behind the long-house instead of on the main road. The shortened trip on the new road took only a day and a half from New Harmonie.

Moving stiffly, Nichol dismounted, walked to the Great Bell, and rang it. She stood by it, eagerly waiting for her children to arrive. Helene and Dinah heard the horses and were the first to greet them.

Everyone in the valley knew of their trip to the former land of Lord Charles and all were eager for word of their visit. People soon arrived and everyone began to ask questions.

Laughing and holding up her hands, Nichol said, "Let us wait for more to arrive and then I can answer all of you at the same time."

Robert went to the road and saw Aiden, Lucette, and Athena running toward him, along with Otto's boys. Leading them was Shadow racing down the hill.

As Nichol looked out over the growing crowd, her thoughts were serene.

These are my neighbors and my friends. Because of them and the shops for their goods that have sprouted up close to the long-house, we are no longer a hamlet. We have become a true village.

Before she could speak, a woman asked, "What were the people like?"

Then another asked, "Did they try to harm you?"

And then a man asked, "Where are Garlyn and Timo?"

Taking a deep breath of relief, she saw that her children had come into the longhouse. Then she began to respond to the questions.

"Garlyn and Timo have stayed behind in New Harmonie. Garlyn will be there for many days to make sure that the men we identified as still siding with Lord Charles are gone. He will also oversee the transition as the villagers learn we mean them no harm and want to help them. He will live in the small castle when he is there and make sure no harm comes to Katharine, Charles' widow."

When she said Katharine's name, several of the women exchanged glances. One murmured, "Maybe he will have a wife at last."

Her words amused Nichol. She continued, "Fifteen of the duke's soldiers have remained behind to support Garlyn. I encourage you to think of New Harmonie as a sister village. Some of the men there offered their labor to help build Samuel's church. As we rode in, it looks like wood has already begun to be placed at the church's site."

Rurik was standing in the back by the children. Speaking up, he said, "It is I who have begun to gather wood for the church."

Hearing his words, she thanked him. Then she said, "Both the church and longhouse need to be completed after our planting this spring. Rurik is skilled in working with wood and he will lead both projects." When she acknowledged him in front of the others, she could see a slight smile on his face.

Nichol continued, "I will miss seeing Timo here each day as he helps New Harmonie. I saw his eyes light up when he saw the land in neglect and poorly used. It reminded me of the Timo I knew as a young woman when he traveled with Moki from monastery to monastery, helping the brothers improve their farming practices. Their land had been poorly planted. Timo helped them so that their surrounding villages would have more food. Now, it's Timo's challenge to make it better for New Harmonie, just as he did for us. He will be back to help with our planting soon."

Shadow couldn't sit still at the back. She pushed through the people to sit beside Nichol, nuzzling her leg as she did. Scratching Shadow's ear, Nichol let her arms drop to encircle her body.

Her belly is full of pups. I can feel one of them pushing against my hand as I touch her.

Lucette, Aiden, and Athena were excited to tell their mother of their journey to Fécamp. Robert had picked up bits and pieces as he met them on the road, but it was their mother who would hear more than just the words they said.

He asked the children, along with Otto's boys, to stay in the back of the room so the villagers could ask questions. "When we are in our home, there is much to tell you … as you have much to tell us."

Touching Aiden on his shoulder, Robert's eyes met his son's and then he moved forward to stand by Nichol.

"There is much work to do in New Harmonie. In turn, it has many who would be willing to come here and help build our church."

Hearing her words, Samuel bowed his head slightly. Nichol was aware Samuel was overwhelmed after the encounter with the three men.

"When I make our next trip to Rouen, I will seek labor there With our growth here, we need more help to build the second longhouse."

Several asked, "When will the duke come to Harmonie?"

"I believe he will be here during the summer." She paused for a moment and then added, "As we traveled back from New Harmonie, we discovered a pathway that could be made into a road.

It will allow everyone here to travel the distance in half the time it does from the road we used to get there a week ago. To be able to use this path and make it into a proper road, we need more labor."

Nichol was tired from the trip back. Knowing that the villagers wanted to hear more, she said, "Let us gather with food and drink tomorrow at this time. Bring some to share. I know many of you have questions about the new village, about the duke, and about our own village. Then Robert and I will be rested from our travel."

As she went through the door, Helene was at her side. "We also have much to talk about. There are changes in the children since they walked with Leiv and to the sea."

Slipping her arm through Helene's, Nichol said softly, "I knew there would be. We will talk tonight."

That night as they sat at the table, Nichol wondered who would start the reveal of what they did or saw. She didn't have to wait long.

Athena said, "I want to sail the sea like Diego and go to the land of Athena, where Zita's manuscripts came from. One day when Diego sailed into Rouen, I heard him talk to you and Granpapa Ezra. He talked about the people and the cities they live in.

"The lands farther to the east, far away where all the spices, books, and beautiful cloth come from. Oh, and I want to go to Cordoba where all the books are kept."

Nichol did not expect to hear the words Athena said. "Cordoba? Daughter, do you have any idea where Cordoba is?"

Athena definitely knew. She had seen the map that Diego gave to Leiv. "Cordoba is in Hispania, Mama. It is where I want to travel to first. And then to all the places Diego goes. Will he let me be on his ship?"

Before Athena could get more words out, Aiden could wait no longer to share his adventures. It was soon clear to Nichol that Aiden had his eyes on working with Leiv.

"I talked many times with Leiv. He said that I could work on the ship but that I must be a good swimmer and have your approval, Mama."

Lucette wasn't going to let her brother and sister have the only words. "I want to go where you grew up, Mama."

Taking in their words, she responded, "I believe all your desires can come true, but there is much to do before any of them can be considered. Did you all notice that Shadow's belly is swollen and growing larger each day? In a few weeks, we will have pups. I do not know how many there will be. You will all be responsible for them.

"Aiden, I promised one of Shadow's pups to Emma long ago. Hers needs to be trained with hand signals and voice commands. When the pup is ready, you will deliver the pup, making sure that he or she knows the signals and will respond to Emma."

Hearing her words, Aiden was thrilled with the challenge. "I can do that, Mama."

Then he added, "When I was helping Leiv unload the ship, he told me that Queen Emma sent word to him to bring Nichol to her again."

Hearing his words, Nichol knew that it had been too long between visits.

Speaking to her oldest, Nichol said, "Lucette, I too desire to go to Marseilles. Your granpapa has made many trips there and will tell us the best way to go. There are several people I want to see, including your cousins."

That got the attention of the three. "Cousins ... we have cousins?" they said in unison.

"Yes, you do. My papa loved a special woman and they had two children. Her name is Elise. I met her at the docks in Marseilles, but didn't know who she was or that she loved my papa."

That got all three of them to sit up straight.

"My children, I see all of you. You are ready to leave for a new adventure. That will be soon, but not yet. Before any of you travel any distance, we will travel together and explore. None of you have the full skills to travel freely yet.

"I've wanted to return to where I was a young girl, and to meet my sister Elise and her son and daughter. Elise was a brewer when she knew my papa and your cousins are close to my age. I think one of our travels together should be to Marseilles.

"Would you like to be with me when the trip is planned?"

All of them nodded their heads. Lucette asked, "When can we go?"

"Not this year. The pups have to grow. You must train them as I trained Shadow. We will first travel back to England with Leiv to see Emma and bring her the pup she wanted." With her words, a grin spread across Aiden's face.

"It is time now to go to bed. Papa and I need to plan what's next for New Harmonie and for the gathering of our neighbors tomorrow at the longhouse. There is much work to do in the fields and help with the building of the church."

With that said, the three went to their room.

Nichol could hear the hushed whispers. They were excited.

Helene had remained quiet and finally spoke, "Are you sure, Nichol? Is it safe for them? Each of them has an unusual mind and skills. I don't think that they recognize them fully, nor do you and Robert."

Nichol paused. "Helene, I too share your concerns. When in Rouen, many times their actions just brought looks and head-shaking. As they grow older, their actions will bring scrutiny from people who are close-minded. To survive, they must learn to temper their words and behavior and choose the words they speak wisely. It is important that they travel. The knowledge and wisdom learned will help keep them safe.

"Learning is like eating to them. They are always hungry. During the summer, we must encourage them to go out … but we must have them tell us every day what they learned."

That night in bed, she lay awake, but it was not New Harmonie that kept her awake.

Helene's words kept repeating in her head.

We must have help. The Lady who was there at their births must also continue to guide them.

eighty-five

Changes

Nichol watched Richard's expression change.
She knew what he wanted.

After the meeting at the longhouse, Nichol knew she must soon travel to Rouen.

The next afternoon Nichol sent the children to tell Otto, John, their wives, and Samuel to meet them at the lake. Nichol and Robert arrived first.

Standing at the lake's shore, they looked down into the valley and saw three children running down the road, a wolf leading them.

Robert put his arm around Nichol and said, "I told them that they could go to the top of the hill but to be back before dark."

"I think of the hill overlooking the valley as their church, Robert. I know that they have had encounters with the *Lady* on that hill from the things that they say and do. She will connect with them and guide them from there."

John, Cara, and Samuel arrived first. Close behind them were Otto and Gabrielle. Nichol directed them to sit in a circle. Nichol wanted to hear from Gabrielle and Cara first.

"Think of what you want to say when I ask each of you to respond to my question. Gabrielle … you start. Do you want to go to New Harmonie to live?"

Surprised with Nichol's question, Gabrielle said, "I have never been asked that question: What do I want?"

Turning to Cara, Nichol asked the same question. "What do you want?"

As she asked the question around the circle, Nichol watched Otto and John for their reaction and was pleased that they appeared to be supportive of their wives' answers.

Each of the women wanted to be with her husband and children.

Turning to Gabrielle, Otto said, "We will tell the boys that we will be moving to New Harmonie as a family. I have seen much opportunity there. John and I, along with Garlyn, will be the eyes and ears for Nichol and Robert when they are not there."

After Otto's response, the conversation went around the circle again, with all contributing thoughts and ideas.

Nichol knew that the winter work in the longhouse had brought the valley together. Nichol's last words were, "Robert and I must go to Rouen to see the duke, Ezra, and Olaf. If Diego is there, we can return with some of his cargo. John will oversee Rurik in the building of the church and work with the other men in the planting of the fields. We leave tomorrow."

In the morning, Otto and family rode north to New Harmonie, with Moki in tow. Moki was loaded with the seeds and other tools Timo requested.

Nichol and Robert rode toward Rouen.

They were in no hurry, taking a full three days to reach Rouen. Once they reached Rouen, their time together would be limited. Riding past the walls that surrounded Rouen, they were immediately recognized and greeted with friendly waves. One shouted, "Where is Shadow?"

Arriving at Ezra's, Robert took the horses to the nearby stables.

Nichol knocked on the door and it was answered by Roger. Roger turned and exclaimed, "It is Nichol!"

Ezra jumped up and approached her with open arms, embracing her just as she entered. "I am glad you are here! We must talk. Where are Robert and the children?"

Nichol smiled. "Robert took the horses to the stables, but he will be here soon. The children are in Harmonie with Helene."

Ezra paused and continued with a sad, distant expression. "I miss her, our conversations, and her insight."

"You can change that, Ezra. Return with us."

"I am needed here."

"Ezra," Roger said, his tone patient. "You have trained Olaf, Marie, and Raisa well. They will take excellent care of E & N while you are gone. Diego is at the warehouse waiting for your list of cargo for his next voyage."

Nichol said, "Tonight we will talk more about this. Robert and I must go to meet with Duke Richard."

On their way to the castle, she told Robert about the need to speak with Ezra tonight and to meet Diego at the warehouse.

As they approached the outer castle wall, Victor greeted them with his usual smile and expressed that he missed her. She gave him a silver coin and was informed that the duke was in the castle.

Thomas the steward opened the door. "Finally, you are here. His Grace asks about you everyday. Go to his solar, and I will tell him you have arrived."

Entering the solar, they stood and waited for Richard. He entered the room, head down, and obviously in a bad mood. Looking up, he gestured for them to sit.

As she did, he noticed that her hand went to her right side to support it.

Nichol knew she must redirect his thoughts. "We are here to tell you that after you left New Harmonie, all went well. We learned quickly that the village has many needs. Garlyn will stay in the castle when he is there. Within a month, he will return to Harmonie and we can discuss what those needs are."

Nichol watched Richard's expression change. Before he could say the words, she knew what he wanted.

"I need you here, Nichol. I have brought lords from Normandy to appear before me. There is one that never answers my questions of him, and I would like you to be here when I question him."

With a concerned look, he sat back in his chair. "Why did you press on your side when you sat down. Are you hurt?"

"When Otto, Priest Samuel, Robert, and I left New Harmonie, three of Charles' men were determined to ambush us. We readied ourselves behind trees when I sensed they were approaching. I nocked an arrow and stepped on the road to face them.

"All three charged at me as I loosed an arrow. Otto and Robert were on the road and attacked the other two riders. My arrow struck the man in the chest and he fell off his horse, but the horse continued forward, knocking me to the ground and spilling my arrows. Samuel handed me one of my spilled arrows.

"With a single blow, Otto killed one of the three and was attacking the other man with Robert. I nocked another arrow and it hit its mark as well, but not before it grazed Robert's arm. I believe they thought with you and most of the soldiers gone, and Robert and I dead, they could take back control of New Harmonie.

"It is good that you left soldiers there to be on guard. The villagers revealed to us as we walked the streets and spoke to them that they felt protected at last. And where we had the encounter with the three men, we discovered an opening in the forest that could be cut back to build a roadway between Harmonie and New Harmonie. As we rode through it, Otto marked the way. It will reduce travel time to one day instead of three.

"Your Grace, I am here now. When should I return for your meeting with the lords? And where do you want me to be? Should I stand next to you or in the shadows?"

"The lords know of you. It would be best if you stand by my side."

Nichol took in his words and then said, "As much as I would like to stand by you, I feel that being in the shadows with all of them will give me the opportunity to observe them as they are. They will be more outspoken and I can deliver you a better assessment."

Duke Richard took in her words. She added, "Next time, I can be more visible. I will return after the lords meet with you. Before I go, I will reveal my observations to you."

"I will send word for you when they arrive."

"I will be at Ezra's or the warehouse at the dock. Robert will be looking for men to come to Harmonie to build another long-house and Priest Samuel's church while we are here. Otto and his family are already moving to New Harmonie and he is bringing seed for Timo."

As she and Robert got up to leave the solar, she added, "Those in Harmonie look forward to you coming to them. They are eager to pledge their loyalty to you."

eighty-six

Ezra

Yes … it is time for me to join Helene.

Nichol and Robert spent several days in Rouen, visiting friends, shops, and merchants. They both realized they longed to return to Harmonie, and their peaceful valley life. Nichol went to the castle and spent an afternoon with Duchess Judith.

She returned to the castle when the duke sent for her. Slipping behind the large tapestry, she observed the lords. She then sat down with the duke, warning him, "Your suspicions are correct. These men are not to be trusted—they are lying."

Absorbing her words, he said, "I agree with your assessment. Before you leave, the duchess awaits you."

Ezra was up early and sitting at a table with a hot cup of water nestled in his worn hands. He was torn between the merchant and moneylending businesses he had always known and moving on … and going to Harmonie to be with Helene and the children.

Was it time for him to leave Rouen … and leave the business to Olaf, Marie, and Diego?

Wresting him from his thoughts, Nichol and Robert joined him in the kitchen, and Achim and Raisa soon joined them as well.

Nichol quietly observed Ezra. Reaching her hand out to him with a stern look, she gently said, "Helene needs you, Ezra. And our children need us as well. Robert and I leave this morning. You should be coming with us."

Knowing her words were true, he still felt words of resistance emerging from his throat. "I am needed here in Rouen. I cannot leave. Not yet."

He could not have guessed the strongest argument to leave would come from his brother. Achim quickly agreed with Nichol.

"You have trained Raisa and I well, my brother. Olaf and Marie know more about the warehousing and merchant trade here in Rouen than even you do. They have become the backbone of the business and know how to deal with the merchants … how to handle them. Both can be trusted. I have watched Diego closely. What he brings in is coveted by the stores here and even in Paris.

"It is time, Ezra. Go to Helene. Roger can stay here until you return and oversee the coin collections for you."

Ezra looked at his family through tear-blurred eyes. He knew Achim was right. He trusted his nephew Robert without question, and Nichol had become the daughter that he and Helene had always desired.

Absorbing their words, he nodded his head. "Yes … it is time for me to join Helene. I want to be there more than here."

Saying that, he stood, squaring his shoulders.

"Achim, you will sort it with Diego, Olaf, and Marie. Let them know I will visit later this fall, but I trust them all to carry on our business. Increase the coinage allotment threefold for Olaf and Marie and yourself. We will do an accounting when I return."

Nichol was pleased with his decision. "Helene will be surprised and happy, Ezra. And the children will be excited to show you what they are doing. I believe that Harmonie will welcome you. I know your wisdom will be needed as we continue to grow."

"I want to get a full day's travel in today. I will bring three horses here. Nichol and I have what we are traveling with already. Ezra, I want to leave soon. Can we go as soon as you are packed? Achim will take care of the warehouse and Diego."

Raisa had already added extra food to their pack by the time Robert returned with horses.

Ezra and Achim came down the stairs with clothes and a cloak. Wrapped inside the cloak were bags of coins.

Ezra said, "You will need coin to pay for work needed in Harmonie. I have already arranged with Joshua this week to travel to Harmonie with skilled men to build what you need, including a new home in Harmonie for Helene and me."

The next two days on the trail, stories flowed. Ezra told of Rouen, and Nichol told of Harmonie and New Harmonie. The conversations between partners were much needed.

When riding there would be times of quiet contemplation. Nichol would watch Ezra. She knew, with enough time to think, nostalgia would occasionally take over his thoughts.

Patiently Nichol and Robert would wait until he was ready to share his thoughts. As she looked at Ezra, her thoughts were practical.

He needs Helene. His unkept hair, beard, and soiled clothing will quickly change when he walks in the door to greet her.

Nichol shared her thoughts with Robert of her final meeting with the duke before they left and why he wanted her present so she could observe the lord's manners and demands of the duke.

"Nichol, did he really need you there when the lord was? Or was there something else? I think … I think the duke desires you."

Ezra was riding behind Nichol and Robert; they both stopped and turned to hear Ezra's response.

"My dear nephew, the moment Nichol stepped from behind you at our home in Paris, a strange feeling came over me. My merchant and moneylending business depended on me, as Nichol says, *seeing* people. The duke wants something he can never have and Nichol will never give. He will either be an ally or adversary.

"I think that both of you should spend most of your time in Harmonie, avoiding the duke. Let me say one more thing. Helene and I were very fortunate that you brought Nichol to our door that day. She has changed our lives … and yours, nephew."

Ezra kicked his horse and rode between them to take the lead.

Late afternoon on the third day, they entered the Harmonie valley.

They saw three children running quickly down the hill, as if they were in a race. Faintly, they could hear Aiden's voice ask of his sisters, "Who is with Mama and Papa?"

Silence … then Lucette exclaimed, "Mama has brought Granpapa home!"

Helene heard the running feet of the children.

Where are they going now?

Hurrying, she stepped out of the house. Watching their diminishing backs as they ran to their parents, she saw an old figure riding with them.

Who is that …

Oh … my Ezra. He has come home.

Now Helene moved as quickly as she could toward the arriving figures, a huge smile across her face.

When Ezra saw her, he slid off his horse and ran to her, embracing her in a tight hold like never before. Both were laughing, overjoyed to see each other.

Drawing back, her nose wrinkled, Helene chided in a gentle tone, "You, dear husband … smell. You need a bath—and more than a bucket of water. We will walk to the lake and while you bathe, you will tell me all that has happened since I last saw you."

eighty-seven

Shadow Gives Birth

You did well, Shadow. It is time for you to rest.

With the first light in the morning, the children were up and tending to their chores. This morning it was Aiden's turn to fetch water, while Athena brought in wood and started a fire under the pot. Lucette cut onions, turnips, and beets, adding it to last night's pot.

Nichol came in from their garden and Robert came in from the forge.

Aiden stirred the pot and said, "It needs meat; I will check the traps. Come, Shadow."

Shadow did not obey. The wolf dog just looked at him. She could not stand still and was panting heavily.

Nichol and Athena went to her and knelt. Nichol placed her hands on her belly. She encouraged her daughter to do the same. Smiling at Athena, she said for all to hear, "Shadow will have her pups today."

"Mama, Shadow should have her pups in our room," Athena cajoled. Lucette and Aiden quickly agreed.

Robert looked at Aiden. "Go check the traps, then come back for breakfast. We all still have work to do today. When you each finish what you have to do, you can come back to be here with Mama and Shadow."

A nesting place was made in the corner of the children's room. Nichol quietly said to Robert, "I want them to see her give birth."

Robert reassured Nichol, "I will keep them close to home and when she starts birthing, they can watch."

After checking the traps, Aiden returned to the house to eat. As he sat at the table, he turned to his sisters. With a big grin, he declared, "I will name my pup Hunter."

Athena quickly said, "Mine will be called Zita." She turned to Lucette. "What will you call your pup?"

Lucette was quiet, deep in thought. Finally, she said, "I do not know yet. I must see the pup. The pup will choose me, and only then I will know the pup's true name."

Turning to her sister, Athena said, "Come with me, Lucette. I want to mix some of my herbs to make a special drink for Shadow. When I felt her belly, there was lots of movement. I think there could be many pups and she will need extra help in feeding them. I know Mama would say it would be good for her."

Telling their father and brother their destination, they agreed to wait for Mama's whistle. The two girls headed for the longhouse where Athena had been storing items that she brought from Zita when she learned about healing herbal medicines.

When the sun was high, they heard it. Four long whistles bellowed out across the valley—meaning *everyone come.*

Lucette whistled back, acknowledging her mother. All were strong runners from the training that John and Otto had put them through and their legs didn't let them down. Each arrived within minutes, with Robert panting behind them.

Moving quietly through the house, they moved to the back room where Shadow lay on her side, still panting. Nichol was at her pet's head, talking to her. Her hand was on Shadow's side. "Everyone is here, Shadow."

Within minutes, Shadow's tail lifted and liquid gushed out like she was peeing. Soon after, she pushed out a shiny lump that wiggled a little. Immediately, Shadow twisted her upper body and nudged it with her nose. She started to lick it, then nip at it gently.

Suddenly, it was alive and they could see little feet and an open mouth.

Shadow licked the pup until it was free of the covering on its fur. Nichol sat back on her heels, feeling Shadow's belly and the movement within it.

"Just watch … there is more to come."

With the pup wiggling, Shadow nudged it toward her belly and settled back down. The lttle pup wobbled as it squirmed, its head pushing forward for a teat to latch onto.

The children were fascinated. Talking quietly amongst themselves, they were excited that different fur colors emerged after Shadow cleaned the pups and moved them close to her belly. Almost at once, each pup would push against her, looking for a teat to clasp onto so it could begin nursing.

Nichol gently stroked the new pups' heads as they greedily nuzzled Shadow's teats.

Over the afternoon, six pups were born.

Aiden said, "I know who Hunter is. He is the biggest one!

Nichol rose. "Shadow has had her pups. Let her rest. Lucette, bring her a large bowl of milk and leave it close by. She will be thirsty."

No one wanted to leave. They were mesmerized by the wiggling little furballs pushing against Shadow as if each were claiming its own territory. Nichol reached down and stroked her pet's head.

"You did well, Shadow. It is time for you to rest."

Turning to her three children, she urged, "Come now. Shadow and her pups will be here when we come in for supper. Let her sleep."

eighty-eight

The Hill

We do not need to run. Lucette is all right.

A single candle was lit the back bedroom where Lucette and Athena were sleeping. Aiden's soft snores sounded close by and Shadow lay curled at his feet.

Suddenly Lucette woke. She immediately sat up in the dark, seized with fear of something that was not present. Her chest pounded as she wiped cold sweat from her brow.

Aiden awoke when she stood up. "Another dream … you cannot sleep?"

She did not answer and stepped over him. Aiden touched her leg. "I want to go with you."

She whispered, "I need to go alone."

It was the summer of her tenth year.

As Lucette cracked open the outside door, a sudden rush of air blew out the only candle.

Hearing Lucette's stealthy movements, Shadow rose from the enclosed area Aiden built to pen up the pups during the night. The space was big enough for Shadow to sleep with them if she wanted. The pups had grown and now were rolling, tumbling balls of fur that played with each other and slept. Now they slept.

Jumping over the barrier that secured them, Shadow moved close to Lucette.

Taking a deep breath, Lucette scanned the starry night sky. Her destination was the hill.

Shadow began to move with her. Lucette raised her hand. "No, Shadow … you stay with the pups. I will be back soon."

With a feeling of urgency, Lucette began to run as she was now accustomed to on the well-traveled road. She was familiar with it in darkness or light.

There was a sense of anticipation for the messages that she knew awaited her. Her mind reeled with questions as she ran. She sought the answers to her recurring dreams that escaped her at morning light.

Sprinting from the base to the top of the hill, Lucette arrived out of breath. Slowly she walked around the top, scanning the stars, wondering if now her *Lady* was among them. As the sun began to chase the stars away, Harmonie and the only road leading into the valley came into full view.

This place had become her hill of solitude: a place of contemplation, enlightenment, and reflection with the *Lady*. Lucette assumed her usual place on a large boulder and prepared to watch the promised sunrise.

At home, Nichol was awake. She was also aware of Lucette's trek to the hill. Rising from her bed, she lit candles while Robert, Aiden, and Athena joined her.

"Something is happening with Lucette, Aiden. I want you and Athena to take food and drink to her. Stay until she wants to come home. No matter what she tells you, do not let her go by herself again. You must now stay together at all times."

Aiden placed a pack of food and drink in the satchel he carried on his back and he and Athena began to run to the hill.

Athena slowed to a walk. Aiden slowed as well and turned back to her, a question on his face. "We do not need to run. Lucette is all right," Athena said calmly.

"Mama's words keep coming back to me. She said, 'No matter what she tells you, do not let her go by herself again. You must now stay together at all times.' What did she mean when she said that?"

Mulling over what Athena said, Aiden replied, "We must talk to Mama and find out. When the duke came to New Harmonie, Mama and Papa began quietly talking to each other and Mama is not herself. She seems worried. Let us hurry and be with Lucette."

The first light began to follow the path to the top of the hill, bringing it into view.

Aiden and Athena ran to the top of the hill. Out of breath, they arrived at the large flat boulder where Lucette was sitting, her place to meditate and invite the *Lady* to be with her.

A serene look on her face told Aiden and Athena she was with the *Lady*.

Wisps of cloud glowed red with brilliant yellow trailing behind as the sun heralded a new day. A red-tailed hawk was perched on a tree branch within Lucette's reach.

There was a tranquil aura around their sister. They were pleased to see she appeared at peace with her thoughts. Quietly they sat down on opposite sides of her as they caught their breath and closed their eyes.

Another world beckoned, a world of knowledge that only a few imagined existed and even fewer possessed. All three were now with the *Lady*, and her thoughts melded into each of them.

What have you learned today and everyday?
What senses are you using?
What do you see?
What do you hear?
What do you feel?
How are you seeing people and their intentions?

Each had become a new strand for the *Lady* in her tapestry of life.

eighty-nine

Summer's Surprises

I knew we did right in coming here.

Timo returned to Harmonie after working with the men in New Harmonie and their land, increasing their food and crop production. As the summer unfolded, everyone knew the yields would be even greater in Harmonie. His apple and walnut orchards brought acclaim to the valley. And the grapevines were producing wines that had become favorites of Rouen and Paris.

Two of the monks from the monastery in Vienne of many years past had found their way to Harmonie and to Timo. During his time with them, he had taught them about planting and growing vines for the monastery's wine. The two had walked north and arrived in Rouen, always asking along the way if anyone knew of Brother Lemur. No one did … until word came to Ezra. He knew that Timo was Brother Lemur.

Making sure that they were not connected in any way to Priest Loupe, he revealed where Brother Lemur was and that he was known as Timo. Excited with the news, the two began the long walk to Harmonie from Rouen, being told to seek out Robert or Nichol. When they entered the valley, they knew at once that Brother Lemur was here.

As they approached what looked like a longhouse that could have been at their monastery, the two exchanged glances and nodded their heads, both saying, "He is here." At the same time, Nichol came out of the longhouse and approached them.

"I have not seen you two before. What brings you here?"

"We are looking for Brother Lemur. He helped us at our monastery with our plantings. Ezra told us that we would find him in Harmonie."

Listening to their words, she knew they spoke the truth.

"Brother Lemur is no longer with a monastery. He lives among us as Timo, guiding us, as he did you, with our plantings and crops. He will return from the outer fields where he is working on our grapevines by early afternoon."

Both were excited with her words. "Is this Harmonie, the village Ezra told us of? Are you the Nichol he said to seek? Do you think Timo would let us work with him?"

Nichol laughed. "I can answer yes to all your questions. You must be hungry from your journey. Come to my home and tell me why you have come to be with Timo … and now it sounds like you may be with us as well."

As they sat on stools in her kitchen, she told them, "Timo oversaw the planting and harvesting of wheat, rye, and oats. He nurtured the grapevines to produce wines that we now sell in Rouen and Paris. His irrigated fields have provided abundant yields and the design of these fields has been copied by other hamlets that he advises. Our residents have found that their personal gardens surrounding their homes have added pleasure to their everyday living as well as to their mealtimes.

"Beehives are his new passion. He has been shadowed over the years by Athena, my youngest daughter, who helps him with the hives. She has no fear and has never been stung. Timo has noticed that she talks and sings to them whenever she approaches the hives. She also talks to Moki, scratching his ears like I used to."

"Moki!" one of the brothers exclaimed. "Is he here, too?"

"Oh yes, Moki is one of our much-loved residents here in Harmonie. When my children were small, Timo would gather them up and load them into a basket on Moki and off they would go for an adventure …"

As she shared this, one said to the other, "I knew we did right in coming here. What Brother Lemur is doing is what we wanted to do: help people in villages to produce food to take care of their families."

Smiling, Nichol extended her hands to the two. "Welcome to Harmonie."

Early one afternoon Nichol was feeding the children when she heard shouts in the distance and went to the open door. Nichol covered her eyes to block the sun's glare and studied the cause of the shouts, a group of approaching riders.

The closer they came, Nichol could see that there were eight armed men in the group.

Nichol began to walk toward the riders and turned back to the children.

"Go ring the bell two times. Wait, then ring two more times and then two more again and then join me."

Nichol extended her arm and waved back and forth.

A familiar face—Richard—broke from the group and rode quickly toward her. Those that saw the armed men approach had also heard the bells ring, and the sound brought the valley's people together. They began to surround the entourage.

The duke dismounted and immediately approached her.

Nichol bowed. "Your Grace, welcome to your valley and the village of Harmonie." With her hand, she motioned to the long-house. "You and your men must be in need of rest and drink."

Then she added, "Where is Judith and your sons?"

"They are at the castle in Rouen. I came here to speak to you in private and, as I promised you, to meet the villagers."

When they reached the longhouse and before entering, Nichol held her hand up and spoke to the people following them. "Let the duke have rest and food, then we all can show the valley to him."

Robert and the children entered, along with Timo and John.

Food was brought to the table; wine and ale served. Fish, cheese, bread, cooked apples, and venison were put on the table. Duke Richard took one bite of the venison and glared at Nichol with a scowl.

"Who has been hunting in my forest without permission?"

The duke's men were immediately on alert.

Nichol stood. "I killed this deer when it was in my garden. You know of my prowess with a bow. Tomorrow we will go to your forest and hunt for deer and boar."

"Yes, I know the truth of your arrows …" here his men laughed, "… and they do as well. But how will we hunt without my dogs to find the deer and boar?"

Richard then took a piece of venison from the table and tossed it in front of Shadow. His action drew the attention of the entire table.

Shadow looked at Nichol as she shook her head, holding her hand up.

Shadow knew that she was not to move … not to eat, yet.

Nichol dropped her hand and reached out to scratch Shadow's ear.

"Shadow, eat." Immediately, the wolf dog devoured the venison and then went to the door to guard the entrance.

The duke's response was a raised eyebrow.

When the duke and his men had eaten, Nichol said, "We use ways to hunt for only meat that will be consumed. Since we have been here, we have learned the ways of land and forest animals. There are times to hunt that leaves them plentiful to breed and increase their size so we can eat heartily as well. Shadow and my children will know where to begin the hunt, and then Shadow will lead us."

On the following day, after the successful hunt led by Shadow and finished with Nichol's arrow into the heart of a stag, Richard's demeanor quickly changed.

Nichol could see that he seemed distracted and upset about something. She felt he needed conversation with a trusted ally; one who listened and was not judgmental.

"I want to show you the lake where the fish you ate came from. Shall we take a walk there?"

Richard turned to his guard. "Follow and watch us from a distance."

Without further conversation, they walked to the lake and found a log to sit on.

For many minutes they sat and just stared at the lake. Nichol waited for Richard to divulge the reason for his visit. She sensed he struggled to find his words.

"You know I have feelings for you: not just as an advisor and you now being Lady Baron Nichol."

"A woman knows when a man has lust in his heart. I have noticed this from our first meeting. I too have feelings for you, but they are the feelings of a dear friend. We both know that nothing can happen between us."

"I do know, but that does not stop my desire."

"Perhaps in a different time or place, but I was not born of nobility. It was not meant to be. Robert is my first and only love, and I would never betray him or your Judith's trust in me."

The duke sighed heavily. "Neither would I."

"There is more you wish to tell me; I sense there is danger. Now tell me the other reason we are here at this moment."

I see you, Richard.

"Tell me, Richard, where is Loupe?"

Richard took a deep breath, looked down at the ground and shook his head. "I do not know. It seems his location is being kept a secret from me."

"You are Duke Richard. Find him."

Immediately Nichol knew she went too far with her words.

Softening her tone, she added, "He can come for me, but not my daughters or son. I will find him and put an end to this. I will no longer live in fear for my family and anyone who lives in Harmonie. I need to eliminate him and the evil around him for the good of all—including you."

Standing, she said, "Your Grace … it is time that the people of Harmonie pledge their fealty to you. Come walk among them and meet them. I will gather everyone to the longhouse and you will be properly introduced."

When Aiden saw her walking down from the lake with the duke, he knew what he needed to do. He went to the Great Bell and rang it, using the signal for all to come to the longhouse.

As it pealed, heads raised in the fields. People came out of their homes. And movement began toward the longhouse. The duke was surprised to see the organization. By the time he and his men were down from the hill, there were many gathered, wondering why they were summoned.

Nichol raised her hand.

"My friends … this is the Duke of Normandy. Robert, Garlyn, Timo, Otto, and I have already pledged ourselves to him. I have asked him to meet you, and to answer any questions you have. And for each of you, we ask that you pledge fealty to him so that he will support you … and Harmonie … if our need arises."

Then she dropped to her knee, followed by Robert and Garlyn.

Almost as one, the villagers all dropped to their knees.

As she looked up at the duke, her eyes encouraged him to speak.

His words came. "I am much impressed with the work and goods you create in Harmonie. I promised Baron Robert and Lady Baron Nichol I would come to meet you and see how you live. Today I learned new things about hunting and your land. Because of Lady Baron Nichol, you have my pledge of protection for those of you who live here."

The duke then turned to the farmer next to him. "Tell me of what you grow …"

For the rest of the afternoon, Duke Richard spoke with anyone who would approach him. Both Samuel and Timo looked on, talking amongst themselves.

As the villagers went back to their fields and homes, the duke saw Priest Samuel and Timo and moved toward them. "Are you pleased to be here?" he asked Samuel.

"I am. The church was built this summer, and the villagers come to it and to me. The longhouse is a gathering place used daily. Timo has been of great help in encouraging them to come. His mastery of the land has made living here desirable. When you return to Rouen, the nuts, apples, and other fruits you take back will be welcomed by those in your castle."

To Timo, he said, "I have heard you are the keeper of bees. When I come back, I will have my sons with me. They know of bees and want to see where honey comes from."

"I will show them the secrets of the bees, Your Grace. Nichol told me that you would bring your sons one day."

Turning to Robert and Nichol, "I am impressed with what your vision has created here for the benefit of all. My men and I will stay here tonight and return to Rouen at daybreak.

"When I return to Rouen, I will remind my brother that any further pursuit of you must stop. You are the Lady Baron Nichol of Harmonie and any attack on you is an attack on me."

He turned to Garlyn. "If you are in Rouen, you are welcome to come to the castle."

"Thank you, Your Grace. We will have food ready for you and your men for your journey. Ezra's wife Helene and I will make sure there is plenty for all."

That evening in bed with Robert, Nichol moved close to him and quietly spoke of the conversation with Richard at the lake.

Robert turned to her and put his arm around her and pulled her to him.

"When you talked about your home in Marseilles and the loved ones you left behind, I knew that you would leave us in Harmonie for a time and go to seek them out. I want to go with you to the places of those memories and dreams."

Nichol kissed him on the lips. Her body went limp in his arms, her anger disappeared and sleep overcame her.

In the morning, Duke Richard mounted his horse, moved to the forefront of the group, and began to trot down the road with his men. All the valley's residents watched as they left.

The older children ran next to them, and Richard watched as Lucette ran next to him. He reached down and offered his hand to her. Without slowing down, he swung her up behind him.

Once he did that, two other soldiers did the same with Aiden and Athena. When they arrived at the crest of the hill, the soldiers stopped and let them down.

It was a day the children and those in the valley would not forget.

ninety

Pup Training Begins

Your pups are you friends and protectors.
And they will warn you of danger.

Throughout the summer months, much activity happened after the duke appeared in Harmonie. The second longhouse was completed with Rurik as the lead carpenter. Ezra had arranged with Roger to pay for the extra labor that had been brought up from Rouen and over from New Harmonie. Ezra also suggested that extra rooms be added so that travelers would have a place to stay.

At that suggestion, Roger said, "That would allow me and Joshua to have a room to stay in when we travel back and forth between Rouen and here." Rurik had added the extra rooms for housing the workers, plus adding a small tavern area within the longhouse for the serving of ale and food for them.

With all the activity, the pups became a common sight with Shadow overseeing them. Aiden knew which one was his on the day it was born. Hunter showed dark gray ears with a silver coat emerging. His once-blue eyes were now a yellow gold.

Athena named her pup Zita after her teacher. With a chest that boasted white fur, the rest of her coat was silver. Lucette was patient in selecting which pup would be for her. As she promised her siblings, she would let it choose her.

When the children watched the pups in play, one always came to Lucette's side when she sat on the ground and plopped down. Picking the pup up, her little tail wagged back and forth at a rapid speed.

"So, you are mine?" Quickly the pup nuzzled her and licked her face. Placing the pup on her lap, she said, "I will call you Sage, with your light-colored ears and silvery fur."

Nichol sometimes stood with Shadow, watching the pups as they moved about and explored their world. One morning, she leaned down and rubbed Shadow, garnering her pet's attention. "It is time to start their training, Shadow. They each need to learn how to communicate like you and I do. Are you ready to work with them and me?"

Approaching the trio of children with Shadow at her side, Aiden looked up at his mother and said to his sisters, "Mama has a different look on her face."

The laughter amongst them stopped.

Lucette asked, "Is something wrong, Mama?"

Smiling at her three, she said, "No … but it is time to start teaching the pups so they will understand each of you as Shadow does me. Remember, they are wolves. Everyone will see them as that and be fearful until you teach them how to present themselves differently. It is my hope they will be with you for as many years as Shadow has been with me."

She then sat down. "Lucette, do you remember when Sage came to you and licked your face? That is what Shadow did to me when she picked me, as Timo and I slept on the forest ground one morning. She picked me, not Timo.

"Your pups are you friends and protectors, and they will warn you of danger. They will do what you tell them to do with your voice and your hands. From now on, when you go to the hill or the lake or anywhere, they will be with you.

"You know that they are eating the meat that Shadow brings to them. They no longer need her milk. As long as they have food, they can be away from her and the other pups for longer periods of time now.

"Each day, you will work with your pup. We start today. At times, Shadow will be with you. In the beginning, I will be with you as well. You know many of my hand signals. Now you will learn them so they become natural and quick for you to do … and for your pup to respond to. And I know that each of you will have special signals and words you create to communicate with your pup.

"Shadow will teach them to hunt. It is how they will eat from now on. I watched Shadow hunt rabbit many times. She would always bring a few home so that I could add them to the pot for a stew or to dry the meat for later eating.

"The other pups should also be worked with. One will go to Queen Emma and another to Duke Richard … "

As soon as she said *Duke Richard*, Aiden jumped up. "I will train the duke's pup. It should be the one that is almost as big as Hunter."

"And Mama," Lucette volunteered, "I will train Queen Emma's pup. I remember her talking to me when I was a little girl in her garden. She will like the one that looks like Shadow the most … I know it."

Not to be left out, Athena said, "I will work with the third pup. I think he might be for Timo to help him in his fields here and in New Harmonie. I've seen how the pup acts around Moki; it is like they are friends."

Hearing the words of her youngest, Nichol laughed loudly. She then stood and reached out her hand to Athena.

"Pick up the smallest one with the star on her forehead. We will find Timo and share which dog you have selected for him."

As Nichol and Athena started toward the fields, they no longer saw Timo out there. He and Moki had returned to the longhouse with baskets of apples. Seeing the two, he called out to them.

Hearing his voice, Athena shouted out, "We have something special for you and Moki."

Timo was curious. *What could they have?*

Then Athena held the smallest of the pups up to him. "This is Moki's new friend. She will chase rabbits from your garden and protect the beehives. And when you walk to New Harmonie, she will go with you. And I will help you train her each day and—"

Before she finished her sentence, Timo was in front of them.

The pup wriggled out of her arms and was on the ground. Looking at the people, she turned to where Moki was and ran as fast as her little legs could carry her. Moki already had his head to the ground and the two were rubbing noses.

"Moki has a friend. And now, you will have a new one too, Timo."

A broad smile spread across Timo's face as he watched Moki and the pup.

"This pup is welcomed. Thank you. I will call her Star. And she can sleep with Moki and me like Shadow did when we walked to Paris many years ago."

With his words, Athena clapped her hands … happy to see her friend so pleased with his gift.

Priest Loupe

I don't talk to women with my concerns.

Timo worked closely with the two brothers in the planting of new vines in Harmonie in the early spring. The orchard with apple and pear trees promised delicious delights for those in the village. In another year, they planned to sell their fruit yield in Rouen and other villages.

When he met with Nichol and Robert at the longhouse, they talked of plans to work with the monastery in Fécamp to host a Timo Fair in a fall month and one in Harmonie that would welcome those who lived in the hamlets that were now growing from the success of Harmonie.

Time continued to pass; soon it was late August. The new vineyards planted in the early spring had taken root and grown better this first year than Timo had expected. The fields in Harmonie were abundant with golden grain as the harvesting began within both the Harmonies. Home gardens of onions, cabbage, and beans were being picked. The children were sent to pick wild blackberries at the edge of the forest, sometimes eating more than what their baskets carried.

Nichol's garden of medicinal herbs and spices was an important part of their diet. Timo's orchards of apple and pears were being harvested and the beehives were tended to by Athena. She took excellent care of the herb and spice garden, and when Nichol wanted to know where her daughter was, it was most likely with Timo, Moki, and Star.

Everyone's senses were overwhelmed with the blessing of such abundance as the men, women, and children came together in celebration. The kitchens and pantries in each home overflowed with spring and summer harvests that were preserved and stored for the coming winter.

Aiden, Robert, Timo, Gideon, and Harald worked in the fields during planting and harvesting. Nichol and Freyja kept Tova, Gunvor, and the older children busy cooking, baking, and preparing to serve the hungry field workers.

Ezra, Helene, Lucette and Athena were constantly chasing the small children from underfoot. The work was hard, the mood was festive, and people were at ease. Harmonie and all in the valley participated in its success.

The Harmonie House was full of activity. With all the doors and shutters open, the welcome breezes chased out the summer's heat.

A large metal pot filled with meat and freshly picked turnips, onions, carrots, beans, and cabbage, and seasoned with herbs from Nichol's garden, hung cooking in the fireplace. The smell of fresh baked bread cooling wafted throughout the building, with cheese and honey already on the tables. Bowls, spoons, and cups were set out and pitchers of cool ale were waiting for the thirsty workers.

When the Great Bell was rung, workers would start streaming in, ready to be fed.

Nichol looked around and pronounced that they were ready to serve. "Ezra, would you ring the bell?"

Ezra went to the door—and abruptly stopped.

With a loud voice, intended to be heard above the children's chatter, he exclaimed, "Nichol, come here!"

She stepped out of the door. Quickly, she turned back toward Ezra and Helene.

In a demanding voice, she ordered, "Take the children and leave at once. Everyone out, *now!*"

Nichol's heart sank.

I knew this day would come.

Approaching the Harmonie longhouse was Priest Loupe.

To her surprise, the people of Harmonie closely followed the priest and his escort of six armed soldiers. In their hands were pitchforks, scythes, and knives.

They raised their implements and shouted, "Go back! Get out! We don't need you here … we have our own priest!"

Robert was at the front of them and made eye contact with Nichol inside the longhouse.

With a forced smile, she held her hand up and waved to him to stay calm.

Priest Samuel was at Robert's side.

Loupe seemed oblivious to the immediate threat from the Harmonie villagers. The soldiers knew better as they placed their hands on the hilts of their swords and watched as the ever-growing angry crowd closed in, moving ever closer.

Sensing the tension, their mounts danced about, restless with nerves.

Reaching the longhouse, all dismounted.

Four of the soldiers immediately unsheathed their swords and stood by the entrance, facing a now-furious mob.

Priest Loupe and the other two soldiers entered the longhouse. He stopped to let his eyes adjust to the light as he looked around the room.

Pointing at a table, the three men moved toward it and sat down. Those still in Harmony House fell silent. Fear invaded the room.

Nichol watched his every move closely. She saw an arrogant, smug smile of joy from one who was feasting on their fear, and that fear pleased him.

One of the soldiers banged his hand on the table and demanded, "We are thirsty and hungry. Bring food for Priest Loupe and his men!"

Loupe had a sinister sneer on his face as he looked about the room, basking with delight at each frightened face as the people ran out, afraid of this stranger who emanated such a threat.

Nichol stood alone in the longhouse.

Loupe's voice was more of a sarcastic snarl. "I see you prepared a feast and celebration on my arrival." His soldiers laughed, knowing that was the response Loupe expected of them.

All eyes were on Nichol, unmoving, her face serene.

Shadow's hackles were up and her soft growl resounded as Loupe glared at her.

Nichol approached with bread and tossed it down in front of them. Moving slowly, she brought cups and a pitcher of ale, spilling some as she placed the items on the table.

The soldiers quickly pulled the bread apart and poured honey on it. Their careless hands spilled the sticky nectar onto the table.

In a voice loud enough for those outside to hear, Loupe bellowed, "Who speaks for this village?" Then he crammed a large bite of bread into his mouth.

Nichol moved to his side, glaring down at him. "I do."

He looked up at her and started laughing—a coarse, bellowing laugh, as he looked at his soldiers. "A woman?" Half-chewed bread spewed from his mouth. "I don't talk to women with my concerns."

"You will talk to me because I represent this village and I know you. I am Lady Baron Nichol." Her voice was calm; her words direct.

Finally, with a village behind me, the man who chased me across France is in front of me, and I do not have my dagger.

Hearing her reply, Loupe seemed to become agitated. In a threatening voice, he said, "I don't know you. Now bring me the man who is the leader of the village."

Positioning her body with legs slightly apart beside one of the tall stools, she said, her voice loud, "If you are looking for a man to talk to you, you best leave, Priest Loupe.

"You have changed since I first saw you at the villa of my father, Alexander, when you were a priest in Marseilles. You have not aged well."

They glared at each other.

Nichol continued to speak, her tone resolute. "I have watched men like you for too long and not spoke out about the injustices they inflicted. You are a small, insignificant man, rotten with ambition and delusions of importance, and the smell of death follows you."

Taken aback at her words, Loupe let out a nervous chuckle.

One of the guards stood and unsheathed his sword.

Nichol's words spewed out, laced with venom.

"You impregnated my mother Astrid with Fredric and then returned to fuck her after she poisoned my father. You chased me from Marseilles and tried to kill me. The head of Fredric was left on your doorstep as a warning that your evil deeds were no longer a secret. And now you bring soldiers into our valley. You are a wretched, foolish coward, not fit to be called a man of God."

His nervous chuckle turned into a bellowing laugh as he slapped the table. Finally, he seemed to recognize her.

"So, you are Lisa or should I call you Nichol? We finally meet face-to-face."

Nichol was surprised at his lapse of memory.

Hmm … he does not remember anything about me since his head hit the stone street in Rouen, only before. Does he not remember Shadow pouncing on him and biting? Does he not remember Lucette's birth at Ezra's home in Paris?

He pointed at her with an accusing finger. "You still have something I want. I want the treasure the whore Astrid told me about and all the tithes that you owe the church. I demand that you donate land so a proper church can be built. It is clear this village needs firm guidance. The people here have wandered away from God."

Nichol's anger continued to grow.

"Neither this village nor I owe you anything, you stupid man. We have a priest that Archbishop William sent to this valley and I know that you have been banished from the kingdom of Normandy. Priest Samuel is standing outside. We are under the protection of Duke Richard.

"As for me, I see you for exactly who you are. You are a thief, a torturer, and a murderer. You lie and you covet. You are not a man of God … you are an evil man of greed and deceit."

The soldier that was standing with his sword unsheathed pushed his stool away and started to move around the table toward her.

Loupe said nothing to stop him.

The villagers outside were getting restless and began yelling insults toward the men who entered and were alone with Nichol.

Several of the Harmonie men started moving toward the guards stationed outside in front of the door, who now pointed their swords toward the villagers.

Inside, the soldier with his sword drawn paused. The angry mob lurking outside outnumbered them.

They were trapped.

Then something happened that halted all movement, inside and outside of the common house.

Out of the shadows, Lucette appeared in a soft light, speaking with a voice so pure in song it mesmerized all but Nichol. The crystalline tones of her voice carried through the door to the people gathered outside.

Robert, Aiden, Athena, Helene, Timo, and John knew the sound of her voice at once. Exchanging uneasy glances, they stood poised outside the longhouse door, alert and ready to enter if Nichol shouted for them.

Loupe's wary gaze followed Lucette as she slowly walked toward him. Her angelic singing overwhelmed the few in the longhouse and wafted to the outside, transfixing the villagers.

When evil comes
Knocking at my door
Come in, I say.
Sit at my table.
Share bread with me and stay.
I will touch your hand.
Do not look away.
Your mind, I will explore.
You will beg me to leave.
Why would I? … You came to my door.
Now you are mine forevermore.

The child moved next to Loupe as he stared at her, seemingly caught in a trance.

Lucette placed her hand on top of his.

Suddenly a light appeared and surrounded Loupe that only Nichol could observe.

The priest's eyes appeared to bulge out of his skull and a grimace of pain spread across his face. Time stood still while the *Lady* invaded the mortal—the invitation that Lucette provided with the touch from her hand.

When she removed her hand and the light slowly faded away, Lucette moved to stand by her mother.

All attention was now on Loupe and the two soldiers at the table.

Loupe's expressionless face bore a blank stare as he rose to his feet, turned, and walked out the door. After a moment, his soldiers followed, confused but staying close to their master.

All of them remounted their horses. As they did, the crowd parted, providing a path for them to ride away. Loupe showed no emotion, his gaze still unfocused and his body movements stiff. One of the soldiers moved to lead their retreat, and Loupe's horse followed, as mindless as its master.

Inside the longhouse, as Nichol tightly embraced her daughter, her only thought was for her child's protection.

Did the Lady allow the priest and protectors to see what happened? What will they report when they return to Rouen? Will they tell others?

She was still puzzled by what happened. After a few moments of reflection, she realized that the *Lady* had acted through Lucette.

The only explanation was that the *Lady* had taken over Loupe's body.

The *Lady* accomplished this through Lucette.

Her hand ...

Moving quietly, people began to reenter the longhouse.

Lingering anger persisted as food and ale were consumed. Voices growing increasingly louder could be heard over the normal conversation. Angry questions rumbled through the crowd.

Why was that evil man here? How did he find the valley?

And finally, the question Nichol dreaded most: *What made him leave?*

Priest Samuel climbed onto a stool and shouted, waving his arms, demanding everyone's attention.

"Today was to be a day of joy, to celebrate an abundant harvest and the success of our valley. Instead, we received a visit, not from a man of God but the opposite. The evil is gone, never to return. Now, let us enjoy this feast and celebrate our success."

As Samuel spoke, Nichol's mind was absorbed in her own thoughts.

Lucette is special. I now can see her gift.

Aiden and Athena must have gifts from the *Lady* as well. When will their full gifts be revealed to us?

Could one of Athena's gifts be that she sees things before others can?

The oldest daughter of Nichol and Robert—the one everyone knew was different—had removed the evil pall that had threatened Harmonie.

ninety-two

The Harvest Fair

I see you now and I know you for the bastard you are.
I have killed better men than you.

It had been ten years since Timo had organized his first fair in Rouen. Each year it had grown and become something that all looked forward to … a celebration of the summer and the preparation for the coming winter Solstice.

Timo's Fair had become the major event at the end of the harvest season. It was now a weeklong event and known as the Harvest Fair. Each year it expanded, bringing people from neighboring villages, towns, and as far away as Paris.

Merchants, food, and ale stalls were numerous. Singers and storytellers entertained the crowds. Farm animals were brought to show, to sell or to trade.

At the center of the fair, the best location to display crafts and wares was a large red cloth cover supported by four poles. Under the red cover were many of the products produced in Harmonie.

On one side of the tent, Robert, Aiden, and Vilfred displayed knives, axes, and farm tools while Vilfred sharpened knives upon request.

On the other side of the main covering, Lucette had a table displaying the bows and arrows she had crafted.

Athena had mastered creating rich colors for dyes by pounding the spring and summer flowers. Each of their tables had a different colored cloth chosen to best display products.

Timo, Athena, and Zita displayed herbs, spices, honey, and wine. Theirs was a multicolored cloth spread over the tables that represented the variety of what they offered. Lucette's cloth was a honey color for displaying her bows and for Aiden, she chose a cloth colored like the dark centers of iris flowers growing wild in their fields.

Over the years, Timo had built a following. He freely gave advice to those who asked for his knowledge of agriculture.

In the center of the red tent, stools were supplied for those who wanted to sit for a few minutes out of the sun. Athena had created a sign with grapes, apples, pears, bread, and cheese painted on it to hang above Timo's table to attract visitors to where he displayed his wines.

All the items were widely sought after and it became the gathering place to drink wine and hear stories—stories of people's lives, their fears, and concerns.

Stalls throughout sold ale. Fair patrons could sit and enjoy conversation with a cup of wine from the Harmonie Vineyards.

Helene was always nearby, feeding and caring for people. It was her idea to add stools and small tables that would encourage patrons to take time to linger. She offered nibbles of bread and cheese to drinkers. This stall had become the hub to find out what was happening in Rouen and surrounding areas.

The more wine and ale that was consumed throughout the day, the better the stories that were revealed. Timo would charge people what they could afford. Duke Richard, Duchess Judith, and Archbishop Williams, as expected, were given free cups.

Rose and Joseph had their own booth; displaying cloth that was made and dyed in Harmonie.

The food, the wines from Harmonie's vineyards under the watch of Timo and the other brothers, and the products and quilts created by the women of Harmonie became essential items in Rouen homes.

Nichol was surprised to learn Leiv had delivered a message from Queen Emma that her brother Duke Richard had sent word about the quality of Timo's wines. He recommended that she stock them for use at her castle.

It was midmorning when people began to arrive and stroll by. Men and boys stopped to look at knives or bows while women stopped at the tent to sample the many herbs, honey, and spices that Timo and Athena offered. Nichol, Helene, and Dinah were already seated under the tent.

Everyone was excited for the first day of the fair.

Wagons of crops were brought for sale from Harmonie's fields. Contests in hatchet, knife-throwing, and wrestling were featured in another section.

Throughout the day, Nichol would listen to her children's conversations with people looking over their work. Aiden was learning from Robert how to sell and together they were very successful.

She observed Lucette as men walked by and looked at her bows. Instead of the bowyer they expected behind the table, they saw a young woman. They questioned her about who made the bows, not about the outstanding craftsmanship.

Nichol, Robert, and Ezra also made it a habit to leave the tables and walk about the fair, talking to all the merchants and visitors, and keeping their ears and eyes opened.

A tall, well-dressed man stopped at Lucette's table. He picked up several bows and carefully looked them over, testing them for strength. He strung each one to feel the force needed to pull the bowstring back.

Something about this man brought Nichol to her feet and moved her to Lucette's table. Nichol's sudden action did not go unnoticed by Helene, who also quickly stood.

The man then turned his attention to Lucette. "Who made these?"

Lucette said, "I did."

A skeptical smile split his well-groomed beard. "You did not make these. Girls do not have the skills for this kind of craft."

Nichol immediately stepped next to her daughter. She snatched the bow from his hand and retorted, "Yes, she did make this bow—and all of them that you see in front of you."

A chill went throughout her whole body.

She turned to Helene. Their eyes met and a slight nod from Helene confirmed her suspicion. In a low voice, she told Helene, "Quickly, go to Ezra and bring him at once."

Nichol turned to the man. She assessed his eyes, his smile, his features, and stature—and she knew … *this must be Aiden's father, the man who raped Marie as a young girl.*

Another chill shook Nichol. She wanted him out of her sight. "This bow is not for sale."

"Do you know who you are talking to?" The man drew himself up. He appeared offended that a woman dared to talk back to him.

Without another word, Nichol glared at him.

"I am Lord Henry … and you will address me as such."

"The bow is still not for sale … not to you. You are blocking others from this table." Nichol made a shooing motion with her hand. "Move on, Lord Henry."

Just then a commotion rippled through the gathering crowds. Nichol and Lord Henry saw Duke Richard and Duchess Judith walking toward the group of tables he was in front of.

The duke's popularity with his people had increased significantly since he had started taking walks among his subjects in Rouen. With Nichol's encouragement, Duchess Judith would join him, always bringing bread and other food to give to children and anyone who looked in need.

With a smirk, Lord Henry said, "I will let the duke punish you. You will never be allowed at this fair again."

The brightly-colored tent cover attracted the duke and duchess, and they moved toward it. As they approached, all bowed.

"You looked angry, Lord Henry. What troubles you?" the duke asked.

"This insolent woman and this peasant girl refuse to sell me a bow."

Duchess Judith looked down to the ground, hiding the smile that had spread across her face. *Clearly Lord Henry does not know of Nichol,* she thought.

She tapped Richard on his hand to get his attention, as if to ask: *What are you going to do, my husband?*

Richard was wondering the same thing. Stroking his beard, he thought, *Has this lord not heard of Lady Baron Nichol?*

Aware that something was happening, the crowd became still; not even a whisper could be heard.

The duke stopped stroking his beard and then spoke.

"You and the woman will shoot arrows at a target I select. The one who shoots with greater accuracy may keep the bow. If you win, Lord Henry, you may choose the punishment for the woman. Her name is Lady Baron Nichol."

Lord Henry's face flushed dark red, but no apology dropped from his lips. Instead, a look of defiance filled his angry face as he glared at her.

"I will accept the challenge."

As he said those words, Helene and Ezra appeared.

Instantly, Ezra recognized the man: a man he knew treated women and children badly. He was also one who did not pay his debts.

Ezra knew how to seize the moment. "If I heard correctly what was said, this sounds like something I will wager on." Taking out his coin purse, he tossed it on the far end of the table of bows. "I bet on the lady. The best two out of three arrows that are the closest to the center of the target's ring wins."

The crowd grew larger. Some knew of Nichol, most did not. More coins and purses came out. Ezra was counting and noting who wagered and for how much.

The crowd laid their coins out. Lord Henry was heavily favored.

Ezra asked Duke Richard, "Your Grace, do you have coin to join in?"

"I think it would be best if I not influence anyone by my choice."

With his words, the duchess laughed out loud, then quickly covered her mouth with her hand, and looked down.

Ezra then said, "Everyone, follow me. There is a mound behind the last stall. We will set up a ring made of a leather strap for Lord Henry and Lady Baron Nichol to shoot at."

As he finished his words, the crowd was already moving in that direction. Lord Henry said, "I do not have my bow with me. I will use this bow from the table."

Before anyone said anything, he picked it up and grabbed three arrows.

Nichol also selected three arrows, saying to Helene, "Stay at Lucette's table. This will be over quickly." To her daughter, she looped her arm through Lucette's, leaned her head close and murmured, "He picked my favorite of your bows. This will bring us much merriment when it is over."

Catching the duke's eye, he winked at her and moved ahead to catch up with the crowd.

When Nichol arrived at the challenge site, she saw the mound with the leather strap in the circle with a diameter of a man's hand. Lord Henry was strutting about in the crowd with a cocky posture, making lewd remarks about Nichol. Seeing her, he grabbed his crotch and thrust his hips at her.

Seeing Robert in the crowd that Ezra had drawn to the event, she saw her husband start to move toward Lord Henry.

Catching his eye, she shook her head *no* and held her hand up to say *stop*. He retreated, his steps reluctant, but remained wary.

Ezra asked if there were any more bets.

Duchess Judith moved toward Ezra. Holding up her hand so all could see, "I have two coins, and I wager them on Lady Baron Nichol to win."

Hearing her words, many of the women added their coin. One said, "I have a pig. I will put it on Lady Baron Nichol if she will take it." The crowd laughed.

"I will gladly take it," was Ezra's response. The crowd laughed again.

Ezra then held his hands up and barked out the rules in a loud voice.

"Lady Baron Nichol and Lord Henry declared a contest. They will each shoot three arrows. The best two out of three will win. I will toss one of these coins and Lord Henry will call what side lands facing up. If he calls the correct side, he can choose if he wants to shoot first or second. If he is wrong, Lady Baron Nichol will choose whether to shoot first or second."

Ezra then tossed the coin in the air and Lord Henry claimed it would land with no stamp side up. Landing on the dirt, sure enough: no stamp.

Ezra, again in his loud voice, announced, "Lord Henry has chosen to shoot the first arrow."

Lord Henry picked up one of the arrows and took a few steps forward, marking a line in the dirt with his boot. He then nocked the bow and raised it, aiming at the leather circle on the mound. Swiftly, the arrow found its target, landing just inside the circle.

The men cheered; the women glared at him.

Stepping back, he pushed the bow at Nichol. She already had her arrow ready and moved toward the line in the dirt. She looked at the duchess with a slight smile, nocked her bow and raised it.

Releasing the bowstring quickly, the arrow sailed toward the target, landing close to the other arrow, but outside the target.

The men cheered.

The duchess shouted out, "You can do it, Lady Baron Nichol!"

Lord Henry approached her in his cocky walk and grabbed the bow.

Nichol stepped back and waited.

Nocking the arrow, his second shot landed next to his first arrow.

Again, the men cheered; the women did not.

Nichol stepped up to take the bow, ready to nock her arrow. Letting her eyes find Lucette and Robert, she nods her head slightly and lifts the bow.

The crowd gasps as her arrow split the shaft of Lord Henry's arrow, causing what remained of the arrow to drop to the ground.

The women cheered louder than the men could imagine. The woman with the pig said, "I have a second pig for you, my lady, if you can do it again."

Lord Henry's mouth dropped open when his arrow was felled. He angrily grabbed the third arrow, his face darkened and eyes narrowed to furious slits as he snatched the bow away from her again. Nocking the bow with his last arrow, he lifted his arm and released his arrow.

The arrow landed within the circle but not centered.

Feeling some courage return, he glared at her as he handed the bow over for the final shoot. "The final shot goes to the lady whore." Many of the men laughed.

Picking up her final arrow, she nocked it and looked at the target in silence.

Then she stepped to his side and murmured in a low voice, "I see you now and I know you for the bastard you are. I have killed better men than you."

She then lifted her arm, thinking: *arrow, be straight and true.*

Maintaining her glare at him, she released the arrow without looking at it or the target.

Her arrow hit the target dead center.

The women exploded in loud cheers, while the mouths of the men gaped open in shock. No one had ever seen shooting like Lady Baron Nichol's.

Lord Henry was vibrating with his expanding anger. No woman had ever spoken to him with such disrespect. He had also never lost a match to someone he felt was inferior. And all women were inferior.

Lifting his hand, he moved to strike her down.

At the same time, the duke yelled out, "Stop, Lord Henry! If you strike Lady Baron Nichol, you will lose your right hand. She has won the match."

Nichol's final words chilled Lord Henry. "Look closely at the crowd. Many men would gladly kill you. Leave Rouen before day's end."

Lord Henry had to push his way through the crowd as he left. No one opened a path for him. One woman threw her ale at him and then ducked behind a man when he turned in anger, seeking his assailant.

Ezra had his hands full settling all the bets. Those who favored Lord Henry got nothing. Those who favored Nichol received five times what they wagered.

The woman with her pig got it back, and Ezra gave her a few of his own coins as well.

When he did, she said with a chuckle, "I will call the pig Henry and think of the Lady Nichol Baron putting him in his place when my family butchers him."

The Women

Tell me your name and about you …

As Nichol walked through the fair the following morning, the women began to follow her.

Some reached out to touch her arm, as if her strength could flow through to them. On the second day, she turned to the many who surrounded her and said, "Come … let's sit over there on the open field and meet each other."

Smiles spread. Heads nodded yes. Nichol led the way to the open spot and turned to them. "Sit down. I am happy to meet you."

As she sat amongst them, she said, "You already know of yesterday. I have three children and am married to Baron Robert. I live in the village of Harmonie and work with the many women there with their quilting and cloth-making. We have two large longhouses where we cook and sew together. We also work in the fields, growing many crops. We teach our children to read and write, and how to protect themselves if they are in danger.

"In the winter, my family comes to Rouen and we live at my family home that Ezra has. His wife is Helene. She is like a mother to me and my most trusted friend."

The women's eyes widened as Nichol revealed so much, so soon.

The first woman that spoke asked, "I saw you make a fool of that man yesterday. How did you learn how to use a bow?"

"When I was a young girl, my father saved me when men were attacking me. He sat by my bed as I healed from my wounds. He gently talked to me and said that he would teach me how to protect myself from anyone who attempted to harm me again.

"What I did not know was that he had contacted a man he was close to who trained men to fight. When I was physically well, I went to a fighting school with my friend Gerhardt every day as Papa didn't want me to go alone.

"Sir Roland became my teacher. The first thing we were taught was that we had to run, and I mean *run* everywhere. Sir Roland said that if one could outrun another, he would survive, then he changed his word to *she* could survive.

"Gerhard and I ran everywhere. And I started to wear boys' breeches so I could run faster. Soon the other girls wanted to dress like me. Their mothers were not happy. Then Sir Roland brought out weapons—daggers and swords—and taught us how to use them and fight with them. Then the bow was shown to me. I felt myself smile as I reached for it; it felt as if it called to me.

"The bow and arrow was my choice. My arm and eyes are strong. The bow always felt like it belonged in my hand. With my special dagger, I have not only saved my life many times, but the lives of others—including the duke."

Nichol fell silent and paused to examine the many faces surrounding her. Some wore smiles; some had mouths agape; and some bore the tracks of tears on them.

Nichol saw and felt their pain. She knew that many had experienced harm and abuse from others, even those they now lived with.

Reaching her hand out to the woman next to her, she said, "Tell me your name and about you …"

Several hours passed as each told who she was. Finally, Nichol stood.

"We will gather again when I return to Rouen at the Solstice. Now I need to return to where the Harmonie tables are. Come see us there."

As she said goodbye and moved away, one of the women said, "We need her … she can help all of us."

Little did Nichol know that she had opened a door to the women.

They began to form their own community and to heal within —one story at a time. There was much for her to do for them. She would help, just as she knew her older daughter would step in to help as well with their daughters.

Daily, Lucette stood behind the bows she made, along with arrows and arm braces.

After her mother's victory over Lord Henry, many came to her table to see the bow that Nichol had used and that Lucette had made. Many spoke to her with praise, at first not believing that someone as young as her could craft bows and arrows as skillfully as she did.

Lucette made targets out of straw tied together in the shape of life-sized deer and boar. On the final day of the fair, an older boy challenged her as she sat in her stall.

"How could a girl make this bow? I don't believe you did."

Standing, she was taller than her mother now. Curves were beginning to show on her young body and looking at her, she was a mirror of Nichol when at the same age.

Her chin lifted. "Sir … I was taught how to make bows by the wise bowyer Hubert of Rouen as his apprentice. My mother trained me in shooting. You have challenged me with your words. I challenge you to a match. Will you accept my challenge?

"You can use your bow or use any that I have on display here. I will use the same bow as you select … either yours, or one of mine."

With a smirk on his face, he picked up one of the bows on the table. Feeling the tension, his eyebrows raised.

Otto's boys were close by and overheard the two talking. Suddenly, one shouted out, "There's a contest! Lucette is going to beat a man with a bow!"

Someone yelled out, "Where …?"

Another exclaimed, "I will wager on Lucette winning."

Word spread quickly and landed on Ezra's ears. Quickly moving to Lucette's stall, he held up his hands and shouted, "Who is the man who has challenged my Lucette?"

The crowd was growing and his eyes landed on the man close to her. "If it is you, then a target is already at the earth mound close by where another challenge was made. This is a place where no one could be hurt and where you both will shoot at the same target."

Speaking to Lucette, he asked, "Is this what you want?"

"Yes, Granpapa. It should be fair to us both." She moved closer and whispered for his ear alone, "I like the eyes on this boy."

Lucette turned to her challenger. "There is a large open area past Rose's and Joseph's stall. Let us all meet when the sun is directly above us there."

The crowd was buzzing with excitement as the word spread that another challenge had been delivered and a contest declared.

Lucette turned to him. "Which bow and arrows shall we use? My name is Lucette."

"I do not have mine with me." Picking up several of the bows from her table, he pulled back on their bowstrings. Finally, he declared, "We will shoot with this one." Looking at her with his green eyes, he said, "My name is Louis."

"You have made a good selection, Louis; you selected my favorite bow. And what three arrows would you like to choose and which targets? We can use some of the stuffed ones I have here … or we can use the leather ring that was used by two others in their challenge."

What is happening with me? This boy makes my neck feel warm.

As the two spoke, the crowd around them was now growing larger.

Ezra was thinking, *we now have another contest. I wonder if anyone wants to bet on who will win? I know my coin will go for Lucette.*

Close by, Nichol noticed what was going on. Moving closer to Ezra, she leaned in and said, "No betting, Ezra. Let them have the challenge. I believe there is something else happening here."

Turning to the crowd, Nichol said, "This will be good to see the skills of our young people. Let's see how they do …"

Turning to her daughter and the young man, she continued, "Merriment is good at the fair. People here like to see challenges. You two may wish to start a regular event for future fairs so that others your ages can show what they can do."

The midday hour came and Lucette and Louis met at the earth mound.

Lucette brought two of the straw-stuffed animals with a small red cloth sewn to each: the arrow's target. She leaned the deer and the boar against the mound.

Stepping away, she handed the bow to him. "We can take turns or you can take your three shots and then I follow you." At the same time, she noticed her mama and papa quietly watching them in the crowd that had gathered. Beside them were Ezra and Helene, along with Otto and John.

As Louis took the bow, his head was swirling with thoughts as he said, "I'll do my three first and then you can do yours."

She is different from all the other girls I know.

As he nocked the arrow, he lifted his arm and began to pull the string back.

Lucette lifted her hand to his arm, gently touching him. "Wait, you need to push your elbow out further, like I do mine and hold your hand closer to your cheek. It will be a better shot for you."

She wants to help me?

Louis did what she told him. His first arrow clipped the deer's ear.

His next arrow took off the boar's front leg.

His final arrow found the deer's tail.

Louis was excited. As he handed her the bow, he confessed, "This is the first time I have ever hit a target."

Lucette smiled at him as she took the bow and began to nock her first arrow. "I thought so. You did well, Louis." Turning to the target, she lifted her arm and quickly released the arrow.

The red cloth split on the deer.

The crowd gasped. Murmurs could be heard. "She is like her mother …"

Nocking the next arrow, she pierced the red cloth on the rabbit and quickly followed it with another arrow next to it.

Lucette won. Silence followed.

Louis turned to her. "You are better than I am with a bow. Will you teach me how to shoot like you?"

"Come back to my table, Louis. I have something for you."

Catching her daughter's eye as she walked away, Nichol smiled at her and reached for Robert's hand.

"Our daughter is no longer a little girl. She will have more ability than I have."

ninety-four

Emma

Nichol saw darkness enter.

Six months had passed since the successful fair.

Much had happened with the pups trained by the children.

Nichol and Lucette sailed to England as soon as it was safe on the channel to see Queen Emma. They delivered the pup that Lucette trained with Nichol's guidance. She had named him Prince.

Before returning to Harmonie, they worked closely with Emma and her sons on how to work with hand signs with Prince. Lucette had written instructions in both English and French with drawings of hand positions for each command for the Queen.

Emma already knew of the fairs. Duke Richard, her brother, had written her of them and how they had created wide recognition for him and Rouen.

"Nichol, he mentions you in his last letter, and he holds you in high regard. He wrote that you are the one person he fully trusts."

Emma paused, and then asked, "Is there more? Is he a problem for you?"

Listening closely to her words, Nichol said, "No. I know he desires me but he has been told it will not be. Because of Duke Richard, I've been allowed to prosper, as my family and the Harmonie community has. I believe he understands that my relationship to him can only be as an advisor."

Nichol then gave Emma a special brooch that Robert had made for her. When Nichol placed it in her hands, Emma's eyes lit up. "Is he making jewelry again?"

"I wish he was, but he has little time. Since the duke named us Lord and Lady, Robert has taken his responsibilities seriously. He rides the land, overseeing the expansion of Harmonie and New Harmonie.

"I know the duke travels with his wolf dog between Rouen and Fécamp whenever he goes. When he spoke with Robert, he suggested that Robert work with Timo and create a new fair for Fécamp this fall.

"If it is done, why don't you come to visit with your sons? The docks have expanded there and I would think the duke would welcome you warmly, along with Judith and their children. And I will get to see you again."

"I would like that. I will ask the King of his thoughts."

This was the final day of her visit and Lucette was with them. Emma asked if they could share Nichol's stone as they had done in the past.

Lucette's eyes expanded as her mother revealed it and watched the two women as they put their hands on it.

Someday, I will have Mama's stone and learn how to use it.

This time, as her hand began to hover over the stone, Nichol saw darkness enter. Not talking about its meaning, she encouraged Emma to touch her hand as well.

She focused on the continued prosperity between Duke Richard's lands and England's, and the future of Emma's sons. The women laughed and then said their goodbyes.

As they walked away, Lucette asked, "What did you see in the stone, Mama?"

"The King will die in a few years. I did not feel she needed the burden of that knowledge right now. One day, this stone will go to you and you will see things that others don't see.

"I know that when you touch others, you will see them as well. When you have the stone, it will bring great power to you. You must use it wisely."

Lucette smiled. "Will Louis be in my future, Mama?"

Nichol laughed. "Let us see what time will tell. Some things are better not known until they are ready to be revealed."

The Rescue

You have saved the children of the kingdom of Normandy ...
and brought great honor to Harmonie and to me.

The summer crops yielded the best harvest that Timo had ever seen.

When the duke had approached him and Robert about creating a Harvest Fair in Fécamp, Timo was reluctant at first.

Now, he saw it as feasible, making it the first fair of the fall season as the leaves would be turning and the Rouen fair in late fall. The productivity of Harmonie had increased significantly so it could supply foods and drink.

However, planning another fair would still be a lot of work.

He knew that the holy relic—a trunk of a fig tree that held the blood of Christ that was displayed at the Abbey—would help bring people to Fécamp to see it and the Abbey itself. He also felt that many would come to a fair just to be seen by the duke.

There was a monastery next to the ducal palace in Fécamp. What was once a small fishing village had increased in size with homes surrounding the abbey and the monastery. The docks had expanded for shipping and Leiv made it a regular stop. Ezra had added a small warehouse to store goods that would be distributed to the local merchants and those with shops in New Harmonie.

Timo decided that the first fair in Fécamp should last for only two days, and he set the date for the first week in October. It was the main topic of conversation in Rouen. A fair in Fécamp would give many a chance to go and see the ducal palace and the church within the abbey.

Since this was to be the first fair for Fécamp, he and Joshua rode to the ducal palace at the beginning of August to seek Duke Richard's permission for the date he had chosen. He knew that there was much to do to prepare for it.

The duke welcomed the shorter two-day festival and listened to Timo's plans, telling him, "I will send messengers to the villages and towns throughout Normandy. Joshua will do the same in Rouen and the Harmonies."

Both the residents of Harmonie and New Harmonie were excited about Timo bringing his fair to their area of the kingdom. As soon as the news was out, merchants in New Harmonie were already planning their table displays. The women in Harmonie increased their sewing and cloth production, knowing that now there would be two fairs to sell goods.

Aiden told his father he wanted to organize contests for the boys and men. He was also ready with a new set of swords and daggers that he made with his father and Gideon, his cousin.

When Timo told Athena that the monastery in Fécamp made large amounts of butter, she made plans for adding her herbs to butter she purchased and then smearing it on different breads to sell at the fair.

Lucette had created several new bows and a new style of arrow and would welcome showing them off in Fécamp.

During the last week of September, people began to arrive. Some came to sell to others, others simply to enjoy being away from their homes and work, and to await the fair to come.

Nichol and her family arrived two days before the official date to visit Duke Richard, and to offer him any assistance. They also wanted to help Timo and began their table setups.

Nichol, Lucette, and Athena wore dresses and covered their hair. When she approached the duke, his large smile greeted her as she bowed.

"Lady Baron Nichol, I see you dressed appropriately for the Harvest Fair. I will not have to defend your dress or actions to the Abbot, Abbess, or any of the bishops."

She heard the humor in his voice. Returning his smile, she replied, "I have instructed my children to not behave as though they are in Harmonie and running with their wolves. They know to be seen, not heard.

"Timo will take Athena to the monastery where she plans to purchase butter for her table display and Aiden is planning to organize contests of strength and speed for the men and boys.

"This is my Lucette, Your Grace. She carves bows and makes arrows to sell. Neither she nor I are planning on contests of our own, as happened in Rouen.

"Is there anything you desire my counsel on while I am here?" As she spoke, she noticed a subtle light surrounding him.

Ah, the Lady is here with us.

She felt herself relax, knowing that she could speak openly with him.

"I have a few matters I want to discuss with you. I think it is important that we define and have the maps of Harmonie and New Harmonie drawn to avoid future challenges by others. Let us meet the day following the fair before you return to Harmonie. Since the ears and eyes of the Abbey are close, it would be wise to have Robert with us."

Absorbing his words and the mention of the Abbey, she said, "I believe you are correct in your thinking. I can walk behind the two of you and speak loudly enough that you hear my words.

When you ask me questions, or respond to what I say, turn your head toward Robert as if you are speaking just to him. He will know to turn his head toward you as we all walk forward."

"I believe that will work. My steward Thomas is with me here. When you and Robert come to the gate, ask for him. He will bring you to me." Then he added, "My sons are still talking about the bees of Harmonie. When I return to Rouen at summer's end, we may come your way first."

With a slight bow and taking a few steps backward, Nichol says, "Your Grace … I will now go help Timo. I look forward to seeing you and Duchess Judith at the fair tomorrow. I believe you will have the same success here as in Rouen. I regret that Queen Emma was not able to be with you."

The first day of the fair, the sun was out and there was a joyous atmosphere. People were arriving throughout the day, many more people than were expected.

Fécamp and the Rouen fairs were on their way to becoming the much-anticipated events of each year in Normandy.

Many had traveled long distances to attend the festival. Already those who were there were saying that they did not want the fair to end. Before the day was over, both Timo and Nichol were thinking the same thing. It would be good to extend it for two more days.

The children wandered over to the banks of the Valmont River that flowed into the channel.

Aiden had created a new contest with the boys. It was to see how far they could skip a rock on top of the water, and how many skips the rock took before sinking.

The winner with the longest skips would receive some of his sister's bread with her special butter and apple and honey spread.

The beginning of day two began with only a few clouds in the sky.

Lucette, Aiden, and Athena were down at the river with their wolves before the crowds started to build. It was not yet time for them to be at their tables.

Aiden had been throwing pieces of wood into the water for the wolves to fetch and return to him. It was a game he did with them at the lake in Harmonie.

Lucette whistled to her brother, sister, and the wolves to come to her.

"More people are coming; we need to be at our tables now. Mama said to me last night that many will want to barter with us this last day."

With her words, the three headed to the fair that was set up next to the monastery, and to their tables, which were positioned under Timo's tent with the red covering.

They didn't see the red-tailed hawk that had perched high on a large oak tree.

Shortly after midday, Nichol encouraged the three of them to enjoy the afternoon, reminding them that they would begin the long walk home the next day after she met with the duke.

Overjoyed, all three called to their wolves and headed to the river.

It was shallow and easy to step into the water. Taking their shoes off, the other children who were there removed theirs as well.

The sky had darkened and storm clouds began to build but went unnoticed. The wolves jumped in and allowed the current to take them downstream and then they would swim out.

Then, a light rain began. It did not deter the throng of children gathering or those that had their feet in the water. For many, it was time to be with other children and just play.

Athena noticed that the water was swelling, growing deeper upstream. Her eyes followed the red hawk as it flew over the river, close to where the children were, and let out a screech, alerting both Aiden and Lucette.

Aiden and Lucette stopped and turned their heads as Athena pointed upstream and at the hawk.

Now they saw the water level rising as well, almost to their knees.

Lucette put her fingers in her mouth and sounded her shrill whistle. The sound was heard by all present, and she motioned with her hands to those around her to get out of the water.

The children began to move in Lucette's and Athena's direction.

Following his sister's lead, waving his arms over his head, Aiden yelled, "DANGER! GET OUT OF THE RIVER! GET OUT! GET OUT, EVERYONE!"

As he shouted, he didn't retreat. Instead, he moved closer to the end of the bank and braced one foot against it. There were several boys in the river, oblivious to the rising water.

Aiden continued to wave his arms and yell, "GET OUT OF THE RIVER NOW!"

Lucette moved those around her to higher ground.

Nichol had heard the whistle her daughter used and knew there was danger.

Grabbing Robert, they ran in the direction of the river, bringing Shadow with them. As she arrived at the top of the river bank, she initially watched what was unfolding and her children attempting to get others to safety.

Now, Robert and Aiden began to run.

All three of the wolves were running beside Aiden. He was giving hand signals to the wolves, moving faster downstream on the bank than he had ever run before.

Robert followed Aiden's movement and followed him downstream, far below where the children were. Both had stripped down to their breeches.

Nichol and Lucette moved to where Robert was, knowing that young lives were now at risk, and the wolves would be needed.

Athena stayed with the children who got out of the river, huddling them together on the bank as the rain was pouring down in thick streams.

Many of the adults now appeared, with more arriving behind them. Distressed screams could be heard from the water and from along the river.

Swollen from the sudden downpour, the river was moving fast, thundering along against the banks, and quickly growing deeper.

The children still in it were caught in the strong current. Despite their efforts, they couldn't move to escape its pull.

They were struggling to get out. Many could not swim. Caught in the turbulent river carrying them out to the channel, they were crying out, "HELP!"

Aiden, standing in the water, was prepared to intercept children who needed help as the river current continued to pick up speed and force. The wolves followed Aiden into the water. His wolf, Hunter, paddled closer and Aiden signaled to him.

Grabbing up the first boy he could reach, he slung the child on top of Hunter. Yelling at the boy so to be heard over the roar of the rushing water, he shouted, "Put your arms around his neck. He will carry you to the shore."

Aiden grabbed the next boy and waited for Hunter to return and help again. Now Lucette's wolf Sage, Athena's wolf Zita, and Shadow are in the water, all of them carrying children back to Robert and Nichol.

The parents focused on moving the wet, frightened children to safety.

Aiden was still in the water, yelling instructions to children and wolves.

Shadow had carried one boy out of the water and turned back toward the fast-moving stream. She was now running as fast as she could toward the water.

One more child remained in danger, bobbing up and down in the water.

Shadow leaped into the river, her attention on the young girl who had not been caught by Aiden yet.

Shadow dipped her head, lifting the child as high as she could in the water, raising her back under her. The girl threw her arms around Shadow's neck and was towed to the shore, where Nichol pulled her out.

Aiden was exhausted.

Seeing his son's fatigue, Robert moved out midstream to catch him and pull him out of the water. His cold stiff hands failed to grab hold and Aiden was swept away in the current.

The river was growing higher by the minute, even spilling over the bank in a few places.

Watching her son's head bobbing in the fast-moving water, Nichol and Shadow were on the run. She noticed that there was shrubbery poking out of the water.

Aiden—grab it and hold on! We can get to you!

Pulling himself out of the water, Robert was panting from exertion. Catching up with Nichol, his eyes scanned the water for his son.

They saw the hawk at the same time, circling close to the ground and emitting screeches.

Over the roar of the rushing water, they heard a faint cry.

"Help! I am here …"

Shadow howled and ran toward the sound, discovering Aiden hanging onto a large shrub with both hands.

Nichol reached down with her hand, extending her other hand to Robert, higher on the bank. Bracing their legs against the suction of the water, the two pulled until their son was out of the water.

Aiden's legs came up and he crawled a short distance away from the river.

The water was still rising.

Robert repositioned on the bank and straddled over his son, lifting him farther away from the river.

Finally, he stopped lifting and pushing Aiden to safety. Dropping on his back on the riverbank by his son, they lay side by side, their chests rising and falling, taking deep gasping breaths.

"I thought I lost you Aiden. What you did, few men could have …"

Suddenly, Duke Richard appears and offers his hands to them both.

Pulling them up, they stood, wet and dripping in front of him.

"You have saved the children of the Kingdom of Normandy … and brought great honor to Harmonie and to me," he exclaimed.

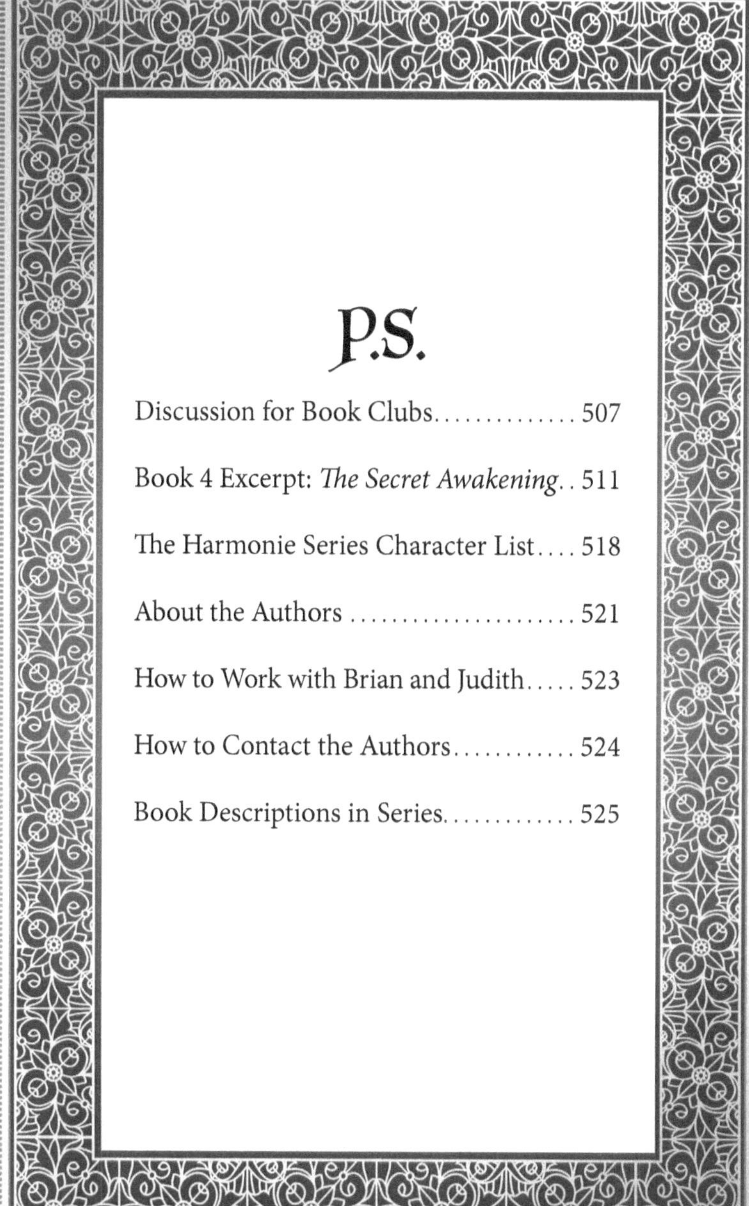

P.S.

Bring **The Secret Rise** to Your Book Club

Book Club Leaders … contact Judith or Brian to participate in a special meeting to discuss **The Secret Rise, The Secret Hamlet,** or **The Secret Journey**—the concepts, the stories, and the evolution of the series. We always encourage readers to post individual reviews on Amazon.com. And thank you.

In-person gatherings are possible if you are in Colorado. Zoom is always an option in any state, and most countries. eMail Judith@Briles.com directly to set a date.

Discussion for Book Clubs

The Secret Rise

Did *The Secret Rise* pull you in? Did you want more?

- Were you satisfied or disappointed with how it ended?

- How do you picture the characters' lives going forward?

- If you were to identify the most important theme within *The Secret Rise,* what would it be?

Do you have a favorite part(s)?

- What was it?

- Were you surprised with its reveal?

- hat would you like to see more of in the next book, *The Secret Awakening?*

What themes surfaced in the story?

- Have you ever been in a situation where you needed someone to save you?

- Have you ever been in a situation where you did not want someone to save you?
- Have you ever had to step in and help someone out of a dire situation?
- Have you ever had to overlook or accept something so that you could have a relationship with someone?
- Has anyone in a church betrayed you?
- Will the duke continue to press Nichol with his desire?
- Have you ever had to trust someone you barely knew?
- If you are a parent, have you ever tried to hold your children back?
- Have you ever allowed yourself to cut off others you knew well because you felt they had become bad?
- Have you ever had inner voices or feelings that guided you?

Do you have a favorite character?
- Who?
- Why?
- Is there anything you particularly liked or disliked about him or her?

What do you think of Nichol's ability to defend herself and others?
- Do you know anyone like her?
- Do you think it's important for a woman to be able to physically defend herself?
- Was it wise for her to encourage her children to be trained with defense skills as she was?

Nichol's vengeful half-brother is finally taken down. Was it just?
- Did you feel any empathy for Fredric?

- Do you think he got what he deserved?

- Were you surprised with who he revealed was after Nichol?

Nichol's Influence with Duke Richard has increased.
Could she be in danger?

- Will her relationship with the duke damage the one she has with Robert?

- Could her children be at risk?

- Will other hamlets and villagers be envious of the support Harmonie gets?

What risks did Nichol undertake when she combined the hamlet of NoName with Harmonie?

- Will the townspeople resent the added exposure?

- Should she and the others create a Timo Fair in Harmonie?

- Will the road that is planned bring in undesirable people?

Could a young woman in the 11th century be a merchant, mother, and confidant of a future queen?

- How can the two women stay in contact when their countries separate them?

- What could Queen Emma do for Nichol?

- Will men seek to destroy Nichol's presence and growing influence?

Does Archbishop William fear Nichol's power?

- Will the archbishop sabotage Nichol?

- Will the archbishop go behind Duke Richard's back to undermine Nichol?

- What does the archbishop fear?

Duke Richard wants Nichol's guidance. Should she continue to give it?

- Should Nichol trust the duke?
- How could Nichol and the Hamlet create an alliance with the duke?
- What danger could Nichol bring to the Hamlet and to her family with her connection to the duke?

The duke has expressed his desire for Nichol. Will he seduce her?

- Did her response to him surprise you?
- Should she heed Ezra's caution about the duke?
- Should she have saved the duke's life?

When Nichol first met Garlyn, he was caustic. He is now the Mayor and Lord of New Harmonie. Will he allow others in his circle?

- Will Garlyn spend more time in New Harmonie?
- Will Garlyn find a wife?
- Will the new road being proposed between Harmonie and New Harmonie create conflict?

If Nichol didn't have the voice of the *Lady* as a support, comfort, and guide … would she have succeeded in her quest?

- Does Nichol need the *Lady* in her life now?
- Should Nichol be cautious as the *Lady* begins to communicate with her children?
- Could the *Lady* abandon Nichol?

Enjoy Book 4 Excerpt of …

the
Secret
Awakening

available 2026

Mapping the Harmonies

I think we must send them away.

Nichol approached Robert as he sat at his worktable by the forge. "Is that a ring you are making for me?"

"Yes, your signet ring. It is a likeness of the *Lady* that you described to me."

Watching him work, she then said, "Make one for yourself. You are Baron Robert and you must have one, too. Have you thought of what it will represent?"

"No, I hope you will think of one for me."

Nichol paused, then gently removed the slim silver braided necklace Robert had made her from her neck. Laying it on the table, she fingered the two rings—one with a raised crest that had deep blue sapphires on it and the other a red ruby. She then let her thumb glide over her treasured rose-colored amulet she held in her hands.

Again, she handled each treasure she carried. it was as though her handling each piece was the first time she had seen them.

"Remember the feather I carried that fell off the chain a year ago? Athena has a feather that she carries on a leather strap around her neck. Yesterday she showed it to me and said that Granpapa dropped it for her the last time she was at the Hill."

Nichol's eyes welled and a single tear rolled down her cheek.

Robert watched her, knowing the cascading memories his wife was experiencing, waiting for her response. She removed Alexander's signet ring from her necklace and offered it to him.

In a voice husky with emotion, she said, "This is your ring." He reached up and wiped her tears away, then stood and embraced her.

Releasing her from his embrace, Robert reached out and clasped her hand, wrapping his hands around hers. "I cannot take this; it is meant for Aiden. We both know that his birth father is a lord and has no recognized sons. He may choose to come forward and claim his legacy someday, and his rightful inheritance."

Nichol pulled her hand back and reversed what Robert had done.

She opened his hand with her fingers and placed the ring in his hand. "It is yours now, husband. You will honor Papa. I know that he would be proud that you should have it and wear it. I want Aiden to have Papa's ruby ring."

Nichol still held Robert's hand. The two gazed lovingly at each other for a time.

Finally, Nichol spoke. "The reason I came here is to ask you a question. Have you noticed Lucette's and Athena's moods of late? They lack interest in their training. Both have become restless after the incident in Fécamp last fall."

Robert nodded. "Yes, I have. Gideon and Rurik have had problems with Aiden's work on the forge. His mind wanders from his work and sometimes he doesn't complete his tasks. I will have a talk with them."

Their intimate mood shifted. "I have a thought. When I returned from Rouen, I remembered Duke Richard's last request, one that is of great importance to us and the Harmonies. With all the immediate tasks in front of us, I did not think to remember it until now. He has tasked me with providing a map of our land. Tonight, I will reveal to the children a way to excite them while at the same time completing Richard's task. For them, it will be an adventure and a quest."

Most nights, Helene and Ezra joined Nichol and family for the evening meal, one that Helene prepared. Sitting around the table, few words were spoken.

Lucette, Aiden, and Athena gazed down, staring at their bowls as they ate.

Nichol put her spoon down.

Robert took her cue, and asked, "What should we do with them? Aiden's work at the forge has almost stopped and Timo said today that Athena's thoughts are not with the task at hand. Lucette that leaves you. What is your excuse for not working?"

Silence.

Nichol winked at Helene and Ezra. She then said, "I think we must send them away." Looking up from their bowls, the children's eyes widened with worried stares.

Nichol added, "Helene, could I have more of your stew? And Ezra, another cup of wine?"

Silence.

"Papa … Mama … you cannot send us away," came from Lucette's low voice.

More silence was met from the adults.

Nichol lifted the cup to her lips, thanking Ezra.

Then she said, "Duke Richard has asked me to perform a special task. The task is important to everyone living in the Harmonies. But now … now I think you three should do it instead of me."

Looking at Lucette, Athena, and Aiden in turn, she added, "Papa and I are sending you to map the Harmonies and beyond."

Smiles returned to the youngsters' faces, and they all started to talk at once.

Nichol held her hand up, quieting them.

Once she had their full attention, she continued to speak.

"Papa and I cannot do what he asks. The three of you must do this for Papa and me. We want the land mapped that we currently have—and more, if it is possible. That means you must be generous with your detail and descriptions. Timo has been planning the trip for days and will join you.

"It is up to us to give the duke a map of the Harmonies and the area around our land. It must be a better map than what exists now and include great detail. Many will protest this map so it will be up to the duke to choose final boundaries for his kingdom.

"Duke Richard may send a man soon to do the same thing. He is aware that we are both involved with the transition of New Harmonie to become part of what we have created here. If he does, we will already have a completed map to hand over to him. Tomorrow morning, we will all meet here to plan your journey. I now see in all your faces excitement but I must tell you this … you cannot fail. The future of the Harmonies are in your hands.

"Now, go tell Timo, John, and Cara to be here early in the morning to help plan your trip."

The next morning before the sun was up, Lucette, Athena, and Aiden were lying in bed talking about the trip.

Aiden suddenly stood. "It is time for everyone to wake up," he mumbled. He put on his breeches and moved quickly to the door. Shadow reached the door at the same time.

Knowing the commotion it would create, Aiden opened the door to the other wolves' greetings. Athena, Lucette, and Nichol were next to appear at the door, followed by Robert.

Nichol knew the reason they were up early and glad to see their new enthusiasm.

It is a new beginning for them.

Timo and Moki arrived at the first light, while John and Cara joined later.

Planning went on all morning. Food and clothing were made ready to pack on Moki the following morning. Parchment, quill and ink, even bows and arrows were organized.

Seeing the bows, the wolves paced as they watched their young masters' every move, awaiting their commands. It was a long day of preparation, and everyone was busy with tasks and lists.

Before the sun rose on the next morning, Nichol, Robert, John, and Cara waved as they watched Lucette, Aiden and Athena walking down the road.

Eager for their adventure to begin, their brisk pace soon caused Timo to fall further behind. He reminded them, "Remember, Moki is laden with supplies. He cannot match your speed."

The Harmonie Series
Character List

BOOK 3: The Secret Rise

Achim Ezra's brother, husband to Dinah, children: Robert, Gideon and Raisa

Aiden Nichol and Robert's adopted son; birth mother is Marie

Alexander Papa and father of Lisa / Nichol, now a presents as a hawk

Amos Inn keeper in Rouen

Astrid Mother of Lisa / Nichol and Fredric

Athena Daughter of Nichol and Robert; sister to Lucette and Aiden

Cara Slave, saved by Nichol on the docks of Rouen, partnering with John

Caterine Daughter of Elise, half-sister to Nichol

Charles Lord Charles, husband of Katharine and Loupe's conspirator

Daniel Young man in New Harmonie

Diego Shipping merchant, that Alexander used and now Ezra's merchant partner to the Far East.

Dinah Achim's Wife, mother of Robert, Gideon, Raisa

E & N Merchant partnership with Ezra and Nichol

Edgar Assassin on ship to England

Edric Lord Charles soldier at the attack on Harmonie

Elise Nichol's half-sister in Marseille and mother to Piers and Caterine

Emma Duke Richard's sister and future Queen of England

Ezra Helen's husband, Achim's brother and Robert's uncle, Granpapa to Lucette, Athena, Aiden

Fredric Lisa / Nichol's half brother

Freyja Wife of Harold and mother of Olaf and daughters Tova and Gunvor

Garlyn Mayor of Harmonie-merged from No Name, now a Lord

Gideon Son of Achim and Dinah, nephew to Robert and Nichol

Harald Husband to Freyja- father of Olaf and daughters Gunvor and Tova

Helene Ezra's wife, Granmama to Lucette, Athena, Aiden

Henry Lord Henry, Aiden's birth father and Marie's rapist

Hubert Bowyer in Rouen and Lucette's teacher of bow making

John Nichol's protector and Cara's partner

Joshua Keeper of secrets, Ezra's cousin and messenger

Judith Duchess and Duke Richard's wife

Katharine Lady Katharine, Lord Charles widow

Leiv Ships captain, Ezra and Nichol's trading partner between England Normandy

Loupe Priest Killian Loupe

Lucette Nichol's first daughter, means "little light"

Margaux Lisa's nanny and villa caretaker in Marseilles

Marie Aiden's birth mother and wife to Olaf

Moki Timo's donkey

Nichol Protector and visionary of Harmonie. Ezra's partner in E & N, married to Robert and mother to Lucette, Athena, Aiden

Olaf Son of Harald and Freyja, husband of Marie

Otto Nichol's bodyguard; wife is Gabrielle; sons Henrik and Siebert

Piers Son of Elise, Nichol's half-brother

Raisa Robert's younger sister, three years older than Lucette, niece to Robert and Nichol

Richard the 2nd Duke of the Kingdom of Normandy

Robert Baron Robert, Nichol's husband/ father to Lucette, Aiden and Athena

Roger Ezra's protector

Rurik Norseman discovered in forest by Lucette, Athena, and Aiden

Sacha Midwife for Lucette's birth in Book 1, *The Secret Journey*

Samuel Priest in Rouen

Shadow Nichol's wolf and protector

Simon Duke Richards Chanselor

Thomas Duke Richard's Steward

Timo Brother Lemur

Urik Man behind attack in Harmonie

William Brother to Duke Richard, the Archbishop of Rouen

Wolves Shadow (Nichol's), Sage (Lucette's), Hunter (Aiden's), Zita (Athena's), Star (Timo's)

Victor Duke Richard's gate guard

Vilfred Blacksmith in Rouen

Zita Healer in Rouen and mentor of Athena

Judith Briles

Briles is the author of 48 books and known as The Book Shepherd to hundreds of authors she's worked with. Her construction tools are her words and imagination.

She is a book publishing expert and coach. Often, she must roll up her writing sleeves and become a "book doctor," juicing up storylines and author words. Judith empowers authors and works directly with those who want to be seriously successful. Her recent books include *Cooking with Judith, The Author's Walk,* and *How to Avoid Book Publishing Blunders.* Her books have all been #1 bestsellers on Amazon. Collectively, her books have earned more than 50 book awards.

Throughout the year, she holds *Judith Briles Book Unplugged* in-person and online experiences: Publishing, Speaking, Marketing, and Social Media. All are intensives limited to small groups.

Join Judith for the "AuthorU: Your Guide to Book Publishing" podcast she hosts on the Toginet Radio Network.

Calling Colorado home, when not writing, she is most likely in the garden … the kitchen … or planning author events.

Brian Barnes

Barnes spent decades in construction. While he built and could fix anything that required a hammer, screwdriver, saw, or drill, his mind filled with stories that only retirement gave him the time to write.

An avid reader of history, historical fiction and a follower of politics and world events, he is appalled when injustice and stupidity are prevalent in the behaviors of those who are in leadership roles. Much of the underlying theme within *The Secret Journey* was ignited by such events and the ignorance of what women are capable of accomplishing and achieving.

The Secret Journey is Brian's debut novel in the Harmonie Books series followed by *The Secret Hamlet* and now *The Secret Rise* due out this fall.

Calling Colorado home, he's known as the "fixit guy" to family and friends. Summers pull him and wife Julie into gardening and maintenance within their townhome community.

Brian and Judith

Book Clubs

Both Brian and Judith are available to book clubs to talk about *The Secret Journey, The Secret Hamlet, The Secret Rise,* and forthcoming books in the series in-person in Colorado or on Zoom.

Judith is sole author of dozens of books. Her memoir, *When Gods Says NO: Revealing the YES When Adversity and Loss Are Present,* is about survival and resiliency. Her many books on writing and publishing are ideal to create a discussion for club members who aspire to write and publish.

Bookstore Signings

Veterans at multiple book signings throughout the year, either or both authors would be delighted to come to your store, creating an event that customers will enjoy. They also create press releases to support their appearances and push out social media, too.

Speaking

Both Brian and Judith would be delighted to speak about the process of writing; creating a series; and creating voices, attitudes, and behaviors for characters in fiction.

Judith has extensive expertise in publishing: how to get published; how to market books; how to use social media; how to create a successful crowdfunding program; how to avoid publishing mistakes; and how to find the author's voice.

How to Contact
the Authors

For Judith

Judith@Briles.com

303-885-2207

 @MyBookShepherd

JudithBriles/

JudithBriles

BookPublishingHelp/

Judith.TheBookShepherd

http://bit.ly/BookPublishingPodcast

https://bit.ly/Author-PublishingTips

TheBookShepherd.com
JudithBrilesBooks.com

For Harmonie Books

@HarmonieBooks

HarmonieBooksSeries

Harmonie Books

@HarmonieBooks

Book 1
The Secret Journey

At 16, Lisa's world unravels. Forced to run to Paris for her survival when her papa is murdered. Will she get there? Will Alexander's partner welcome and help her? Will she discover who killed her papa? Will the Voice that invades her sleep continue to guide her? Will she ever feel safe and loved again? The year is 1000 AD.

Winner of multiple book awards.

Book 2
The Secret Hamlet

With a priest coming for Nichol and her growing family, the *Lady* forewarns her that she must leave Paris at once and seek a new and distant land ... one that will bring peace and prosperity. Nichol's skills and movements are called upon repeatedly to protect them from thieves and the priest as they move toward their destination, the new hamlet of Harmonie.

Winner of multiple book awards.

Book 3
The Secret Rise

Harmonie has prospered under Nichol's leadership and vision. With Ezra's partnership, their commercial ventures have grown greater than her papa's were. The power of Duke Richard and the church threatens to destroy them and the business success they have created. Once again, Nichol must outsmart and out maneuver those in power and her evil half-brother Fredric. Lucette and Athena display skills that their mother doesn't possess.

Book 4
The Secret Awakening

The light that the *Lady* has surrounded Nichol with has extended to her daughters. The New Land, a land where women are not subservient to the church or to men, is the final destination with a port expanding trade to neighboring kingdoms and countries for the goods they produce. Available in 2026.

Your Book Review Matters ...

Thank you for discovering the historical fiction Harmonie Book series. The first book, **The Secret Journey** was followed by **The Secret Hamlet,** book 2. Now book 3 emerges, **The Secret Rise.** We hope you enjoyed reading them as much as we did in creating the story and bringing Nichol's story to life.

On the checklist of every author is to create a story that readers fall into. Also, on the checklist is to gather book reviews from reading customers for Amazon's detail page. Why? Because they become an essential part of encouraging other readers to discover books of epic fantasy.

All books are available in print, eBook and audiobook. If you are an Amazon Kindle Unlimited member, you can download all the books to your digital library.

We would be honored to have your review. Did the characters draw you in? Did the suspense pull you in? Was the story engaging? Would you recommend **The Secret Rise** to others?

Please post your thoughts on *Amazon.com* by searching the title, then click on "customer ratings" and add your review.

Brian and Judith

* 9 7 8 1 9 5 9 7 3 7 9 0 2 *